NO ESCAPE

A strong swimmer, Kevin quickly righted himself underwater and kicked hard to the surface. More cold than scared, he looked up, waiting for someone to appear at the rail with a rope.

"Kevin, hold—" Devon saw the end of the nylon rope tied off on the rail and started pulling in the slack, the life ring appearing from across the deck. Grabbing the flotation device, she tossed it overboard.

The ghostlike demon had reappeared. Gliding gracefully on its side, it opened its mouth, its lower jawline moving silently across the surface.

Kevin's smile disappeared as he saw the expression of terror on his sister's face. He turned around.

The ivory head, lying on its side, was barely visible. A small wake closed, revealing a black hole in the sea, outlined by pink gums and sickening teeth.

A rush of panic washed over him. Ignoring the life ring, he tried to swim away, but an overpowering current grabbed him, dragging him backward in the water.

Dragging him into the Megalodon's open mouth . . .

STEVE ALTEN

THE TRENCH

MEG 2

PINNACLE BOOKS
Kensington Publishing Corp.
www.kensingtonbooks.com

PINNACLE BOOKS are published by

Kensington Publishing Corp.
119 West 40th Street
New York, NY 10018

All Kensington titles, imprints, and distributed lines are available at special quantity discounts for bulk purchases for sales promotion, premiums, fund-raising, educational, or institutional use.

Special book excerpts or customized printings can also be created to fit specific needs. For details, write or phone the office of the Kensington Sales Manager: Attn.: Sales Department. Kensington Publishing Corp., 119 West 40th Street, New York, NY 10018. Phone: 1-800-221-2647.

PINNACLE BOOKS and the Pinnacle logo are Reg U.S. Pat. & TM Off.

First Printing: August 2023
ISBN: 978-0-7860-5030-7

ISBN: 978-0-7860-4685-6 (ebook)

31 30 29 28 27 26 25 24 23 22

Printed in the United States of America

For Mom and Dad,

For always being there . . .

ACKNOWLEDGMENTS

It is with great appreciation that I acknowledge the wonderful people whose time and effort led to the completion of this book since it was first published.

Thank you to Ken Atchity, and his team at Atchity Editorial/Entertainment International for their tireless efforts. To Dave Angsten, who worked so hard on the manuscript, and to Ed Stackler of Stackler Editorial, thank you both for your contributions. A special thanks to Robert Leininger, whose editorial suggestions and technical expertise were invaluable.

Many thanks also to the great people at Kensington/ Zebra, especially Senior Editor John Scognamiglio and copyeditor Stephanie Finnegan. It is a pleasure to be associated with your team.

Also my sincere thanks to my talented personal editor, Barbara Becker; my gifted cover artist, Erik Hollander; and my webmasters, Doug and Lisa McEntyre at Millennium Technology Resources, as well as to my social media director, Kelly Rollyson.

Big thanks to my friend and producer, Belle Avery, who is working on the movie sequel, *MEG 2: The TRENCH*, which will be released in August 2023. Thanks as well to my literary agents, Danny Baror and Heather Baror, at Baror International.

To my wife and partner, Kim, our children and grandchildren, and to my readers who have stood by me over the past 22 years. Your comments are always a welcome treat, your input means so much, and you remain this author's greatest asset.

—Steve Alten, Ed.D.
meg82159@aol.com

Deep Pressures

Retired navy deep-sea pilot Barry Leace wiped the sweat from his palms as he checked the depth indicator of the *Proteus*. Thirty-four thousand, seven hundred and eighteen feet. Nearly seven miles of water above their heads, sixteen thousand pounds per square inch of water pressure surrounding them.

Just stop thinking about it . . .

Barry glanced around the tight quarters of the four-man submersible. Racks of computer monitors, electronics, and a bewildering jungle of wires filled the pressurized hull. The watertight coffin barely had room for its crew.

Below the navigation console, team leader Ellis Richards and his assistant, Linda Heron, stared out through tiny portholes in the floor of the *Proteus*'s bow.

"See those animals with the furry green pelt?" Linda

asked. "Those are Pompeii worms, capable of with-standing temperature variations from twenty-two degrees all the way to eighty-one degrees Celsius. The hydrothermal vents supply sulfur for bacteria to live off, which in turn are digested by the tubeworms—"

"Linda—"

"—which are a source of food to all sorts of bizarre-looking life-forms."

"Linda, enough with the biology lesson," Ellis said.

"Sorry." Embarrassed, the petite geologist turned back to the porthole, cupping her hands around her eyes to eliminate glare.

Smiling to himself, the sub's fourth crewman, Khali Habash, looked down from his control console at Linda. The girl loved to talk, especially when she was nervous, a quality the Arab never hesitated to exploit.

Khali's real name was Arie Levy, a Jew born and raised in Syria. It had been nearly ten years since the day Arie had been recruited by MOSSAD, Israel's covert intelligence agency. Since that time he had led a double life, spending half his time in Israel with his wife and three children, traveling around the Arab world and Russia the rest of the time, posing as a plasma physicist. It had taken four hard years of sacrifice for the agent to infiltrate Benedict Singer's organization, but here he was, seven miles beneath the Pacific, about to learn secrets that could change humanity forever.

Arie checked the external temperature gauge. "Hey, Linda, can you believe the water's seventy-eight degrees?"

The girl perked up again. "Incredible, isn't it? We call it hydrothermal megaplumes. The hot mineral water pumping out of these black smokers is seven hundred degrees. As it rises, it warms the freezing seawater column until it reaches neutral buoyancy at about twelve hundred feet above the floor of the Trench. Ocean currents then spread the plume laterally. The floating layer of soot from the minerals creates a ceiling that acts like insulation, sealing a tropical layer of water along the bottom of the gorge."

"The layer never cools?"

"Never. These hydrothermal vents are 'chronic' plumes. They've been active since the Cretaceous period."

Ellis Richards checked his watch again. As the project's team leader, he was perpetually worried about falling behind schedule. "Christ, three hours and it seems like we've barely made any headway. Linda, is it just me, or does it seem like this pilot has no idea what he's doing?"

Barry Leace ignored the insult. He checked his sonar and cursed under his breath. They had moved too far ahead of the *Benthos*, Geo-Tech Industries' (GTI) mobile deep-sea lab community and submarine docking station. The billion-dollar mother ship resembled a domed sports arena, with a false flat surface for an underbelly, dangling three mammoth shock absorbers for legs. Hovering just above the turbulent seafloor in neutral buoyancy, the 46,000-square-foot titanium structure reminded Leace of a monstrous man o'war as it followed them north through the most hostile environment on the planet.

Barry Leace had served on three different submarines during his tenure in the Navy. He had long ago become accustomed to living in claustrophobic quarters beneath the waves. Not everyone could make it as a submariner. One had to be in tip-top mental and physical shape, able to perform while knowing that drowning in darkness within a steel ship hundreds of fathoms below the surface was just an accident away.

Barry had that fortitude, that mental toughness, proving it time and again during his twenty-six years of service. That's why he was so surprised at how easily his psyche was unraveling within the Mariana Trench. Confidence that had been nurtured through thousands of hours of submarine duty had suddenly dissipated the moment the *Proteus* cleared its abyssal docking back aboard the *Benthos*.

Truth be known, it wasn't the depths that unnerved him. Four years earlier, through man's intervention, *Carcharodon megalodon*, a prehistoric sixty-foot species of great white shark, had risen from this very trench to wreak havoc. Although the albino nightmare had eventually been destroyed, and its surviving offspring captured, at least a dozen people had died within its seven-foot jaws. Where there was one creature, there might be more. Despite all of Geo-Tech's precautions and technical innovations, the submersible pilot was still a bundle of nerves.

Barry pulled back on the throttle controls, slowing the main propulsion engine. He had no desire to get too far ahead of their abyssal escort.

"What is it now, Captain?" Ellis asked. "Why are we slowing?"

"Temperature's rising again. We must be approaching another series of hydrothermal vents. The last thing I want is to collide with one of those black smokers."

The team leader squeezed his eyes shut in frustration. "Dammit—"

Barry pressed his face against the porthole, eluding Ellis's tirade.

The submersible's lights illuminated a petrified forest of sulfur and mineral deposits, the towering stacks rising thirty feet or more from the bottom. Dark billowing clouds of superheated, mineral-rich water gushed from the mouths of the bizarre chimneys.

Arie watched Ellis Richards move menacingly toward the pilot's navigational console. "Captain, let's get something straight. I'm in charge of this mission, not you. My orders are for us to cover no less than twenty miles a day, something we'll never come close to at this snail's pace."

"Better safe than sorry, Mr. Richards. I don't want to get too far ahead of the *Benthos*, at least not until I get a feel for this sub."

"*A feel for* . . . I thought you were an experienced pilot?"

"I am," Barry said. "That's why I'm slowing down."

Linda looked up from her porthole. "Exactly how far ahead of the *Benthos* are we, Captain?"

"Just over six kilometers."

"Six kilometers, that's all? Benedict Singer's going to flip." Ellis Richards looked like he was about to have an aneurysm. "Look, Captain, the *Prometheus* and *Epimetheus* are expected to arrive topside early next week. Neither submersible can even begin its work until we complete ours."

"I know that."

"You should. GTI's paying you a king's ransom to

pilot the *Proteus*. We can't keep waiting for the *Benthos* to play catchup every time we go out. We'll add another thirty days or more to our timetable, which is completely unacceptable."

"So is dying, Mr. Richards. My job is to keep us alive in this hellhole, not take chances so you can earn your bonus for coming in ahead of schedule."

The team leader stared at him. "You're scared, aren't you, Captain?"

"Ellis—"

"No, Linda, I'm right."

Arie watched the dynamics unfold. In the few weeks he had been in the abyss, the MOSSAD agent had observed Ellis Richards to be an obstinate man who preferred the use of bully tactics rather than concede he might be wrong. Though mankind knew more about distant galaxies than about the Mariana Trench, Richards proclaimed himself an expert on the abyss, somehow knowing everything from its hidden geology to its mysterious life-forms.

To Arie Levy, Ellis Richards's pompous attitude made him a dangerous man.

Captain Leace glared back at Ellis. "I have a healthy dose of fear inside me if that's what you mean. It's obvious that neither one of you fully appreciates the dangers of working in thirty-five thousand feet of water. Try to understand, if something should go wrong, if we should accidentally hit something . . . or if something hits us, there are no watertight doors to seal and no standard operating procedures to follow. In the event of a hull breach, you won't even have time to bend over and kiss your ass goodbye."

"Sounds to me like you've lost your nerve," Ellis said.

"What did you say?"

"What do you think, Habash? Has our captain lost his nerve?"

"Considering that the surviving descendants of *Carcharodon megalodon* are living somewhere within this gorge, I must respect the captain's opinion," Arie said. "At the same time, we have more than sixty thousand square miles of seafloor to search. Our surface ship's towed sonar array was designed to alert us to any approaching life-forms in plenty of time to retreat back to the safety of the *Benthos*."

"Plenty of time?" Barry shook his head in amazement. "How the hell do we know the speed at which a life-form might approach? Besides, the *Titan's* in the midst of gale-force seas. Topside interference is disrupting communications."

"In that case, I suggest we collect our first samples here and give the *Benthos* a chance to catch up. Once the weather calms, I'm sure you can find a way to make up for lost time."

Barry shot Linda an exasperated look before returning to his control console. He double-checked the acoustic transponders, took another quick glance out his viewport, then engaged the lateral thrusters. Maneuvering between several black smokers, the *Proteus* descended slowly, establishing neutral buoyancy just above a cluster of glowing tubeworms. The entanglement of mouthless, fourteen-foot life-forms writhed in the current like the serpents on Medusa's head.

"I'm initiating our gas chromatography detectors,"

Arie said. "We could cut our mission time in half if we can detect helium isotopes leaking from these hydrothermal vents."

"Fine, fine, just do it," Ellis said, struggling with the laptop controls that operated the sub's robotic arms. Using the sub's underwater camera to see, Ellis began manipulating the two central control knobs, causing the twin robotic arms to extend from beneath the sub. Gingerly he directed the pincers of the left arm, snagging the isotherm sampling basket from its storage area.

Captain Leace watched the robotic arms extend toward the seabed, their movements stirring the bottom into clouds of mud. He closed his eyes and tried to relax, listening to the hydraulic whine of the pincers.

"Move to your left," Linda said, directing Ellis from her viewport. "Just beyond the tubeworm cluster."

Loud warning blips from the sonar caused the pilot's heart to skip a beat. He grabbed the acoustical printout, then checked the sonar screen in disbelief.

A tight cluster of objects had materialized. Large objects.

The captain felt his throat tighten. The others continued working, not even bothering to look up.

"Habash, we've got company."

Arie turned. "What is it?"

"Sonar reported three unidentified objects, bearing two-one-five. Range seven-point-four kilometers. Speed, fifteen knots and closing. Heading directly for us."

"Any word from the surface?"

"I'm trying now. No response. We're on our own."

"What do you suggest?" Arie suddenly felt a bit claustrophobic himself.

Barry stared at the sonar console. "I say we get the hell out of here. Richards, retract the robotic arms, we're returning to the *Benthos*."

"You've got to be kidding."

"Captain, are you certain?" Linda registered a knot of fear in her stomach.

"Look for yourself. Whatever those creatures are, they're accelerating through the Trench in our direction. Richards, I said retract those mechanical arms."

"And I'm saying, screw you. It's taken me twenty minutes to collect these samples and I'll be damned if we're going anywhere before I secure the bucket back on board."

Arie moved to the sonar console, staring at the three images. He thought back to his training sessions. *Were Megalodons pack hunters?*

"Maybe it's just a school of fish," Linda suggested. "Try to stay calm—"

"A school of fish? Stick to geology, Linda. Sonar indicates that these things are more than forty feet long. Out of my way—"

Barry ignited the lateral thrusters. *Steady. Not too fast. Don't hit anything, or you'll rupture the hull.* The sub spun counterclockwise. A bone-rattling jolt shook the *Proteus*.

"Dammit, Leace," Ellis yelled. "You nearly tore the mechanical arm off. I just lost every sample."

"I told you to retract the arms." Barry accelerated the *Proteus* to its top speed of 1.8 knots. He knew the *Benthos* was moving toward them, somewhere out there in the darkness.

The blips grew stronger.

ETA thirty-two minutes, Arie thought. *We're too far out . . .*

"Captain, listen to me," Linda said, grabbing his arm. "They're not sharks."

Barry stared ahead. "So, you're a biologist now?"

"I think Linda is right," Arie said, trying to reason with his own fear.

"Listen, Habash, whatever these things are, they're a hell of a lot bigger and a helluva lot faster than the *Proteus.*"

The blips grew faster; Arie's heart raced to keep pace.

"This is absurd," Ellis said.

Barry ignored him and leaned forward, staring through the porthole into the abyss. The smoke rising from the hydrothermal vents made it difficult to see beyond the perimeter. He shielded his eyes and strained to focus.

Long minutes passed in silence.

A darting movement ahead. Another to starboard. Very swift. Very large.

"They're here," the captain whispered, a lump in his throat. *Fast suckers . . .*

For a long moment, no one said a word, the only sounds coming from the *Proteus*'s propeller.

With a sudden jolt, the sub pitched to starboard. Barry crashed face-first into his console.

"What's happening?" Ellis asked. "What did you hit?"

"I didn't hit anything. They hit us." Barry struggled with the navigational controls. "She's not responding . . . something's wrong."

"Shhh. Listen," Linda whispered.

From above their heads, they heard a faint sound—metal groaning.

"Oh, Christ, one of them is on top."

Arie listened at sonar, studying the screen.

"Leace, do something," Ellis ordered.

"Hold on." The pilot swung the submersible hard to port, then back to starboard, trying to shake the creature off.

"Captain, stop," screamed Linda. "That plate's loosening!"

The sound of grinding metal screeched along the top of the hull. The pilot reached up and touched one of the titanium rivets welded into the plate above his head. He felt moisture and tasted his fingers. "Seawater," he moaned. He leaned forward, praying for the *Benthos* to appear in his viewport.

The sound of shearing metal grated in their ears as the *Proteus* dipped sideways.

"Son of a bitch." The captain wiped the sweat from his face. "They're tearing the whole tail fin loose."

Linda pushed her face against her viewport. "Where's the *Benthos*?"

Something huge broadsided the sub, hurtling stacks of recording equipment against the far wall.

"Captain, I think I know what they're doing," Arie shouted. "The two smaller ones are driving us to their larger companion."

"These things are intelligent?"

"Look!" Linda yelled, pointing out the porthole.

Barry could just make out an ominous shape moving toward them. "It's the *Benthos*—"

"You don't have time to dock," Arie warned. "Signal the *Benthos* to open the hangar doors!"

"It takes five minutes to flood the chamber," Linda shouted.

The pilot grabbed the radio. "Mayday . . . Mayday . . . *Benthos*, this is *Proteus*, request you open hangar doors immediately—"

"Proceed to docking area, *Proteus*—"

"Dammit, open the hangar doors, *now*—"

Standing beneath the loosening rivets, arms above his head, Arie Levy felt the titanium plate reverberate against his sweating palms. "Whatever these things are, they're tearing this entire section loose—"

A whistling sound infiltrated the cabin.

"What's that?" the team leader whispered.

Barry Leace looked up. "We're losing the integrity of the plates."

"Captain," Arie yelled, "the third creature—"

A tremendous force struck the sub's bow, flinging Linda and Ellis to the floor. Barry Leace plunged over his navigational console, his head striking the viewport glass. Blood flowed from his brow. He wiped it clear, staring in horror.

A luminous crimson eye peered in through the glass.

Arie pushed his palm futilely against the titanium plate reverberating above his head. He thought about the information he had fought so long to acquire but had not been able to report. He thought about his wife and children, whom he had forsaken in the line of duty.

The whistling sound above his head ceased. A pair of twisted rivets spit into the cabin like five-caliber machine gun slugs.

The MOSSAD agent's head imploded before the rivets hit the floor.

Waking Nightmare

Flickering sunlight penetrated the gray-green depths. Jonas Taylor plunged nose-cone-first into the void, struggling to draw breaths, his chest constricted, his throat burning. He opened his eyes wide, pressing his hands against the LEXAN pod.

The ocean turned black. He continued descending, spiraling downward into the gorge, all the while searching the darkness below.

A swirling vortex of soot appeared in the sub's headlights. An object rose out of the muddied current, another LEXAN pod. His light revealed a woman's body lying inside. Her face was obscured in shadows, but Jonas could make out her long black hair flowing like silk. For a brief moment, he caught a glimpse of her dark almond eyes—vacant eyes staring through him.

Terry . . .

He accelerated toward her, the sub barely moving, struggling against a strong current. He screamed her name again, a feeling of dread washing over him.

From the swirling current of debris behind her, a luminescent glow appeared. The unearthly light turned Terry's features to gray silhouette.

Jonas stopped breathing as Angel's monstrous head appeared. The demonic grin cracked open, a cavernous mouth revealing a stretch of pink gums and rows of serrated triangular teeth.

Jonas tried to scream, but had no mouth.

Her eyes flashed open in recognition—and fear.

"Jonas," she whispered—as the beast took the entire pod into its mouth.

"Jonas."

"No!" Jonas shot upright in bed, his chest heaving, his hands shaking uncontrollably.

"Honey, it's okay, it's okay." Terry sat up, stroking his hair, her own heart racing following her husband's sudden screams.

Morning sunlight streamed through the wooden shutters, illuminating the familiar bedroom as Jonas came out of the night terror. He turned and kissed Terry's hand.

"Are you okay?" she asked.

He nodded, struggling to find his voice.

"Was it the same dream? The one where you're back in the Trench?"

"Yes." Jonas lay back in bed, allowing his wife to use his chest as a pillow. He stroked her long silky black hair, then let his hand drift down the small of her back to her smooth bare behind.

"It isn't getting better," she said. "You should see Dr. Wishnov before you give me a heart attack."

"Post-traumatic stress disorder—I already know what he'll tell me. He'll tell me to quit the Institute."

"Maybe you should. Four years studying that monster is enough to give anyone nightmares, especially after all you've been through."

The ring of the phone made them both jump. They smiled at each other. "Guess we're both a little on edge," Jonas said.

She rolled over and snuggled naked against him. "Don't answer it."

Jonas pulled her close, nuzzling her neck as he ran his hands across her breasts.

The phone continued ringing.

Jonas swore and grabbed the receiver. "Yes?"

"Doc, it's Manny. Sorry to bother you, but I think you ought to get back to the lagoon."

The tone of his assistant's voice caused Jonas to sit up. "What's the problem?"

"It's Angel. Something's wrong with her. You'd better get down here."

Jonas felt his heart pounding in his throat. "Give me twenty minutes." He hung up, then slipped out of bed to get dressed.

"Jonas, what is it?"

He turned to his wife. "Manny says something's wrong with the female. I have to go—"

"Hon, take it easy. Maybe you should eat something, you look as pale as a ghost." To her surprise, he stopped getting dressed and sat down on the edge of the bed to hug her.

"I love you," he whispered.

"I love you, too. Jonas, tell me what's wrong? I can feel your arms trembling."

"I don't know. I think I just had déjà vu, like my absolute worst nightmare is about to become real."

It had been eleven years since Jonas Taylor had first encountered *Carcharodon megalodon*, the fiercest predator ever to have lived. He had been nearly seven miles down in the Mariana Trench, the deepest and most unexplored location on the planet, piloting the Navy's three-man submersible, the *Sea Cliff*. On the last of the top-secret dives, the exhausted argonaut had been staring into the pitch-black waters below when the unearthly white glow had appeared. Mesmerized by what he first took to be an aberration, he quickly found his thoughts turning to fear as the sixty-foot great white shark's luminescent torpedo-shaped head began rising at them from the depths, the demonic smile opening to reveal seven-inch teeth.

A primordial panic had seized him, changing his life forever. Disregarding protocol, he had jettisoned the vessel's ballast and raced the sub back to the surface, the rapid rise causing a malfunction in the pressurization system. Both scientists aboard the sub had died, and Jonas's career as an argonaut was over. Or so he had thought.

Over the next seven years, Jonas became obsessed with proving to the world that the creature really existed. Returning to school, he earned advanced degrees in paleobiology while his first wife supported them. Research over the mysterious disappearance of the Megalodon species soon led to a controversial theory and several publications. Jonas surmised that many of the prehistoric great white sharks had migrated to the warmer abyssal waters of the Mariana Trench in order to avoid the cold surface temperatures brought about by the last ice age. Despite the scientific basis for his conclusions, his research was dismissed by colleagues as utter fantasy, his papers banned from many institutions.

Four years later, the opportunity to return to the Mariana Trench was offered by Masao Tanaka, an old friend and mentor. The founder of the Tanaka Oceanographic Institute had not been interested in Megalodons or Jonas's theories about the creature's possible existence. Masao was building an artificial lagoon off the Monterey coast, a man-made habitat in which to study whales. To finance the project, he had entered into a joint-venture agreement with the Japanese government to deploy an array of seismic detection robots, called Unmanned Nautical Information Submersibles (UNIS), along the floor of the Mariana Trench. Something had gone wrong with several of the devices, and Masao needed Jonas's assistance in order to retrieve one of the instruments. At first, the former deep-sea pilot had refused, unable to face his fear. But with his first marriage falling apart and his career in disarray, the thought of redemption became too seductive to pass up.

And then there was Terry.

Masao Tanaka's only daughter was as beautiful as she was rebellious. If Jonas would not accompany her brother on the mission, she would go in his place. And so Jonas had returned to the gorge, this time descending in a one-man submersible. Once more, fate would deem that he cross paths with one of nature's most prolific killing machines. Tanaka's son died within one of the creature's jaws, while another, a huge pregnant female managed to rise from its purgatory in the depths. In the end, Jonas had been forced to kill the very creature he had wanted to save, his heroics becoming the stuff of legend. Once the target of ridicule and scorn among his peers, the paleontologist suddenly had his career vindicated, and literally overnight became an international celebrity: *The man who killed the Meg.* Talk shows, television specials, reporters—it seemed everyone wanted a piece of him—as well as a peek at the female Megalodon pup that had been captured within the Tanaka lagoon.

He and Terry had wed. Masao Tanaka made his new son-in-law a partner at the institute, and a year later, the most popular live exhibit in the world had opened for business in Monterey.

But fame is fleeting, and celebrity, with all its perks, also makes one an easy target. Eight months after the lagoon had opened, Jonas and the Tanaka Institute found themselves defendants in a $200-million class-action lawsuit, filed by grieving relatives of those who had perished within the jaws of the Megalodon. Terry was four months pregnant when the trial began, a media frenzy rivaling that of the O.J. Simpson hearings:

"Would you explain to the court, Professor Taylor, why you risked so much to capture a creature we've heard described as the most dangerous predator of all time?"

"We had the means to contain the Megalodon and study it."

"Tell us, Professor, when you had actually succeeded in sedating and capturing the monster

*in your cargo net, did you ever consider kill-
ing it?"*

*"No. We had it under control. There was no
reason—"*

*"No reason? Isn't it more accurate to say that
you and the Tanaka Institute simply made a business decision not to kill it? Money, Professor, it
was all about money, wasn't it? You decided not
to slay the goose when you had ample opportunity to do so, only because you wanted its golden
eggs. In the end, your greed cost innocent people
their lives. And now, the offspring of the creature
that violently slaughtered my clients' loved ones
is reaping millions of dollars in profits for the
Tanaka Institute. Is that your idea of justice, Professor?"*

In the end, the jury had awarded damages exceeding
everyone's expectations. When the courts refused their
appeals, the Tanaka Institute had been forced into
bankruptcy. Then, out of the blue, the Japanese Marine
Science Technology Center (JAMSTEC), which had
first lured Masao Tanaka into the Mariana Trench, offered the Institute a way out of their financial fix. Concerned about the rise in seismic activity along the
Philippine and Pacific tectonic plates, the Japanese
once again gave the Tanaka Institute an opportunity to
deploy an entire array of UNIS robots along the Mariana Trench floor. The contract was lucrative, but the
dangers of returning to the abyss forced Masao Tanaka
to seek the help of billionaire energy mogul Benedict
Singer, who was in the midst of constructing his own

fleet of deep-sea submersibles to explore the world's trenches. A partnership was formed and Masao was forced to give up controlling interest in his beloved Institute in order to fulfill the JAMSTEC contract and keep the doors of his attraction open.

Jonas drove past the giant billboard advertisement of the Meg:

He turned down the employee access road, waved to the guard, then pulled into his parking spot.

The haunting sound of baritone drums began pounding from the loudspeakers of the outdoor arena. He checked his watch and saw that the ten o'clock show was moments away from starting.

Viewed from above, the man-made Tanaka lagoon appeared as an oval lake surrounded by a concrete arena, which ran along the shoreline of the Pacific Ocean. Connecting this enormous aquarium to the sea was an eighty-foot-deep, thousand-foot-long channel at the midpoint of the lagoon's western wall. Consisting of two concrete seawalls running parallel to each other, the canal was cut off from the ocean by a set of mammoth double doors of reinforced steel, which prevented the lagoon's star attraction from escaping.

As Jonas entered the ten-thousand-seat stadium, a hush fell over the impatient capacity crowd. All eyes, all camera lenses, turned to focus on the south side of the aquarium where a five-hundred-pound headless carcass of beef was now being attached to a thick chain dangling from an enormous A-frame. Somewhere deep within the three-quarter-mile lagoon, still remaining out of sight, lurked Angel, the monster they had paid theater-ticket money to catch a glimpse of. The moment they had waited for would soon be upon them. Breakfast was being served.

Jonas followed the arena's circular walkway until he came to the concrete platform supporting the steel winch. He glanced up to see his assistant, Manny Vazquez, swing the raw carcass carefully into position above the tranquil blue water.

Below the concrete platform was a steel door marked "AUTHORIZED PERSONNEL ONLY." Jonas noticed that the steel safeguard protecting the locking mechanism had been partially pried back. *Damn kids* . . . He made a mental note to have it repaired, then unlocked the door and entered the dank stairwell, slamming the door closed behind him.

Jonas inhaled the familiar cool dampness, taking a moment to allow his eyes to adjust to the dim light. He descended the two flights of stairs slowly, the voodoo-like drumbeats growing fainter as he moved deeper into the bowels of the facility.

The stairwell emptied into a subterranean semicircular corridor that ran along the southern circumference of the enormous tank. Eerie reflections of blue-green light illuminated an otherwise dark passage. Jonas moved slowly to the source of the light, turning to face the fifteen-foot-high, six-inch-thick LEXAN bay aquarium windows.

He was now thirty feet below the surface, staring into the crystal-blue waters of the man-made lagoon. Jonas looked up, reading a newly created sign above his head: "DANGER. NO MOVEMENT WHILE MEGALODON IS PRESENT."

He pressed his palm against the LEXAN glass. Its

cold surface reverberated from the underwater acoustics being pumped into the tank, calling the beast to its meal. Drops of crimson blood from the dangling carcass dispersed along the surface of water above his head.

Jonas gripped the rail.

Deep within the farthest confines of the ocean-access canal, a pure white triangular head the size of a small house continued its side-to-side mantra of movement, rubbing its conical snout raw against the porous gateway of steel. As the inflowing current of water from the Pacific passed through the pores of the gateway, the to-and-fro movements of the creature's head siphoned the scents of the sea into its nasal capsule. Miles away, pods of whales were migrating north along the California coastline. The seventy-two-foot prehistoric female great white could smell their sweet, pungent scents.

The deep bass of the underwater acoustics intensified, stimulating the highly sensitive cells running along the creature's lateral line. The reverberations meant food. The female turned away from the gate, remaining deep to avoid the electrical field being discharged from an array of pipes extending out along the upper inner portion of the seawall, all that prevented the sixty-two-thousand-pound behemoth from simply leaping sideways out of the canal.

A great roar rose from the crowd as a prodigious wake accelerated into the lagoon. Ten thousand hearts fluttered as the seven-foot ivory dorsal fin appeared, cutting across the azure surface. The moving girth of the submerged leviathan sent fourteen-foot waves crashing over the eastern seawall of the tank.

The fin disappeared as the fish descended to circle below.

The audience breathed a collective sigh.

"Ladies and gentlemen, say hello to Angel, our own white Angel of Death!"

With a whoosh, the beast suddenly exploded from the tank. Murderous jaws stretched a full ten feet, rows of six-to-nine-inch teeth hyperextending away from its mouth in slow motion, sending screams rippling through the crowd. For a heart-stopping moment, its upper torso remained suspended out of the water, defying gravity, as the monster shark latched onto the entire carcass in one horrific bite.

The A-frame groaned, bending as the creature twisted from side to side in exaggerated throes of its humongous head, attempting to free its meal from the steel clamp. Mountains of frothy pink waves slammed against the Plexiglas shielding the spectators. And then the carcass tore free, the steel support snapping back into place as the ghostly prehistoric predator claimed its prize.

The crowd swooned as the pale monstrosity slipped back into its tank and submerged. The cleanly picked clamp continued to dance at the end of the swinging chain, the steel girders of the A-frame reverberating like a giant tuning fork from the force of the attack.

Through the myriad of bubbles and swirling shards of beef, Jonas stared at the creature's ghastly alabaster belly as it chewed its food, the violent muscular contraction from its jaws sending great ripples gyrating down its underside and gills.

Waves created by the feeding behemoth pounded the glass, causing the sheet of LEXAN to rattle in its frame. Jonas stared in awe at the female's girth, which had surpassed even that of its deceased parent. Angel's lifelong existence in highly oxygenated surface waters had obviously had an impact on her size, as well as her ravenous appetite. Like her parent, her entire hide was luminescent white, a genetic adaptation the shark's ancestors had acquired to lure prey in the perpetually dark waters of the Mariana Trench.

Jonas remained motionless, staring at his waking nightmare. The soulless gray eye rolled back into place as it ravaged its last bite.

A red phone on the wall rang. Jonas reached for it.

Detecting movement, the Megalodon arched its back. Sculling forward, it pushed its snout against the LEXAN glass as if looking in.

Jonas froze. He had never seen the female so agitated.

"Hello? Doc, are you there?"

Sweat trickled down Jonas's armpit as Angel continued pressing against the underwater bay windows, staring at him. The LEXAN began bending.

Jonas recalled the words of the facility's engineer. *Bending is normal. Flexible plates actually become stronger as they bend. If the window does shatter, the doors in the outer corridor will automatically seal.*

Angel pressed the side of her massive head against the window. The cataract-gray eye focused on him.

Jonas felt an exquisite eeriness. Only six inches of LEXAN separated him from death. What if the engineer had been wrong? After all, the tank was originally designed to harbor whales.

The Meg turned and disappeared into the lagoon, heading straight for the canal.

Jonas released his breath, his limbs shaking. He leaned back against the wall, out of sight, trying to fathom what had just taken place.

"Doc, are you there?"

"Yeah, Manny. Christ, I see what you mean about our girl being a bit wound up."

"Better join us in the control room, boss. You're gonna want to see this."

Jonas exited the underwater viewing area, heading across the open-air arena to the administrative wing. Not bothering to wait for the elevator, he dashed up the three flights of stairs two steps at a time, pushing through the double doors of the lagoon's master control room.

Manny Vasquez was standing over two technicians seated by a computerized control board. From here, operators could oversee the lagoon's environment, electronics, security, and sound system. Six closed-circuit monitors were mounted above the board.

Manny pointed to an underwater image appearing on one of the monitors. Jonas could see the outline of the giant steel double doors that secured the canal from the Pacific.

"What am I looking at?"

"Keep watching."

Jonas stared at the monitor. A minute passed, and

then a white blur shot past the camera, accelerating toward the gateway faster than a tractor-trailer, moving at more than one hundred feet per second. The head of the leviathan slammed into the sealed double doors, causing the televised image to shake violently.

"Oh, Jesus—she's attacking the gate."

Manny nodded. "No doubt about it, Doc. That fish of yours wants out."

Preparations

Sadia Kleffner walked over to the bay windows of the executive office and yanked open the Venetian blinds, revealing the lake-sized aquarium shimmering three stories below. She turned back into the room and, for a long moment, stared at her employer.

"Professor Taylor, are you all right?"

Jonas looked up from his work. "Yes. Why?"

"You have dark circles beneath your eyes."

"I'm just tired. Do me a favor and page Mac for me. I need to speak with him right away."

"Okay, boss." His secretary pulled the double doors closed behind her.

James "Mac" Mackreides burst in unannounced ten minutes later. At just under six feet four, Mac had the square-cut jaw, regulation crew-cut, and muscular upper body that gave the impression this fifty-one-year-old ex-Navy sailor was still on active duty. Ironically, it was only after being kicked out of the service that the maverick helicopter pilot had decided to work out and shave on a regular basis.

Mac sprawled out across Jonas's couch. "You beeped?"

"We've got a problem, Mac. Angel's trying to break out of the canal again. She's been bashing her head against the gate all morning."

"What do you need me to do?"

"I'm finishing up a proposal. I want Geo-Tech to reinforce the gate as we talked about doing several years ago."

"How much to do the job?"

"About three million. We'd also have to close down and sedate the Meg for about ten days."

"Celeste will never go for it. She doesn't care about safety, or this institute for that matter. Hell, it's been over a year since Benedict made her CEO, and how often has she even bothered to visit?"

"Then we need to take matters into our own hands."

"Like we talked about last year?" Mac smiled. "It's about time."

"How long will it take you to get the necessary equipment?"

"I'll contact my buddy right now. The transmitter should be no problem. The weapon may take a week or two."

They were interrupted by the intercom. "Professor, Masao needs to see you in his office, right away."

Jonas stood to leave. "I'll talk to Masao about the Megalodon, but let's keep everything else just between you and me."

* * *

Masao Tanaka finished reading the fax for the third time when his son-in-law entered his office.

"Morning, Jonas. Sit down, please."

Jonas noticed the somber tone in the elder man's voice. "What's wrong?"

"I've just received word from Benedict Singer that the *Proteus* imploded in the Trench. Four people died in the accident."

Jonas felt his blood run cold.

"Singer is insisting that you meet with him about the *Titan* immediately. He's sending a private jet to take you to Guam. His chopper will meet you there—"

"Masao, I can't . . . I can't go. We have an emergency of our own here. The Meg is trying to escape."

Masao took a deep breath. "Are you certain? I thought we went through this last year. Once the whales completed their migration north, the creature calmed itself."

"She's a lot bigger now. It's time we sealed the gates permanently."

"You're planning an inspection of the gate?"

"Tomorrow morning."

Masao closed his eyes, deep in thought. "Jonas, I also received a call this morning from Dr. Tsukamoto, JAMSTEC is insisting that we conduct our own investigation of the *Proteus* accident. They specifically requested that you board *Titan* and analyze all sonar records of the event. Failure to complete our report on a timely basis will lead to termination of our UNIS contract."

"Christ."

Masao opened his eyes. "Now you see the importance of your journey. Can I count on you?"

"I understand JAMSTEC's wanting my input as a submersible pilot, but why is Benedict Singer insisting that I go?"

"I don't know. Truth be known, he can be a bit eccentric. I thought it best not to ask."

Jonas shook his head. "I can't go, Masao. Not now."

"Jonas, no one is asking you to descend into the Trench, merely to meet with Singer aboard the *Titan* and analyze his ship's data."

"I understand, I just can't go."

"You realize the awkward situation you are placing me in?"

Jonas looked him straight in the eye. "I know."

Masao walked around his desk, placing his hand on his son-in-law's shoulder. "I understand your hesitance in accepting Benedict's invitation. Terry has told me about your dreams. At some point, you have to stop living in fear."

Jonas felt his temper flaring. Standing, he walked over to the bay windows and raised the Venetian blinds, revealing the lagoon below. "You want me to stop living in fear? Let's drain the lagoon and kill the damn monster before it escapes. Do that, and I'll sleep a whole lot better."

Masao shook his head. "Killing the shark is not the answer. The demons that haunt your dreams come from your past. The sooner you realize this, the sooner you can get on with your life." Masao sat back in his chair. "However, since you refuse to make the trip, I have no choice but to go in your place."

Jonas nodded. "I'm sorry, Masao."

Masao watched him leave.

An hour later Jonas was still thinking about Masao's request as he drove south along the Pacific Coast Highway. Over the last four years, he had been offered no fewer than a dozen opportunities to return to the Mariana Trench. Some requests were to pilot submersibles, others were merely to appear in documentaries aboard a surface ship. No matter what the request, he had refused them all.

After all he had been through, no one could blame the paleobiologist for being afraid of the abyss. But Jonas's fears ran deeper. No psychiatrist could alleviate his anxieties, just as no medication or hypnosis could subdue his ongoing nightmares. Even Masao's request to meet with Benedict Singer aboard a surface ship went beyond his phobia. The truth was simple: Jonas Taylor was convinced it was his destiny to die in the Mariana Trench. As miserable as his life had become, he had no intention of putting his theory to the test.

Pulling into his driveway, he was surprised to find a cab waiting in front. A driver emerged from the entrance to his home, carrying two suitcases.

Jonas pushed past him as his wife appeared.

"Terry, what's going on? Where are you going?"

"Don't get upset—"

"Upset?"

"I'm going with Masao to meet with Benedict Singer."

For the second time that day, Jonas was over-whelmed by a sense of trepidation. "Terry, listen to me. I don't want you to go. Please . . . can we at least talk about this?"

"What's to talk about? You already told my father that you refuse to go, despite the fact that Benedict Singer specifically requested that you meet with him."

Jonas heard the anger in her voice. "Did your father happen to mention *why* I can't go?"

"Yes, I heard all about it. We both think you're over-reacting. We went through this same scenario last year. The creature struck the gate for about a week and then calmed down." She shook her head. "I have to tell you, Jonas, I'm really disappointed in you. You know Dad is too old to be making these trips by himself anymore. Where's your sense of responsibility? My father treats you like his own son."

"Sense of responsibility?" Jonas felt his temper flar-ing. "Let me tell you something, it's only because I've felt a sense of responsibility that I even stayed with the Institute this long."

"And what's that supposed to mean?"

"It means I've wanted to quit for a long time, but I stuck around because I knew Angel was getting too big to handle. How do you think I'd feel if the shark es-caped? The lagoon's simply not strong enough to hold her, and something has to be done about it before she escapes."

"Then fly out to the western Pacific and discuss the matter with Benedict Singer. It's his shark now."

"And what if he disagrees?"

"Jonas, it's not your call. Singer owns the Meg now, not you."

"Then I'll kill her before she can escape. Let him sue me—"

"You want to kill the shark?" Terry stared at him in amazement.

"Better the shark than . . . better than allowing it to escape."

"Jonas, listen to yourself. This obsession of yours is—"

"Is what? Is making me crazy? Go ahead, say it."

"Jonas, it's okay to be scared. Look at what you've been through."

"It's not my death that scares me, it's the thought of losing you. In my nightmares, you're in the Trench. Angel appears—"

"Enough!" Terry grabbed him by the shoulders. "Here's a news flash, Jonas. You *are* losing me."

The words seemed to pierce his soul. "What do you mean?"

She averted his eyes, wondering how much she should reveal. "I'm not happy, Jonas. I feel like we've grown apart."

"Terry, I love you—"

"Yes, but you spend more time with that damn shark than you do with me. What happened to us? These last few years have been hell, and it wasn't just losing the baby. Even when we're together, your mind is elsewhere. What do I have to do to be the only female in your life?"

For a long moment, he remained silent, allowing her words to sink in. "You're right. Who would want to be with someone who constantly thinks about death?"

"Jonas, it's not that I don't love you—" The taxi's

horn interrupted her. She glanced back. "I really have to go—"

Jonas grabbed her arm. "Terry, wait, please! Look, I'm sorry. I don't want to lose you. I can change. Just tell me what to do and I'll do it."

She wiped back a tear. "For starters, make an appointment to see that psychiatrist."

"Done. I'll make an appointment right away. What else?"

"I think it's time you changed your career. Eleven years of studying these monsters is enough."

"Agreed. I'll quit the Institute. Just let me make sure the Megalodon can never escape."

She pulled away. "Damn you, Jonas, you're hopeless, do you know that?" She pushed past him, walking toward the cab.

"Terry, wait—"

"No more talk. I have a plane to catch."

He strode after her. "At least promise me you'll stay aboard the *Titan*."

"Leave me alone. Go play with Angel—"

He grabbed her, spinning her around. "Terry, please—"

She looked at him, anger flashing in her eyes. "Fine. I promise I won't be descending with Singer into the Mariana Trench. If you're so worried, you can come with me."

"I can't. Not now, not this time—"

The cabbie honked again, calling out, "You okay, miss?"

"Fine." She pulled her arm free and climbed into the rear seat, refusing to look back.

Benedict

Terry Taylor made her way toward the rear of the Sikorsky AS-61 helicopter to where her father, Masao Tanaka, was stretched out across two seats.

"Sip this, Dad." Terry handed him the can of ginger ale as he sat up. "Are you feeling any better?"

"A little. I hate flying in these contraptions. How long until we arrive at the *Titan?*"

"The copilot says another fifteen minutes."

"I haven't been great company, have I?" Masao asked.

"It's okay. You needed the rest, and I needed time to think."

"Don't be so hard on Jonas. He's been through a lot."

"All of us have. I think he's having a nervous break-down."

"He needs your love and support."

"I do love him. I'm just not sure how much more of this I can take. I'm actually glad you invited me to come with you. I think Jonas and I needed a break."

Masao shook his head sadly. "By the way, Celeste will be onboard the *Titan*."

Terry groaned. "So much for my R and R."

"You dislike the woman?"

"I can't stand her. The way she struts around, flaunting her looks, you'd think a camera was on her twenty-four hours a day. She treats her staff horrendously, then she openly flirts with every man she meets."

"Including Jonas, I take it."

"Jonas more than anyone. Why the hell did Benedict have to appoint that Russian concubine CEO of the Institute?"

Masao smiled. "Benedict refers to her as his protégée."

"I don't know what she is, but I can't stand her, or that peroxide hairdo of hers."

"It would be best for all concerned if you made an effort to get along."

"It's degrading—"

"Try. For me."

"Fine. I'll try." She gazed out the windows at the glass-like surface of the Pacific. "You know, I'm actually looking forward to meeting Benedict. What's he like?"

"Benedict? A brilliant man. European-bred. A man of great wealth and power who is quite skilled in the art of manipulation. He is fluent in a dozen languages, though he prefers to impress with quotes in Latin and

French. I find him to be a bit eccentric, with a prodigious fondness for hearing himself speak. Some might even say he's mad. We must be tactful, Terry, very diplomatic. We cannot afford to set him off any more than we can ignore the requests of the Japanese."

"How do you think he'll react when you tell him JAMSTEC is threatening to cancel our contract unless we investigate the *Proteus*'s accident?"

"That depends on us. Outcome is often determined by the manner in which something is presented."

The helicopter banked sharply. Terry glanced out her window as an enormous gray warship appeared beneath them.

The *Titan* was a decommissioned Kirov-class Soviet missile cruiser donated by the Russian government to Geo-Tech Industries as part of a twenty-year contract to develop and supply alternative-energy resources. The ship was aptly named: at 813 feet long, with a ninety-one-foot beam, it was the largest research vessel in the world.

Fitted with a hybrid power plant, the *Titan* combined nuclear and steam to drive its two sets of turbines and twin propellers. Battle armor removed, the vessel was capable of maintaining cruising speeds of thirty-three knots. More importantly, the *Titan* had the size and power necessary to transport and deploy Geo-Tech's enormous deep-sea laboratory, the *Benthos*.

The Sikorsky bounced twice before settling down on the helicopter pad located at the stern. Terry followed her father and the copilot out of the chopper to where a stunning woman in her late twenties was waiting impatiently for them. Deeply tanned, she was dressed in a white skintight bodysuit that revealed an athletic build. Long platinum-blond hair blew wildly in the wind, revealing her high Slavic cheekbones.

"You're late," Celeste said to the copilot, shouting to be heard over the wind.

"We ran into some weather—"

"Enough with the excuses. You were late getting out of Guam. Take their belongings to our guest quarters and get down to the galley. You have thirty minutes to eat before heading back out."

"Tonight?"

Celeste turned her back on the man to face Masao.

"*Dobryi dyen*, Mr. Tanaka, we weren't expecting you. Where's Jonas Taylor?"

"He sent his better half instead," Terry said, climbing out of the chopper.

Celeste's eyes flashed anger. "Benedict insisted on Jonas. This is not good."

"The Megalodon's been attacking the gate again," Masao said. "Jonas felt he needed to remain at the Institute. He asked us to deliver a proposal he'd like you to read."

"Very well. Benedict is waiting to meet with us in his stateroom."

Without waiting for a reply, Celeste started walking across the open deck of the stern, heading for a steel-gray superstructure of multiple decks and towers bristling with sensors.

Masao eyed two barren platforms located on either side of the deck. "Celeste, could you tell me what these structures are?"

Without turning, she said, "At one time they were used to support the ships' two one-hundred-millimeter dual-purpose guns. The Russians removed all the weapon systems, but when this ship was armed she was a mean one."

Just like you, thought Terry.

Celeste led them up a short flight of stairs onto a second deck and into the ship. They followed a steel corridor to a spiral stairwell and ascended two more levels, stopping at C deck.

"From here on out, most of what you see has been gutted and redone," Celeste said.

Unlike the watertight corridors they had just come from, C deck had been refashioned into a wide paneled hallway, its floors a deep-blue all-weather carpet. The interior resembled an office building more than a research vessel. Celeste walked to the end of the hall. She knocked, then opened a set of cherry wood doors, beckoning them inside.

Benedict Singer had his back to them, the crown of his cleanly shaven head just visible above a brown suede chair. Terry and Masao sat down on a matching couch along one wall, listening as the billionaire CEO of Geo-Tech Industries completed a business call in Russian.

Benedict hung up, then stood to greet his guests.

"Ah, Lord Tanaka, *Ogenki desu ka?*"

Masao smiled. "Well, and you?"

"Alive, which always beats the alternative. But where is Professor Taylor?" For the briefest second, rage passed across Benedict's face.

"Unable to attend, but he sends his deepest apologies. This is my daughter—"

"The beautiful Terry Taylor. *Bonjour, madame*, how wonderful to finally meet you," Benedict said, recovering quickly. He took her hand, kissing it as he bowed. "Benedict Singer, at your service." He flashed a yellowed smile. His grayish-white goatee, the only hair on his head, flickered upward at the corners.

Terry stared into unearthly emerald eyes that seemed to lock onto hers, refusing to let go.

"You're wondering about the unusual color of my eyes. The result of an industrial accident suffered some years ago. The contact lenses are permanent, tinting what had once been blue irises. I find I like the emerald color, unfortunately, as you can see, the accident also permanently singed away my eyelashes and brows."

He turned to Masao. "Dinner is in an hour, but I thought we'd speak first. Celeste, have you offered our guests a drink? Some red wine, perhaps? Chateau Neuf du Pape 1936."

"Nothing for me," Masao said.

"The wine sounds good." Terry watched Celeste glide over to the bar, annoyed as she casually strutted her perfect physique.

"So, my friend, let's talk. As you can imagine, all of us are still in shock over the tragedy that befell the *Proteus*. We lost four good friends and valued personnel. One was our project manager. He'll be sorely missed."

"Have you any idea how it happened?" Masao asked.

"The last word we received was the pilot reporting a hull breach. Celeste believes the accident was more likely the result of pilot error than a malfunction."

"The man lost his nerve," Celeste said, obviously disgusted. "He probably panicked down there and collided with a black smoker."

Benedict shook his head. "*De mortuis nil nisi bonum*, my dear. Of the dead, say nothing but good."

"Then I'll say nothing. The loss of the *Proteus* more than doubles the timetable of this entire project."

"Unfortunately, Celeste is correct. Without the *Proteus*, the *Prometheus* and *Epimetheus* will have to complete their own geological survey of the seafloor before the UNIS seismic detectors can be deployed within the Trench. I had wanted to speak directly to your son-in-law regarding his experiences, anticipating that his insight could save us some time. I do hope your friends at the Japan Marine Science and Technology Center will be understanding regarding our delay."

Masao cleared his throat. "I'm certain they will, once they receive a full report regarding the incident."

Terry saw Celeste's blue eyes flash venom. "GTI filed a report two days after the accident occurred," Celeste said. "What more do they want from us?"

Masao held up his hand. "Please do not shoot the messenger. This is a sensitive issue that involves all of us. As you know, this area of the Mariana Trench is part of an exclusive economic zone, bringing it under American jurisdiction. It is only because of our ongoing contract with JAMSTEC that the Tanaka Institute has been permitted to reenter the Trench."

Benedict stood. "Have you traveled across the Pacific to insult me, Masao? My organization invests more than a billion dollars to create the *Benthos* and its fleet of submersibles so that mankind may finally access the last unexplored frontier on this planet, and JAMSTEC demands I pay homage to them? Perhaps we should simply tear up our joint-venture agreement.

GTI will use the *Benthos* to explore other deep-sea trenches while the Japanese wait for another earthquake to strike without warning."

Masao broke eye contact. "That is not our desire, or our intention, Benedict-*san*. The Japanese are very appreciative of your generosity and ingenuity in being able to access the Mariana Trench. They need our UNIS systems to be deployed but only desire a more thorough report on our part regarding the incident. The last thing any of us wants is to insult you or your great company. However, if you do not wish to comply with JAMSTEC's request, then I must regrettably relay your response back to the Japanese, who most certainly will terminate our agreement."

Benedict made his way to the bar and poured himself another glass of wine. "Exactly what is JAMSTEC asking for?"

"Examination of the wreckage—"

"There's little wreckage to see," Celeste said. "The sub imploded. The currents have scattered the debris."

She's lying, Terry thought. *Slow-moving currents wouldn't carry hunks of titanium anywhere.*

"Then they'll wish to examine all documents recorded by the *Benthos* and the *Titan*, including sonar grams recorded by your towed array," Masao said.

Benedict glanced at Celeste, who shrugged. "*Nivazhna*—it doesn't matter."

"Very well, Masao. Give us a day or two to pull together *Titan's* records. But we can't get down to the *Benthos* until the *Prometheus* and *Epimetheus* arrive."

"When will that be?" Terry asked.

"Not until the end of the week," Benedict said. "Of

course, you're both welcome to say for as long as you'd like."

"Very kind of you," Masao said.

"Now that that's out of the way, let's talk about Angel. From what my protégée tells me, the shows continue to sell out as our monster continues to grow."

"She's an amazing creature."

"Your son-in-law seems to think she's too dangerous, even in the lagoon," Celeste said, holding up Jonas's proposal. "He's asking GTI to front another three million dollars to reinforce the gateway."

"Jonas can be a bit paranoid," Terry said. "He's been through a lot."

"Hope everything's okay at home." Celeste flashed a smile.

"Couldn't be better." Terry didn't miss a beat. "Thanks for asking."

Benedict laughed. "Ah ... *Amor vincit omnia*, eh, Masao?"

"I'm sorry?"

"You really must brush up on your Latin, my friend," he said, pouring himself another drink. "Love conquers all things."

Child's Play

SeaWorld animal-care supervisor Pete Soderblom patted Tootie lovingly on her bumpy snout, then stood in the eighteen-wheeler's open cargo container to stretch his legs.

"Hey, Andy, looks like we're pulling into Bruceport Park."

Zoologist Andrew Furman continued attaching the first of two radio transmitters to the nineteen-thousand-pound, thirty-one-foot gray whale calf. "It's about time," he said. "I've been carsick for the last two hours."

"Better not get sick now, there are about two dozen news vans waiting for us by the dock," Pete said. "Hey, remind me to put up the 'SeaWorld Rescues' banner before they start filming."

"Did you see the shirts Anheuser-Busch had made just for today's event? There's a picture of Tootie on the front, above the caption, 'HELP US SAVE THE

WHALES.' SeaWorld's logo's on the back. They want us to pass them out to the first two hundred people in attendance."

"At least it's not a picture of Tootie drinking a six-pack."

The truck maneuvered its cargo beneath a towering crane positioned at the edge of the dock. The Coast Guard Cutter, which would be escorting Tootie out to sea, was already in place, and a flotilla of pleasure boats was waiting for them a hundred yards offshore.

Pete watched as a stocky man wearing an NBC *Today Show* windbreaker approached the truck.

"Hi, I'm Brian Dodds. Which one of you is Pete Soderblom?"

"Right here."

"Nice to meet you, Pete. Here's what's going to happen: I want to get some footage of the whale inside the truck so our viewers can get a good look at . . . what's the whale's name?"

"Tootie."

"Tootie." Dodds wrote the name down. "Good. Anyway, we'll continue shooting right up until she's released. How far are you planning to take the calf out to sea?"

"About two miles."

"Fine. From here, I understand you're flying out to our studios in New York."

"Yeah, I'm supposed to be doing a live interview with Matt Lauer tomorrow morning. I gotta tell you, I'm really nervous about that—"

"You'll do fine, Matt's a terrific guy. Before we begin, how about we do a quick preinterview so I can get some background information about this whole rescue operation." Brian signaled his cameraman over. "Don't look at the camera, just talk to me. You ready?"

"Uh, I guess—"

"Brian Dodds, *Today Show*, interviewing Peter Soderblom, animal supervisor with SeaWorld. Pete, how did this whole rescue operation come about?"

Pete forced himself not to look at the remote camera. "About fourteen months ago, Tootie, that's what we named the calf, was found stranded about fifteen miles south of here in Ocean Park. She was in really bad shape, probably less than a month old. Lifeguards and bathers loaded her into a U-Haul and drove her up to our facility in Seattle."

"And how large was she when you first saw her?"

"She only weighed about fifteen hundred pounds. In fact, when she finally arrived at SeaWorld, she was comatose. Fortunately, our animal-care specialists were able to revive her. Within a few days, we had her eating again. From that point on, she gained a good two pounds a day."

"And now how much does she weigh?"

"She's up to nineteen thousand pounds. By the time she's full-grown, she should weigh close to sixty-thousand pounds."

"Why release her now?"

"We believe she's strong enough, and the timing's right. For the next few months, thousands of gray whales will be migrating up the Pacific coast to spend the summer months feeding in the Bering Sea. Releasing Tootie at this stage gives her a chance to join up with one of the whale pods."

"Will she be in any danger?"

"If she can stay with the pods, she should be okay. Hopefully, she'll be able to learn to feed fairly quickly and avoid killer whales. My assistant is attaching two remote radio transmitters to Tootie, which will allow us to keep tabs on her over the next several months."

"Great, that should do it. Anything else you'd like to add?"

"Yeah," Pete said, slightly embarrassed. "Could you make sure our banner's in the shot when you begin filming? Our corporate sponsor's pushing a new 'get back to nature' campaign. I think they want Tootie to become the next Spuds McKenzie."

Tanaka Lagoon
Dusk

On the beach side of the arena, sixteen-year-old Jake Howell took a long drag on the joint before flicking it at his buddy, David Caine. The two teenagers were sitting on the private beach located directly behind the Tanaka lagoon's arena. Fifty yards north, the concrete seawall of the access canal stretched out into the Pacific like a highway off-ramp.

"Cop—"

David buried the joint in the sand as a security guard crossed behind them.

"Asshole, that's not a cop. Look what you made me do—"

Jake snickered, rolling on his back.

The security guard turned. "You boys shouldn't be back here."

Jake smiled. "We're waiting for our parents, Officer."

"Move—or I'll have you moved."

Jake stood, rubbing the back of his shaved head with his middle finger. The two boys followed the beach south past the arena until the guard was out of sight.

"Hey, idiots—"

They turned to see David's cousin, Doug, running toward them. He held up a crowbar.

"Come on. I found a way in."

Jonas watched as the crimson glow of the setting sun faded behind the brightly lit arena. From the open bay window, he heard the crowd noise escalate as the underwater tank lights flickered on, turning the dark lagoon waters a bright teal.

He turned to face one of the technicians. "Is she still in the canal?"

"Yeah, but she stopped pounding the gate about an hour ago. Probably has a headache."

Jonas put the binoculars to his face. There were no lights in the canal, making it impossible to see the Meg underwater. He turned to his left, watching Manny and another assistant struggle to hook an immense side of beef onto the chain of the A-frame.

Moments later, the outdoor lights were dimmed and the deep baritone recording of timpani drums began, ushering the visitors to their seats.

Mac took a seat next to Jonas. "I spoke to my guy; I'll have the transmitter by tomorrow morning. Here comes your fish."

An enormous phosphorescent mass glided into the lagoon.

* * *

The three teens listened for the crowd's crescendo before prying open the fire door. They jogged past souvenir stands and had already entered the outdoor arena before the first guard noticed the alarm bells ringing.

In the southern end of the lagoon, rising waves slapped against the Plexiglas barriers.

Jake pointed to the concrete structure supporting the A-frame. "See that door? It leads to an underwater observation room down below."

"How do you know?"

"Saw it on TV. Doug, give me the crowbar."

Jake led David and his cousin to the steel door. They stood behind him, shielding his movements from the crowd while he pried open the lock.

Jonas focused his binoculars on the pallid beast as it viciously tore the remains of its meal from the chain. As he pulled back to locate Manny, something caught his eye.

He trained the glasses on the observation room door.

"What is it?" Mac asked.

"I don't know. Probably nothing. I thought I saw the door leading down into the observation area swing open." Jonas handed him the binoculars.

"Hard to tell from this angle. Want to take a look?"

"Yeah, maybe we'd better."

The teens ran down the stairs and into the corridor.

"Whoa, Jake, check this out."

The three boys stood before the underwater bay windows, staring into the depths of the lagoon.

David pressed his face against the glass. "Where's the shark?"

"Gone, moron. The show's over."

"Bull," Jake said. "This show's about to begin." He banged against the LEXAN glass, the others following suit. "Here Angel—here girl!"

Jonas followed Mac down the concrete steps of the upper deck. He looked up to see the Megalodon glide slowly back toward the canal. As they made their way to the southern end of the outdoor arena, the creature suddenly turned.

"Here she comes!" Doug yelled.

"Hey, Caine, watch this." Jake pulled his baggy JNCO shorts and boxers down and pressed his bare buttocks against the window.

David and Doug fell down laughing as the Meg accelerated toward the viewing window. Jake ducked beneath the window frame, laughing as he rolled on the damp concrete floor.

The creature slowed, then banked sharply, slapping its great caudal fin hard against the reinforced glass. The LEXAN rattled within its frame.

"Hey, Jake, check out this sign. No movement while the Megalodon is in the area."

Jake stood, pressing his face against the glass. The creature was circling, its back arched. "I think she wants to play."

Jake and Doug banged on the glass while David took out a can of black spray paint, laughing hysterically.

Mac led Jonas through a crowd congregating around the southern end of the lagoon. Instead of leaving, people seemed to be moving toward the tank, jostling to get a better view.

"Jonas, what's going on?"

"I don't know. Something's drawn Angel back into the main tank. Oh, hell, look at the door. Somebody broke in, all right. You better get security down here."

David stood back and admired his handiwork. "Here she comes—"

All three boys stood by the window, wide-eyed, adrenaline pumping. The Megalodon accelerated toward them like a Boeing 747.

"Now!"

The juveniles dropped to the floor.

Losing its prey once more, the creature slowed, swiping the glass barrier with its snout and upper row of teeth and gums.

"Oh, man—what a rush?" Jake said.

David stood—then stopped laughing.

Just above the freshly painted words, "BITE ME," a blazing slate-colored eye was staring at him.

The Meg turned, moving off into the lagoon.

Jake and Doug stood, ready to play again.

"No, wait," David said, "maybe we ought to go."

"You go. I've gotta do this one more time. You in, Doug?"

"Hell, yeah. Come on, man. Don't be a pussy." They started banging.

David watched the creature approach. He felt his hands trembling. What had started out as fun and games was becoming dangerous. Still, he didn't want to chicken out. "This is it, the last time, okay?"

"Fine," Jake said. "Let's wait until the last second—wait until you see her ugly-ass eyes."

The three boys readied themselves, hearts pounding, staring into the charging face of the sixty-two-thousand-pound monster.

"Now!" The boys ducked below the window, laughing.

The Megalodon struck the LEXAN window like a locomotive plowing through kindling. Shards of glass and bone-chilling water exploded into the corridor as the creature's snout and upper jaw slammed into the back wall, knocking out a dozen teeth.

David and his cousin registered the white torpedo a split second before its crushing girth drove them backward against the concrete wall.

An icy torrent lifted Jake off his feet. He squeezed his eyes shut and curled up as his body was tossed within the corridor.

Jonas ran down the steps as a deafening crash rocked the stairwell. Racing down the corridor, he was greeted by an incoming wall of frothing water. He turned and ducked, the eight-foot wave pummeling him against the concrete floor, sliding him back toward the stairwell. Before he realized what was happening, the flow ceased. He opened his eyes, lying on his stomach in a pool of water, gasping to regain his breath.

Yellow lights flashed through the corridor.

Jonas stood, dripping wet. The emergency doors had activated, sealing off the viewing area from the rest of the corridor. He sloshed over to the steel door, looking through its eighteen-inch porthole.

Angel, what have you done?

What he saw made him nauseous.

Jake's lungs were on fire, his limbs like lead weights. He felt his body floating up from the floor and opened his eyes.

The image jolted him awake as if he'd been struck by lightning. He opened his mouth to scream, gagging on seawater as the cavernous maw surrounded him. Thrashing about, he paddled and kicked furiously, slipping out of the monster's closing jaws, trying to surface.

Jake's head struck the ceiling. The realization of his predicament sent a surge of panic through his limbs. Through blurred vision he searched the flooded corridor, only to find himself pinned against the back wall.

The Megalodon pushed forward, homing in on the vibrations.

Jake felt his body being sucked backward in a vacuum of water. With nowhere to maneuver, he ducked instinctively as the nine-foot maw jutted forward and clamped shut over his head.

In pitch darkness, he gasped a putrid breath as the

water momentarily drained away from his face. He gagged, then registered his own muffled screams within the creature's mouth as unseen scalpels sliced and pulverized his body into mincemeat.

Through foamy swirls of pink Jonas saw the creature shake its imposing head, retracting its body from the underwater viewing room.

"Dammit!" Jonas ran up the stairs, emerging outside in time to see Angel surface, the remains of a lower body held aloft in her jaws.

Screams rent the night. News crews jostled for camera angles, nearly pushing one another into the tank. Rising to the surface, Angel shook her head to and fro like a mad dog, tearing apart the carcass as her twisting upper torso sent great swells in every direction.

The beast disappeared, submerging somewhere beneath the floating pool of blood and mangled limbs. Then the hyperextended jaws rose majestically from the tank and, in one horrific bite, engulfed the remains from below.

Change of Plans

Positioned parallel to each other on two enormous hydraulic ramps at the *Titan's* stern were the sister submersibles, *Prometheus* and *Epimetheus*. The identical cigar-shaped vessels, both painted white with red trim, were sixty-eight feet long, with sixteen-foot beams and five-foot-high conning towers. In contrast to the somewhat barren dorsal surface, the subs' bellies contained an array of high-tech gadgets, the centerpiece being a spherical observation pod. From within this eight-foot structure, a single operator could manipulate a pair of robotic arms, cameras, lights, and a vacuum hose for gathering samples along the bottom.

Terry and Masao watched from the stern as the hydraulic ramp supporting the *Epimetheus* rolled into position beneath a massive winch along the *Titan's* transom.

Benedict Singer joined them.

"The late arrival of our subs forces a change in

plans," Benedict said. "The air purifiers and scrubbers onboard the *Benthos* must be replaced before carbon dioxide levels become too high. The *Epimetheus* will descend immediately with supplies and a partial replacement crew, returning topside in two days with our A-team. The rest of B-team, along with myself, will descend aboard her sister ship, the *Prometheus*, following their return. We're scheduled to begin a week-long mission in the abyss to deploy no fewer than three of your UNIS robots.

"I shall inform JAMSTEC," Masao said, admiring the *Epimetheus* as she rolled by. "Tell me, the inscription beneath the subs' names—"

"*Resurgam*. I shall rise again."

"And the vessels' names?" Terry asked.

Benedict smiled, relishing the opportunity to pontificate. "According to Greek mythology, the Titan god, Epimetheus, was charged with distributing gifts to all of the animals in the world, gifts necessary for survival. Unfortunately, Epimetheus ran out of gifts by the time it was humanity's turn. And so his brother, Prometheus, stole the Sun's energy and gave it to man. Zeus was so angered that he had Prometheus chained to a mountain, where vultures tore away at his liver for a thousand years. Prometheus means forethought; Epimetheus—afterthought."

"Will the *Epimetheus* be returning with the information JAMSTEC requires?"

"Those are my orders, Masao, but I expect you'll be disappointed. I doubt the *Benthos* records will reveal any more than the *Titan's*."

"Benedict Singer, please contact the control room at

once." Celeste's metallic announcement echoed across the deck.

"Excuse me." Benedict removed his walkie-talkie, moving away from them as he spoke.

Masao watched the man's face closely. "Something is wrong."

Terry leaned over the rail, watching a team of divers ride the *Epimetheus* into the sea. "Dad, how much do you trust Singer?"

"You are suspicious?"

"I think he's hiding something. Why would a billionaire energy mogul be so interested in bailing out the Tanaka Institute, let alone take on the UNIS contract?"

"I asked Benedict the same question when we first met. He claimed to have found himself drawn to the Megalodon's sheer power and grace. He says he became challenged with the idea of building a fleet of vessels capable of exploiting the creature's trench."

"And you believed him?"

"GTI has invested more than a billion dollars for sea exploration—"

Benedict returned, looking grim. "We have a situation. There's been a terrible accident at the Tanaka lagoon. The creature attacked and killed three teenage boys who had broken into the viewing corridor."

Terry saw her father go pale.

"Chaos abounds, Masao, and the media are circling. As president of the Institute, I suggest you return with Celeste to Monterey at once. Terry can remain on board to obtain the information for JAMSTEC."

Masao's knees buckled.

"Dad—" Terry grabbed his arm, feeling him shaking in convulsions.

Benedict reached for him as he collapsed on deck.

Four hours later, Celeste joined Benedict on the uppermost deck of the *Titan* beneath a sea of stars.

"Doctor says the old man should be okay. We'll leave for Monterey at first light."

"Such a beautiful night." Benedict stared up at the twinkling sky.

"Funny how things work out sometimes, isn't it?"

"We sail where fate directs. Still, I'm concerned with our timetable. JAMSTEC and the Americans are already suspicious. If we remain in the Trench for more than a month, they may investigate themselves. We can't risk the *Titan* being boarded."

"How long will you be able to keep Terry on board without arousing suspicion?"

"She'll leave only after you persuade the information out of Jonas Taylor." Benedict smiled. "*Festina lente*, Celeste. Make haste slowly."

Celeste leaned her head against her mentor's chest, running her fingers along his stomach. "I do find him rather attractive. Does this make you jealous?"

Benedict grabbed her by the hair, yanking back hard, forcing her to look into his piercing emerald eyes. "Never forget your place!"

"*Prastitye*—"

Benedict released her. "Gain Taylor's trust and obtain the information. But if he suspects the truth, kill him."

Differences of Opinion

Tanaka Oceanographic Institute

The late afternoon shower sent ripples across the aqua-green waters of the Tanaka lagoon. Jonas watched the rain from his third-floor office. The arena was deserted, the facility closed, pending the results of the police investigation.

Every few minutes, a hollow, metallic boom echoed across the manmade lake.

That's three. If she sticks to her pattern, she'll circle back into the main tank and wait another ten minutes before having another go at it.

As if on cue, the eight-foot wake rolled in from the canal, a white blur gliding into the lagoon.

The intercom buzzed. "Ms. Singer and Mr. Tanaka are ready to see you."

Jonas left his office, walking quickly down the corridor to Celeste Singer's office. The secretary gave him an antiseptic smile. "Go ahead inside. They're waiting."

Masao greeted him as he entered the suite. Jonas hadn't seen him since he had returned earlier that morning. He looked as if he had aged ten years.

"Masao, how do you feel?"

"I'll survive. Come, take a seat. We have much to discuss."

Celeste emerged from her private washroom wearing a black skirt and white blouse, her platinum-blond hair pulled up in a tight bun.

"Jonas, darling, I'm so glad to see you again." She kissed him on the cheek, then took her place at the head of an oval conference table, where a well-built gentleman in his late thirties was already seated. Steely-eyed, all business. A legal pad and miniature tape recorder sat ready on the table in front of him.

"Jonas, this gentleman is Lee Udelsman, a partner with the law firm of Krawtiz, Udelsman, Kieras, and Pasquale. Since we can anticipate getting hit with a lawsuit from the parents of the dead teenagers, I thought it best to be prepared."

"Professor, I'm well aware of the class-action lawsuit you and the Tanaka Institute have had to endure over the last eighteen months. I want to begin by putting your mind at ease regarding this incident. The three teens involved were juveniles with rap sheets as long as your arm. We know they didn't pay to enter the arena and we have a dozen eyewitnesses who saw them break into the locked facility where the attack took place. We're looking at a clear case of contributory negligence and assumption of risk—"

"Which is just our defense," Celeste interrupted. "Those little bastards not only trespassed, but their actions cost our company more than a million dollars in damages and lost revenues. I told Lee I want to go after their parents and countersue."

"Of course, that's your decision," Lee said. "We are looking at a breach of a duty of supervision. At the very least, a negligent supervision claim."

Jonas shook his head. "These boys paid with their lives. Isn't that enough?"

"No," Celeste said. "You lost two hundred million dollars before GTI took over because you weren't prepared. There are dozens of attorneys out there circling like sharks, waiting to take a bite out of the Tanaka cash cow. I say we go after them."

Jonas looked at his father-in-law. "Masao, what do you think?"

"Masao agrees," Celeste answered. "Lee, let's talk spin control. I'm scheduled to address the media in another hour to announce the reopening of the arena tomorrow morning. I want you to join me. Prepare a few carefully worded remarks about how these juveniles broke into our facility. Mention their rap sheet and how they infuriated our little Angel, inciting her to attack."

Lee wrote furiously on a legal pad. "I can do that, Celeste, but I think we should be cautious—"

"Forget cautious. You can't win on the defense; you have to attack."

"Is all this really necessary?" Masao asked. "Ticket sales have jumped since the incident. We're sold out through August."

"Celeste, there's something more important, much more urgent we need to discuss," Jonas said.

Lee stood. "Let me give you some privacy. I need time to make some notes anyway."

Jonas shook Lee's hand, waiting until the door

swung closed before he began. "Celeste, we've got a major problem, and I'm not talking about any lawsuit. You've read my report and proposal. The Meg has been trying to break out. Unless we do something quickly, she'll escape—"

"*Padazhditye*—wait, slow down. Did you say 'escape'? Jonas, darling, have you even conducted a visual inspection of the outer hinges?"

"No, not yet. I had planned on doing it yesterday, but the police had other ideas. We'll get to it first thing tomorrow morning."

"And what does your plan to reinforce the doors involve?"

"Again, it's all in my proposal. The construction work would take place along the outside of the gateway. Pilings would be driven into the seafloor to prevent the doors from opening. Then a four-four wall of concrete would be poured in sections along the outer doors and pilings."

"And the lowest bid you received was three million?"

"Three million, two. Angel will also have to be doped up for at least ten days to complete the work. You'll probably have to shut down the arena."

Celeste glanced down at the proposal. "I think I want to hear more about this before I just say yes. Masao, may I steal your son-in-law for a business dinner?"

"Sorry, I can't," Jonas said. "Too much work."

"It's all right," Masao said. "I'll take care of things here."

"Excellent." Celeste hit a button on her phone. "Margaret, have my car brought around."

Jonas gave Masao a long, hard look.

* * *

The maître d' showed them to a table facing the water. Celeste ordered drinks, then excused herself to use the ladies' room.

Jonas looked around the Victorian dining room, noticing couples smiling and laughing together. He ran the tips of his fingers above the candle's flame, staring at his wedding band. He thought of Terry, and his heart ached for her. He had been caught off guard the other day when she confessed her unhappiness. Were things really that bad? How could he have missed the signs?

You missed the signs because you're selfish . . .

He tried to recall the last time he and Terry had laughed together, or had made love when it hadn't seemed an obligation. When was the last time they had spent time away together from work?

Jonas felt a lump in his throat. His obsession with the Megalodon had made him blind.

He detected Celeste by her jasmine scent moments before she brushed past him to take her seat. She smiled at him, the candlelight dancing in her eyes.

This one's poison in a million-dollar wrapper.

"I'm tired," she cooed, slipping her sandals off. "My feet could use a massage." She ran her toes up Jonas's pant leg. "So what are you hungry for? I bet they have great lobster here."

"Stop."

She smiled at the brush-off.

"Celeste, this is supposed to be a business dinner."

"It is. I'm working on employee morale."

He pushed her foot away again. "Employee morale. That's a laugh. The last time you blew through town, you showed nothing but contempt for our entire staff."

"Not you." She drained her martini. "Maybe you can help me to mellow?"

"I doubt it. I think you get off on controlling people."

The words seemed to affect her. She gazed out the window, lost in thought. "You're right, Jonas, I can be harsh. *Oderint dum metuant . . .*"

"What does that mean?"

"One of Benedict's favorite expressions. 'Let them hate, so long as they fear.' I only know one way to do things, and that's the way my guardian has taught me. I've spent more than half my life being groomed by Benedict to take over his organization when he retires. He's given me a set of—how do you say—brass balls. I'm his partner and confidante, the son he'll never have, the mistress he'll never marry."

"How is it that you and Benedict met?"

"My father was a Russian nuclear engineer. He and Benedict met at a seminar at Oxford in 1970 and became friends. My mother was a beautiful Russian woman. Benedict actually introduced her to my father. I was born in England, but my father moved us to Byelorussia when I was eight to take a position at Chernobyl."

She looked up at him, tears welling in her eyes. "April 26, 1986 was the last day I saw my father alive. My mother and I were relocated after the accident, but Benedict truly saved us. He moved us into a small apartment in Moscow. He would visit us when he came to the city on business, which was frequent back then.

"A short time later, Benedict introduced my mother to another man, a powerful member of the Politburo whom many felt would become the new Minister of the Interior. They began seeing each other—discreetly. The man was married with a family. Two days before my eleventh birthday, I came home from school and found someone had shot my mother and her Politburo lover while they were making love in her bed."

"Did they ever find out who did it?"

"I have my suspicions. I remember it being a huge political scandal. But my bigger concern at the time was trying to survive on the streets of Moscow, only twelve years old, with no family or money. Benedict found me eight months later. I was working as a prostitute. He sent me to America to a boarding school. On vacations I'd return to one of his homes in California, though he was usually gone, flying to one country or another on business."

"Then, when I turned fourteen, everything changed. I was home for summer break, just sitting outside by the pool when I saw him staring at me from inside the guest house. At the time I had no idea what he was doing, but I remember liking the fact that I finally had his attention. I even teased him, removing my bikini top, rubbing oil over my breasts."

"We never spoke of what happened, but he pulled me out of school to travel with him around the world. He hired a woman to tutor me. Her name was Anne Barry. I remember her having one of those real twangy Tennessee accents. Anyway, Anne traveled with us everywhere. At first, I thought she might be Benedict's mistress. Then one night, just after my fifteenth birthday, Anne slips into my room and crawls into bed with me."

"What did you do?"

"Well, I certainly wasn't into women, but I was confused. Anne was the first person who had shown me any affection since my parents had died. She desired me and was gentle, and I needed the warmth of another human being, so I let her use me. Anyway, those little conjugal visits went on until Benedict found us naked in bed together."

"What'd he do?"

"Benedict's an opportunist, and he never lets his emotions impair his judgment. He was furious at Anne, but decided to use her to teach me one of life's most important lessons—how to deal with one's enemies. The next morning we boarded his private jet to fly to England. On the way over, he had one of his personal staff, a former KGB agent, take Anne into a private compartment and work her pretty good—"

"In front of you?"

"No, Sergei liked his privacy. Probably gave Anne the first heterosexual experience she ever had. Halfway over the Atlantic, the Muskovite brought her out, her arms bound behind her back, bruises everywhere. Benedict pulled the gag from her mouth and told her to apologize to me. I'll never forget the look in her eyes—a frightened, insane animal. The next thing I know, the jet drops to three thousand feet, and Sergei's opening the outer door. Benedict grabbed Anne by the hair and said to me, 'Celeste, my dear, always remember to keep your enemies close, so that you can dispose of them properly when the time is right.' Then he stepped back and kicked her right out of his jet."

"My God . . . he murdered her? Just like that?" *Is she playing me again? I can't tell.*

"Yes, Jonas, just like that. Cold, calculated, and efficient, that's my guardian. The truth is, I was flattered.

It was the third time Benedict had come to my aid. As far as I was concerned, Anne had crossed the line and deserved to die. I even remember running to the window, hoping to catch a glimpse of her body smashing against the water. Then I gave Benedict a hug. What? Tell me what you're thinking?"

Jonas exhaled. "I don't know what to think. I guess you've had a pretty twisted childhood."

"Perhaps, but is this not better than a twisted adulthood? *Nivazhna*." She drained her drink. "It turns out the real reason Benedict was so angry at Anne was because he wanted me for himself. He came to me two nights later. From that moment on, our relationship changed. I became his trusted confidante. And he realized that I had not only inherited my mother's looks, but my father's intelligence. Benedict became my personal tutor in the school of the real world. By day, he taught me how to be ruthless in a corporate world ruled by men. At night, he taught me the art of love. I'm a product of Benedict Singer, his creation."

"Does he allow you to see other men?"

"I've been with other men, if that's what you mean, but only for business. Benedict's not crazy about sharing his toys unless he gets something back." She looked at him with a sad smile. "I've never been in love, in case you were wondering. Never had the chance."

"Why did you change your last name to Singer?"

"Benedict's idea. He knew his men would respect me more as Celeste Singer than Celeste Alekseyev." She signaled the waiter for another drink. "Now you talk. I heard you were once one of the top deep-sea submersible pilots in the world until the Navy accident in the Mariana Trench."

Jonas shot her an icy glare.

"Darling, give us a little credit. We did a thorough check of every principal involved with the Tanaka Institute before agreeing to buy in. You'd be surprised what we know."

"That was a different life. My piloting days are long over."

"I just told you my deepest, darkest secrets. Now I want to know. What happened to that cocky young submersible pilot I remember seeing on PBS when I was seventeen?"

"Christ, now I really do feel old."

"Come on."

He leaned forward. "About eleven years ago, I was piloting a three-man submersible for the Navy. It was a top-secret dive, almost seven miles down in the Mariana Trench. I was tired, it was my third dive in a week, and I knew I shouldn't have been down there, but they had no one else. It's a long, five-hour descent in total darkness, so your mind tends to wander. I remember staring into the pitch, several thousand feet from the bottom, when a white glow appeared, then disappeared before my eyes. The other two scientists on board saw nothing. I continued watching, when all of a sudden this monstrous white head appears out of nowhere, rising out of the abyss—"

"The Megalodon?"

"At the time I had never even heard of a Megalodon. All I knew was that we were about to die, so I jettisoned all of our weight plates and raced the sub to the surface. On the way up, something went wrong within the dive pod and we lost pressurization. One man hit his head, rupturing a blood vessel in his brain. He bled to death before we hit the surface. The other man died in sickbay. I spent three weeks recovering, then was shipped to a psychiatric ward for evaluation. That's where I met Mac."

"And then you changed your career?"

"Yes. For the next seven years, I became consumed with trying to prove to myself and everyone around me that the creature really existed, that it wasn't some aberration of the deep like the Navy said. I gave up piloting submersibles, the one thing I truly loved, to become a paleobiologist."

"But you went back down. You proved everyone wrong."

"I was foolhardy. I allowed my ego and emotions to impair my judgment. Meg or no Meg, entering the abyss in a one-man submersible was just plain stupid. Masao Tanaka convinced me to go. He needed me to escort his son into the Trench to retrieve a damaged UNIS robot. I let him talk me into it . . . hell, the truth is, I wanted to go."

"And you ran into the creature again."

"Two of them. The first attacked us, killing Tanaka's son. It became entangled in the submersible's cable, and the surface ship unknowingly began hauling it topside. And then a second creature appeared, a larger female, who began devouring its helpless mate, ascending through the icy waters in the warmth of the dead male's blood."

"Angel's mother?"

Jonas nodded. "Attempting to capture the Megalodon instead of killing her was the biggest mistake I made."

"Nonsense. If it wasn't for you, we wouldn't have our star attraction. You're responsible for the greatest show on earth."

"What I'm responsible for is a lot of innocent people dying, like those three boys." Jonas felt his patience wearing thin. "Celeste, I need to know. Are you going to reinforce the gateway, or not?"

"Tomorrow you'll determine if the doors are being damaged. Tonight we'll get better acquainted." She slipped off her sandal and rubbed his leg again with her toes.

Jonas stood. "Since you've already checked me out thoroughly, I think I'd prefer a good night's sleep. *Dasvidaniya*."

Celeste swore under her breath as Jonas headed out the door.

Tokamak

Western Pacific Ocean

Terry kicked the sheets away in frustration. Despite having gone to bed more than three hours ago, she could not sleep, her concern over her father refusing to allow her mind to rest.

She looked at the digital clock: 2:38 a.m.

The hell with it . . .

She climbed out of her cot and unlatched the cabin's porthole, breathing in the brisk night air.

Go for a walk. Clear your mind and cool off.

She slipped into her jogging suit and opened the door to her cabin, carrying her tennis shoes in hand. Barefoot, she entered the deserted corridor, emerging five minutes later on the starboard deck of the *Titan*.

She pulled her shoes on and began walking at a brisk pace. A tapestry of stars sparkled against a black velvet sky, soothing her soul. Unexpectedly, an ocean breeze whipped across the deck, sending shivers down her spine, breaking the trance. Pulling the jogging suit up around her ears, she stared at the *Titan's* pyramid-like superstructure rising above her head and listened to the cold wind as it howled through the maze of steel.

She passed a steel turret, the remains of what had been the missile cruiser's thirty-millimeter Gatling guns. Continuing forward, she crossed the wide-open space of deck leading to the *Titan's* massive bow, the only visible structure being a series of steel hatches that had once covered several dozen missile silos.

Terry leaned against the bow's guardrail, staring at the lead-gray sea. Four years ago her brother, D.J., had descended into the Trench with Jonas, only to be devoured by a species of shark her family now earned a living exploiting. She and her brother had been so close. How could so much have changed so quickly?

The wind blew tears across her face. She thought about her father, how the last few years had aged him. The Tanaka lagoon had been his life's dream—an aquarium so large that a pod of whales could swim in and out without restriction. Not only would the facility never house a single cetacean, but financial difficulties over the Megalodon's capture had forced her father to turn over control of his organization to Benedict Singer. It had been the final straw that had crushed his spirit.

She thought about Jonas, realizing she had probably been a bit harsh. Her husband had suffered as much as anyone, yet, for some reason, her love for him had grown cold over the last year. Deep down she knew she still blamed him for the loss of her stillborn, as well as her father's diminishing health. She wondered if their relationship was salvageable.

Terry's teeth began chattering from the cold. Turning to head back, she heard the sound of hydraulics coming from one of the steel hatches. Ducking behind a wall of stacked life rafts, she watched three men in white lab coats emerge from what appeared to be a stairwell built within one of the missile silos.

The men stretched, inhaling the night air as if they had been below for quite some time. Terry heard dialect that sounded Russian. One of the men removed a bottle of vodka from his lab coat, took a massive swig, then offered the bottle to his comrades. They waved him off, heading aft without him.

The man with the vodka spotted the stacks of life rafts. Barely able to stand, he removed a small device from his breast pocket and aimed it at the open stairwell, swearing aloud until the hatch sealed. Then he drained the remains of the bottle and staggered toward the spot where Terry was hiding.

She moved to the opposite side of the stack, remaining out of sight. The Russian collapsed on deck, leaning back against one of the life rafts.

Several minutes passed. The man began snoring. Terry emerged from hiding and leaned over him, gagging at his breath. She stared at the hideous scar slicing horizontally across the base of the man's throat. Then she noticed the remote-control device in his hand.

Gently she pried open his fingers. The man stirred. She froze as he opened his eyes halfway and flashed her a drunken smile. "*U minya tasnit—*" He passed out.

Terry removed the device from his hand and looked around. The foredeck was deserted. Moving to the sealed hatch, she pressed the green button on the remote control. The hatch lifted, revealing a steel stairwell that disappeared below deck. A shot of adrenaline coursed through her. She recalled the words she had spoken only days ago to her father: *Dad, how much do you trust Singer?*

Descending several steps, she turned around and pressed the red button, sealing the hatch behind her.

The hum of a powerful generator filled her ears, the noise coming from somewhere down below. She descended two flights of stairs, coming to a sealed door. Terry turned the circular housing counterclockwise, then pulled the hatch open, revealing a brightly lit, antiseptic-white corridor.

She secured the door behind her and moved quickly down the passageway. At the end of the hall was an imposing steel security door. She felt disappointed, realizing that a personal identification card was necessary in order to enter.

Swearing under her breath, she turned to head back down the corridor when a loud buzz startled her. The hydraulic door began opening outward.

Oh, crap, what have you gotten yourself into?

Totally exposed with no time to flee, Terry squeezed out of sight behind the steel door as it swung open with a metallic hiss. She flattened herself against the adjacent wall, the back of the door pressing tightly against her face and chest. She heard men's voices speaking in an Arabic dialect, diminishing as they continued down the corridor.

Terry felt the security door crushing her rib cage when the pressure ceased, the door retreating away from her face. Without hesitation, she slipped inside, the door locking into place behind her.

She had entered a large lounge. To her left, several

chairs and sofas faced a flat-screen television and DVR. To her right, a kitchenette with sink, microwave, and refrigerator. Directly ahead was a closed door.

She pulled it open gently. A blast of humidity hit her square in the face. To her surprise, she found herself standing in a large locker room. Sinks and toilets to her left, lockers on the right, a passage leading into the showers directly ahead.

She heard men's voices in the showers.

Terry exited the locker room, only to hear the familiar buzz of the steel security door reopening. Racing back into the locker room, she ducked into one of the toilet stalls and locked the door. Heart racing, she sat on the seat, drawing her feet up to her chest, praying that no one would notice her.

Several minutes passed. Terry heard the slapping of bare feet against tile. Peering through the crack between the door and frame, she saw a naked man standing directly in front of her stall, facing the sinks. Dark-complexioned, with thick mats of black hair along his back, he turned on the water and proceeded to shave. Another man spoke to him in Arabic from the changing area.

The Arab finished shaving and moved out of sight. The men continued speaking, occasionally laughing. Moments later, Terry heard them exit the locker room through the lounge door.

She waited another few minutes. Then, drenched in sweat, she opened the stall door and tiptoed out of the bathroom. The locker room was empty, but she could hear the television playing in the lounge.

Damn . . .

Trapped, she walked past the shower stalls, entering

a small alcove ending at a watertight door mounted within a framework of rubber insulation. Above the door was a white sign with red lettering, its message written in English, Russian, German and Arabic:

"WARNING: ALL PERSONNEL MUST
SHOWER BEFORE ENTERING LAB."

Terry pulled hard on the door, which opened outward, a powerful hiss of air pushing at her back. *What kind of lab is designed to prevent air from escaping? Is Benedict dealing with viruses?*

She stepped into an antechamber, which appeared to be a changing area. White tile lined the floor, walls, and ceiling. Stacks of fresh towels sat on shelves above two large laundry baskets and a row of benches. Suspended from hooks were dozens of pressurized bodysuits.

At the end of the room was another pressurized door with a warning sign posted above it:

"NO ONE MAY ENTER TOKAMAK LAB
WITHOUT A PRESSURIZED SUIT."

Sweat poured down her face, her nerves quivering from the tension. She swore at herself, wishing she had remained in her room. She also realized she should have urinated while in the bathroom stall.

You came this far. Finish it.

Searching the racks, she found one of the smaller pressurized suits and laid it on the ground. Removing her shoes, she stepped into the suit, slipping her feet into the attached rubber boots. Pulling the rest of the bulky suit onto her shoulders, she tucked her shoes into her jogging-suit pockets, then slid her arms into the sleeves, struggling to push her fingers all the way into the attached rubber gloves.

Terry reached behind her neck and pulled the hooded headpiece into place, then zipped the front of the suit up. A popping sound filled her ears. The faceplate steamed up, blinding her. She unzipped the suit, gasping, then noticed an orange hose attached to a machine along one wall. Resealing the zipper, she grabbed the end of the hose and connected it to a valve on her suit.

A rush of air filled her ears as the suit inflated around her, clearing her faceplate. She detached the hose, then opened the pressurized door and stepped inside.

Terry gawked at her new surroundings. She was on a narrow catwalk towering five stories above a vast interior that spanned the entire forward compartment of the *Titan*. What had once been vertical launching silos had been gutted out, creating a ten-thousand-square-foot high-tech chamber, the centerpiece of which was an enormous object, shaped like a giant metallic ring.

Terry gripped that rail in front of her, unsure of what to do next.

Two technicians exited the strange object. Both wore pressurized suits and air tanks. One looked up in her direction. Terry waved and they moved on. She proceeded down the spiral flight of stairs, wondering how she had gotten herself into this mess.

She approached the doughnut-shaped vacuum chamber, an enormous circular tube of steel towering twenty feet above the floor. Thick copper coils encircled its outer hull. Numerous cables ran from the machine, attaching to computer terminals and high-tech equipment situated around the perimeter. Within the farther recesses of the lab were massive generators, their deep thrumming sounds causing the steel floor to vibrate beneath her feet.

Terry looked around. The two technicians were nowhere to be seen. She located a computer terminal whose monitor was on and sat down, engaging the mouse. A program menu appeared:

GTI TOKAMAK

Alpha particles	Electromagnetic Force
H-mode	Ionization Chamber
Magnetic Well	Neutral Beam Injectors
Neutron Energy	Particle-in-cell (PIC)
Absorber	Program
Passive safety systems	Poloidal Field Plasma
Primary Transformer	Current
Superconducting	Reactor Fuels: Deuterium
Magnets	Tritium
Target chamber	Toroidal Field Coils
Turbulence	Vacuum Vessel

Terry looked up from the monitor. The technicians had returned and were staring at her from across the room. One motioned to the other. They approached.

Terry stood, realizing that the air within her pressurized suit was diminishing. Walking casually toward the spiral staircase, she kept her head low to hide her face. The men followed her. Nearing the stairs, she broke into a run, climbing two steps at a time.

Men's voices shouted in her headpiece, first in Russian, then in English. "Whoever you are, stop now! Identify yourself."

Terry reached the catwalk, out of breath. She lunged

for the pressurized door, her pursuers gaining on her. Passing through the changing area, she reached the pressurized door and pulled it open, stumbling awkwardly into the showers, her rubber boots skidding out from under her. She fell hard onto her back and slid across the wet floor.

Russian voices filled her ears.

Get up, girl—move your butt!

Regaining her feet, Terry ran into the lounge. Four men, all dressed in surgical gowns, looked up from the television.

Concealing her face with her gloved hands, Terry darted through the lounge to the security door, searching desperately for the means of opening it. She located a green button and pushed it as the Russian technicians came bolting out of the locker room.

Terry squeezed through the door and ran through the connecting corridor. She pushed open the watertight door and ducked inside, smashing her forehead painfully against the steel casing. Slamming the door closed behind her, she secured the hatch as the Russian voices grew louder in her ears.

As she dragged herself up two flights of stairs, Terry began stripping the pressurized suit from her body. Her lungs ached from the physical exertion; her heart pounded in her ears. At the top of the stairs, she reached for the remote control in her jogging suit, groaning as she felt it slip into her right boot.

Terry could hear the Russian technicians panting in the headpiece's earphones. Pulling her legs free of the pressurized suit, she reached into the boot for the remote, then pressed the green button. The hatch swung open above her head.

The Russians pushed through the watertight door, ascending the stairs as Terry emerged on deck. She turned and sealed the hatch behind her, still dragging the pressurized suit.

The drunk!

She ran to the life rafts, relieved to find the man passed out on deck. She pulled his shoes off, then shoved his feet into the boots, working the suit up his back.

She heard the hatch opening.

Terry shoved the man's arms roughly into the suit's sleeves as a half-dozen men emerged from the open hatch.

She ducked behind the pile of rafts and looked around desperately. The foredeck was all open space. With nowhere to hide, she ran across the deck to the rail and climbed over, clenching the lowest of the three bars as she dangled precariously along the *Titan's* outer hull, forty feet above the dark Pacific.

Men shouted. They had found the drunk.

Terry pressed her bare feet against the cool steel plates. Hand over hand, she made her way aft along the hull, her goal, to make it to an immense steel turret, all that remained of one of the missile cruiser's big guns.

Her hands and feet were numb, her fingers too small to wrap completely around the rail. After twenty feet she had to stop. Pulling herself up, she squeezed between the railing, hearing men running on deck.

Terry crawled along the outside of the turret, remaining out of sight. Now only forty feet of open deck lay between her and the ship's superstructure.

Crawling on hands and knees, she reached the maze of steel and climbed up to the next deck. Hearing activity below, she entered the ship, then ascended another level.

Five minutes later she arrived at the entrance to C deck. Hearing voices, she peered around the corridor. Benedict Singer was in his bathrobe, speaking with the two Russian technicians from the lab. They were standing in front of her stateroom, glancing at her door.

Terry hurried back outside and crawled along a narrow deck situated beneath her cabin. Looking up, she verified that the porthole of her stateroom was still open.

Okay, you can do this.

She jumped, wincing as her raw, numb fingers gained a grip along the outer edge of the open porthole. Pushing her feet against the rail to gain leverage, she shoved her head through the hole, the rest of her body still dangling outside.

Her shoulders were too wide to squeeze through.

She heard a knock on the door.

Terry pulled her head out, slid one arm through the porthole, then pushed her head back through the opening. Wiggling and twisting her shoulders, she managed to squeeze inside, falling headfirst in a heap on the cabin floor.

The knock came again, this time louder, more urgent.

"Just a minute—"

Terry closed the porthole, then stripped off her jogging suit. Naked, she tore a sheet off the bed and wrapped herself in it, concealing her bleeding fingers and dirty feet.

She opened the door, feigning grogginess. "Is it time to leave already?"

Benedict and the two technicians looked at her.

"No, my dear, not yet," Benedict said. "We had a little disturbance earlier and just wanted to make sure you were all right."

"What kind of disturbance?"

His penetrating emerald eyes shot Terry an icy glare, then caught sight of the back wall. "It's not important. Go back to bed."

Terry gave a tired smile and closed the door. She paused to listen, hearing Benedict spout orders in Russian to his men before closing his own door. Satisfied, she limped over to her own bed. She was cold, sore, and felt utterly exhausted.

What was Benedict hiding?

Too tired to care, she lay down, smiling at her own daring. Just before drifting off, she reached for a pen and pad of paper off the night table. She scrawled the word "TOKAMAK," then tore away the sheet, crumpling the paper into one of her shoes.

A minute later, she fell into a restless sleep, unaware of the trail of black fingerprints she had left along the porthole wall.

Unhinged

"**D**id I mention that you're out of your mind?"

"Yes, Mac. Several times. Cut the engines. I don't want to spook the Meg."

"Spook the Meg? Forget the Meg, pal, you're spooking the hell out of me."

Mac switched off the Mercury outboard, allowing the thirty-foot pontoon to drift toward the outer edge of the canal's seawall. He reached out and grabbed the exposed ledge of the submerged concrete barrier, securing the flat-bottomed vessel against it.

The design of the ocean-access canal consisted of an eighty-foot deep-dredged channel bordered by two concrete seawalls running parallel to each other, sixty feet apart. Running from the western wall of the lagoon, the canal extended like a highway offramp across a short stretch of beach, continuing out into the Pacific another thousand feet. The eighty-foot-high steel doors that sealed the canal were positioned at the three-quarter mark, seven hundred and fifty feet offshore.

During low tides, the upper two to three feet of seawall were visible, resembling a narrow sidewalk running into the sea. But at high tide the wall became submerged, its presence identifiable only by a dozen orange buoys and signs warning trespassers away.

Jonas pointed to a double helix of barbed wire mounted between the two seawalls. "The barbed wire marks the location of the gateway."

"Christ, here she comes," said Mac. An eight-foot wake surged through the canal, heading for the barbed wire. With a resounding boom, the creature struck the doors, the impact unleashing powerful reverberations along both seawalls.

Mac rubbed his hands nervously across his crew cut. "Damn, Jonas . . . are we safe sitting here?"

"That's what I intend to find out."

"You'll be sure to let me know before your fish escapes, right? Just out of curiosity, which way were those gates designed to swing open?"

"Fortunately, from the outside in. Masao originally designed them to lure migrating pregnant humpbacks and grays into the lagoon to breed. The doors are porous, so ocean water moves freely back and forth into the tank."

The distant sound of timpani drums echoed across the canal.

"Afternoon show's getting ready to start," Jonas said. "I'd better get my gear on."

Mac watched his friend squeeze into the neoprene wet suit.

"Jonas, I know life's been brutal lately, but what you're about to do—well, it's just insanely dangerous."

"If you know of another way to assess the damage to the gate, I'm all ears."

The squawk of the walkie-talkie interrupted them.

"Go ahead, Manny."

"Doc, we just increased the underwater acoustics. I'll let you know the moment she enters the canal."

"Thanks."

The drums grew louder. Jonas realized his heart was beating in sync with the voodoo-like cadence.

"Jonas, we've been friends for what, eleven years now, right? You know you're my closest friend."

"Here I thought I was your only friend." Jonas smiled. "What's on your mind?"

"Actually, it's what's on your mind that worries me. Terry's right. You've become obsessed with this damn monster. Haven't you had enough?"

Jonas stared across the beachhead, focusing on the packed open-air arena. "More than enough."

"Then get out. I'll bet these nightmares of yours go right away within a week after you leave the Institute."

"I plan to, very soon. First, there's still a thirty-one-ton loose end I need to tend to. Do you have that transmitter?"

"Right here." Mac removed a six-inch dart-like object no wider than a bullet. A four-inch barbed harpoon protruded from one end.

"Seems kind of small. What's its range?"

"It varies, depending on ocean depth and topography. Figure three to five hundred miles. It emits a subaudible acoustics signal that can be instantly identified by SOSUS, allowing you to track your monster anywhere in the world."

Jonas inspected the instrument, impressed. SOSUS was the Navy's fifteen-billion-dollar underwater SOund-SUrveillance System, which for decades had been used exclusively to track enemy ships and submarines. Consisting of more than thirty thousand miles of undersea cable and microphones, the global array was now used by scientists to listen to whale song, monitor seaquakes, or detect icebergs cracking apart from thousands of miles away.

Jonas handed the dart back to Mac. "How long will the batteries last?"

"The transmitter contains a lithium primary battery along with a nickel-cadmium booster. You should be good for up to six months."

"Where's the gun?"

Mac removed a small handgun resembling a starter's pistol from his jacket. He screwed a plastic adaptor into the end of the barrel, then loaded the transmitter within the adaptor, handing it to Jonas.

"For a handgun, this weapon carries quite a kick. Be sure to aim and fire using both hands. Unfortunately, the gun only has an effective range of about a hundred yards. Beyond that, I doubt the transmitter would be able to pierce the Megalodon's thick hide. If you give me another two weeks, I can come up with something that would attach to a rifle."

"We don't have that much time. I want to tag her today."

"Doc, come in."

Jonas grabbed the walkie-talkie. "Go ahead, Manny."

"Angel just entered the lagoon. If you're going to do this, you'd better move."

Jonas grabbed his fins. "Keep the boat here. I don't want the Meg to see it when she returns. After I inspect the hinges, we'll pull up along the outside of the canal and tag her."

"Yeah, whatever. Hey, Jonas, you know what the definition of a moron is?"

Jonas positioned his face mask, staring into the blue water. "No, what?"

"A moron's a guy who sees a pile of crap on the ground, knows it's a pile of crap, but steps in it anyway. Go play with your stupid shark, moron."

Jonas looked back at his friend, then stepped off the boat. He plunged feetfirst, a curtain of bubbles momentarily blinding him as he fell into the turbid waters.

Leveling out at thirty feet, he remained close to the interior of the seawall on his right, the concrete facing camouflaged behind a slick layer of vegetation. A strong current pushed him through the channel. Within moments he was at the gate.

Looming out of the misty blue sea, a pair of sealed steel doors dwarfed his presence. Dark and ominous, the submerged barrier ran as far as his eyes could see, disappearing eighty feet into the murk below.

A thin veil of rust and barnacles ran along the sheer wall of metal. Jonas reached out and poked three fingers inside one of the pores. A good five inches of steel. Unable to resist, he peered through the three-inch opening, staring at the other side of the canal.

A chill ran down his spine. *Stop wasting time, moron* . . .

Jonas approached the seawall to his right and

switched on his powerful underwater light. He aimed the beacon at the hinges that connected the door frame to the concrete canal wall.

The damage began ten feet down, becoming more pronounced as he descended. The three-foot steel hinges had already started buckling outward under the force of the creature's head-on blows. Although they remained in place, Jonas knew it would only be a matter of time until the joints were torn free. Once the first few went, the rest would follow quickly.

He set off to inspect the other door when a flash of movement caught his eye.

Fifteen feet below, a broad lead-gray back glided silently along the gateway. Reaching the concrete sea-wall, it banked sharply, disappearing in the murk.

Jonas turned his head. From out of the mist, a second shark emerged directly ahead of him. A wave of adrenaline washed over him. It was another great white, very large. An eighteen-footer, well over a ton.

Fighting to remain calm, Jonas sculled backward until his air tank clanked against the steel gate. The eighteen-footer continued moving toward him slowly. Horizontal pectoral fins flared like midwings on a jet fighter. The great white closed to within twenty feet, homing in on his scent.

Jonas directed his light forward, the beam illuminating dark holes peppering the underside of the shark's snout.

The ampullae of Lorenzini. The predator was zooming in on the faint electrical field given off by his pounding heart.

Jonas waved his arms wildly, yelling into his regulator. The shark closed to within four feet . . . then veered off; the big male showing Jonas its twin claspers.

He looked down.

Three more sharks circled below. All great whites.

Jonas remained frozen against the steel door. Two more predators crossed his vision in front, both males.

So many of them . . . all males. Why are they here?

The sharks began circling faster, clearly becoming agitated. One of the larger animals lashed out at a competitor. For a heart-stopping moment, the two whites tore into one another's thick hides, four-thousand pounds of muscle twisting and writhing as one before separating.

Jonas had never witnessed behavior like this among *Carcharodon carcharias*. He felt incredibly vulnerable, a lone sheep among hungry wolves. He checked his depth—sixty feet.

Jonas flattened himself against the steel door, minimizing himself as a target. It didn't work. The sharks began their attack.

Mac couldn't see the show in the lagoon but knew what was happening by the crowd's reaction. Minutes passed. What the hell was taking Jonas so long?

A three-foot charcoal dorsal fin shot past the boat, its caudal fin slapping along the surface. Mac watched it move into the canal before realizing what he had just seen.

"Dammit, Jonas . . ."

Mac gunned the engine, accelerating through the canal toward the barbed-wire barrier. A second dorsal fin appeared to his left, then another. Frantic, he searched the surface for air bubbles. He looked up at the last second. Too late.

"I'm screwed!"

Mac slammed the throttle into reverse, sending a suffocating cloud of blue smoke into his face. Caught in his own wake, the boat surged forward, the flat bow sliding beneath the spiral barrier, lodging itself in the barbed wire.

"Stupid idiot!" Mac grabbed an oar and pushed against the fencing, desperate to free the boat.

Movement ahead caused him to look up. An eight-foot wake curled out of the lagoon, bearing down on him.

Jonas saw Mac's boat. He began ascending, frantically looking in all directions as the sharks took turns making runs at him.

He paused again at thirty-five feet. A 1,600-pound flesh-seeking missile glided in on him, slowing as it neared the wall. Jonas knew the shark's ampullae of Lorenzini were being scrambled by the fluctuating AC fields given off by the hydraulic steel doors. Closing within ten feet, the great white's remarkable sensory system became confused. Rather than retreat, the prodigious predator opened its gruesome mouth, extending its jaws and scalpel-sharp ivory teeth, rolling on its black eyes back into its head.

Having lost sight of its prey, its receptor system temporarily disoriented, the great white struck the wall to Jonas's right, opening and closing its hideous mouth in powerful gnashing bites as it blindly searched for its meal along the steel door.

Quickly Jonas released air from his BCD vest, sinking beneath the oncoming mouth. The monster's head passed directly over him, its jaws continuing to open and close as it slid its face sideways along the gate.

The fifteen-foot male gave up and retreated back into the mist. Jonas scissors-kicked, ascending to thirty feet. He looked down.

Another male—the twenty-footer—rising directly beneath him.

Jonas kicked harder. The slack jaw opened. Black eyes rolled back, ivory teeth distended, and Jonas knew the beast had him.

The shark struck him with the force of a small truck, its mouth engulfing his left leg up to his hip.

Jonas bit through his regulator and tongue, his body sizzling as if hit by a live wire. He lashed downward with his left hand, striking the shark squarely on its snout with the blunt end of his flashlight. The jaws opened. Jonas paddled, twisting to squirm his leg from the terrible mouth.

The big male paused, shook its head, then was upon him again, jaws stretched open . . .

It turned and darted away.

Jonas registered the luminescent white glow, followed by a deafening explosion of metal, as the Megalodon struck the steel doors like an eighteen-wheeler hitting a police barricade. The impacted doors slammed hard into Jonas's air tank, driving the breath from his chest as the tanks exploded in his ears.

A horrible screech of metal echoed all around him

as the face of the steel door continued to open, thrusting him face-first toward the seawall.

The monstrous girth of the Megalodon pushed its way through the widening gap.

The ruptured tank, now emptied of air, pulled Jonas down like an anchor. Blinded, with his mask hopelessly flooded, he gagged on a mouthful of water as he continued to sink out of control, unable to kick with his lacerated leg.

Pony bottle!

Jonas tore the small cylinder of air from his belt, exhaled, then sucked in a life-giving lungful of air.

Struggling to locate the latch of his weight belt, and blinded by his own blood, Jonas reached around his waist, feeling his lower body going numb. Finally he managed to grab the plastic latch and pull. The weight belt slid away, smashing his mutilated leg on its way to the bottom.

He began rising in a mist of blood that seemed to hover along the facing of the mangled steel door.

Jonas cleared his mask and felt woozy from the effort. Realizing he was moments from passing out and bleeding to death, he focused on swimming to the surface—then stopped, looking into the face of his worst nightmare.

Angel's gray eye was staring at him, her luminescent head less than fifteen feet away. The demonic smile—slightly agape—opened and closed in small spasms as if talking to him.

Jonas froze, absolutely terrified. Blackness started closing in on his vision.

Angel remained motionless before him, momentarily sizing him up.

She recognizes me . . .

Jonas felt himself rising. His left hand reached out, touching the unhinged steel door.

Move!

In one adrenaline-enhanced muscular contraction, Jonas pulled himself behind the mangled door, squeezing between the torn-off hinges—a split second before his "Angel of Death" launched her open jaws upon him.

The Megalodon's snout smashed into the inner facing of the door, driving it back against the concrete seawall.

Jonas heard the steel door groan at his back, shielding him from Angel's jaws. Too weak to care, he shut his eyes and continue rising through the trail of his own blood, buoyed by what little air remained in his BCD vest.

Mac stood over the engine mount, staring into the swirling blue waters. He knew the Megalodon had bludgeoned its way through the gate. What he didn't know was whether Jonas was still alive.

An alabaster glow appeared.

The dorsal fin broke the surface, moving out to sea.

Mac aimed the pistol with two hands and fired.

The dart struck the base of the dorsal fin.

And then something struck the bottom of the pontoon boat with a thud.

Mac ran to the noise. A head bobbed, then disappeared in a pool of blood. Mac lunged over the side, grabbing Jonas by the hair. He pulled, then grasped Jonas beneath his arms, hauling him into the boat.

"Oh, God . . ." cried Mac, gagging, as blood gushed from a mangled appendage he could no longer identify.

Mac stole a quick glance over his shoulder to verify that the Megalodon was moving out of the canal. Then, with a trembling hand, he reached his thumb and index finger into one of the gaping holes in his friend's leg. Feeling the noodle-like vessel bleeding out along his fingertips, he pinched, holding on desperately as he started the engine with his free hand and raced the pontoon boat into the lagoon.

A Magnificent Hell

Western Pacific

Terry leaned back against the rail, allowing the morning sun to warm her face. Having barely slept, she would have preferred to spend the rest of the day in bed, but that would have aroused suspicion.

Tokamak? What was Benedict working on in his lab? Could it have something to do with the Benthos?

She opened her eyes as the *Epimetheus* broke the surface fifty yards off the *Titan's* stern. A diver rode the winch's cable down to the sea, attaching several clips along the submersible's hull. Minutes later, the sixty-eight-foot cigar-shaped vessel swung into place and was lowered onto its docking platform.

Benedict gave her a wave as he crossed the aft deck to greet the members of his A-team. Half of the B-team were already on board the *Benthos*, having made the journey to relieve their companions two days early. In less than three hours, Benedict and the remaining members of the crew would board the *Prometheus* for a week's mission in the Trench.

Terry watched Benedict through heavy eyes, wondering if he knew it was she who had broken into his lab.

Just get the sonar records and get off this ship . . .

Something was going on. Terry stood away from the rail, the surge of adrenaline snapping her awake. Across the deck, Benedict was engaged in a heated discussion with the A-team's captain. The two men looked over in her direction.

Terry met Benedict halfway across the deck.

"Is there a problem?"

"It's my fault, forgive me," Benedict said. "The captain has correctly pointed out that the *Benthos* computers were specially designed and are not compatible with the *Titan* or anything JAMSTEC would possess."

"What does that mean?"

"It means that before the sonar records JAMSTEC requires can be brought topside, they must be converted to an acceptable format on board the *Benthos*."

Terry felt herself getting angry. "Fine, convert it. do whatever's necessary."

"Unfortunately, these things take time. The *Benthos* has been functioning with a skeleton crew. Converting the required information is not very difficult; in fact, you could do it yourself after ten minutes of instruction, but it means tying up one of our people for at least two, perhaps three shifts. The good news is that I'll be aboard the *Benthos* over the next week. I give you my word that I will do my best to isolate and convert the necessary data, or, at the very least, complete a significant percentage of it."

"That means I'm stuck on board the *Titan* for at least another week?"

"Perhaps two if I cannot finish the work. I'm sure JAMSTEC will understand the delay."

Terry shook her head in protest, feeling her fatigue getting the best of her. "No, Benedict, they won't understand. In fact, if I repeat what you just told me they'll probably cancel our contract immediately."

Benedict looked surprised. "Why would they do such a thing? Do they not trust us?"

"No, nothing like that. I think the Japanese just tend to be suspicious."

"Suspicious of what?"

"I don't know. It doesn't matter—"

"It matters to me. I conduct business in good faith all over the world. Wherever I travel, my word is my bond. How dare the Japanese question me?" Benedict's face turned beet-red, the veins in his neck throbbing. *"Nemo me impune lacessit*—no one attacks me with impunity! I will not allow myself to be bullied in any way by any nation. I shall cancel our contract—"

"No, wait—" Terry panicked, her mind racing. She couldn't allow the JAMSTEC contract to be canceled. She also wanted to learn more about Benedict's secret lab. "Benedict, what about me? What if . . . what if you showed me how to convert the data?"

"You?" Benedict shook his head. "You would have to join us aboard the *Benthos*. After what happened to your brother, your father would have me shot if he knew I had taken you into the Trench."

"He doesn't have to know. Benedict, please, it's the only way. If JAMSTEC cancels, it would ruin my father. Please—"

Benedict stared out to sea, enjoying the mind game. "I don't see how . . ."

"Benedict, look at how much time and money GTI has already invested in this project. It's too important to just walk away. Give me a chance to satisfy JAM-STEC. I'll collect the data and stay out of your way."

"Very well," Benedict said, moving in for the kill. "But so there is no bad blood between your father and myself, I want you to write a letter by your own hand explaining that this is your decision entirely, absolving me of all responsibility."

"Thank you. I'll prepare the letter, then I'll pack. How soon do we leave?"

"Two hours. Pack light. There's not much room on-board the *Prometheus*."

Terry trotted across the deck, heading back to her cabin.

Terry descended carefully through the conning tower into the main cabin of the *Prometheus*. The sub's four-man crew were at their stations, the remainder of the *Benthos's* B-team lying about or playing cards in the tiny galley.

Benedict looked up from his workstation. "Ah, our guest of honor. Welcome aboard. Are you nervous, my dear?"

"Excited, actually. It's been a dream of mine to dive into the Trench."

"Then this is a fortunate day. Come with me, I've reserved the best seat in the house for your first descent."

Benedict led her through the tight cylinder, the walls lined from floor to ceiling with computer consoles and electronic gadgetry. A dozen steel pipes ran overhead. At the center of the vessel, the grated walkway widened. Terry could see light coming from below.

Benedict bent down and removed a two-foot square of grating from the floor, revealing the entrance into the spherical observation pod located beneath the main cabin.

"Go ahead. Climb down and make yourself comfortable. When you get bored with the view, activate the computer and type in 'GUEST.' The program will take you on a guided tour of the *Benthos*. Touch nothing else. If you get cold, there's a blanket beneath the seat."

Terry climbed down a short ladder, stepping into the one-seat pod. The spherical structure hung suspended beneath the submersible's hull like a World War II fighter plane's gun turret. An eight-inch porthole set at a forty-five-degree angle lay directly in front of her. A rush of adrenaline coursed through her. This was going to be fun.

A metallic double clang and the track began moving. Moments later, the winch attached to the enormous steel frame reeled the *Prometheus* above the deck. The entire mechanism pivoted backward, swinging the vessel up and over the *Titan* in a long, graceful arc. Terry watched the sea rush up at her as the submersible was released into the water.

Swells tossed the vessel to and fro. Divers disconnected lines and inspected the array of gadgetry and rows of weight plates secured under the hull. One frog-man gave Terry a wave before disappearing in an effer-vescence of bubbles.

The *Prometheus* began sinking, descending slowly on its six-hour journey into the unknown.

Terry stared out at a blue world illuminated by the beams from a half-dozen underwater lights. She could see the tips of the robotic arms' mechanical fingers folded beneath the hull, as well as a series of cameras clustered below the bow. As they descended farther, the sea darkened from a deep shade of blue to a purple hue before going utterly dark.

Cold began to press in on her. She pulled out the blanket and wrapped it around her shoulders.

Like its sister ship the *Epimetheus*, the *Prometheus* was designed with a double hull of six-inch-thick tita-nium. In order to descend, the sub's main ballast tanks were flooded with seawater, making the vessel nega-tively buoyant. Upon reaching the Trench, several steel plates secured along the underside of the hull would be jettisoned until the sub achieved neutral buoyancy. To surface, the remaining weights would be released.

As they passed the two-mile mark, Terry saw a twinkling of tiny lights beneath her window. Two brown anglerfish appeared, each possessing enormous heads and frightful-looking jaws of needle-like teeth. From the top of their skulls a fleshy projection dangled out and over their mouths, at the tip of which was a glowing light, used to attract prey. The anglers darted back and forth in the sub's lights, eventually losing interest.

Making herself comfortable, Terry pulled the com-puter's keypad onto her lap and typed in the word, "GUEST." The program booted. A Geo-Tech Industries emblem appeared, offering the user a choice of user languages. Terry manipulated the arrow to "ENGLISH," pressed "ENTER," then waited for the program to begin.

"Welcome aboard the Benthos," crackled a feminine dubbed-in voice, *"Geo-Tech Industries' crowning achievement for deep-sea exploration."*

A computer-animated image of the *Benthos* appeared, the vessel resembling the northern hemisphere of an enormous globe, cut in half along its equator. Three claw-like legs dangled from beneath the ship's false flattened undercarriage.

A scale replica of a six-story building materialized next to the *Benthos*, only to be dwarfed by the dome-shaped object.

"The Benthos *is a marvel of engineering and technology. The largest submersible ever built; it measures two hundred thirty feet from the peak of its dome to the bottom of its three retractable shock-absorber legs. The diameter of its circular undercarriage extends a full three hundred feet across. Submerged, the entire ship displaces sixty-four thousand six hundred and fifty tons.*

"The Benthos *hull is composed of eighteen layers of six-inch titanium, one hundred eight inches thick, capable of withstanding compressive forces in excess of ninety-six billion pounds. The hull of the vessel is actually a perfect sphere, its flattened underside a nonpressure cowling designed to support its ballast tanks.*

"The interior of the Benthos *is divided into seven decks, each self-contained. In the unlikely event of a hull breach on one deck, the remaining decks would maintain integrity."*

The computer image of the *Benthos* changed, its outer casing dissolving to reveal its internal compartments.

"As we can see, each deck is linked by a sealed stairway, or companionway, as well as an access tube that runs as a vertical connecting shaft down the very center of the vessel. Watertight hatches capable of withstanding pressures in excess of sixteen thousand pounds per square inch separate each adjoining level.

"Our tour begins at the top, or A deck. This domed section, which we call our observation deck, contains an additional interior shell composed entirely of ten-inch-thick LEXAN, a clear, impenetrable, plastic. Thirty percent of the outer titanium hull along A deck can be retracted like the dome of a telescope, revealing the unexplored beauty of the deep Universe.

"B deck contains the bridge, or command center, of the Benthos. *Our computer and engine rooms are located directly below the bridge on C deck. D deck, the central and largest deck in our spherical sub, contains our galley, dining area, and recreation lounge. Crew quarters are located on E deck, along with the ship's stores. Deck F is where the* Benthos's *nuclear reactor is housed, as well as a variety of equipment and mechanical rooms. The sub's single screw can also be accessed from here. The lowest level, its dimensions identical to the observation area, is G deck. It is here, at the bottom of the sub, where all entry into the* Benthos *takes place.*

"Situated beneath the Benthos's *hull is an abyssal docking station designed for the vessel's submersible transport ships, the* Proteus, *the* Prometheus, *and the*

Epimetheus. *A pressurized vault originates just below G deck. Mechanical docking arms located in the undercarriage position the submersible, lifting its conning tower up and into the flooded docking bay. Once the sub is sealed in place, this compartment drains and repressurizes, a feat made possible using the combined efforts of ten, five-hundred-horsepower pumps, creating over two million two hundred and forty thousand foot-pounds of force per cubic foot. G deck also houses a one-thousand-eight-hundred-square-foot underwater hangar, which can be pressurized or vented using massive hydraulic ram pumps located on level F, allowing for deployment of heavy equipment or robotic operational vehicles into the abyss.*

"*Designed as both an exploratory vessel and deep-sea submarine docking center, the* Benthos *can remain within the deep at neutral buoyancy for months at a time. The ship's flat undercarriage is composed of two different types of pressurized ballast tanks. Gasoline-filled, pontoon-like tanks provide positive buoyancy while pressurized tanks filled with seawater can be adjusted to achieve both negative and neutral buoyancy. Forward maneuverability is made possible by our nuclear-powered S8G reactor, which provides steam to drive the electrical turbo generators and motor that turn* Benthos*'s single-propeller shaft—*"

Terry turned the computer off, wrapping herself tighter within the blanket. They had been descending for more than three hours now, more than four miles of ice-cold ocean above their heads. She closed her eyes.

* * *

Terry woke with a start, feeling as if she were falling. Flailing her arms out to her sides, she grabbed hold of a console until she regained her equilibrium.

Two more hours had passed. She glanced at the depth gauge above her head: 34,487 feet. The view from her porthole had turned murky. She realized that the temperature within the pod was rising.

The *Prometheus* descended through a layer of dense sediment-like clouds, an abyssal ceiling of superheated water and minerals originating from beneath the sea-floor. Spewed forth from towering hydrothermal sulfide chimneys, the suspended minerals helped maintain an insulated layer of warmth over many areas of the Mariana Trench.

Minutes passed, the water gradually clearing. Another fifty feet and they descended into a canyon of shimmering black water whose temperatures varied from fifty degrees along its abyssal plains to upwards of seven hundred degrees directly above the mouths of its hydrothermal vents. They had reached bottom.

An unfathomably large shadow loomed ahead. Terry could make out docking lights flickering on and off.

The *Benthos*.

Staring wide-eyed out the porthole, she watched in fascination as the long bow of the *Prometheus* slid within the docking assembly mounted along the undercarriage of the *Benthos*. With a groaning of rubber against metal, the sub stopped. Hydraulic sounds reverberated all around her as the docking assembly's arms raised the submersible into position. Terry could hear a pressurized sleeve being fitted over the sub's conning tower, and then a great whoosh of air as the compartment was sealed and repressurized.

Benedict ducked his head into the pod. "To the extreme, at last."

Terry climbed out of the spherical compartment, then followed Benedict up the conning tower ladder into a small chamber, its circular white walls still moist with seawater. They exited out a pressurized vault door, entering G deck of the *Benthos*.

A barrel-chested man in his forties greeted them. Benedict shook his hand, turning to Terry.

"Terry Taylor, this is Captain Breston Hoppe."

"Welcome aboard the *Benthos*, Mrs. Taylor. We'll stow your gear in cabin eight, which is on E deck, two levels up. We only have a few rules for our guests, but we ask you to follow them to the letter. There are only two passages leading to adjacent decks. When passing through, please be sure to secure all watertight doors behind you. In the unlikely event of a hull breach, titanium doors will automatically seal all hatches and the access tube, but the watertight doors must remain closed for the seals to lock into place. You may feel free to access any part of the vessel, with the exception of certain high-tech areas marked 'authorized personnel only.' We also don't allow smoking on board."

"Not a problem."

"Captain, I'll join you in a few moments in the bridge," Benedict said. "First, I want to show our guest the observation room."

Benedict bypassed the companionway stairs, choosing to ascend directly through the core of the vessel by way of the vertical access tube. Terry followed him into the ten-foot-diameter chute, then up the steel ladder, her arms aching by the time they reached A deck.

The circular room was just over a hundred feet

wide, its dome-shaped, cathedral-like ceiling rising thirty feet above their heads. Plush violet carpeting lined the expanse of floor. Suede chairs and luxurious down sofas ringed one half of the room, with a large oak conference table, chairs, and a bar along the opposite side.

Benedict moved to the wall behind the bar and reached for a series of switches mounted on a sophisticated control panel. The lights dimmed.

"From the moment we first descended from the trees, man has been an explorer," Benedict said, his voice echoing throughout the room. "We have conquered every corner of the world and have circumnavigated the globe. We have probed the distant reaches of the galaxy and explored the nucleus of the atom. We've set foot on the face of the Moon, landed on Mars, and have dispersed spacecraft to all the planets within our solar system. And yet for all our accomplishments, we have barely penetrated the void that covers sixty-five percent of our own world's surface.

"Since the days of Galileo, millions have glimpsed the heavens, yet only a handful have gazed into the abyss. But it is here," he raised his voice, "here, within the deepest recesses of the ocean, that life truly originated. Since time began, an elixir of chemicals, the components of life itself, has been spewing forth from these unexplored depths. The answer to life's riddle is here, Terry; yet man, for all his bravado, continues to fear the deep, terrified by its dark secrets and primal chaos."

Terry sensed a controlled madness in his voice.

"Audientes fortuna juvat—fortune favors the bold. Like the great explorers before me— Marco Polo, Co-

lumbus, Magellan, Galileo, Hubble, Armstrong, Beebe—I dare to fail greatly so that I may achieve greatness."

Benedict hit a switch, extinguishing the interior lights. A deep rumbling reverberated overhead, and then a section of the domed wall began retracting.

"Behold, man's last, greatest unexplored world!"

Terry stifled a scream, her heart racing in flurries as the titanium hull parted. She stared into the black heart of the abyss and thought of oblivion.

Benedict's soothing voice came out of the pitch. "Let there be light."

An eerie incandescent-red glow ignited from the *Benthos*, the powerful lights revealing a vast alien world like nothing Terry could have ever imagined. The view overlooked a petrified forest of countless black smokers, whose chimney-like formations silently bellowed superheated water and smoke from their primordial stacks. At the base of the structures, some of which towered more than six stories, were clusters of albino clams and mussels and crustaceans, sprawling in worship around their source of nourishment. Freakish specimens of glowing fish wove in and out of the hydrothermal vents, swirling like pixie dust within the Trench.

It was a magnificent hell.

Benedict stood before the window, his arms outspread, emerald eyes blazing as he reveled in his glory.

"I am the master of my fate, the captain of my soul. *Veni, vidi, vici*," he whispered, "I came. . . I saw . . . I conquered."

Propositions

"**D**octor, quick. he's awake."

Still in the throes of his nightmare, Jonas sat up, thrashing, tearing the tubes from his arms. He tried to scream, gagging in the effort.

"We need some help here," called the nurse. An orderly joined her. Together, they managed to strap Jonas's wrists to the guardrails.

The doctor steadied the IV, injecting the hypodermic needle's serum straight into the tube.

Jonas felt lead seeping into his body. He floated backward, eyes half-closed, staring up at the nurse.

A man's face appeared. A dull light shone in one of his eyes, then the other.

Jonas tried to protest, but his mind fell back into the abyss.

Jonas opened his eyes. Sunshine. An enormous weight was lying on top of his left leg. He tried to kick it off.

The sensation of a thousand daggers stabbing his leg sent a jolt of pain coursing through every nerve of his body. In agony he thrashed back and forth in bed, gagging on the object lodged in his throat.

The doctor appeared overhead. "Hang on. Let's get that tube out of you. When I count to three, blow out hard. One . . . two . . . three—"

An object slid out of Jonas's throat. He gagged, then gasped a huge breath.

"What—" Jonas rasped, his raw throat unable to voice the words.

"Try not to talk right away. You're in a hospital. You were attacked by a shark. We were able to save your leg, but you lost a lot of blood."

A wave of nausea washed over him. He closed his eyes and took several breaths, then tried to sit up.

"Wait, let me get those straps." The physician unbuckled the leather bands from around his wrists.

Jonas sat up. He stared at his left leg, which was heavily bandaged.

The physician pointed to a series of moist orange-red dots where blood had oozed through the thick gauze packing.

"When they brought you in, you had two-to-three-inch holes running from your midquad to just below the calf," the physician said. "I believe we counted twenty-one tooth marks, requiring one-hundred and eighty-three stitches, including a dozen just to close the femoral artery. By all rights, you should have bled to death."

Jonas whispered, "Mac?"

"Your friend? Yes, he saved your life. Actually reached into your leg and pinched off the artery with his fingers. We've had you on antibiotics over the last three days to prevent infection. Sharks' teeth tend to be havens for germs."

"Three days?"

"The worst is over. You'll be discharged tomorrow morning. The pain should begin letting up in about a week. Until then, it's painkillers and bed rest, crutches if you need to move around. And I don't want you back in the water for at least another two months."

A nurse entered. She handed Jonas a cup of water. "Your friend's outside, and there must be a dozen reporters downstairs waiting to speak with you. You shouldn't be speaking to anyone right now. You need to rest."

Jonas shook his head. "Just Mac," he rasped.

The doctor motioned his friend in, then followed the nurse out of the hospital room.

Mac sat on the edge of the bed. He looked exhausted. "Hey, moron."

Jonas smiled.

"You sure look like hell. How do you feel?"

"Like Swiss cheese." Jonas held out his hand weakly. "I really owe you this time."

"Yeah, yeah, I'll put it on your tab."

"The Meg?"

"Gone." Mac handed him a paper from earlier in the week. Jonas examined the front page.

MONSTER SHARK ESCAPES
by Mike Clary, Los Angeles Times Staff Writer

MONTEREY—*Carcharodon megalodon*, the 72-foot, 62,000-pound prehistoric cousin to our modern-day Great White, yesterday demolished the steel canal doors that had held it in captivity at the Tanaka Oceanographic Institute since its capture four years ago. A stunned capacity crowd of 10,000 could only watch as "Angel" fled her tank, escaping into the Pacific Ocean. Just as the creature freed itself, Jonas Taylor, the controversial paleobiologist from the Tanaka Institute, managed to tag the beast with a small transmitter. Authorities at the Institute are now tracking the Megalodon, which appears to be heading north along the California coastline.

In response to the creature's escape, authorities have ordered all Monterey beaches closed and have issued a small craft advisory, warning all boaters to stay clear of the area. (See complete coverage on page 6A.)

Jonas put the paper down, staring at the ceiling.

Mac smiled. "Notice they gave *you* all the credit for tagging the shark. Hey, Jonas—"

"Huh, sorry, Mac. What did you say?"

"What the hell happened to you down there? All those great whites—what were they all doing in the canal?"

Jonas closed his eyes. "I know why the Meg's been agitated. I know why she escaped."

"So do I. She was hungry and she probably smelled all those delicious whales swimming by."

Jonas shook his head, looking at his friend. "Angel's in estrus."

"Estrus? You mean she's in heat? How do you know that?"

"The great whites, they were all males. She must be giving off some kind of powerful scent. I guess I got caught in their mating ritual."

"Those puny twenty-footers think they're gonna impregnate *that* female?" Mac scoffed. "You'd stand a better chance of breeding a Chihuahua with a Rottweiler."

"Those sharks don't want anything to do with the Meg. They were just lured into the area by their prehistoric cousin's scent."

"So what do we do now?"

Jonas closed his eyes. "You're going to get us a weapon, something that can stop a tank. Once I heal up a bit, we're going to track our little Angel down and kill her."

"Ahh, dammit!"

The stabbing pain snapped him out of his night terror. He lay back, catching his breath as he took in his new surroundings.

He had absolutely no idea where he was.

An adjoining door opened. He was shocked to see Celeste Singer emerge, wearing only a man's white dress shirt. Her long, silky legs moved toward him.

"Dobraye utra."

"Is that good morning? My Russian's a bit rusty."

"Da. Are you all right? You were screaming."

"Yes . . . What are you doing here? Christ, where the hell am I?"

"Just take it easy. I had you moved to another room, one more private. The press can be difficult. I'm staying next to you in the adjoining room. Let me help you sit up."

"I can manage."

Celeste sat down on the edge of his bed. He caught a glimpse of beige silk underpants beneath the shirt.

She squeezed his hand. "Jonas, darling, I really need your help."

Jonas felt himself becoming intoxicated by her scent. Her platinum-blond hair dangled over the nape of her neck, covering the swell of her breasts. He stared at the movement of pulse at the base of her throat. Looking at her mouth, her lips . . .

Stop it! "I need to use the bathroom." He swung his bandaged leg over the side of the bed, registering the painful throb from the rush of blood.

Celeste grabbed his arm, helping him to his feet.

Jonas stood, breathing heavily. He took a few painful steps to the bathroom.

"Do you need any help in there," Celeste asked playfully.

"I can manage."

Jonas closed the door, locking it. He relieved himself, then stared at his reflection in the mirror.

He looked pale, his face gaunt. The thick brown hair was graying quickly around the temples. He needed a haircut and a shave.

The nightmare's real, Jonas. Find the creature and kill it—before it's too late . . .

He emerged fifteen minutes later to find his breakfast laid out on a table before him.

"Hope you're hungry," said Celeste. "The nurse said the doctor will be stopping by in about an hour to check on you before you're released."

"Why are you here, Celeste?"

"I need your help recapturing our fish."

"Our fish? Sorry, I'm not interested."

"I've arranged for a research vessel to meet us in Monterey. Everything we need will be on board and ready to go in two days."

"Forget it—"

"I already ordered the contractors to begin repairs on the canal doors. They'll be working day and night while we track Angel down."

"Celeste—"

"Jonas, you and Mackreides tagged it, that's half the battle right there. The shark's heading north. We have to recapture it, unless you'd prefer to stand by and watch it eat a few more people."

Jonas felt dizzy. He sat down on the edge of the bed and rubbed his forehead. Reality had suddenly become his worst nightmare. He felt as if destiny were dragging him down an inescapable vortex, which could only end in death.

Celeste massaged his shoulders.

"Don't—"

"Relax," she cooed. "I won't bite. Your shoulders are in knots."

Jonas winced as her fingers worked to loosen his muscles.

"Thanks, that's fine. I need to get dressed."

"Me too." She stood and walked toward the adjoining room. "I brought you a change of clothing, just things you had left in your office. Everything's in the bathroom. Oh, here's your shirt."

She unbuttoned the shirt and slipped it off her naked shoulders, then tossed it to him with a smile.

The late-morning air was damp and cold, the heavy spring clouds threatening rain. The orderly wheeled Jonas out the front door to where a limo and a throng of reporters were waiting.

Placing his foot gingerly on the gravel, he balanced himself on his crutches and stood before the open car door, turning to face the press. Celeste moved beside him.

"Professor Taylor, how's the leg?"

"Hurts like hell—"

"Can you confirm that it was a great white shark that attacked you?"

"Yes. A twenty-foot male."

"There's a rumor going around that the attack occurred within the Megalodon's canal as the creature broke free. Is that true, Professor?"

"Yes."

A female reporter from Channel Five pushed through the throng. "Professor, Gail Simon, *Channel Five Live*. In recent weeks several marine biologists have publicly stated that the Megalodon's presence in the lagoon posed a clear and present danger to coastal populations. Now that the creature has escaped— would you feel responsible if others died?"

"The Tanaka Institute is tracking Angel as we speak," interrupted Celeste. "Professor Taylor will be assisting us in recapturing her and permanently sealing her within the lagoon."

She pushed him inside the limo, climbed in next to him, and slammed the door shut.

"Get us out of here. Are you okay, Jonas?"

The reporter's words continued to echo in his ears.

"So, Professor, what's it going to take to convince you to help us track down and recapture your fish?"

"Funny. I thought it was *our* fish."

"I'm not the one haunted by a guilty conscience."

Jonas stared at her. "What's that supposed to mean?"

"These night terrors of yours."

"Who told you about that?"

"I read your medical records. I heard you screaming this morning."

"It's none of your business—"

"Jonas, darling, face it, something's terrifying the hell out of you at the subconscious level. You know what I think? I think you still blame yourself for what happened in the Trench eleven years ago."

"Don't play amateur psychiatrist, Celeste, it's not your calling."

"Life is not so complicated, Jonas. Your feelings of guilt over the deaths of the two scientists aboard the Navy submersible still haunt you. You think it's normal to wake up screaming every night?"

"You're way off base." Jonas stared at his bandaged leg. "Besides, I'm dealing with it."

"Really? Look at you. You're exhausted; your second marriage is ending in divorce—"

"What did you say?" Jonas grabbed her by the wrist.

"Oh, I love it when you get rough." She leaned her face close to his, taunting him.

Jonas pushed her away. "Don't play games. Who said I was getting divorced?"

"Your wife. Terry happened to mention that the two of you are having marital difficulties. The way she talked, it's all over."

"You're lying. Since when does Terry talk to you anyway? She can't stand you."

"We were the only two women aboard the *Titan*. Who else was she going to talk to?"

Jonas felt confused, unable to focus. He adjusted his leg, which continued to throb painfully. "Celeste, don't mess with me, okay? I'm not in the mood."

"Sorry, darling. I know it's none of my business, but I happen to care about you. Not that it matters, but she also mentioned the two of you had recently lost a child."

Jonas stared at her.

"It's true?"

"There were some complications with the pregnancy. The baby died in the womb during the eighth month."

"And this all happened during the trial?"

"Yes."

"It's unfair, but it's my guess that Terry blames this on you." She shook her head. "Benedict says American women don't handle stress very well. Your wife has convinced herself that her marriage to you is over, that the love is gone—"

"Shut up, Celeste. You know what? You're about the last person on Earth I'd accept marital advice from."

"Shoot the messenger if you wish, but—"

"Enough!"

They rode in silence for several minutes.

"Jonas, forget Terry for a moment and think about the Megalodon. I'm offering you the chance to finally put this shark business behind you. Help me recapture the female and I promise you, I'll seal her up in the lagoon forever."

"Forget it."

"I'll pay you enough to retire, and you can finally get on with your life, with or without Terry."

"Mac?"

"Jonas? Where the hell are you?"

"I'm home. Listen, forget about hiring a vessel. We're going with Celeste."

"Celeste? You're jerkin' my chain. Who's this on the phone? What happened to Jonas . . .?"

"Just hear me out. Celeste wants my help recapturing the Meg. I negotiated a deal for both of us."

"Listen, Jonas, all kidding aside, you tell that witch to go screw herself and the horse she rode in on. I don't trust her as far as I can throw her."

"Mac, Angel's tasted human blood and she's moving into populated coastal areas. Celeste's vessel is ready to go. We can't wait any longer, we need to move quickly."

"Wake up, pal, she's using you."

"No, Mac, this time I'm using her. Just get ahold of that weapon of yours. We leave port in two days."

Feeding Time

California Coast

Propelled by the supple movement of its great tail, the female glided in silence through the depths. Despite its prodigious size, nature had endowed the Megalodon, its most supreme hunter, with speed. From the tip of its blunt triangular snout, the muscular body tapered back, allowing it to soar through the water with minimal resistance. Beyond the vertical gill slits were the creature's massive horizontal pectoral fins, which worked like the ailerons of a jet fighter, controlling the creature's roll, yaw, and pitch. Pelvic fins maintained the shark's elevation, while the ominous seven-foot dorsal fin, a gracefully curving sail, held the creature steady as it moved through the sea.

Propelling the Megalodon through its environment was its powerful caudal, or tail, fin, at the base of which was the muscular peduncle, twice as wide as it was deep, which served as a keel, adding stability and strength to the tail. Just ahead of the caudal fin were two smaller fins; a secondary dorsal fin and an anal fin. These slight protrusions increased laminar flow across the predator's tail, helping to diminish drag further.

Even the Megalodon's skin contributed to its hydro-dynamics. Made up of sharp scales, or denticles, the skin channeled the flow of water, decreasing drag while allowing the fish to move silently through its environment.

Cruising just above stall speed, the female continued its journey north along the California coastline. Snakelike movements of its head allowed water to flow through grapefruit-size troughs along the underside of its conical snout. Entering the nostrils, the seawater passed into the nasal cavity, coming in contact with a series of lamellae that allowed it to detect even the smallest traces of chemical odor in the water.

The predator rose through the thermocline, picking up the scent of its prey.

The humpback pod remained close to the surface, swimming in majestic up-and-down movements created by their colossal horizontal flukes. Every so often, a forty-ton cow would breach, exhaling a towering spout of moist air before sucking in a breath through twin nasal blowholes.

Haunting groans and squeals echoed beneath the waves as the pod communicated with its own. Having detected the powerful scent of the advancing hunter, the whales closed ranks, mothers nudging their young closer to the surface.

It was not long before the wolf entered the arena to circle the flock. Sensory cells peppered beneath the shark's snout detected the faint electrical fields generated by the whales' beating hearts and swimming muscles. The hunter quickly targeted the young, moving in for the kill.

Walls of heaving blubber crashed down upon the charging female's snout. The inexperienced hunter veered away, then darted back into the fray. Pushing its nose through the surging behemoths, the shark attempted to latch its teeth into the nearest calf. The cows turned upon the intruder, attempting to ward off the shark with head butts and powerful slaps from their flukes.

The Megalodon retreated, then circled again.

Half Moon Bay Beach
18 miles south of San Francisco

Ken Berk finished setting up the lounge chair for his wife, Emily, who was busy applying sunblock to the faces and shoulders of their three young children.

"You can play by the water but don't go in," she warned.

"But it's hot, Mommy," the youngest complained.

"Daddy will take you in later."

"Daddy's reading his newspaper," Ken said, lying back in his lounge chair. "Hey, guys, look at all the whales in the water."

Broad lead-gray backs rolled across the churning surface eighty yards offshore.

The Megalodon closed again, this time approaching from beneath the fleeing pod. The hunter targeted one of the calves and accelerated, barreling its way through a sea of foam and slapping flukes. Unable to reach the calf, the frustrated predator snapped its jaws upon the enormous tail of a sixty-eight-thousand-pound cow.

Dragged back from the surging pod, the humpback cow groaned, twisting in ponderous contortions to reach its calf, which was floundering alone along the surface.

The Megalodon shook its head like a dog engaged in a tug-of-war, grinding its serrated teeth through the whale's muscular tail in seconds. Blood gushed from the mutilated appendage. The distressed whale moaned in agony. Propelling itself with canoe-size flippers, the adult struggled to the surface, attempting to nudge her calf into shallower waters, even as it bled to death.

The Megalodon followed the blood trail. The hunter rolled sideways, propelling itself along the surface, then opened its mouth and inhaled the trail of blood into its gullet until its jaws clamped down on the remains of the fluke.

Writhing in its death throes, the dying mammal lurched forward, repeatedly pushing its offspring to shore.

"Daddy, can you carry me out to pet the whales, too?"

The child's voice startled Ken from his catnap. "What? Honey, what did you say?"

"It's not fair. Michael's petting them."

Ken sat up to see his twelve-year-old wading out into chest-deep water. "Oh, my God . . . Michael! Michael, get back here!"

Ken ran into the ocean and grabbed the boy around the waist.

"Dad, wait, the baby's stuck—"

Ken watched the stranded fourteen-foot creature

struggle to free itself. The enormous head of its mother bobbed up and down from behind, as if trying to reach its young.

Ken felt a surge of undertow pull on his legs. "Okay, Mike, here's the deal. I'll try to help her, but I want you to stay onshore with your mother." Ken carried his son into shallower waters, then waded back out in water up to his chest. Hesitantly he reached out and touched the calf along its pectoral fin as he eyed the larger cow, straining to reach its offspring thirty feet back.

Ken pulled on the fin, quickly losing his balance. "What the hell am I doing? I can't do this myself."

The mother raised its head, contorting her upper torso.

"Okay, I'm trying!" Ken looked into the calf's huge brownish-red eye. He placed both hands against the side of the animal's head and pushed, slipping as the undertow gripped him again.

A woman in her early twenties and her two male companions joined him. "Hold on, man, we'll give you a hand." Together they began pushing the struggling calf away from the sandy bottom.

"Hey, buddy, are you bleeding?"

"Huh?" Ken looked at his chest, which was covered in blood. "Oh, God—"

"No, it's coming from the mother," the woman pointed out.

The cow's mammoth head rose out of the water and let out a deep moan.

Behind the beast, something was battering the surface waters, spraying great froths of lather in all directions.

* * *

The Megalodon snaked its way along the sloping sandy bottom, straining to reach its prey. Twisting sideways, a pectoral fin slapping above the waves, the hunter bit down on the whale's bleeding muscular peduncle and attempted to drag the beached behemoth, tail first, back out to sea.

Ken's feet slipped away from the bottom as the powerful undertow dragged him into deeper water.

"Hey, man, can you tell if the calf's fluke is free?"

"Its fluke? You mean its tail?" Ken asked. Cautiously he moved behind the calf. "I can't see a damn thing, the tail's submerged." Feeling the undertow pulling him into deeper water, he dove forward, swimming hard against the current while trying to stay clear of the adult humpback thrashing ten feet behind him.

The Megalodon registered the vibrations of the new life-form. Releasing the cow, it flailed along the surface in twenty feet of water, its nostrils snorting the surface like a mad bull.

Ken looked up to see the two men abandon the calf, pulling their female companion into shallow water. Back on the beach, two dozen onlookers were waving frantically. He saw his wife—heard her scream.

A wave of fear tingled through his stomach.

He turned to look over his shoulder, allowing the current to drag him backward another five feet.

"Oh dear God—"

The freakish great white thrust its head forward, snapping its jaws ten feet behind him.

Ken lunged forward and swam against the powerful undertow.

The Megalodon's sickle-shaped tail slapped the surface, its garage-size head twisting to and fro.

Exhausted, the out-of-shape forty-year-old was forced to rest, barely able to raise his arms. As he drifted backward, his left foot made contact with something that felt like sandpaper.

"Oh, hell—"

Adrenaline surging through his body, Ken dove forward and swam with all his strength, keeping his head underwater to streamline his upper torso as he distanced himself from the creature's snout. Swimming blindly, he rammed his head against the side of the calf, gasping as he came up for air. Pushing off the stranded whale with two feet, he dove forward, managing to catch an incoming swell.

A pair of arms reached out for him. He swam through them, continuing until his chest literally scraped along the bottom. Then he stood, the world spinning, as he staggered onto the beach and collapsed next to his sobbing wife and children.

The adult humpback reared up onto its flippers, lifting its head above the waves. In its final moment of life, the beast managed to trumpet its death call, an agonizing exhalation of pink spray.

A hushed crowd of onlookers watched in awe as an imposing pale white dorsal fin, streaked with smears of scarlet foam, zigzagged across the surface. The monstrous shark slammed into the submerged carcass of its dying prey, the exposed upper lobe of its crescent moon-shaped tail thrashing wildly about, dousing the mutilated whale with its own innards.

Ken shivered, his heart beating rapidly, as he watched the tortured mammal being towed backward into the sea, its head disappearing beneath a pool of blood.

Bad Karma

Docked along a stretch of pier, the 163-foot research vessel, *William Beebe*, glistened beneath the cloudless morning sky, its three upper decks buzzing with activity. Technicians in the bow were busy mounting a towering twenty-five-foot satellite communications antenna, designed to link the ship to SOSUS, the Navy's network of undersea microphones. Low-frequency signals emitted by the transmitter attached to the Megalodon's hide were already being detected by the underwater sound-surveillance system. Traveling by way of fiber-optic cable, the sounds fed into a global arrangement of processing stations situated along the Pacific coast. With the antenna in place, the working stations could uplink the acoustical information via satellite to computers onboard the *William Beebe*, allowing the crew to track the animal nearly anywhere in the world.

Jonas made his way slowly along the wooden pier, limping heavily, a duffel bag slung over his right shoulder. The morning sun felt good on his face. He found the cawing of gulls and the creak of boards beneath his feet somehow comforting.

As he approached the vessel, he noticed a familiar figure seated alone on one of the benches facing out to sea.

"Masao?"

Without looking up, the elder Japanese patted the bench, signaling his son-in-law to take a seat.

Masao stared at the bandaged leg. "Why are you doing this, Jonas?" he asked, his voice raspy and weak.

Jonas noticed Masao's hands were shaking. "I think we both know the answer to that."

Masao continued staring at the Pacific. "There is much bad karma surrounding this voyage. You have looked death in the face twice now. I've already lost one son because of this monster. I do not wish to lose another."

Jonas looked into the old man's almond eyes. "I began this, only I can end it."

"In your mind, I know you believe that to be true. There's too much hate in your heart to see clearly. There's no reason to jeopardize your life again. If you can't think of yourself, then think of my daughter."

"I am."

They watched the one-man submersible, *Abyss Glider-I*, as it was lowered onto the aft deck of the ship. The sight caused Jonas's heart to race. "Why is that being loaded onboard?"

"Celeste says the sub is needed to secure the creature in its harness once it has been harpooned and drugged." Masao saw fear wash over his son-in-law's face. "What is it?"

"I . . . never mind. It's nothing."

"Tell me."

Jonas rubbed his bloodshot eyes. "The night terrors I've been experiencing . . . in a lot of them I'm piloting the *Abyss Glider* into the Trench."

Masao squeezed Jonas's hand. "Terry told me about your dreams. That is why I would only permit the AG-1 to be loaded on board, not its deep-water version."

"Thank you."

"Still, I don't want you to pilot that sub—"

"He doesn't have to." Celeste came strolling down the pier, accompanied by a man in his late forties. "Meet Richard Diefendorf, our new submersible pilot. Dief, this is Masao Tanaka and Dr. Jonas Taylor."

"Hey, Doc, a real pleasure to meet you." Diefendorf placed his cigarette into his mouth so he could shake Jonas's hand.

Jonas couldn't help but stare at the man's partially bald scalp that brandished a fresh sunburn and knot-like welt. "Richard, have you ever piloted one of these one-man subs?"

"Hey, call me Dief, all my friends do. Yeah, I've piloted the *Abyss Glider* a few times, but never in water as deep as you have. Celeste tells me this job is fairly routine. I'm curious why you guys even need me along?"

Jonas looked up at Celeste. "There's nothing routine about capturing a seventy-two-foot shark."

"Don't let him worry you, Dief," she said. "The creature will be drugged long before we lower you into the water."

"If it's so easy, why not have Dr. Taylor—"

"We need Dr. Taylor on board to coordinate the shark's capture," Celeste said, flattening the short gray hairs sticking out along the side of Dief's balding head. "Besides, Jonas is wounded."

A deep thrumming echoed off the water. They looked up to see a small white helicopter with green trim circling down to the forward deck of the *William Beebe.*

"Is it really necessary to bring Mackreides along?" Celeste asked.

"We need Mac to help us pinpoint the Meg's location."

"No offense, Jonas, but I don't trust the man. I'd prefer my own helicopter and pilot."

"Mac and I are a team. If he doesn't go, neither do I."

"Fine, fine, just get on board already." Celeste marched off toward the ship, Dief in tow.

Masao stood. "I wish you'd reconsider."

"I'm sorry Mas. I'm sorry about a lot of things. It was my fault you had to sell the institute to Singer."

"Stop. No one is to blame. Since you won't listen to reason, go and do what you must, just come home in one piece. Terry and I will be waiting."

Jonas started to say something, then thought better of it. He squeezed the old man's shoulder and headed for the end of the dock.

As the newest addition to the Woods Hole Oceanographic Institution's Shipboard Science fleet, the *William Beebe* was a floating laboratory designed for a wide range of ocean research missions. The vessel was divided into three upper and three lower decks. An enormous mast rose high at its center, holding lights, navigation antennas, a crow's nest, and the ship's radar. Below the mast, occupying the smallest of the upper decks, was the control room and pilothouse. One deck below was the officer's quarters, followed by the third or main deck, which housed the staterooms and ship's labs. At the stern of the main deck stood an enormous A-frame and winch designed to raise and lower heavy equipment overboard. Two motorized rubber rafts hung suspended on either side of the ship, along with a heavy cargo net. The net would be used to tow the captured Megalodon back to the lagoon. Scientific storerooms, the ship's galley, the sickbay, and an enormous engine room comprised most of the lower decks.

Jonas boarded at the stern, pausing to watch a high-tech harpoon gun being mounted into the deck. When readied, the barbed head of the harpoon would be filled with a massive dose of tranquilizers.

Two of the ship's officers approached.

"Professor Taylor, I'm George Morgan, Captain of the *William Beebe*. This is my first officer, Harry Moon. Harry's had quite a bit of experience with SOSUS back at Woods Hole."

Harry extended his hand. "I know you've been through this before. Any advice you care to share with us?"

"Yes. After you harpoon the beast, move your vessel away as fast as you can."

"Why?" Harry asked, tugging at a gray hair in his bushy eyebrow.

"The drugs caused the first creature to react violently. It attacked and crippled the *Kiku*, which was a lot larger than this vessel."

"That's because you had no idea what you were doing." A man in his late twenties joined them. He was wearing a tie-dyed shirt, his shoulder-length brown hair pulled back into a tight ponytail.

"Professor Taylor, this is Mike Maren—"

"*Doctor* Maren, if you don't mind. I'm an ichthyologist. You amaze me, Taylor, you really do. Four years ago you shot up an adult *Carcharodon megalodon* with near-lethal doses of Ketamine and pentobarbital, and you wonder why the fish went ballistic on you. Unbelievable."

Jonas felt his temper flaring. "At the time, no one could have predicted how the creature would react."

"You should have tested your concoction on smaller sharks first, or, at the very least, contacted us at Woods Hole. If you had, we would have advised you against using the pentobarbital. It's amazing your little chemical cocktail didn't kill the animal. Instead, it wore off prematurely, allowing the fish to slaughter a few more innocent people—"

Jonas stepped forward, pushing Maren backward with one hand. "Do you have a problem?"

"Yeah, I have a problem with gutless stupidity—"

Jonas grabbed Maren by the shirt collar with both hands and lifted him off his feet.

It took the combined effort of Captain Morgan and Harry Moon to get Jonas to release his grip on the stunned scientist, whose tie-dyed T-shirt was torn apart in his assailant's hands.

"You're nuts, Taylor!" Maren yelled. "And you're dangerous. It's your fault all those people died—"

"Maren, get out of here," the captain yelled.

Jonas pointed a finger menacingly at the younger scientist's face. "Stay out of my way or I'll shove a hook into you and use you for bait."

Mac joined the group as Maren skulked back to his lab. "Damn. Looks like I missed all the fun."

"I want to apologize for Maren's behavior," Captain Morgan said. "You should know that he's as brilliant as he is obnoxious."

"He's devised a method to feed medication continuously into the Megalodon, once we harpoon it," Harry added. "It's like a giant IV tube. We won't have to worry about the creature waking, and the mixture of drugs should put it to sleep right away—without the violent side effects you had to go through."

"Wonderful," Jonas said. "When do we get underway?"

Captain Morgan checked his watch. "Twenty minutes. Harry, would you show these gentlemen to their quarters."

Jonas picked up his duffel and followed the first officer inside.

Trapped

Mariana Trench

Terry felt the eyes of the *Benthos* crew upon her as she sat alone at the small table, picking at her powdered eggs. The excitement of being aboard had quickly turned to anxiety and a strange, foreboding sense.

The depths did not frighten her. It was Benedict. The man had changed, his entire persona undergoing a frightening metamorphosis since their arrival in the abyss. A dark monomania had emerged, a hidden malignity freed within the confines of the *Benthos*. Narcissistic rage was slowly being released in a fine madness; a madness she was certain was fueled by Benedict's true purpose for being in the Trench.

Terry knew she had stumbled on something vastly more important to Benedict when she had invaded the *Titan's* lab. Although she still had no idea as to its significance, she now realized that Benedict had lured her into the deep. He had baited the trap, and she had plunged in willingly, and now everything in her being told her that Benedict Singer was intent on keeping her captive.

The Russian stood over her, a sheepish grin plastered on his sea-worn face.

"Benedict wants you."

Terry recognized the scar slicing across the man's throat. *The drunk Russian technician aboard the* Titan. She felt herself shudder. "Where is he?"

"I take you."

Her heart pounded heavily in her chest. She stood, nodding to the Russian to lead the way. As he turned his back, she grabbed a steak knife from her plate, slipping it nonchalantly into the back pocket of her jeans.

The Russian pulled open the watertight door of the companionway, beckoning her inside.

He motioned down the steps. She began descending the narrow stairwell, pausing at E deck. He pointed downward with his index finger, smiling as if toying with her.

They exited on G deck, the lowest level of the *Benthos*. The Russian led her through a brightly lit, antiseptic corridor. Benedict was waiting for them at the end of the passage.

"Ah, there she is, an angel in the depths of hell. Did you sleep well?" The emerald eyes glittered down at her.

"Yes, thank you. I'm actually anxious to get back to the sonar records. Everything looks to be in order," she lied, "just as you said—"

"Of course, my dear, but first, a brief distraction before you continue your toil at the computer." He pointed to the thick titanium door leading into the hangar.

"What's inside?" she asked, unable to disguise her fears.

"Are you nervous about something?"

"No, it's just . . . well, doesn't the hangar lead directly outside?"

Benedict smiled at the Russian and translated. Both men laughed. "Come with me," he said, pushing open the door.

The hangar was a circular chamber, sixty feet long and thirty feet deep, its concave ceiling rising twenty feet above the bowl-shaped flooring. To their right was another door leading into a small control room sealed in nine feet of titanium and portholes of LEXAN glass. Moving beyond the control room, Terry located two massive inlets constructed beneath the hangar floor, each of the five-foot openings covered by titanium grating. An array of powerful air ducts lined the ceiling.

Benedict walked across the chamber to an immense titanium door. "Come here, Terry, I want to show you something."

She joined him, aware that the Russian had entered the small control booth.

"Touch this door. It's six-foot-thick titanium, paper-thin in these depths, and all that separates us from instantaneous death." He pressed his face to the metal. "Can you feel the pressure behind it? It's searching—probing our technology for the tiniest flaw to exploit."

Benedict slapped his palm against the titanium. Terry jumped. He smiled, placing a heavy arm across her shoulder, pulling her ear close to his mouth.

"Look here," he whispered, pointing to the grating

on the floor. "With a flick of the switch, Sergei can vent this chamber."

The Russian smiled back at her from behind the control-room window.

"To hold such power over life, even for a moment, is to play God, is it not?" Benedict could feel her shaking. He smiled, releasing his grip on her shoulder, walking away. "*Quos dues vult perdere dementat,*" he mumbled to himself. "Those whom a god wishes to destroy he first drives mad."

He strolled to the far end of the room where two dozen UNIS robots were lined up in rows of four. "Your father's inventions, standing in line like little children, waiting to board a school bus. Give me a hand," he said, his demeanor changing.

Terry joined him. Using a specially designed forklift, they secured one of the five-foot-high by four-foot-wide titanium barrels and pulled it across the room, positioning it next to the hangar door. Attaching a custom-made fitting to the end of a drill, Benedict unbolted the robot's watertight, pressurized seal as if removing lug nuts to change a tire. Having removed the bolts, he proceeded to unscrew the two-and-a-half-foot titanium lid, pulling it aside to reveal the complex inner workings of the hollow UNIS device.

Benedict motioned to the insides of the deep-water robot. "Would you do the honors?"

Terry reached inside the shell, located the main control panel, and activated the sonar device. Once buried within the seafloor, the Unmanned Nautical Submersible would begin recording and tracking seismic disturbances in the Mariana Trench. By dispersing the twenty-five robots at selected intervals, the Japanese would have an array of seismic detectors providing them with an advanced warning system to predict and prepare for earthquakes along their island chain.

Benedict resealed the top of the UNIS. "We'll leave the robot close to the hangar door. The *Prometheus* will extract it from the flooded chamber using its mechanical arms, then transport it to the designated coordinates. I'll be heading out this morning with the sub. I'd invite you to come along, but I know you're anxious to return to your work."

She followed Benedict toward the exit. "I have an idea," he said. "Why don't you watch us extract the UNIS from inside the control room? It really is quite fascinating, and I'm sure Sergei will enjoy your company."

Terry's pulse raced. "Perhaps another time. JAM-STEC really is waiting for—"

"Nonsense. Seize the day." Benedict pulled open the control room's heavy titanium door, motioning her inside.

Sergei grinned.

Benedict closed the hydraulic door behind them, then exited the chamber. Terry watched the Russian unlock a large valve on the control console, turning it a half-dozen times in a counterclockwise motion.

On the other side of the LEXAN window, thousands of gallons of seawater blasted upward from one of the two circular gratings on the floor of the hangar. Within minutes, the entire chamber filled with water.

Sergei turned to her. With the hangar flooded, the two of them were trapped together in the control room. "We must wait for the sub," he said, grinning.

Terry tried to make conversation. "How is the *Benthos* able to drain the chamber so quickly? It must take an ungodly amount of power to—"

"Water is not sent directly to sea. From chamber, it is pumped into smaller catches, then pumped out over several hours using hydraulic rams on F deck." He unbuckled his pants. "Enough talk."

The pulse in her neck throbbed. She reached behind her back, grasping the handle of the steak knife. "Sergei, don't—"

Sergei lunged forward, grabbing her by the hair, pulling her face to his, and buried his tongue in her mouth.

Terry bit down hard, tasting his blood. She spit it out onto his chest, then stabbed him above his knee.

Sergei screamed, swearing in Russian as he slumped onto the floor in agony, blood streaming from his thigh and mouth. A hunting knife fell out of his hand.

Terry snatched it up.

"Prometheus to hangar control room, we are in position. Open hangar doors."

Sergei stared up at her, his eyes burning.

"Open it," she said, brandishing a knife in each hand.

Sergei reached up and turned a small key two clicks to the right. A red light flickered on.

The hangar door began opening. The titanium walls inside the chamber groaned.

Bright lights from the *Prometheus* illuminated the inside of the flooded hangar. A pair of mechanical arms extended from the sub, latching onto the UNIS robot.

"We have the UNIS. Close hangar doors and depressurize."

Sergei continued staring at her, not moving, testing her resolve.

"Do it."

"Screw you—"

Terry plunged the steel steak knife into the Russian's right calf muscle, retracting it quickly. Sergei screamed in pain, pulling his wounded legs toward him.

"Want some more? The one in the middle's next."

The Russian spat blood at her. Then he reached up and closed the hangar door. As it sealed, the red light turned green.

"Now empty the chamber."

The Russian pulled himself off the floor. Leaning over the console, he closed off the open vent, activating another series of controls. Pumps within the floor began draining water from the hangar bay, sending it on its way to dozens of holding areas throughout the ship.

Terry's and Sergei's eyes remained locked through the entire process.

It seemed to take forever for the chamber to drain.

Terry moved forward, a knife clasped firmly in each hand. "The next time you get near me, I'll reopen that wound along your throat. You understand?"

His bloodshot eyes burned hatred into her soul. He whispered a death threat in Russian.

Terry felt her resolve buckling. She activated the control room door and backed out, then pulled open the door leading into the outer corridor. Hustling to the companionway, she ran up the two flights of stairs leading to E deck and quickly located her cabin. She locked herself in, then sat on her cot, her body trembling in fear and frustration.

A rancid taste filled her mouth—the slightest hint of vodka, mixed with blood from the Russian's tongue.

Terry ran to the toilet and retched.

An abrupt knocking woke her. She sat up in bed, with a dull ache over her left temple. Checking her watch, she was surprised to find she had only slept for an hour. She heard the knock again on her door.

The Russian?

The thought sent her heart racing. She reached into her boot and retrieved Sergei's hunting knife.

"Who is it?"

"A friend."

Terry cracked open the door and saw a well-built black man in his early forties. He was looking up and down the corridor, appearing nervous.

"I don't know who you are—"

"Heath Williams. Jonas and I taught together at Scripps. Let me in before someone sees me talking to you."

She stepped back, allowing him to enter.

"I was in the galley when I overheard the Russian talking about what happened between the two of you. Are you all right?"

"I'll be better when I get off this ship."

"Your life is in danger. I came to warn you that Sergei is talking about killing you."

Terry went pale. "Where's the captain? I have to tell him what happened—"

Heath shook his head. "Won't do any good. I've only been on board a few weeks, but from what I've seen, I can tell you that on the *Benthos*, the only laws observed are Benedict's. You and I may think we're guests, but as far as Benedict and his crew are concerned, we're outsiders who don't belong here."

"I kind of figured that out."

"It's worse than you think. There's a hierarchy among the men. Sergei is one of Benedict's personal staff, one of his piranhas. They have access to all parts of the ship, especially the secured holds on G deck."

"So it's all right if that sleazeball Sergei rapes me?"

"Rape, murder, anything goes down here. And don't expect Benedict to take sides with you against Sergei. In fact if I were you, I wouldn't even confront him about the incident. Don't give him any cause to believe you might go to the authorities once you return topside. Benedict considers himself above the law. To avoid a mess, he may kill you himself."

Terry felt nauseous. "My father knows I'm down here, so does JAMSTEC. If they don't receive my report within the next two weeks, they'll shut down this entire project. Benedict can't just . . . he can't just kill me."

"He can *and will* if he considers you a threat."

Terry took a long breath, trying to calm herself. A thought occurred to her. "Heath, have you ever heard the term 'Tokamak'?"

"No," he said, giving her a strange look. "What's a Tokamak?"

"Never mind, I'm just scared. I think maybe you're right. What should I do?"

"Try to stay calm. You're scheduled to return topside in six days. It'll be difficult, but you have to avoid Sergei."

"How the hell am I supposed to do that?"

"He'll try to find you when you're alone outside of

your quarters. There are certain areas he won't attack you. Most of the technicians in the command center are decent guys, so you'll be safe while you're collecting your data. Try to avoid the galley, you may find yourself eating among a small group and then everyone abruptly gets up and leaves."

"What am I supposed to do for food?"

"My lab is on the same level as the galley. I'll bring food up to you after the piranhas have eaten. Oh, and whatever you do stay away from the lower two levels."

"Why?"

"Sergei spends most of his time there, working in the high-security areas on G deck."

"Okay. What about you? What brings you aboard the *Benthos?*"

"I'm a paleobiologist, just like your husband, except my area of specialty involves ancient marine reptiles. Benedict contacted me at Scripps about a week before the *Proteus* went down."

"Why?"

"The seafloor of the Trench dates back hundreds of millions of years. I guess Benedict decided he needed a paleobiologist on board to examine fossils his subs will be dredging up during the UNIS burial process."

He checked his watch. "I'd better go."

"Heath, what should I do once my report to JAM-STEC had been completed?"

"Talk to Benedict. Maybe he'll allow you to come with him aboard the *Prometheus*. At least you'd be away from Sergei. Right now, I suggest you clean yourself up and get back to your workstation on the bridge. Try to act as if nothing happened."

Heath opened the door, checking the corridor. "Terry, do you have a weapon of some kind?"

"Sergei's knife."

"Good. Keep it on you at all times. If you should find yourself alone with the Russian, don't hesitate to use it."

Terry felt the knot of fear return to her stomach. "Heath, what do you think—I mean, how far will the Russian really take this?"

Heath gave her a dead serious look. "If you have to, kill the scumbag, because after he rapes you, that's what he'll do to you."

The bridge, control room, and ship's computers were all located on level B. Lining the circular walls of the enormous oval room were high-tech navigational computers and electronics. Forward, a dozen manned stations formed a small arc around the captain's plotting area, the central feature of which was a floor-to-ceiling computerized bathymetry map highlighting the topography of the underwater canyon. Closed-circuit monitors lining one wall revealed high-resolution images taken from cameras mounted along the *Benthos*'s hull. Next to these monitors was the helm, a navigational station that looked like the driver's side of a stripped-down automobile. A large steering wheel rose out of the console along with several pedals which controlled the ship's single screw and rudder. Next to the helm were the ballast control panels and communication system, linking the *Benthos* to the *Titan* via fiber-optic cable. Both systems were monitored around the clock by the chief of the watch.

To the right of the ballast controls were four sonar stations, the ship's eyes. Terry sat at one of the stations. Popping a thumb drive into a computer that had been jury-rigged to the station, she listened through headphones as she formatted yet another set of sonar recordings displayed on the console before her. In addition to the acoustics coming over her headphones, the B2Q5 echo sonar system's monitor presented her with a graphic visual of any object that had been detected within the *Benthos*'s sonar convergent zone.

Terry closed her eyes. As much as she tried to relax, she couldn't stop her hands from trembling. Her mind was overwhelmed with one consuming thought: She was trapped within an escape-proof prison with an insane guard who wanted to rape and murder her.

And the warden had encouraged it.

Each breath brought an acrid taste of stress.

She opened her eyes as the sound of an approaching object echoed in her headphones. A light vertical line representing the unidentified object materialized on the solid green monitor. Numerical coordinates indicated the object's range to the *Benthos*.

Twenty thousand yards. She heard a rapid series of strange sounds . . . and then the acoustics simply disappeared.

What the hell . . .

"Excuse me," she said, tapping the shoulder of the sonar operator seated closest to her. "Can you help me?"

The technician removed his headphones and rolled his chair toward her.

"What's the problem?"

She rewound the sonargram. "Do you recognize this?"

The technician listened for a brief moment, then removed the headphones. "Forty-two hertz. It's the *Proteus*."

"That's what I thought. But why does its signature suddenly disappear?"

"According to the catalog date of this sonargram, this recording was made just prior to the sub imploding. Keep listening and you'll hear it."

Terry watched the digital chronometer on the blank screen. The sonarman watched for a moment, then wheeled himself back to his station.

Seven minutes and forty-seven seconds elapsed in utter silence, and then a sickening detonation reverberated in her ears.

"I don't get it," she said. "Why all the dead space before the implosion?"

"The *Proteus* went down in an area heavy in black smokers. The mineral stacks often interfere with our sonar's reflective waves, limiting the convergence zone. The pilot probably hit a black smoker head-on and lost integrity of the hull."

"Still, the *Proteus* was close enough to the *Benthos* to have left some kind of signature. This sonar recording sounds blank."

The man shrugged, returning his headphones to his ears.

Terry looked up in time to catch stares from the other men.

She rewound the tape to the series of strange sounds occurring just before the recording had gone blank. Then she programmed the computer to break the signature down into smaller segments so she could analyze what few clues were on the tape. Instead of completing her request, the screen flashed a warning:

> "THIS PROGRAM HAS PERFORMED
> AN ILLEGAL FUNCTION AND
> WILL BE TERMINATED."

She rolled her chair next to the technician. "Sorry to bother you again, but my terminal just shut down and—"

"Miss, are you aware that the *Benthos* is presently following the *Prometheus* through the Trench and it's my job to keep us from smashing into the canyon wall? Or would you actually prefer to end up like the *Proteus*'s crew?"

"I'm sorry. Just tell me, is my computer capable of breaking down these sonargrams into smaller bites?"

"No. Only this terminal or the one aboard the *Prometheus* can perform that function. Now, please—"

"Okay, okay." She returned to her station.

Terry inserted her own thumb drive and recorded the sounds that appeared on the sonargram just before the mysterious gap. When she was finished, she nonchalantly slipped the recording into her boot, then left the bridge and returned to her quarters.

Awkward Moments

The **William Beebe**

Alone at the bow, Jonas watched the last rays of daylight darken to crimson and violet. The wind sprayed mist across his face, howling its high-pitched metallic ring as it whipped across the forward deck.

The fiberglass bow crashed through four-foot seas as the vessel pushed north along the Oregon coastline. Jonas inhaled the salty air, wiping the moisture from his brow. He stared at the ocean, mesmerized by its unrelenting swells.

Why must I fear the very thing that brings me such joy . . .?

He was startled to see Celeste standing by his side.

The wind whipped her platinum-blond hair and pressed the gray windbreaker to her figure. She remained quiet, respecting his solitude.

Several minutes passed. They watched the horizon turn charcoal gray.

Celeste moved closer, nuzzling against his chest. "I'm cold."

Jonas started to put his arm around her, then thought better of it and pulled away. "Maybe you should go inside."

"Are you afraid of me, Jonas?"

"I don't trust you."

"Maybe you don't trust yourself." She stood before him, her back to the sea. "It's a terrible thing to live in fear, isn't it?"

"What do you mean?"

She moved closer. "I'm just trying to speak honestly with you, Jonas, I know you think I'm a conniving witch, but there's another side to me, and the truth is, I could use a friend."

Jonas searched the vixen's eyes. She inched closer. He noticed goosebumps on her exposed upper thighs.

"I want to tell you something very personal, something I've never mentioned to anyone before."

"Why share it with me?"

"Because I think you can relate to what I have to say. How do I explain this? Jonas, have you ever felt trapped by your own destiny?"

Jonas felt cold beads of sweat trickle down his armpits. "Why? I mean—do you feel trapped?"

She broke eye contact. "Never mind. This is stupid. Forget I mentioned it."

She walked away, wiping her eyes.

"Celeste, hold it, wait a second—"

She waved him off, then jogged across the deck and disappeared into the ship.

* * *

Jonas entered the galley fifteen minutes later. He grabbed a tray and silverware and stood in line behind a half-dozen men waiting to be served.

The cook slapped a roasted half chicken and a side of mashed potatoes onto his plate as Jonas moved through the line. He grabbed a can of soda and an apple, then joined Mac and Richard Diefendorf at their table.

"Where have you been?" Mac mumbled, his mouth full of food.

"Just enjoying the night air. Have you seen Celeste?"

Mac finished swallowing. "No, I didn't know it was my turn to watch her. Hey, get this. Dief here worked for Singer."

"I thought you were in the Navy," Jonas said.

"Served on the *South Carolina* for six years," Dief said, pointing to the knot-like protrusion at the center of his receding hairline. "Had a little mishap and received a medical discharge. After I left, I took a job designing and testing submersibles for a private outfit in Santa Cruz. Benedict Singer bought out the owners a few months later. I was on the design team that built the *Benthos*. I was also the pilot who completed the shallow-water test runs aboard the *Proteus*."

"The sub that went down in the Mariana Trench?"

"That's the one."

"What do you think happened to her?" Jonas asked.

"GTI claims the implosion was caused by a piloting error, but I have my doubts. I knew the pilot. Another ex-Navy man. If anything, he was overly cautious, just the type you'd want maneuvering under the weight of thirty-five thousand feet of water. Personally, I think GTI's covering up something."

"Then why work for them now?" Jonas asked.

Dief grinned. "What can I say? They pay well, and I need the money."

Harry Moon spotted them from across the galley. "Gentlemen, when you're through, the captain would like to see you on the bridge."

The bridge of the *William Beebe*, located on the up-permost deck of the ship, was divided into two compartments. A small, somewhat barren pilothouse lay forward of the command center, which housed the vessel's high-tech computers and electronics.

Captain Morgan stood over a fluorescent tabletop in the middle of the command center, examining a map of the northwestern coastline. "Professor Taylor, gentlemen, come in. We've just received another transmission from your shark. Looks like she's continuing north along the coast."

"How far behind are we?" Jonas asked

The captain referred to the map. "This is our present location, two miles southwest of Newport. Your fish is approaching Cape Lookout, approximately forty-five nautical miles due north."

Dr. Maren entered, noisily sipping a cappuccino. "Obviously she's following the cetaceans as they migrate to their summer feeding grounds," he said. "If we let her, she'll lead us right into the Bering Sea."

Captain Morgan looked at Jonas. "What do you think, Professor?"

"I don't know. Four years ago I predicted this creature's mother would follow a winter migration pattern. Instead, we wound up losing her for several weeks. Let's not forget, tracking a rogue female that is also in estrus—"

Maren rolled his eyes.

"You have a problem?" Jonas asked, feeling his blood pressure rising again.

"No, no, do go on, this is really fascinating," Maren said sarcastically. "Just keep in mind that while you're lecturing us, *Carcharodon megalodon* is moving into populated waters."

"What are you suggesting we do, Dr. Maren?" Captain Morgan asked.

"Cut the shark off now, before it moves farther north, or it may never survive the extended return trip to the lagoon. I've studied the SOSUS transmissions. The predator has been feeding once every thirty-six to forty-eight hours and almost always at night. If she sticks to her schedule, she'll feed again tonight, which gives us the opportunity to catch up with her by morning and capture her here." Maren pointed to the map, his index finger on the mouth of the Columbia River, which divided Oregon and Washington along the Pacific Ocean.

"That's Cape Disappointment," Jonas said. "You couldn't have picked a more dangerous place to attempt a capture."

"Jonas is right," Mac said. "You're looking at waves that punish the hell out of—"

"I'm sorry, and you are?" Maren asked, obviously annoyed.

"Mr. Mackreides is our chopper pilot," the captain answered.

"Well, pilot, just so you know, I'm not into playing 'guessing games' like Professor Taylor. My recommendations are based on SOSUS data and painstaking calculations that take into account everything from the predator's average day and nighttime cruising speeds, distances traveled, feeding patterns, even the average time it takes her to stalk, kill, and feed upon her prey. And unlike Taylor, here, I have no interest in attempting to handle this creature when it's hungry. By the time *Carcharodon megalodon* reaches Cape Disappointment, which I've estimated to be between seven and nine tomorrow morning, she should be well-fed and slightly sluggish."

"Going after the Meg in those waters could be a tragic mistake," Jonas said.

"Professor Taylor may be right," the captain agreed. "Sailors call the area the 'Graveyard of the Pacific,' and rightly so. There's a storm front moving in from the west. We'll be facing fifteen-to-eighteen-foot waves of sheer white water."

"Captain, I'm sure the *William Beebe* is large enough to handle a few waves."

Jonas felt himself losing his temper again. "Listen, pal, what you're not taking into consideration is that Dief will be in the *Abyss Glider*, trying to wrap a cargo net around the Meg in rough seas."

"Enough of this," Maren said. "Captain, I was hired by GTI to organize this recapture. What I don't need is some cowboy paleontologist and his pilot sidekick to tell me how to do my job."

Jonas took a menacing step forward.

"What, are you threatening me again? Go ahead,

tough guy, hit me. Hit me and I swear to Christ I'll sue you for everything you've got."

Jonas hit him.

Maren fell backward, spilling his cappuccino across the map table. He pulled himself from the floor, blood trickling from his nose.

"That's quite enough, Professor," the captain bellowed. "Dr. Maren, are you all right?"

"All of you are witnesses," rasped Maren, pinching his nose to stifle the bleeding.

"Sue me, you little nitwit. Take me for everything I've got—"

Mac grabbed Jonas by one arm, signaling Dief to grab the other. "Come on, Jonas, let's get some air."

Mac and Dief led him down two flights of stairs and onto the main deck. They huddled beneath one of the Zodiac rafts as great gusts of wind threatened to tear the shirts from their backs.

"Man, Jonas, I've never seen you so uppity. Stop letting that little jerk push your buttons."

"It's not just him, Mac. I feel like I'm losing my mind."

"You're exhausted. You need a good night's sleep."

"Yeah, well, I'm afraid to sleep—"

Mac grabbed him by the shoulders. "Listen to me. You know what needs to be done and you'll do it. Once you do, the nightmares will end. In the meantime, let the hotshot fish expert do his job and capture the shark. He'll place the Meg right in your gunsight for you, then we'll see who laughs—"

"No!" He stared Mac hard in the eyes, the wind howling in his ears. "You and Dief—I want you guys to get off this boat."

"Whoa, slow down, pal—"

"Mac, listen to me—we're never going to capture that monster, do you understand? She's way too big. She'll sink this boat and kill everyone on board. This is my battle, not yours. I want you guys to go. Take the chopper and—"

"He's losing it, Dief, grab his arm, let's get him inside."

"You're not listening!" Jonas pushed Dief back.

Mac overpowered his friend, pinning him against the A-frame. "Now you listen to me. You're exhausted, do *you* understand? Your brain's fried, and you're babbling like a little schoolgirl. So I'm giving you two choices. You're either going to come with us and get very drunk, or I'm going to knock you out myself."

Jonas closed his eyes. "Mac, my life's already damned. I just don't want you guys to die, too."

"How noble of you." Mac grabbed Jonas by his arm, leading him inside. "Now that you've officially christened this the 'Voyage of the Damned,' I think it's high time we got drunk."

One deck up, Celeste stood out of sight, listening intently to their conversation. She waited until they had left before returning to her cabin.

Cape Disappointment

Under a gray morning sky, the U.S. Coast Guard rescue vessel, *Chinook*, raced head-on to meet another fifteen-foot wall of raging white water. With a bone-rattling smash, the wave stopped the vessel in its tracks, lifting its bow as it dropped more than twenty tons of sea onto the four-man crew.

Lieutenant Eric "Big Daddy" Wisdom smiled from his vantage behind the pilothouse as he watched cadets Geary and Richardson hold on for dear life. Both men were trainees enrolled in the Coast Guard's heavy-surf and weather rescue course, taught exclusively in the waters off Cape Disappointment. Wearing protective helmets and heavy weather gear, the two cadets were harnessed to a steel rail mounted behind the open pilothouse. Today marked the two trainees' first initiation to what Big Daddy called "challenging waves," and Mother Nature was cooperating beautifully.

Fed by fierce Pacific storm centers, ferocious waves race across thousands of miles of open ocean, often traveling a week or more before arriving at the Northwest coastline. Approaching Cape Disappointment, these powerful swells become enormous walls of churning sea, battering anything in their path. More than two thousand vessels have sunk off Cape Disappointment since the early 1800s, making the waters off the Oregon/Washington coast some of the fiercest in the world.

Big Daddy Wisdom leaned forward to shout to his pilot. "Deacon, how do we look?"

"Winds at thirty-one knots, waves at thirty-three miles per hour. About a seven on the Beaufort scale."

"Perfect. Take us out a bit farther. We'll teach our boys here a little more about humility, then let them get acquainted with Oscar."

Deacon flashed him a thumbs-up, then yelled out, "Starboard bow—starboard bow, hold on, we'll push!" The wall of white water crashed into the boat, lifting it clear over its swell before slapping the airborne vessel thirteen feet down into the ocean.

"Hang on, kiddies, hang on. Two more coming, negative front—"

Geary and Richardson ducked behind the pilothouse as the *Chinook* rose up over the swell, its entire hull exposed in mid-flight.

"*Woo-hoo!*" yelled Big Daddy as the vessel plunged bow first back into the sea. For a frightening moment they were in up to their waists, and then the craft righted itself, bobbing like a cork in an ocean of lather.

"Hold on," Deacon yelled, fighting to realign the bow before the next blow. The pilot wiped foam from his face, bracing himself against the wheel as yet another thunderous wall of water rushed at them head-on.

The Megalodon moved lazily through the thermocline, its caudal fin just barely keeping the big fish above stall speed. Mouth slightly agape, its slack lower jaw quivered reflexively as it breathed in the sea, which rushed through its mouth and gills. Shards of blubber hung from gaps between the predator's serrated teeth, all that remained of the 7,600-pound male elephant seal the shark had devoured only hours earlier. Satiated for the moment, the monster continued its northward trek.

Beneath the creature's teeth-like skin, running from head to tail along either side of its muscular torso, was a sensory canal known as the lateral line. Connected to the surface of the skin by small tubes, this canal contained specialized cells called neuromasts. Variations in pressure within the predator's environment stimulated thousands of cilia within this incredibly sensitive movement detector, which was capable of registering even the faint heartbeat of an animal moving through water miles away.

The Megalodon remained within an acoustics waterway resonating with the vibrations of a thousand migrating whales. The pods were well aware that the hunter was close, just as a herd of zebra knows when a lion is about. But the cetaceans could also sense the predator had recently fed, and therefore, would not attack unless provoked. Still, they gave the beast a wide berth as it followed them north along the Oregon coast.

As the shark moved past Cape Disappointment, its

lateral line detected a different kind of reverberation along the surface, one too massive to ignore. Aroused, interpreting the buffeting vibrations of the *Chinook* as a direct challenge, the Megalodon deviated from its course to respond.

"Stand by, Captain," Dr. Maren called out from his SOSUS station. He readjusted his headphones, listening intently.

Jonas could see beads of sweat form on the man's forehead.

"The predator just changed course. She's now heading due east. Damn, her speed's increased, too. Something must have spooked her."

"Or gotten her attention," Jonas said. "Captain, how close are we now?"

"Just under five miles, but we'll have to make a course change if the Megalodon's moving into shallower waters. Harry, take us farther out to sea. We'll circle back and approach from the west."

Maren looked up, obviously annoyed. "Is that really necessary, Captain? We're so close—"

"Coast Guard reports fifteen-foot breakers. I can't risk taking those waves broadside."

Jonas left the control room and descended two flights of stairs, emerging on the main deck. He jogged to the stern, where the *AG-I* submersible was being readied by two crewmen.

Mac and Dief were standing next to an immense hunk of whale blubber suspended from the large housing and winch fastened to the stern's deck. They waved him over.

"How's your head?" Mac asked.

"Pounding like a son of a bitch. Sorry about flipping out last night."

"Forget it. Where's your fish?"

"Moving toward shore. I take it the bait's for luring her topside. Where'd you get the whale meat?"

"Fished it out two nights ago," Dief said, taking a drag from his cigarette. "All that remained from one of her previous meals."

"You nervous, Dief?" Jonas asked.

"Hell, yes," he smiled. "Any last words of advice?"

"Yeah, don't go."

"Thanks a lot."

Mac slapped Dief on the back. "You'll be fine. Just don't enter the water until we contact you from the copter. Jonas, if you don't mind, I want to be airborne before those waves slam into the *William Beebe*'s stern."

"Hold on, boys," Big Daddy yelled.

The wall of white water exploded over the bow with the power of a raging river.

"Okay, Cadet, toss Oscar!"

Geary reached down and unclasped the life-size training dummy from its leash. "Man overboard, starboard bow," he yelled, tossing Oscar into the sea.

"Stand by," Deacon yelled. "We'll come around the moment we get a hole."

"Hang on," Big Daddy said, "here comes a widow-maker!"

Deacon drove the *Chinook*'s bow into the barrier of

water, hitting the swell just before it broke. The small boat catapulted over the wave, the twin screws spewing water into the air. And then the boat righted itself as the blades gained a foothold on the sea.

Deacon spotted the next swell approaching on the horizon. "Hold on, I'm coming about."

He turned hard to starboard, pointing the bow east against the incoming wave.

"There's Oscar," Geary yelled, pointing off the port bow.

"Richardson, stand by with your rescue hook," Big Daddy ordered. Staring over the transom, he watched the approaching swell race toward them from behind. "Faster, Richardson, go—go—"

Richardson reached over the starboard bow and hooked Oscar, pulling him back on board just as the fifteen-foot torrent of ocean burst over the transom, knocking him flat on his back.

"What the hell happened to Oscar?" Big Daddy held the dummy up, inspecting what little remained of its upper torso.

"Jesus, Lieutenant, it looks like something bit it in half."

"Oh, Christ Almighty . . ." The memory of the seventy-two-foot great white feeding in the Tanaka lagoon flashed in his mind's eye. Big Daddy had taken his family to see the monster only four months earlier. He broke into a cold sweat, his mind overcome by fear. "Deacon, take us in now!"

With a tremendous thud, the Megalodon's head struck the hull of the *Chinook*, cracking four of its support ribs and caroming the boat sideways.

Deacon fought to regain control.

Big Daddy Wisdom looked to his left, swearing aloud as he ducked.

The churning fourteen-foot wave barreled into their exposed port side, pushing the vessel forward as it lifted, then rolled the boat upside down.

Big Daddy felt the breath explode from his chest as he was dragged underwater, the thunderous roar of the ocean above his head overwhelming his senses. He opened his eyes to find himself submerged, caught within his safety harness as a powerful force tried to tear him away from the deck of the inverted *Chinook*.

Locating the line of his harness, he pulled his way to the safety clip and freed himself. Pushing away from the inverted deck, he surfaced, shivering from the cold.

Deacon appeared a moment later. "Lieutenant, behind you—"

Big Daddy turned to see an orange helmet bobbing at the surface. He swam to Geary, who was barely conscious, his life vest barely keeping his head above water.

"He's still attached to his harness," Big Daddy yelled to Deacon. "I need to free him before the next wave hits. Find Richardson."

Deacon saw another wave approaching fast. He ducked his head and surface-dived.

The Coast Guard captain had to kick hard to descend beneath the capsized hull, the cold water biting into his skin, making every movement doubly hard. Grabbing onto the boat's rail, he pulled himself down another five feet until he was level with the inverted deck.

He spotted Richardson.

The cadet had become entangled in his harness. Deacon stared at the bulging eyes of the corpse, now bobbing against the submerged deck. The face was a frozen mask of terror.

A strange glow caused him to look down.

Deacon tried to scream, expelling his air as his mind snapped. Overwhelmed by primal fear, he paddled upward in maddening strokes, slamming his head hard against the submerged deck.

Rising vertically, the Megalodon opened its mouth and gently plucked its struggling victim away from the boat.

Deacon felt daggers clasp onto his kneecaps, pulling him away from the *Chinook*. Grabbing the rail, he tried to hold on.

With an agonizing snap, his legs severed in the demon's mouth.

The Angel of Death rose, stretching her unfathomable jaws wide open, chomping down on Deacon's upper torso and three feet of aluminum rail.

Big Daddy shook Geary until the cadet moaned. "Wake up, son, and hold on!" He ducked underwater, dragging himself below by the leash of Geary's safety harness. The safety line led him straight to the inverted steel rail. He grabbed Geary's safety clip in his numb fingers and strained to unfasten the line.

Then his eyes bugged out in absolute terror.

Suspended vertically, hovering directly beneath the capsized boat, was a stark-white creature at least twice the size of the *Chinook*. The gargantuan head shook, its hideous mouth gnashing upon Deacon's freshly mangled remains.

Big Daddy pinched his nose, choking back the acidic bile that rose in his gut. A flash of orange showed from above—Richardson's drowned corpse. Still secured to the boat by its harness, the dead cadet bobbed against the submerged decking.

Wisdom's heart ticked like a bomb ready to explode.

A menacing gray eye glanced up at him. In his feverish madness, Big Daddy heard Angel's demonic voice speak to him as her quivering jaws opened and closed. *Yes, Big Daddy, I'll be with you in just a moment . . .*

A deafening roar in the distance broke the spell.

The Megalodon ascended toward Richardson's bobbing corpse.

Afraid to move, Big Daddy gulped, his lungs screaming for air. The roar from above thundered like a freight train. Fighting to hold his breath, he closed his eyes as the prodigious mouth closed on Richardson's body.

A thought came to him. He opened his eyes, then ever-so-gently unclipped Geary's harness from the rail.

The gray eyeball turned, registering movement.

Big Daddy hastily wrapped the freed end of Geary's leash around his forearm and clenched his teeth as the eye searched for him.

Geary snapped out of his delirium to gasp at the roaring horizon of white water bearing down upon him. He gulped a breath and ducked instinctively, pulling himself below by his leash.

Big Daddy spun around, Geary's actions tugging him upward.

Homing in on the movement, the Megalodon rose majestically toward the source.

Paralyzed by fear, Big Daddy could only watch as the creature's mouth seemed to yawn open before him, stretching out below him like a tunnel. A current sucked him closer. He closed his eyes.

Through blurred vision, Geary saw the albino's glow. Fear drove him back toward the surface, his mind oblivious to the roar.

The wave slammed into the cadet, capturing him within its rolling vortex.

Launched upward by the arm he had wrapped in Geary's harness, Big Daddy opened his eyes—horrified by hideous pink gums and an upper jaw that seemed to jut forward at him. The lieutenant's heart seized in his chest as the nine-foot mouth slammed shut upon empty ocean; Wisdom literally yanked out of the jaws of death by another incredible force of nature.

The wave hauled Geary and the trailing Eric Wisdom two hundred yards inland before releasing them. Big Daddy surfaced, gagging and screaming and hyperventilating, his shattered mind gone beyond reason.

Something grabbed him and he lashed out blindly, striking Geary on the nose, drawing blood.

"Lieutenant! Lieutenant, calm down—" The cadet located the cord on Wisdom's life preserver and pulled it, inflating the orange vest.

Big Daddy stopped thrashing.

Geary saw the terror in the lieutenant's eyes just before the older man lost consciousness.

"Mac, to your left . . . I see something floating at the surface." Jonas focused his binoculars on the object bobbing in the sea as Mac angled the helicopter closer. "Damn, it's the hull of a capsized boat," Jonas said. "I don't see any survivors."

"I'll radio the Coast Guard," Mac said.

Another powerful swell churned past, the hull disappeared beneath it.

"Mac—"

The wave had rolled the boat back into an upright position. Floating atop the sunken deck, tethered to a rail, was a bleeding, half-eaten human corpse.

As Jonas watched, the Megalodon surfaced next to the rail, pushing its snout sideways in an attempt to snare the gushing remains.

"Oh, Christ." Shaking with rage, Jonas leaned out of the cockpit and screamed, "I'm going to kill you, Angel, you hear me!"

Mac grabbed him by his elbow and yanked him back inside, shocked by the expression of madness on his friend's face.

Jonas turned to see the caudal fin slap across the surface as the creature abandoned the sunken craft. "Where's she going? She's moving toward shore—"

"Jonas, calm down."

"Mac, move, go . . . head east, hurry! There might be someone else out there."

Mac spun the chopper toward shore.

Jonas watched the gray-green waters as the helicopter's shadow passed over an ivory blur. He grabbed the binoculars and searched the sea. "Mac, there." He pointed to an orange life vest being waved above the surface and knew the Meg was racing toward the same spot.

Jonas ducked into the rear of the chopper and slid back the cargo door, his leg throbbing from the effort.

"Hold on," the ex-Navy pilot yelled, accelerating ahead of the fifteen-foot wall of churning sea. The airship dropped precariously to soar just above the surface.

Mac braked hard, nearly tossing Jonas out of the cargo area as he spun the chopper in a tight circle to face the incoming barrage of water. "Move it, Jonas!"

Jonas was already out the door, both feet positioned precariously on the landing struts. He heard the roar to his left as he grabbed the unconscious lieutenant by the life vest, hauling him on board as the other man pushed from the water. The cadet lunged, grabbing Jonas's wrist with one hand, the landing struts with the other— as a heart-stopping glow rose up beneath him.

"Go!" Jonas screamed.

Mac yanked the joystick back, causing the airship to leap skyward as the creature's head rose above the surface, eyes rolled back, jaws fully hyperextended to engulf the legs of the dangling cadet.

A wave exploded against the Megalodon's upper torso, driving the beast back into the sea. A river of foam buffeted Jonas, the cadet's hand sliding within his grasp.

A scream—as the young man slipped from the landing strut.

Jonas watched him plummet thirty feet into the sea. "Mac, we lost him! Go back—"

Grabbing the rescue harness, Jonas shoved his arms inside and released the safety catch on the spool of steel cable. Spotting the orange life vest, he jumped.

"Dammit, Jonas!" Mac yelled.

Jonas plummeted feetfirst into the cold Pacific. He sank six feet before the cable nearly dislocated his shoulders, then kicked hard to the surface, the soaked bandages on his injured leg weighing him down.

Geary wrapped his arms around Jonas's neck in a suffocating bear hug.

Jonas saw Angel's dorsal fin appear behind the cadet. The glistening snout broke the surface, two huge nostrils flaring as the fish snorted the sea like a mad bull.

The bruising noose of steel cable wrenched Jonas and his passenger into the air, driving the breath from his chest, crushing his rib cage. The combined weight of the two men sheared the skin along Jonas's armpits, the canvas flailing in the wind.

Unable to activate the winch, Mac could only watch as the two men dangled helplessly from forty feet of cable.

A blur caught Jonas's eye.

Angel breached, attempting to snag her prey just as she had in the lagoon. Jonas caught himself staring down into her yawning gullet as the man in his arms began sliding and slipping from his grip.

Jonas dug his fingertips into Geary's life vest just as the helicopter lurched to a higher altitude.

The Megalodon disappeared.

Icy tears clouded Jonas's vision as the wind tore into his face. His arms felt numb. He squeezed his eyes shut, struggling to maintain his grip.

Geary continued slipping, his face sliding past Jonas's chest.

Jonas lunged forward, biting into the cadet's life vest and coiling his good leg around the man's waist in a vain attempt to stop him from falling.

The cold wind howled in Jonas's ears. He heard the cadet whisper, "Can't . . ."

They seemed to slow, and then the deck of the *William Beebe* miraculously appeared below their dangling legs.

Fabric tore from Jonas's teeth as Geary's limp body slipped from his grasp. The cadet fell twenty feet to the main deck. Jonas slipped out of the noose, dropping in a heap to the deck seconds later.

Lying on his back, too numb to move, Jonas stared up at the swirling gray skies, listening as the chopper landed somewhere to his left.

Footsteps bounded across the open deck.

A beautiful face blotted out the sky, blond hair blowing in the wind. Warm hands embraced his frozen cheeks—soft lips parting, pressing against his in a perfect embrace.

Mediation

Mariana Trench

Terry squirmed on the lumpy cot, unable to get comfortable. She folded the mildewed pillow in half, propped her head, and stared at the locked door, her breathing labored, the pounding of her heart and her perpetual thoughts keeping her awake.

For the thousandth time, she recalled Heath's words of warning: *Benedict considers himself above the law. To avoid a mess, he may kill you.*

She sat up in bed, on the verge of hyperventilating.

You'll be okay, just stay calm. Three more days and you'll be topside. Four days and you'll be home. You'll hug Jonas and tell him that you're sorry, that you understand what he's been going through.

For the first time, Terry really did understand. Her husband lived in constant fear, his mind consumed by premonitions of his own violent death. What she had dismissed so casually as paranoid delusions were real to him. Isolated in the *Benthos*, at the mercy of Benedict and his Russian goon, she realized only now how overwhelming the power of fear could be.

God, I miss him. How could I have been so callous . . .

She jumped at the knock at the door, gripping the knife by her side. "Who is it?"

"Benedict."

She slipped the hunting knife into her boot and opened the door.

"Were you sleeping, my dear?"

"No, I—"

"Good, then may I come in?" He entered without waiting for her reply.

Benedict took a quick look around the tiny room, then stared into her eyes. "You look positively exhausted. Are you all right?"

"Just tired."

"And perhaps a bit stressed, I'd imagine. Yes, I heard what happened between you and Sergei, and I cannot tell you how sorry I am."

Terry felt hot tears flow down her face.

"Did he hurt you?"

"He tried to . . ." she answered, but then remembered Heath's warning. "It's all right. It's forgotten."

"Forgotten? Why you seem positively terrified."

"I'd rather just forget the whole thing, assuming he leaves me alone."

"Nonsense, I shall report him to the authorities once we—"

"No!" She grabbed his arm, then let go. "No, just let it go. Please . . ."

Benedict eyed her warily. "As you wish. Tell me, how is your work progressing? When will your report be ready to submit to JAMSTEC?"

She hesitated. "Everything seems consistent with the *Benthos*'s earlier report. I suppose I could finish in a day or so—"

"Good. Now sit, for I am the bearer of bad news. Our white Angel of Death, as I've taken to calling her, escaped several days ago from its lagoon."

Jonas! Terry felt the blood drain from her face. "How?"

"Broke through the gates like a rampaging bull. Your fearless husband injured his leg during the incident but shall recover. Fortunately, the beast was tagged with a homing device before it disappeared. Jonas and Celeste are now tracking her in an attempt to recapture—"

"Wait, Jonas is with Celeste?"

"And working well together, from what I understand. The two have become inseparable. But I'm sure your marriage is sound, *n'est-ce pas?*" Benedict paused, relishing her pained expression. "Are you all right?"

"Fine." Terry imagined Celeste flaunting her million-dollar figure at her husband, worming her way into his heart through conniving and seduction. *God, I hate that woman.*

"I can understand your concern," Benedict said, reading her thoughts. "Celeste possesses a beauty that can be intoxicating to any man."

"I happen to trust Jonas."

"A man of virtue, is he? Still—"

"Was there anything else?"

"Just an invitation to join me aboard the *Prometheus* after you finish your report to JAMSTEC."

"Yes, I'd like that."

"Then best to get a good night's rest." Benedict

turned to leave, pausing at the door. "Oh, I'd almost forgotten. The Russian's knife."

Terry's heart fluttered. "The knife?"

Benedict's eyes became emerald lasers. "Yes, my dear, the knife. May I have it?"

Terry hesitated.

"The knife—now!" His eyes blazed.

Terry jumped. She reached into her boot and extracted the blade.

"And I believe you relieved the galley of a steak knife."

She stared at her feet, feeling helpless.

"Terry?"

Feeling like a schoolgirl chastised by her teacher, she walked over to the desk and removed the knife from a drawer, handing it to him.

"Thank you. I shall return this utensil to its proper place. Now get some sleep."

The door clicked shut behind him.

Benedict followed the main corridor of E deck until he entered a more elaborate wing that housed his personal staff. Coming to Sergei's stateroom, he entered without knocking, and in one motion, hurled the hunting knife at the sleeping Russian.

Sergei shot up in bed, the knife still reverberating from the frame of the painting hanging above his head.

"Idiot. I told you to frighten her, not kill her."

The Russian looked pale. "I did what you asked. She caught me by surprise. I was not expecting—"

"The alcohol has made you weak and sloppy. It was your fault the girl infiltrated our lab aboard the *Titan*, and now, against my very orders, you threatened to kill her?"

"You told me she was mine—"

"If and when I say, and only when I say!" he bellowed, his tone causing the Russian to shrink. Benedict took a deep breath and ran both palms along his smooth head, calming himself. "Sergei, listen to me carefully. Our contacts in Tokyo have sent word that the surface ship *Neisushima* is preparing to leave port. The deep remote vessel *Kaiko* was seen being loaded on board. I cannot afford the Japanese breathing down our throats. I need the girl alive to submit her report to JAMSTEC. She may also prove to be invaluable as a hostage in the event Celeste fails to coerce the information we require from Jonas Taylor."

Sergei felt his will buckle under Benedict's piercing gaze. "I understand."

"Good, because I won't be explaining it again."

"Were you successful today?" the Russian asked, attempting to change the subject.

"No, we're still in the wrong area," said Benedict, glancing around the room. He walked into the bathroom and lifted the basin cover from behind the toilet. Reaching into the cold water, he removed both bottles of vodka.

"*Nyet, nyet*," Sergei protested, "it is for my nerves. Benedict, please, I cannot tolerate the depths—"

Benedict unscrewed the caps and poured the contents of both bottles into the toilet.

"Sergei, I know you have more of this poison stashed around the *Benthos*. Heed my warning carefully, my friend, or I shall personally feed you to Satan himself."

Benedict left. He walked to the double doors at the end of the corridor and entered his stateroom. Taking a seat behind the mahogany desk, he lit a cigarette, then picked up the phone and dialed the bridge. "Yes, Captain, please contact the *Titan* and have them patch me through to the *William Beebe*. I wish to speak to Celeste at once."

True Confessions

"Jonas, wake up!"

"Terry!" Still in the throes of his nightmare, Jonas stumbled out of bed, the pain from his wounded leg instantly snapping him awake. He yelped in pain, then staggered to the cabin door and opened it for Celeste.

"Jonas, are you okay?"

Jonas slumped back onto his bed, out of breath.

Celeste adjusted her white bathrobe and knelt down beside him, affording him a glimpse of her tanned cleavage. "I heard you screaming from next door. Are you all right? Do you want something to drink? Water?"

"No." His chest stopped heaving. He realized he was wearing only sweatpants.

"How often do you wake up screaming like this?"

He looked at her through bloodshot eyes. "Lately, almost every night."

"Sure you don't want a drink? I could use a nightcap."

"No, thanks. Have you heard anything more about the Coast Guard survivors?"

"The man who was in shock should be okay. The cadet broke his leg from the fall. Mackreides flew both of them to a local hospital a few hours ago."

"Where's the shark?"

"Moving north again along the coast. Maren says she'd increased her speed. He and the captain are setting a new course to cut her off, hopefully before she feeds again.

"Feeds again? Wait . . ." Jonas rubbed his eyes, trying hard to remember. "The capsized boat . . . there was someone else on board—"

"Two others," Celeste said. "One drowned. Angel ate the other."

"Damn it . . ." The memory flooded back to him, the bile rising from his gut.

"Are you okay?"

"No!" he snapped, standing up. "Are you okay? Does it bother you that two more people died today because this creature escaped from our facility? Is there any part of you that feels even a little responsible? Think about it—two more families torn apart because of—"

"Go screw yourself," she spat back. "Who the hell are you to criticize me? Will my weeping bring back the dead? Will my guilt? I came in here because my room is next door and I heard you screaming. Next time, I won't bother."

Jonas grabbed her arm as she went for the door. "Wait, I'm sorry—"

"Leave me alone."

"Celeste, please . . . My brain's fried, give me a break."

She looked into his eyes. "You know, Jonas, the other night, when we were alone together on deck, I wanted to trust you. For the first time, I thought here's someone who might be able to understand what I'm going through."

"Tell me what you were going to say."

"Not now, I'm not up to it."

Jonas placed a hand on her shoulder. "Celeste, it's no excuse, but I'm stressed out. I really am sorry. Now come on, the other night you started to tell me why you felt trapped by your own destiny. What did you mean by that? Tell me. I honestly want to know."

She sat on a small couch, pulling both feet up on the cushions. "How well do you know Benedict Singer?"

"I've met him a few times." Jonas sat opposite her, propping his bandaged leg on the bed. "I got the impression he likes to be in control."

"Control is an understatement. Benedict likes to play God. He seeks out desperate souls, people who have hit bottom, then recruits them, putting them to work in his private society. He restores value—his values. He offers salvation, but always at a price. Loyalty is a virtue he demands. If he finds it lacking, he uses fear to restore it. Once Benedict takes you under his wing, you're under for life."

"Does the same go for you?"

"Yes and no. Benedict knows he won't live forever. About fifteen years ago he suffered an accident that not only injured his eyes but made him sterile. As his ward, I'm the closest thing he'll ever have to an heir. He's made it my destiny to take over his operation."

"And you feel trapped by that?"

"Not at all. In fact I love wielding power. I love it as much as Benedict. But I have another calling, one I think you can relate to. More than anything, I want to avenge my mother's death."

"You know who killed her?"

"Yes, and I've been obsessed with murdering this monster for as long as I can remember."

"But you've restrained yourself."

"The timing wasn't right. I didn't want to screw things up with Benedict."

"I take it he wouldn't approve."

"Would Benedict approve?" A wicked smile spread across her face. "Benedict has no problem with me killing someone—as long as it's good for business. In this case, he'd probably disagree. Benedict and I have a strange relationship. I love him, but he still frightens the hell out of me."

Like you frighten the hell out of me.

Celeste seemed to read his thought. "I take it you don't approve?"

"It's not my place to judge. My mother wasn't the one murdered."

"Benedict would say I'm nursing an everlasting wound within my breast. I'm biding my time, keeping my enemy close."

"Then you are going to go through with it?"

"One day." She lay back, placing a bare leg atop the couch in a seductive pose. "What I said scares you, doesn't it? Well, at least I face my fears instead of waking up screaming every night."

Jonas felt a cold sweat break out along his back. He

reached across the bed and grabbed his T-shirt, slipping it over his head.

"Now you talk," Celeste said. "I want to know what's really haunting you. How long have you been having these nightmares?"

"They started about two years ago, during the trial. Imagine sitting in a courtroom, week in and week out, having to face the surviving parents and spouses and children of innocent people who died brutal deaths, all because you were trying to capture a shark."

"The trial was a sham. Everybody knows the judge railroaded you."

"Maybe, but the pressure became overwhelming. I'd go home and stay up all night, my insides torn apart from guilt. Terry was pregnant at the time. We'd been so excited, our first child and all. But the stress of the trial and the media coverage really took its toll. Just before the verdict came in, the baby died in the womb during the eighth month of pregnancy."

"I'm sorry."

"The night terrors began right after that. The psychiatrist labeled it posttraumatic stress disorder, brought on by feelings of guilt manifested during the trial. For a while, the medication worked, but recently, the dreams have been coming back, this time worse than ever. That's when I realized what was really happening."

"I don't understand."

Jonas took a deep breath. "I knew as far back as two years ago that the Meg's offspring was growing way too large to control. I think the nightmares were my subconscious telling me to get off my butt and do something before it was too late."

"So why didn't you?"

"I did—or rather, I passed the buck. I told Masao, warning him that one day the creature would escape, that we needed to permanently seal her in the lagoon. He agreed, but we just didn't have the funds. Out of left field, the judge slapped us with a cease-and-desist order, closing the Institute down and freezing our assets. We couldn't do anything but pay attorneys and feed the damn shark. It was as if the powers that be wanted us to go bankrupt."

Jonas stood and limped to the porthole, opening it to take in some fresh air. "I blew it, Celeste, three times I've blown it. First, aboard the *Sea Cliff*, then by trying to capture the Megalodon instead of killing it, and now, by allowing its offspring to escape. How does the saying go? A coward dies a thousand deaths, a brave man dies but one. That's me. I should have drained the lagoon and drowned the Megalodon two years ago."

"Kill the Meg? Are you crazy?"

"A good question. I'm beginning to wonder."

She stood, moving next to him. He could smell the jasmine fragrance on her skin. He stared at her, feeling himself getting aroused as she nonchalantly undid her robe.

"Celeste, you better go."

She moved closer. "I don't have to."

"You're a beautiful woman, but I'm married—happily married."

"You don't seem very happy."

"You're right, but I love my wife. Now please—"

"Okay, but you still haven't answered my question."

"You mean about feeling trapped?" He closed the

porthole, distancing himself from her. "Eleven years ago, I cheated death. I think I was supposed to have died aboard the *Sea Cliff*."

"That's nonsense. Why say such a thing?"

"Because I've seen my death and it has closure. In my dreams, I'm descending in the deep-sea model of the *Abyss Glider*. Angel appears out of the blackness, and this time, I can't escape. I know it sounds crazy, but I'm convinced it's my destiny to die where I should have years ago, in the dark recesses of the Trench."

Kindred Souls

Mariana Trench

Terry stared at the computer screen, rereading for the fourth time the report and technical data she was contemplating emailing to the Japanese Marine Science Technology Center.

> TO: Dr. Tsukamoto, Director
>   JAMSTEC
> REF: File MT
>
> Careful review of all pertinent data regarding the May 22 accident within the Mariana Trench indicates that no other vessels or predatory life-forms were involved. My evaluation of sonargrams from both the *Benthos* and its surface vessel, *Titan*, indicate nothing out of the ordinary prior to the (*Proteus*) submersible's loss of hull

integrity (see enclosed sonar records, ref.
#5/22.10:34.17 through #5/22.10:56.04).

It is my opinion that piloting error was responsible for the submersible accident,
most likely caused when the starboard
bow plane struck a black smoker (see enclosed photos of debris field).

Geo-Tech Industries has already begun
the process of restitution in regard to the
four victims' surviving families. It is our request that deployment of the UNIS array
be allowed to continue, and, unless further
information is requested, the Tanaka Institute will consider the matter closed.

Terry Tanaka-Taylor
Exec. Vice President
TANAKA OCEANOGRAPHIC INSTITUTE

Terry printed a copy of the letter for Benedict, then
typed in JAMSTEC's email address.

It's a lie, she thought, *but it's the only way Benedict
will let me off this ship.*

Maneuvering the mouse, she emailed the report, via
the *Titan*, to JAMSTEC headquarters.

Bells sounded without warning. The chief of the
watch ran to his station and grabbed the radio.

"Chief of the Watch here. Go ahead, *Titan*."

"Towed array has detected four bioforms moving
south by southeast through the Trench. Bearing zero-
one-eight, speed, just under twelve knots. Range to *Pro-*

metheus . . . fourteen-point-three kilometers and closing fast."

Terry's heart raced. *Four objects had momentarily appeared on the* Benthos*'s sonar records seven minutes before the Proteus had gone down. But Jonas had told her Megalodons don't hunt in packs.*

"Dammit," Captain Hoppe swore, taking up position behind his two sonar technicians. "How far ahead is the *Prometheus?*"

"Nineteen kilometers, sir."

"Chief, contact the *Prometheus*. Inform them of the situation and tell them to hightail it back here at once. Helm, full speed ahead."

Terry felt the vessel leap forward, achieving its maximum speed of five knots.

"Captain, *Titan* now reporting that the objects have increased their speed to eighteen knots."

"Christ."

"Sir, *Prometheus* has come about. ETA with *Benthos*, forty-six minutes. This one's going to be close, Captain."

This one? Terry saw the sonarman wipe his brow.

The captain grabbed the phone from the wall and went on loudspeaker. "This is the Captain. All personnel, prepare for an emergency docking. This is not a drill."

"Captain, bioforms have just come into sonar range, now appearing on my screen."

The captain moved to the sonar station, swearing under his breath. "Damn it, I warned Benedict not to venture too far out of range—"

Terry saw the man's expression change from frustration to fear. She turned around in her chair.

Sergei was standing behind her, his dark eyes furious.

"Why is she here?" he spat.

Terry went limp.

"She's assisting us at sonar," the captain lied.

Sergei swore at him in Russian.

"Sergei," ordered the captain, "you're needed at the docking station."

Terry felt herself thrown off balance as the Russian grabbed her hair from behind. She gagged at the smell of alcohol on his breath as he pushed his cheek right next to hers, his whiskers scratching her face. "Tonight, we finish our business, *da*?"

She twisted sideways and fell to the floor as the captain stepped forward.

"Off my bridge, mister. Now!"

Sergei grinned at Terry. He pursed his lips, making a kissing sound. Then he disappeared down the access tube.

"You okay, miss?" The captain helped her to her feet.

She nodded, unable to find her voice. She forced herself to remain at her station for several minutes, then crossed the bridge and locked herself in one of the bathrooms.

Her hands had stopped trembling when she returned to the sonar station thirty minutes later. Not one crewman would look up as she walked by.

"Captain, the bioforms have broken off," sonar reported.

The captain joined the chief at the sonar station.

"Probably sensed the *Benthos* and decided we were a little too big to mess with," the chief suggested.

"Maybe. How close were we to the *Prometheus* when they broke off?"

"Just under a kilometer, sir, but their last recorded speed was twenty-two knots. Whatever they were, they wanted to get to the *Prometheus* before we did."

"Agreed. Notify me when the sub docks." He turned to Terry. "Mrs. Taylor, why don't you join me upstairs in the observation room? We'll watch the *Prometheus* as she returns."

Still a bit shaken, Terry followed the captain up the access tube's ladder and onto level A. He sealed the hole behind him, then moved to the bar.

"Drink?"

She nodded.

He poured her a scotch, then activated the mechanism to retract the outer titanium dome.

Terry drained her glass as the heart of the Mariana Trench opened before her.

The *Benthos* soared majestically through the netherworld like an abyssal blimp. Somewhere below, unseen hydrothermal vents spewed blue-black mushroom clouds of searing hot mineral water at them directly from the furnaces of hell. Enormous patches of spaghetti-like tubeworms danced through the undulating waves of heat. Directly ahead, a patch of sea shimmered luminescent-blue, as a school of deep-sea bioluminescent jellyfish made their way through the canyon.

Terry stood mesmerized as a plethora of orange, red, and purple objects flowed past the window in every conceivable size and shape.

The captain pointed to a ghostly translucent-blue figure that resembled a screen-saver pattern more than a life-form. "Those are called *Kiyohimea*. I'm told they're a species of ctenophore named for a mythical Japanese princess. Bizarre, aren't they?"

"Beautiful. And those?" Terry asked, pointing to a shimmering blotch of bright orange.

"Deep-ocean herbivores. They're actually translucent, but the ship's red light gives their mucus filters an orange glow."

"They're wonderful."

"And dangerous," the captain said. He refilled her glass. "Sergei is not one to trifle with, especially when he's drunk. You'll be safe on the bridge and in your quarters, but don't venture below E deck. I'm sorry. I wish there was more I could do to protect you. I may be Captain, but this is Benedict's ship. We live by his rules down here."

He stared into the abyss. "Look. Here comes the *Prometheus*."

A flash of lights, and then the white cigar-shaped sub appeared, moving in surreal motion through dense clouds of rising smoke. They watched the vessel descend beneath the *Benthos*, disappearing from view. Moments later, a metallic ring reverberated around the ship as the submersible docked into place.

"Captain, those objects chasing the *Prometheus*? Did they also attack the *Proteus*?"

"I don't know. Yes, it's possible."

"Possible?" Terry moved in front of him, forcing him to make eye contact.

"Look, I don't know what they were, only that they hunt in packs."

"Why is Benedict so quick to risk his life and those of his crew? I know it's not just to deploy the UNIS robots. What's the real mission? What's out there that's so damn important?"

He's uncomfortable. He wants to talk, but he's scared.

"It's not my place to discuss our—"

"Frightening our guest, Captain?" They turned to see Benedict himself climbing up through the access tube.

"Just sharing my opinions."

The emerald eyes flashed a warning signal. "*Quot homines, tot sententiae*—there are as many opinions as there are men. Don't allow our *kapitan's* opinion to sway your scientific objectivity, my dear."

"What was it that was after the *Prometheus*, Benedict?"

Benedict seemed to ignore her, moving to stand before the bay window, his back to them. A six-foot eel-like creature came into view. Jet-black, it slithered its elongated body against the dome just above Benedict's head. Terry stared at the creature, which trailed an iridescent bulb attached to its lower jaw by a long antenna.

"A black dragonfish," Benedict said, moving his fingers to and fro across the glass. The creature stared at his hand with its translucent eye, then opened its jaws nearly 180 degrees as it tried to bite down upon the barrier, displaying row upon row of needle-like teeth.

Benedict seemed to relish the performance. "Lovely, isn't it? Are we still on Earth, or have we traveled to an alien world? Is there a difference? Like futuristic astronauts, we journey through a hostile environment, kept alive only within the fragile confines of our vessel. We are the true explorers of our century, delving into the unknown, facing death at any moment. The seven miles of sea above our heads might as well be seven light-years, eh, my dear, for who could possibly rescue us in a real emergency?"

Benedict turned to face Terry. "You ask me what is out there. My answer is, the unknown. We know far more about other planets than we do about this parcel of ocean that has remained unchanged for hundreds of millions of years. Yes, Terry Taylor, there *are* undiscovered life-forms living in this hellhole. Some are beautiful, others frightening, as our captain would tell us, yet all have survived the ravages of time while remaining confined within this glorious purgatory. I cannot tell you what is out there but as scientists and explorers, I know it is our duty and our mission to learn."

"How many lives must be lost in that mission?" Terry asked.

"I take it you are referring to our four departed souls lost on the *Proteus*. I believe your report to JAMSTEC indicated the vessel imploded due to pilot error."

"What about those life-forms chasing the *Prometheus?*"

"What about them?"

"Don't play games with me, Benedict. It's fairly obvious that whatever chased the *Prometheus* could have also destroyed the *Proteus*."

"And you can prove this?"

The statement caught her off guard. "No, but had I known—"

"Had you known what? That undiscovered life-forms may exist in the abyss that could threaten our lives? Didn't your husband prove that years ago?"

"Yes, which is precisely why the United States and Japan have been hesitant to allow other groups to explore the Trench. If JAMSTEC suspected that the crew of the *Proteus* was killed—"

"They'd be obligated to inform the Americans, who would order an investigation and delay the mission for months," Benedict finished. "Knowing what you do now, do you wish to change your report?"

"I—No, I didn't say that—"

"Then, what are you saying?"

Terry rubbed her forehead. "I guess what I'm saying is that I just don't want to be lied to anymore."

"Lied to? You accuse me of lying?"

"I think everyone aboard the *Titan* and *Benthos* knew these creatures attacked the *Proteus*. I believe you altered the sonar records so I'd provide JAMSTEC with a clean accident report."

"Then it was you who lied."

"What are you talking about?"

"Come, my dear, which one of us is playing mind games now?" Benedict turned to face her, his glittering eyes mesmerizing her as headlights paralyze a deer. "If you suspected that the sonar records had been doctored, then you lied to JAMSTEC. And do you know why?"

"No," she whispered.

"Because the outcome justifies the deed. Like it or not, you and I are cut from the same cloth. Two explorers who have descended into hell to complete a lost mission, your mission. You ask me how many more lives must be lost and I say—as many as it takes. Would you ask a general at the dawn of battle how many men must die for victory to be secured? The hazard of war is uncertain. Yes, four good soldiers perished under our watch, but are we not here, risking our own lives, so that thousands more might survive. *Pro bono publico*, for the public good. Wasn't that the purpose for creating the UNIS array?"

"There's a difference between acceptable risk and foolhardiness," Captain Hoppe said. "You're sending the *Prometheus* too far ahead of the *Benthos*."

Benedict gave the captain a long, hard look. "*Et tu*, Breston? Do you question my judgment?"

"What I question, sir, is your need to complete a six-month mission in sixty days. What I protest is your willingness to place the crew in danger."

Benedict turned to Terry and shrugged. "They condemn what they do not understand."

"You may quote your Latin at me, sir, but I still maintain my belief that you are taking unnecessary risks."

"And you, Captain, are a coward," Benedict snapped. "You allow your emotions to whittle away at the foundation of your character until there is nothing left but fear. Did Columbus delay his journey, or return to Spain upon hearing the first mutinous whispers among his men? Did Lewis and Clark cancel their expedition after sighting their first grizzly? Did NASA cancel the space program when seven lives were lost aboard the *Challenger*?"

He turned to Terry. "You and I are explorers. We push the extreme and refuse to yield to misfortune, for we know that fortune favors the bold. We cannot bring back the dead, but we can honor them with our triumphs. I know you feel this in your heart, for your own brother died in these waters, did he not?"

"Yes," she whispered.

"If he were still alive, would this noble explorer have turned in fear at the first sign of danger, or pursued his course of action, ever the more determined?"

"He'd have continued on," she whispered, hot tears welling in her eyes.

"As would I, and I shall not allow the deaths of our compatriots to be in vain. We shall press on into the unknown, prepared in mind and spirit to face the challenges that await us. Are you with me, madam?"

"Yes—"

"Then join me now. Captain, order the crew of the *Prometheus* back on board the sub immediately."

"So soon? Sir, at least allow whatever life-forms may be out there to vacate the area."

"No, Captain. I will not allow man or beast to dictate the timetable of my affairs. He who does not advance loses ground. There is much work to be done and we are already far behind schedule."

"But sir—"

Benedict moved closer to the captain, the two men's noses almost touching. "You have your orders, Captain." The emerald eyes displayed menace. "Question me again, and I will have you permanently relieved."

"Aye, sir."

Benedict turned to Terry and placed his arm around her. "Come, my kindred soul," he said, leading her toward the companionway. "The unknown awaits."

Deep Terror

Masao Tanaka stood before the bay windows of his office, feeling the tightness return along the side of his neck. Crumpled within his fist was a fax he had just received from the *Titan*, informing him that his daughter, against his wishes, had entered the Mariana Trench nearly a week ago.

How could I have allowed her to remain behind with Benedict?

He massaged his neck, staring out across the dark blue surface waters of the canal. At the end of the waterway, between the two concrete seawalls, floated an immense barge, on top of which stood a mobile construction crane, towering one hundred feet in the air. A thick steel cable trailed from the crane's boom and disappeared beneath the sea.

A dozen local reporters and their camera crews had gathered along the seawall and western bleachers. Two news choppers circled noisily overhead.

Masao watched as a half-dozen scuba divers emerged from the canal and climbed aboard the barge. Moments later, the cable grew taut as the hydraulic winch began retracting it from the sea. For a while, it appeared that the submerged object might win the battle. Then, a massive wall of steel rose majestically out of the sea, the lower section of which was mangled beyond recognition.

Masao stared at the battered canal door. He tried to imagine the relentless pounding the creature must have delivered to have caused such damage.

Feeling dizzy, he returned to his desk and fell back into his chair. A strange numbing sensation began traveling up his left arm. He felt short of breath.

And then a vise gripped his chest and he fell sideways onto the floor.

Mariana Trench

Legs quivering from adrenaline and her overwrought nerves, Terry made her way through the pressurized docking chamber of the *Benthos*, then carefully down a ladder and into the *Prometheus*. Benedict followed her, placing a fatherly hand on her shoulder.

"Relax, my dear, we'll be fine. Come, we'll find you a seat at a station that has a window. I'd invite you to sit in the observation pod, but Ivan Kron, our robotics expert, needs to operate the mechanical arms to prepare a burrow in the seafloor for the next UNIS system."

He led her through the cramped bridge to a computer station situated against the midstarboard side of the sub. A six-inch window made of reinforced LEXAN was to her right.

"Watch from here, but again, touch nothing," Benedict warned.

He left her to speak with the sub's captain.

Terry felt as if the sword of Damocles was hanging over her head. She looked into the faces of the *Prometheus* crew, shocked to see so many expressions of fear. She realized that many of these men, like her, had simply been brought on board to do a job. They were not soldiers at war and they had not signed on with GTI to foolishly risk their lives. Here they were, seven miles beneath the Pacific, as helpless as sheep being led to the slaughter. Something was waiting for them out there, something large enough to have destroyed the *Proteus*. Yet, despite the obvious danger, despite the fact that four of their comrades had already died, none would step forward to challenge Benedict's decision.

Terry stifled a scream as the submersible pushed away from its docking sleeve. Pressing her face to the window, she stared into the abyss, her heart pounding furiously. Why had she again allowed herself to be manipulated by Benedict?

The sub lurched forward. Terry gripped the armrests of her chair. A distant memory came flooding back to her. She closed her eyes and remembered a time long ago when she had been a teenager, flying alone aboard a commercial airliner in stormy weather. At thirty-five thousand feet, the airbus had tossed about violently, unable to climb above the storm. Every bump, every sudden dip in altitude had caused her to squeeze her eyes shut and grab onto the armrests of her seat. She had felt helpless, alone, and vulnerable as she and those around her prayed that the fragile vessel that held them would continue to perform in the face of Mother Nature's fury. Without warning, a bolt of lightning struck the plane. All power shut down, every light within the cabin extinguished. For a terrifying, surreal moment, there was absolute silence. And then the plane fell from the sky, plunging nose first, and Terry and the other passengers screamed and screamed and waited to die like helpless sheep—until a higher power had intervened and the engines miraculously restarted. It would be years before Terry would board another plane. Then, when she was twenty-one, Masao pushed her into taking flying lessons. Understanding the technology had removed her fear, and she had gone on to become an outstanding pilot.

Terry opened her eyes, beads of sweat trailing down her face. Almost twenty years later, the memory still jolted her. She recalled the scent of her father's cologne as he had embraced her tightly in the airport. She heard the sounds of passengers weeping as their loved ones greeted them. But most of all, she remembered the expression of desperation and terror that had been lodged on the passengers' faces just before the plane had fallen from the sky.

Terry realized it was the very look she now saw on the faces of the crew of the *Prometheus*.

When it came to the sea, Terry had never known fear. Like her older brother, D.J., she loved the adrenaline rush of piloting a submersible, the deeper, the better. At one time, she had actually fought with her father to allow her to pilot the *AG-II* into the Mariana Trench.

Now, everything had changed, and yet everything felt the same as it had twenty years before. Once again she felt helpless, a passenger aboard a vessel, this time vulnerable at a depth of thirty-five thousand feet.

"Sorry, miss—mind if I squeeze in here?"

Terry opened her eyes. A tall rail-thin man in his late twenties was leaning over the computer station before her.

"I'm sorry." She stood, allowing the technician to take her seat.

"Only be a minute or two," he said, booting up the computer.

She glanced over his shoulder as the screen lit up. A menu appeared below the GTI symbol. She scanned the list—

Tokamak!

The menu disappeared as the technician typed in several commands, pulling up a navigation chart. He copied several coordinates onto a small clipboard, then shut the computer down.

"Thanks," he said, returning to his station.

Terry sat again, staring at the computer, her fear momentarily replaced by curiosity. A wild idea crossed her mind. She dismissed it, tucking it away for later.

The submersible increased its speed, moving silently along the canyon wall. Terry peered out her window. Unlike the *Benthos*, the exterior lights of the *Prometheus* barely cut through the blanket of darkness surrounding the vessel. A dull patch of light coming from beneath the sub illuminated the seafloor, revealing a landscape of deep gray. They passed over a cluster of clams, all snowy-white, lying in great lines along the bottom. Every so often, an albino lobster or crab could be seen scurrying about, appearing almost translucent within the beam.

But in every direction was total darkness.

Terry felt strange, as if the abyss were closing in upon her. She broke into a cold sweat, her hands shaking out of control. She began hyperventilating and, on the verge of screaming, she turned from the window and stood, positioning her face just below one of the air conditioning vents above her head.

"Feeling a bit claustrophobic?" Benedict asked.

She shook her head. "I—I just can't believe we actually allowed Jonas and my brother to dive to these depths in a one-man sub."

"Ah, yes, the great Jonas Taylor. Your husband was once quite a pilot. Alas, the pressures associated with the abyss can steal the nerve of even the strongest men."

"Try facing a sixty-foot great white shark in these waters, and we'll see how anxious you'd be to dive again—"

Benedict smiled. "It seems I've struck a nerve. I assure you that I have but the highest regard for Professor Taylor, especially in light of his most recent interest in my protégée."

"Excuse me?" Terry felt her blood boiling. "Are you purposely baiting me?"

"I don't understand," he said, feigning innocence. "Celeste has informed me that your marriage is all but over."

"Your concubine is misinformed. Jonas and I may have had some problems, but we'll resolve them."

"Of course you will. I'm sure her newfound relationship with your husband is purely platonic."

"As I told you before, I trust Jonas. I know he loves me—"

"You don't need to convince me. Marriage can be a difficult partnership to maintain, especially when faced with the sort of stress the two of you have had to endure. No doubt the last several years have been difficult. As I recall, you gave birth to a stillborn. A tragic experience that leaves a mark on even the strongest of marriages, I should think. Pain like that simply doesn't go away, does it my dear?"

Terry gripped the rail above her head, her knuckles turning white. She recalled the image of her doctor's face as he had informed her, four weeks before her due date, that her baby had died in her womb. Jonas had been consumed with guilt, blaming himself for the emotional burden he had placed on her. And Terry had done nothing to ease his pain.

She focused on Benedict's bizarre emerald eyes, trying her best to stem the rising tide of emotions.

Benedict leaned closer. "You know, some women were simply not meant to bear offspring. My own mother, for example, died giving birth to me. A miracle she lasted that long. I'm sure Jonas was heartbroken at your inability to carry the pregnancy to term." He smiled. "Now Celeste, on the other hand, has an inner strength—"

"Stop. Please—"

"—one day she'll bear children, of that I'm certain."

She felt herself losing control, exhaustion getting the better of her. Tears streamed down her face.

"Ah, but I envy the man who claims her as his own. She's a prize, unlike any woman I've—"

"Shut up!" Terry shrieked. All heads turned, eyes staring at her as if she were standing before them stark naked.

A triumphant look appeared in Benedict's eyes, the point of his goatee quivering slightly as he suppressed a smile.

"Sir," the captain interrupted, "we've reached the location we were forced to abandon earlier."

Benedict's eyes continued unraveling Terry's willpower. "So, shall we resume excavating the location for the next UNIS?" he asked her as if nothing had happened.

Damn you, Benedict . . .

"The crew of the *Prometheus* awaits your orders, Taylor-*sama*."

"Do it," she snapped, pushing past him to move into the stern. She located the bathroom and locked herself inside.

Ten minutes passed before she calmed herself. She stared at her reflection in the tiny square of mirror taped to the barren bathroom wall. Tears had left her almond eyes swollen red, her jet-black hair disheveled, her bangs matted to her forehead from perspiration.

Terry felt the vessel reverberate beneath her feet as the *Prometheus* began preparing a hole within the seafloor.

"All right, girlfriend," she said aloud, "time to toughen up. From now on, you're stone. Nothing gets to you anymore—nothing. Benedict and his Russian minion can go screw themselves."

Terry washed her face, then pulled her hair into a tight bun. A large seven-foot-tall aluminum locker stood to her left. She opened it, removing a roll of paper towels, drying her face. Then she left the bathroom, and instead of returning to her seat, headed for the observation pod.

Ivan Kron, one of Benedict's personal staff, was seated within the spherical pod, manipulating the robotic arms. Terry could see a long titanium tube originating from somewhere beneath the sub, running down to the seafloor ten feet below.

"What is that—a vacuum?" Terry asked.

The technician ignored her.

"Hey, comrade, you deaf or what?"

The man looked up, rage burning in his eyes.

Benedict joined her. "Is there a problem?"

"Your man down there doesn't seem to want to answer my questions. Since I'm still an officer of the Tanaka Institute, I think I have a right to know what's going on."

Benedict smiled at the girl's sudden show of strength. "But of course. What would you like to know?"

"It looks like that tube is sucking up sediment from the bottom."

"That's correct. As you know, each of your UNIS robots must be buried into the trench floor in order to monitor seismic activity. The vacuum is infinitely more efficient to complete this task than the sub's robotic arms—"

A screech of metal filled their ears as the *Prometheus* was jolted sideways.

"Report," the captain ordered.

"Nothing on sonar—"

"Engines still online, Captain."

"It was the vacuum," Ivan called out from within the pod. "We're caught on something buried beneath the sand. Feels heavy."

"Can you free us?" the captain asked.

"Not without tearing the vacuum loose."

"Which is not an acceptable option," Benedict said. "Ivan, if we move closer, can you extract this object using the robotic arms?"

"I'll try."

The *Prometheus* descended to within four feet of the seafloor, Ivan extended the two robotic arms away from the sub, the claws digging into the seafloor like a giant crab.

The noise rattled the ship, the echo reverberating against the canyon wall.

The forty-six-foot reptilian creature hovered along the pitch-dark seafloor as her brood chased their prey in her direction. Sensing movement, the big female closed her luminous eyes to conceal her presence.

The giant squid swam into range, its eight stout arms and two tentacles reaching out as if groping the darkness.

With a synchronized downstroke of her four appendages, the big female lunged upward, snapping her flat jaws shut upon the arrow-shaped mantle of her prey. Immediately, the two-ton squid's tentacles latched onto its larger assailant, the sucker pads and toothlike rings tearing at the scaly reptilian hide. A life-and-death struggle began, the two titans rolling over and over one another.

But *Architeuthis* was no match for the big female, whose T. rex-size teeth tore life from the giant squid in a crushing embrace.

The three smaller creatures quickly appeared, ravaging what little remained of the carcass.

A length of tentacle still dangling from its mouth, the big female paused in midbite. Familiar vibrations beckoned from the darkness ahead.

Finishing its meal, the thirty-three-thousand-pound beast slithered out ahead of the pack, its brood falling into formation behind her.

After nearly thirty minutes, Ivan had outlined a furrow around the mysterious object, measuring almost eight feet long and five feet across. There was still no telling how deep the object was buried.

Terry saw the radio operator jump. She watched his face go pale.

"Captain, the *Benthos* reports unidentified bioforms moving in our direction."

Everything stopped. Everyone on board looked at Benedict.

"How close?" the captain said.

"Five kilometers due west and closing fast, ETA . . . nineteen minutes. The *Benthos* is thirteen minutes southeast—"

"Continue digging," Benedict ordered. "We cannot and will not tear apart the vacuum."

The crew looked from Benedict to the captain.

"You heard Mr. Singer's orders," the captain yelled. "Sonar, let us know when these life-forms to be . . . Jesus, they're half the size of the *Prometheus*. Sir, they've increased speed, ETA now fourteen minutes."

The captain turned to Benedict. "Sir, we have to abandon the vacuum—"

"Are you suffering from hearing loss, Captain?"

"No, sir."

"Perhaps a lack of nerve then?"

"No, sir. My concern is not for myself, but for my crew—"

"Here I am, here I shall remain—until the task at hand is completed."

"ETA—ten minutes," sonar reported.

"*Benthos* still twelve minutes away," the radioman said.

Terry took her seat by the computer station, her heart pounding. *Damn you, Benedict, why are you doing this? Is this a macho thing, to show all of us how tough you really are, or do you just get off on toying with everyone's emotions?*

She gripped the armrest, frustrated at finding her life, once again, resting in his hands.

"I'm underneath the object," Ivan reported.

Benedict looked down into the pod. "Can you raise it?"

"I'll try." Ivan began retracting the hydraulic arms.

Terry pressed her face to the window. She could see an enormous black object dispersing bucket loads of sediment as it rose from its primordial burial ground.

Several long minutes passed while the mechanical arms struggled to withdraw its prize.

"One minute, Captain!"

"Vacuum's free, Benedict," Ivan reported. "Should I release the object?"

"Yes," the captain said.

"No," Benedict yelled. "Secure the object beneath the sub."

Terry felt claustrophobic. The walls of the submersible seemed to be closing in. She thought of the *Proteus*, how the slightest breach in the integrity of its hull would have caused it to implode.

"Object secured," Ivan said.

"You may take us to the *Benthos*, Captain," Benedict ordered.

Terry held on as the sub dropped, rolling to port.

"Dammit." The captain squeezed his way forward to the ballast controls. "What the hell is that thing, Ivan? Must weigh over five hundred pounds." The captain released ballast, the sub righting itself.

"Sir, two life-forms off the port bow, the others circling. Range—fifty meters. I think they mean to channel us away from the *Benthos*."

Terry pressed her face to the glass. She could see nothing but blackness.

"*Benthos* now within view, Captain," a relieved chief shouted.

"Life-forms moving away, distancing themselves."

The captain smiled nervously. "The *Benthos* is too big to pick a fight with. Chief, request hangar doors be opened. Maneuver the *Prometheus* into position to deposit the object we've extracted from the seafloor, then prepare the sub for docking."

Terry breathed a sigh of relief. She released her grip from the armrest and whispered a prayer of thanks.

Then she remembered Sergei was waiting for her on board.

Trapped

SeaWorld animal-care supervisor Pete Soderblom sneaked a peek at the gathering crowd from behind the auditorium's backstage curtains.

"Christ, Andy, what the hell's going on? It's like a media feeding frenzy out there."

Zoologist Andrew Furman handed him the newspaper. "Take a look at the front page."

Pete scanned the headlines of the *Seattle Times*.

ESCAPED MEGALODON
SIGHTED OFF LEADBETTER POINT

OYSTERVILLE, WA—Carcharodon megalodon, the 72-foot monster shark that only days earlier attacked a Coast Guard vessel, killing two, was sighted by fishermen off Leadbetter Point early yesterday evening. "We were heading in when this huge white dorsal fin started circling the boat," said Cal Cambronne, a local fisherman. "Damn thing followed us right into the bay before heading out to sea. Scared the hell out of the entire crew. Our boat's only a 50-footer."

In a related story, scientists at Sea-World report that Tootie, the 18,000-pound gray whale calf released into the wild weeks earlier, appears to have abandoned its attempts to migrate north to the Bering Sea. The newborn, which had beached itself four months earlier along Ocean Shores, was spotted feeding in Grays Harbor yesterday by whale watchers. Biologists at SeaWorld tracking the calf's movements by radio transmitter confirmed Tootie's position to be less than 25 miles from where the Megalodon was last sited.

Animal-rights activist Gay Gordon expressed concern that the newborn whale was in danger. "While we commend Sea-World for saving Tootie's life, we believe that officials should have delayed the calf's return to the wild until after the Megalodon's recapture."

Pete Soderblom, SeaWorld's animal-care supervisor, could not be reached for comment.

"This is garbage," yelled Pete. "I was in the office all night and no one called. And this reporter doesn't even mention the fact that we released Tootie at least a week before the Megalodon even escaped. How the hell were we supposed to know—"

"Forget that, Pete, we've got bigger problems," Andrew said. "I spoke with Jonas Taylor about an hour ago. He's tracking the Megalodon aboard the *William Beebe* and confirmed that the creature could reach Grays Harbor within three hours. We have to face the reality that the Meg could enter the bay and slaughter the calf."

Pete wiped the sweat from his brow. "Christ, we're looking at a public relations disaster."

"I got a call this morning from Anheuser-Busch, and, to put it lightly, they are not happy campers. Apparently, associating beer with a defenseless whale calf being eaten by a seventy-foot shark is not what they had in mind for their new 'back to nature' campaign. Pete, we need to get down to Grays Harbor with the tractor-trailer and get her out of there."

"Are you certain Tootie's still in the bay?

"According to our last radio fix. Why? What are you thinking?"

Pete smiled. "If the Megalodon does enter Grays Harbor to go after the calf, we could use some gill nets to seal off its exit and trap it within the bay. In fact, we could coordinate the Megalodon's capture with Tootie's rescue."

"You want to use Tootie as bait?"

"Unfortunately, her presence near the Megalodon makes her bait. But picture this: Tootie's safe in the cargo truck, the Megalodon's been captured, thanks to SeaWorld, and we're all celebrating with a cold one. Think I could sell that to Anheuser-Busch?"

"Beats the hell out of Spuds MacKenzie. What do you want me to do?"

"Arrange for the cargo container and harness to rendezvous with us at the Westport Marina. That truck needs to be on the highway within the next hour. I'll set up a conference call between Jonas Taylor, myself, and the harbormaster. We need to minimize the boating traffic and see if there are any gill nets available to seal off the mouth of the bay."

"What about the calf?"

"When you contact Westport Marina, rent us a fishing trawler, complete with nets. We'll locate Tootie and drag her into shallow water before the monster can get to her. Once she's safe, we'll either wait it out or transport her back to SeaWorld, depending upon what happens with the Meg."

"We'll need a crane then." Andrew motioned to the auditorium. "Don't forget about the press."

"I'll handle them. In fact, I'll brief them regarding our intentions. Then I want to speak to Jonas Taylor."

Jonas shielded his eyes against flying debris as the helicopter touched down on the helo-pad of the *William Beebe*. He waited until the rotors stopped before greeting Mac.

Mac slid out of the chopper and looked Jonas up and down. "You seem to have recovered well. Guess you have your private nurse to thank for that."

"What's that supposed to mean?" Jonas asked.

"We need to talk, pal, but not here. Give me a hand. I've got the equipment you requested in back."

Mac led him to the cargo bay. He slid open the door, revealing two wooden crates, each marked "TANAKA OCEANOGRAPHIC INSTITUTE."

Mac opened the first crate, removing a bizarre-looking rifle. "One Olin RAAM rocket-boosted rifle grenade. It's not bulky, like a LAWS rocket, and it can be launched from the muzzle of any NATO-standard rifle."

"Yes, but is it capable of killing an animal this size with one shot?"

"Hell, yes. The charge was designed to go through four hundred millimeters of armor at a range of two hundred fifty meters. One good shot broadside and your shark is fricassee. What's inside this other crate?"

"A portable acoustics transmitter, tape recorder, and a set of underwater microphones."

"Planning a deep-sea concert?"

"More like an underwater dinner bell. Let's leave the grenade rifle inside. We'll stow the sound equipment in the stern."

They carried the crate aft, locking it in one of the storage compartments adjacent to the ship's A-frame.

"So talk to me, Mac. What's on your mind?"

Mac stared out at the Washington coastline. "Explain to me why you have a death wish."

"A death wish?"

"Don't play me for stupid."

"I have a death wish because I jumped in after that cadet? What was I supposed to do? Stand there and watch him get eaten?"

"You didn't just go in after him, you went in with

reckless abandon like you didn't give a damn if you lived or died."

Jonas spit into the sea.

"I recognize the symptoms, Jonas. I've been there myself. You're suffering from a classic case of survivor's guilt."

"I already have a psychiatrist."

"Now you have two. I guess you're forgetting that I went through the same thing in the Navy."

"How is this the same?"

"Hey, pal, no one volunteers for a third tour of duty unless their brain's been seriously messed up. Third week I was overseas, I led my platoon straight into an ambush. Lost more than half my men. I blamed myself, just like you. Hell, I must have relived that night in my dreams a thousand times."

"Do you still have the dreams?"

"Once in a while, but they're nowhere near as intense. I don't wake up screaming anymore." Mac put his arm on Jonas's shoulder. "You're going through the same stuff I went through, except you've declared war on this creature. Of course, the creature doesn't know it, being just a dumb animal trying to survive, but you—hell, you're as obsessed as Captain-freaking-Ahab. You blame the last eleven years of your life and everything you've lost on this monster, and you won't be satisfied until you kill it."

"I didn't realize all those sessions in the loony bin had taught you so much."

"Joke if you like, just don't be so quick to throw your life away. Just because you can't see the forest for the trees right now doesn't mean you won't find your way out. I did, and I was in deep."

"I know the way out. I've seen the way my life ends—"

"They're just nightmares, Jonas. I used to dream about getting killed all the time, too. Don't turn them into a self-fulfilling prophecy."

"I'm not trying to, believe me."

"Bull." Mac slapped him playfully across his head. "Jumping in to rescue that cadet? Who are you, Batman?"

Jonas smiled. "Okay, that was a tad risky."

"Yeah, a tad. So, these nightmares of yours—how does it happen—your death?"

Jonas looked Mac in the eye. "I'm in the *Abyss Glider*, descending to the Mariana Trench. For some reason, I seem to be searching for Terry."

"Terry's in the Trench?"

"Yes. She dies with me right after I find her."

Mac slumped down onto the deck.

"What?"

Mac leaned back against the rail. "I was waiting to tell you. When I stopped by the Institute to pick up your toys, I was told Masao suffered a heart attack."

"What?"

The blood drained from Jonas's face. "When?"

"Yesterday afternoon. Sadia found him unconscious in his office. They transported him to Valley Memorial. The doctor says he's stable, but he was still unconscious when I stopped by to see him. He looked pretty bad."

"I need to call the hospital . . . has anyone contacted Terry?" Mac averted eye contact.

"Now what?"

Mac looked pale. "There's more. Masao had just received word that your wife descended into the Mariana Trench with Benedict Singer. She's aboard the *Benthos*."

Jonas took it like a punch in the gut. His eyes shut, all the strength drained from his body.

"Jonas, she'll be okay."

Jonas shook his head. "It's happening, Mac. My nightmare's playing itself out like some bizarre déjà vu. Terry and I will both end up in the Trench. The creature will appear and—"

"Take it easy, pal—"

Jonas became enraged. "I begged Terry not to go. I begged her—"

Mac stood, grabbing him by the arm. "Jonas, listen to me. Terry will be back onboard the *Titan* in a few days, and the Megalodon is thousands of miles from the Trench. Thousands of miles! Don't let your guilt get to you. Terry descending into the Trench is just a coincidence. I'm telling you, she'll be topside by the end of the week."

"I don't know anymore, but I can't think rationally. Maybe—maybe that's all it is, just a coincidence, but I can't take a chance. I need to kill this monster and remove all doubt."

"Agreed. Once the shark's dead, you and Terry will ride off into the sunset."

Jonas exhaled a deep breath. "You're assuming, of course, that she'll still have me."

"She'll have you. You guys were meant to be together." Mac looked up to see Celeste approaching. "Just stay away from the temptations of the wicked queen."

"Why don't you do us all a favor and fly that bucket of bolts somewhere else," Celeste said.

Mac smiled at her. "Beats the hell out of flying a broomstick—"

"Will the two of you knock it off."

Celeste turned to Jonas. "I came to tell you that one of the directors over at SeaWorld is on the radio. He says he knows how we can trap the Meg."

Jonas spread the chart of the Pacific Northwest out on the light table, circling Grays Harbor with a red erasable marker. "According to SeaWorld, the calf they released has taken up residence here, in Grays Harbor. If the Meg stays on her present course, she'll detect the calf and home in on her. SeaWorld's plan is for us to follow the Megalodon into the bay. Once inside, the harbormaster would drop the gill nets into place across the inlet, which will hang vertically under the sea like giant curtains. The depth in this area is only fifty to sixty feet, the inlet about three miles across. The Meg would literally be confined within the bay."

"Sounds good," Celeste said.

"It's not going to be easy. There are also some financial considerations. Before Westport Marina moves their fishing vessels into place to spread the nets, they want Geo-Tech to guarantee to pay for any and all damages incurred, plus an additional ten thousand dollars to cover labor and expenses."

Celeste scoffed. "They should be paying us for the publicity we'll be bringing to their damn harbor. What do you think, Maren?"

"I say do it. We'll never get another opportunity like this. The costs involved are a drop in the bucket compared to what the Institute's losing every day."

She looked at Jonas. "Do you agree?"

"The plan could work, but it's risky as hell. We're not allowing the harbor police much time to clear away boating traffic."

"I disagree," Maren said. "SOSUS indicates the Megalodon to be less than two miles ahead, moving north at only three knots. At her present speed, she won't even arrive at the mouth of the bay for another ninety-four minutes."

Jonas scoffed. "Let me tell you something, Maren, the moment Angel detects that calf, she'll be racing through the ocean like a runaway freight train. Her top speed's sixty-eight miles an hour. So you better get that slide rule of yours back out and rethink this whole plan. My vote is to keep this battle at sea. Cornering any animal, let alone a seventy-two-foot great white, is a dangerous proposition. Angel's spent her entire life in captivity. She's not going to be real happy about being confined again."

"I remember when the first shark went berserk off the coast of Monterey," Mac said. "Plenty of boats went down that afternoon. A lot of people died."

Maren rolled his eyes in disgust. "We're wasting time. The harbormaster is waiting for our call."

"This whole discussion seems moot," Celeste said. "Like it or not, there's a good chance the creature is going to detect this baby whale and go after it. If it enters the bay, we'd be foolish not to attempt to capture it there."

"Finally, a voice of reason." Maren grabbed the radio to contact the harbormaster.

Captain Morgan studied the map. "The inlet may be narrow, but Grays Harbor is huge. Harpooning that monster once she enters won't be very easy—we still have to find her. SOSUS will be useless to us once we're in the bay."

"The bay's shallow," Jonas said. "Mac and I should be able to spot her from the air."

"Just locate the baby whale and Angel will follow," Celeste said.

"SeaWorld just radioed," Maren said. "Their rescue team has arrived in Hoquiam. They should be heading out into the bay aboard a fishing trawler within the next twenty minutes."

Celeste turned to him. "Tell them not to remove the calf before the creature enters."

"SeaWorld's first priority is to save the calf," Jonas said. "In my opinion, they're already cutting it close. I'm telling you, once Angel homes in on that whale, she'll enter the bay faster than you think."

"Well, if she does, it'll be *arrivederci*, Tootie," Celeste said.

"Doesn't matter," Maren said. "As long as the wolf enters the pen, who cares if it happens to eat the sheep?"

Mac shook his head. "You can bet the sheep cares."

The gray whale calf known to SeaWorld as Tootie continued plowing the muddy bottom of Grays Harbor. Unable to keep up with the other migrating whales, the calf had sought shelter in the bay, attracted by the vast quantities of food located along the seabed. Sucking the turbid water into its mouth, the calf filtered out sandhoppers and other bottom-living organisms from the silt through its baleen before sucking the food to the back of its throat. After several minutes Tootie would rise back to the surface to blow, then inhale another breath before returning to feed again along the bottom.

The predator moved silently along the seafloor, its bioluminescent skin casting a dull glow on the murky bottom. Baleful eyes, cataract-gray, searched the sea in vain for an object its primal senses insisted was somewhere ahead.

Short, powerful sweeps of the crescent tail propelled the giant into a higher gear. Soaring in from behind its darting prey, the leviathan rolled onto its side and opened its jaws, creating a vacuum of sea that sucked a six-foot octopus and its inky trail down into its immense gullet.

Swallowing the morsel whole, the shark righted itself, its bulk sailing effortlessly along the bottom. Once more the predator slowed, returning to automatic pilot, its senses keeping it on the trail of migrating whale pods.

Two hundred yards to the south, seven predators, ranging from fourteen to twenty-two feet in length, reduced their speed almost as one. Aroused by the intense scent of their primordial cousin, the male great whites had continued to follow the gigantic female as she made her way north, feeding off the remains of her kills, yet always remaining a safe distance behind.

* * *

Moving at a velocity just above stall speed, the Megalodon entered a state of rest as close to sleep as nature would allow. The rogue hunter knew the males were shadowing her, having registered their presence ever since she had escaped the lagoon. With prey readily available, the female tolerated the sharks—provided they moved no closer.

As the Megalodon coasted along the bottom, distant vibrations coursing along the seafloor began stimulating nerve fibers along the creature's flank. Rapid signals transmitted to its brain, activating a primeval alarm. Aroused from its stupor, the Megalodon's posture changed. Rapid movements of its head and snout engaged its olfactory sense.

Breathing the sea, the monster shark isolated the direction of the whale calf's scent.

Like a guided missile, the planet's fiercest predator raced across the ocean floor, stirring great gusts of sediment in its wake.

Pete Soderblom followed his acoustics specialist across a long boardwalk owned by the Westport Marina, home to one of the largest commercial fishing fleets in the area. The vantage offered him a panoramic view of the entire harbor. Directly ahead loomed the Grays Harbor lighthouse, rising 107 feet in the air. Just to its left was the Pacific Ocean, connected to the bay by way of a three-mile inlet. From here, Grays Harbor opened to a vast expanse of shallow water, stretching to the north and east as far as the eye could see. Nine cities dotted its banks, along with four modern marine terminals equipped to handle even the largest cargo ships in the world.

A police escort assisted them in getting through the crowd. Officers instructed fishermen to reel in their lines as thousands of onlookers jostled for positions along the pedestrian esplanade. Hundreds more stood on viewing platforms, a lucky few even managing to reserve vantages from the Marina's three-story observation tower. Brown pelicans balanced on pilings, sandpipers and blue herons strutted along the water's edge. Heavy bass from a calypso beat mixed with the cawing of seabirds and the aroma of fast food, all adding to the carnival atmosphere.

The police officer led Pete and his technicians down a long fishing pier, where hundreds of empty boats floated in their berths. The bright silver surface of the sea sparkled up at them, forcing them to squint. Normally a hive of activity, the bay was now off-limits to all but the harbor patrol and two fishing trawlers, which, at that moment, were moving into position at the center of the inlet.

Pete noticed another fishing trawler tied at the end of the pier. Over ninety feet in length, the trawler's deck was an open expanse used for hauling in nets filled with massive quantities of fish. With the exception of the pilothouse, the only other prominent features of the trawler were three steel arch-like buttresses rising twenty feet above the deck. These overhead structures supported two steel cables that ran from the fishing nets across the top of the arches, then into two hydraulic winches situated behind the pilothouse. Once the nets were full, the cables would be hauled in, dragging the trawl up the angled stern deck directly from the sea to the ship's hold.

Pete climbed aboard and spotted Andrew Furman speaking with a deeply tanned, very tall man in his late thirties.

"Pete, this is Greg Dechiaro, the ship's captain. He says Tootie's been seen feeding about a mile out."

"Great. How soon till we're underway?"

"My crew should be finished rigging the trawl net within the next ten minutes. How much this whale of yours weigh?"

"I'd estimate nineteen thousand pounds," Pete said. "Can your rig handle that?"

"Long as she don't thrash about too much. What I told your assistant here, is we'll use the otter trawl. The net itself is weighted so it'll spread open like a giant parachute when we tow it. We'll scoop your whale up, then drag her to shore."

Andrew pointed to the shoreline, where a thirty-foot harness dangled from an immense crane. "That's where we need to be. The cargo container's already in place and partially filled with seawater."

Pete glanced up at the growing crowd. "I have a feeling these people didn't just come out here to watch a whale being rescued." He checked his watch nervously. "I think we'd better go get our calf."

Jonas watched Dr. Maren replot the latest SOSUS coordinates for the fourth time in five minutes.

"Is there a problem?" he asked.

Maren looked up at Jonas, ashen-faced. "I—I think you were right." He shook his head in disbelief.

"Where is she?"

"According to these coordinates, she just entered the bay."

"Dammit." Jonas grabbed the radio. "Andy, come in—"

A voice bathed in static said, "Go ahead, Jonas."

"Andy, the Megalodon just entered the bay. Have you netted Tootie yet?"

"Jonas, repeat, please. It sounded as if you said the creature's already in the bay."

"Affirmative. Have you netted your whale?"

"No . . . not yet, but we've closed to within two hundred yards. Stand by."

Pete stood in the pilothouse scanning the bay through a pair of high-power binoculars. His acoustics man was to his right, listening to the dual transmitters fastened along Tootie's upper torso. "She should be just ahead of us," the man said. "Both signals still coming in, loud and clear."

Pete saw a lead-gray head break the water, the snout covered in kelp. "There she is, directly ahead!"

The captain signaled for the otter trawl to be released. Several seconds later, the net began feeding out behind the ship.

Bobbing along the surface, Tootie scooped kelp into her mouth, using her baleen to strain the myriad of tiny sea creatures attached to the long leaves. Swallowing the morsels, the gray calf took another breath and submerged.

Descending gracefully through the murk, the newborn suddenly registered another presence closing quickly. The calf stopped swimming.

A luminescent blur streaked toward her along the seafloor. Sensing danger, the calf turned, retreating to the surface.

Pete watched his radio technician frantically adjust the acoustics receiver.

"Damn it, I just lost one of the transmitters," the technician said. "The other's functioning, but the strength of the signal just dropped in half. Tootie's moving away from the bottom, about one hundred yards off the starboard bow."

"Pete, Jonas says the Megalodon has entered the bay," Andy reported. "We gotta get Tootie out of the water, now!"

"Give me the whale's exact location," the captain ordered.

"One click to starboard," the technician said. "That's good, we're right on line. She's still deep, we'll pass over her—now!"

The captain made a slight course adjustment, then cut his speed in half.

"Got her," yelled the technician, slapping Pete's high five.

Seconds later, the entire ship shuddered as the otter trawl scooped up an immense life-form.

"Take in the slack, boys," the captain ordered his crew.

The two hydraulic winches strained to haul in the submerged load.

*   *   *

The *William Beebe* slipped into Grays Harbor as the last one hundred yards of gill net was dropped into position across the inlet.

Jonas ducked beneath the whirling rotors of the helicopter and climbed in. "Did you ready the weapon?"

"All set," Mac said. "Hold on—"

The chopper lifted away from the deck, soaring out ahead of the ship.

Jonas found the Olin-RAAM rifle grenade hidden beneath a pile of blankets. Verifying a grenade was already loaded into the barrel, he returned to his seat with the weapon.

Mac handed him the radio. "SeaWorld."

"Andy?"

"Jonas, we just bagged our whale. We're towing her in now, but she's really struggling, the Meg must be circling close by."

Jonas could hear men yelling in the background. "Stand by, Andy—"

The chopper flew over the trawler, hovering at two hundred feet. Jonas saw the submerged net, as well as an ivory shape at the midst of what appeared to be a battle raging below the surface.

"Andy, the Meg's right behind you. Haul in the calf!"

Peter stood next to the trawler's captain and a dozen of his crew, watching as the fishing net was slowly hauled up from the bay along the steep incline at the stern.

The ship shuddered, the incline actually dipping deeper into the water.

"Dammit," the captain swore, "the girders are bending. No way this calf only weighs nine tons."

Andy ran over to them, out of breath. "Jonas says the Meg's right behind us—we've got to haul Tootie on board—"

The captain grabbed him by the arm and pointed above their heads. "See that? We pull any harder and those arches will collapse."

Black smoke billowed across the deck.

"Now what?" the captain yelled. "Smells like the bearings are burning up."

The trawler continued shuddering; the engines unable to push the ship forward. A high-pitched metallic screech rent the air.

"Kill the engines," the captain ordered.

Incredibly, the stern began dipping into the sea, the water level rising to within four feet of the transom.

Pete braced himself, staring down the steep incline, praying for Tootie to emerge from the sea. The calf was putting up a terrific struggle.

The stern suddenly righted, the strain on the cables momentarily easing. The trawl net began rising.

"Here she comes," Pete announced, making his way down the ramp as if to greet his whale.

Angel's ghostly white face rose vertically out of the bay, her mouth stretched open as if the creature were screaming. Tootie's scarlet blood outlined the jaws like smudged lipstick. Shards of whale blubber dangled from murderous rows of teeth. Angel's upper torso, entangled in fishing net, remained suspended clear out of the water up to her wing-like pectoral fins.

Pete's eyes bugged out, horrified, yet mesmerized by the size of the beast. Pinned against the transom, too heavy to be hauled aboard, the monster remained upright in the water, one of its gray eyes locked on the trawler.

Then, with unfathomable power, the Megalodon began twisting her ensnared torso from side to side in violent spasms. Each jolt caused the fishing trawler to lurch, tightening the stranglehold of netting across the creature's body. Enraged, the beast fought harder, each sweeping movement of her colossal head exaggerated in great arcing movements, back and forth along the surface, her fury rolling towering swells of ocean in every direction.

Pete could only hold on as tons of churning water and shards of fishing net splattered on his head. He heard a sickening groan of steel—followed by men yelling—as the forward support arches collapsed onto the deck.

Jonas and Mac stared at the surreal scene below.

"God, what a monster," Mac whispered.

"She's tearing the vessel apart." Jonas positioned the grenade rifle onto his shoulder. "Mac, get us closer. It's time to end this nightmare."

The chopper dropped, hovering forty feet above the trawler.

Jonas aimed.

"Damn it—she's thrashing around too much to get off a clean shot."

At that moment, one of the two steel cables supporting the trawl net tore loose from its hydraulic winch, the free end sent lashing through the air. Striking the back of the helicopter, it shredded the whirling rotors from the tail assembly.

"What the hell was that?" Mac yelled. "I'm losing control."

The chopper began twirling in dizzying circles.

The remaining cable tore loose, splaying across the deck. It struck one of the crewmen across his elbow, severing his arm in two, then caught itself around the remaining steel support in the stern.

Spinning out of control, Mac lost altitude and plummeted toward the deck of the trawler. Jonas held his breath as the landing struts collapsed onto the remains of one of the ravaged steel supports, the airship nearly toppling overboard before coming to rest on the pile of mangled metal.

With a final sweep of its head, the Megalodon's sharp denticles shredded the remains of the bonds along its upper torso, allowing the shark to fall back beneath the surf.

Pete scrambled up the slick incline in time to see the helicopter crash on deck.

Andy reached down and grabbed his hand. "Where's Tootie?"

Pete struggled to catch his breath. "That monster must have eaten her, transmitter and all."

"Oh my God—"

"Look at my ship!" the captain yelled. "Who the hell's going to pay for this—"

The trawler lurched backward, knocking everyone off their feet.

"Jesus Christ, now what?" Andrew yelled.

Pete stared at the stern. Waves sloshed against the incline as the trawler was pulled back through the sea.

"I don't believe this," Pete said. "That thing's towing us."

The captain spotted the end of the remaining cable wound around the stern support. He ran to the pilot-house and grabbed an ax. As he braced himself to sever the cable, the line suddenly snapped, the enraged animal tearing itself free from the last of its bonds.

The *William Beebe* churned slowly across the inlet, patrolling the three-mile stretch of bay now cordoned off from the ocean by the vertically hanging gill nets. Six hundred pounds of half-frozen, rotting whale blubber floated forty feet behind her, attached by steel cable to the big winch in the stern.

Harry Moon peered over the top of the harpoon gun, staring at the trailing fish. With one hand he nervously fingered the trigger of the weapon, with the other he held a portable headset to his ear. "Dief, what's happening up there?"

Standing precariously atop a slender steel grate five stories above the deck, Richard Diefendorf held onto the central mast as he focused his binoculars on the bay.

"Looks like she's freed herself of the trawler. I can't see . . . wait, there's the dorsal fin. Harry, stand ready, she's heading this way, Captain, we need to be farther south. Another two hundred yards."

Listening on his own headset, Captain Morgan relayed the instructions to his helmsman.

"Celeste, Dr. Maren, Dief says she's coming," Harry reported.

Standing along the portside rail, Celeste and Dr. Maren searched the sea, waiting for the alabaster hide of the Megalodon to show itself.

Dief spotted her first. "Captain, she's sixty yards off the port bow and closing fast. I can't tell which—wait, she's breaking toward the stern!"

"Let's give Mr. Moon his shot," the captain said. "Helm, all engines stop."

Angel streaked along the muddy bottom, close to exhaustion. Although the denticles along her rough hide had minimized the damage from the trawl net, veils of blood trailed from her head and abdomen, where razor-like lacerations now zigzagged across her shiny, pale skin.

Self-preservation was now the creature's overriding instinct. Vulnerable in the shallows, she headed for deeper water, racing toward the inlet.

Having detected the object at the surface, the Megalodon hugged the seafloor to avoid another confrontation. From somewhere ahead in the murky water came the death throes of two of the male great whites, both having become hopelessly entangled in the gill net. Sensing the dangerous obstruction, the Meg banked sharply, whipping its head away from the barrier as it soared along the netting, searching for a way out.

"The shark's moving south along the net, looking to escape," Dief reported.

"She's ignoring the bait," Harry said, "and she's way too deep for me to take a shot."

Dief followed the blur with his binoculars until the behemoth raced out of sight. "This is impossible," he said. "We need the chopper. What the hell's Mac doing?"

Mac and Jonas covered their eyes as the harbor patrol helicopter landed on the deck of the disabled trawler. The wounded crewman was quickly loaded on board, his severed arm in a plastic bag, packed in ice.

"We'll send another chopper for you boys as soon as we can," the copilot shouted as the airship lifted.

The trawler captain waited until the noise of the rotors dissipated before starting in on Jonas and Pete Soderblom again.

"That otter trawl will cost you $100,000," he yelled, "and there's no telling how much damage was done to my engines—"

"Captain, relax," Mac said. "I'm a witness. I heard Celeste Singer agree to pay for all damages. Geo-Tech has more money than they know what to do with. If I were you, I'd sue the crap out of them."

Jonas ignored them, focusing on the harbor through binoculars. "Captain, what is that?" He pointed north.

A tall wooden sailing ship was heading toward them.

The captain stared at the object with his own binoculars. "That's the *Lady Washington*, a replica of an eighteenth-century Tall Ship."

"Yeah, but what's the boat doing in the bay? Andy, you better get the harbormaster on the radio."

*   *   *

"The Meg's coming around, heading right for us," Dief shouted. "Harry, I can see the tip of her caudal fin. She's just below the surface. Captain, she'll pass under us on our starboard side within thirty seconds. Give her some room."

Dr. Maren rushed over to Harry Moon. "Take the shot; it may be the only one you get."

Harry spun the gun around, the point of the harpoon facing the open ocean. He stared down the barrel, waiting for the shark to appear behind the ship.

Dief held his breath, watching the pale shadow streaking just below the surface. "Damn it, she's sounding—"

"There she is," Maren pointed, excited by the sheer size of the creature gliding beneath the boat.

Harry saw the cream-colored object sail by. He fired.

The harpoon exploded from the gun with a loud bang, trailing steel cable through a cloud of silver smoke.

The Meg was in sixty feet of water when the point of the harpoon struck the base of her dorsal fin. Slowed by the sea, the lance lacked the power required to pierce deep enough into the shark's thick skin.

Registering the attack, the Megalodon twisted along the bottom, shaking the harpoon from its hide before the anesthetic could be delivered.

Cornered and wounded, the animal went berserk.

Uninvited Guest

Captain James H. Locke, known to friends and crew merely as "Flagg," stood on the poop deck of the *Lady Washington*, nodding to the guests of the bride and groom as the ship's pursers led them to their seats. He felt a cool spring breeze at his back, watching as the wind filled the square-rigged main- and foresails that stretched out high above his head.

The Douglas fir brig, *Lady Washington*, was a full-size reproduction of an eighteenth-century Tall Ship, the first American-flagged vessel ever to sail around Cape Horn. She had an overall length of 112 feet and a twenty-four-foot beam, and her two masts, each containing three sails, towered eighty-seven feet above the main deck. Normally at this time of day, Washington State's "Tall Ship Ambassador" could be found at port, offering dockside tours to the public. On this particular afternoon, however, the *Lady Washington* had been privately chartered to host a wedding ceremony, a fact not realized by the harbormaster.

Three bells signaled half-past one. The guests quieted.

Flagg waited, listening to the calming sounds of the sea and the comforting flapping of canvas. He glanced at the groom, a well-built man in his mid-thirties dressed in a slate-gray tux.

"Are you ready?"

The groom nodded, flashing a nervous smile.

Flagg nodded to one of the crew. Wedding music began. The crowd stood, turning in unison to gaze at the bride and her parents, who were escorting her up the steps from the quarterdeck.

"A perfect afternoon for a wedding," the captain declared, at the same time wondering why the bay appeared so empty.

Whipping its crescent tail in frenetic sweeps, the Megalodon zigzagged along the murky bottom in a continuously widening pattern as its senses probed the bay for an alternative escape route. Trapped in a maze, the crazed animal raced inland like a mad bull, only to be forced back by the shallows. Banking sharply, the fish then headed for the inlet, veering off at the last moment as it approached the gill nets, scattering the five remaining male great whites trapped within its presence.

Jonas, Mac, and the crew of the damaged fishing trawler watched in fear and amazement as the eight-foot wake created by the submerged leviathan continued rolling across the surface of the shallow bay.

"She's trapped and she knows it," Mac said.

Jonas eyed the *Lady Washington*, now closing to within five hundred yards of the trawler. Through binoculars he could see the vessel's one hundred seventy tons displacing water as she rolled in full splendor along the glass-smooth surface.

"Angel will go after the sailing ship," Jonas whispered.

"Why?" Mac asked. "The *William Beebe*'s about the same size and she hasn't gone after that."

"The *William Beebe*'s steel and has churning propellers. The *Lady Washington* moves up and down through the sea like a big whale. Angel's panicking. Her sensory system is so overloaded right now that her instincts will be to attack anything that crosses her path."

Approaching the Westport Marina pier, the Megalodon banked sharply, forced to retreat once more from the shallows. Moving into deeper waters bordering the inlet, the predator raced along the curtain-like gill net, snaring a sixteen-foot twenty-two-hundred-pound great white in its jaws. With a violent chomp, Angel's teeth severed her distant cousin into three mangled pieces, the male's tail and head spinning toward the seafloor. Without slowing, the exhausted hunter banked again, homing in on a new source of vibrations from a larger adversary moving along the surface.

* * *

". . . then, with the power vested in me by the State of Washington, the United States Coast Guard, and as Captain of the *Lady Washington*, I now pronounce you husband and wife. You may kiss your bride."

Caught in the background, Flagg held a frozen smile as a photographer clicked off a half-dozen pictures of the newlyweds kissing. He watched the couple make their way down the aisle to the reception area on the main deck, then turned to his left, a movement in the bay catching his eye.

"What in the hell?" The rogue wave seemed to be rolling straight for them.

Flagg stood at the guardrail, catching sight of a pale object streaking below the surface seconds before the *Lady Washington* was hammered broadside with a resounding thud. Before he could react, the wake washed over the main deck amid the sounds of splintering wood, the great ship rolling sideways.

Screams filled the air as startled passengers fell hard onto the wooden deck. The buffet tables tumbled over, a butane burner actually starting a small fire before an alert guest smothered it.

The ship's boatswain and one of her pursers ran to Flagg.

"Captain, what hit us?"

"I don't know. Keep the passengers calm. I'm going below deck to check the damage."

Flagg climbed down through the hatch in the quarterdeck, descending to the middle deck.

Water sprayed in through tiny gaps along splintered planks just above the floorboards. Grabbing a flashlight, he headed below to the lower deck.

"Oh, Christ—"

The lower deck was already submerged in seven feet of water. Flagg climbed down, then ducked underwater, focusing his light along the far side. It didn't take him long to find the damage. What had once been the wall of the galley was now an eight-foot gaping hole rapidly venting the ship to the sea.

Flagg emerged from the water and gasped for air, shaken by the sight of the damage. What could have caused such an impact? He realized that he had to seal the upper hatches right away, knowing the ship could be on the bottom within minutes. He started up the ladder.

Without warning, the *Lady Washington* was pummeled sideways as if struck by a runaway locomotive, the jolt tossing Flagg backward into the water. Opening his eyes, he was shocked to see a second hole in the splintered wall. He swam over to the gap and peered through.

The captain's heart pounded in his ears as his eyes focused on the luminescent-ivory snout. The creature shook its head, then glided away through the murky water.

Flagg dragged himself back up the ladder just ahead of the rising sea, slamming the hatch closed behind him. For several seconds he simply stood there, doubled over and dripping wet, his mind trying to fathom the size of the monster that was attacking his vessel.

He looked up as the boatswain and purser descended from the main deck.

"Captain, what's hitting us?"

"You don't want to know. Listen to me, both of you. This boat's going down very fast. I want you to seal every hatch, then get back up on deck and start loading everyone into life rafts."

The purser, a volunteer who worked for room and board, seemed bewildered. "Sir, we're abandoning ship?"

"No, son, the ship's abandoning us. She'll be on the bottom in less than five minutes—now move!"

The crew of the trawler watched helplessly as the sail-like dorsal fin rose above the wake, circling the crippled sailing ship.

Jonas crouched in the cockpit of the downed chopper, yelling over the radio. "Damn it, Maren, I said I want to speak with Celeste."

"Forget it, Taylor, we're not retracting the nets. The Megalodon's exhausted, and the *William Beebe*'s on the way to harpoon her. We'll pick up any passengers in the water, but we're not—"

Dief entered the pilothouse and tore the radio away from Maren.

"Jonas, it's Dief. What the hell's going on?"

"The chopper lost its tail assembly, Dief, that sail ship's going down fast. There must be fifty passengers on board. You've got to retract those gill nets. The Meg's going berserk."

"I'm on it."

Jonas rejoined Mac on deck. Two hundred yards away, the *Lady Washington* had managed to turn leeward, its prow straining to reach the disabled fishing trawler, its eleven-foot draft now less than two feet above water.

"They'll never make it," Mac said. "Crap, here she comes again!"

Jonas cringed as the wake barreled into the *Lady Washington*, the ship shuddering as it absorbed yet another tremendous blow. He could hear the screams of the passengers.

A tremendous crack—and the towering mainmast toppled forward like a fallen redwood. Terrified passengers looked up and saw they were about to be crushed. To their relief, the collapsing mainsails struck the foremast, causing the fractured mainmast to twist sideways and slam into the bay with a tremendous splash.

Seventy-eight-year-old Emily Wheeler struggled to her knees, the bride's grandmother attempting to free herself from the fallen topsail that held her pinned to the deck.

"Help me, please—"

"Mom? Mom, where are you?" Hugh Wheeler, the father of the bride, pulled aside the canvas, lifting his frail mother off the *Lady Washington*'s deck, which was now listing at a thirty-degree angle to starboard.

Wheeler saw Flagg turning toward two life rafts and practically tackled him. "Captain, I demand to know what the hell is happening!"

"What's happening? What's happening is that there's a very large shark out there who doesn't seem to like our boat."

"A shark? I can't believe a shark could—"

Flagg saw water rising out from several hatches. "Mr. Wheeler, there's no time to debate the issue. I need help getting your guests in the life rafts."

Wheeler took his mother by the arm, practically carrying her across the flooded deck. His wife and daughter waved at him from one of the two inflatable life rafts, already crammed with hysterical passengers.

Flagg blew his whistle as loud as he could. "Now listen here. The *Lady Washington* is about to sink. I want everyone seated in a life raft within the next thirty seconds. It's vital all of you remain as calm and quiet as possible. There's a very large shark out there, and the last thing I want is to let it know where we are."

The *William Beebe* raced across the bay, five hundred yards and closing fast on the dying sail ship. Harry Moon and Dr. Maren quickly reloaded another tranquilizer into the barrel of the harpoon gun while Dief and Celeste supervised the emergency launch of the *Abyss Glider*.

As Dief opened the rear hatch of the tiny Kevlar submersible, he turned to Celeste and Captain Morgan. "I'll lure the Meg away and give you a chance to rescue those people, then lead her back around so you'll get a good shot."

He crawled into the LEXAN pod of the AG-1, sealing himself in.

Through binoculars, Jonas focused on the white dorsal fin as it rose up behind the *Lady Washington*. Water now covered the ship's main deck; the passengers and crew hovering in two life rafts lashed to the foremast.

Mac grabbed Jonas's arm, pointing to the research

vessel now gliding alongside the sinking Tall Ship. "Jonas, check out the *William Beebe*'s stern. Are they launching the *Abyss Glider*?"

Jonas redirected his glasses in time to see the one-man submersible plunge into the sea.

Filled to capacity, the two life rafts remained lashed to the foremast, floating just above the submerged deck of the *Lady Washington*. Flagg and his passengers stared behind them, horrified by the sight of the wake rolling in behind them. A pearl-white fin emerged from the moving mound of water—and kept rising. The snout appeared.

Screams—as the monster struck the submerged poop deck with a heart-stopping crunch. The impact shattered the keel and fractured the foremast, which toppled backward like chain-sawed timber.

Flagg watched the sickle-shaped caudal fin slash back and forth among the floating debris less than twenty feet away. The creature was searching the perimeter of the sinking ship, which now began to spin, caught within a slow-moving whirlpool.

One hundred feet of sea separated them from their would-be rescuers.

"The *Lady Washington* will drag us below," he yelled. "Lose the lines and paddle toward the rescue ship."

Abandoning the harpoon gun, Harry Moon helped his crew position a cargo net over the port side of the ship as the two overcrowded life rafts paddled toward them.

"Damn," he muttered. The dorsal fin had turned, homing in on the vibrations.

Lying prone, secured within the pilot's harness, Dief grabbed the twin joysticks and ignited the sub's main thrusters. Diving at a sharp angle, he descended quickly to the shallow bottom, approaching the hull of the sinking wooden Tall Ship.

"Jesus . . ."

An immense hole stared back at him, so large he could have maneuvered the sub straight through and out its fractured keel.

"Okay, shark, where . . . oh, hell—"

Seeing the glow, Dief wrenched the joystick hard to his left as a head, the size of a small house, glided out from behind the wreckage. Momentarily panicked, Dief accelerated too quickly, nearly burying the nose of the swift sub in the muddy seabed.

Ignoring the sub, the shark ascended.

Flying along the bottom, Dief frantically searched the murky water for the monster. Looking up, he saw a frightening silhouette glide like a jumbo jetliner along the sunlit surface, closing slowly on a yellow life raft.

Her decks now completely submerged, the *Lady Washington* swirled in a great counterclockwise circle, pulling her downed mainsails with her. Flagg and his passengers hung on as the two life rafts converged with the surface debris, revolving in the vortex of the sinking mother ship.

With a sudden jolt, the ship's splintered keel twisted into the shallow muddy bottom. The towering foremast remained upright, marking the sunken ship's position, high above the waves.

Emily Wheeler sat shivering at the rear of the life raft, her new dress soaked in seawater. Hugh removed the jacket of his tux and wrapped it around his mother's shoulders.

"You okay, Mom?"

She nodded, her lips blue.

"Just hang on. We'll be on that rescue boat in—"

Without warning, the Megalodon's snout rose beneath the back of the raft, pushing it upward and out of the water.

Twenty-eight passengers shrieked, clinging to each other in desperation as they were flipped upside down and tossed into the sea.

Emily plunged sideways into the water, the sudden cold shocking her system. Buoyed by the life jacket, she surfaced quickly, struggling to catch her breath.

Hugh surfaced next to his wife, hearing her scream, "Carrie can't swim!" Ducking underwater, he saw his daughter flailing below without a life jacket, her long wedding gown spreading out like a parachute, its weight dragging her toward the bottom.

Dief looked up to see the Meg bite down on the rubber raft, bursting it in a shower of bubbles as it shook its mammoth head from side to side like a dog, tearing the craft to shreds.

Before the predator, spread out along the surface, was a feast of kicking legs and paddling arms. Dief gasped in horror as he saw the bride sinking feetfirst, her wedding gown and train now entangled around her legs in a death grip.

Hugh surface dived and kicked hard, straining to reach his daughter as she continued to sink in twenty feet of water. Missing her arm, he managed to grab a handful of her long hair, momentarily stopping her descent. Gaining a grip on her wrist, he towed her to the surface, struggling to move in clothing that weighed him down like an anchor.

As his head broke the water, Hugh was relieved to hear his daughter choking as she gasped for air. Tossing his arm over her chest, he began towing her toward the rescue vessel. He saw the dorsal fin emerge.

"Oh, God—Mom! Mom!"

Hugh cried out in agony as the hellish creature rose directly behind his mother.

Directing the nose of the sub at a gap of sunlight, Dief launched his craft between the Megalodon's snout and the figure of an old woman. With a loud yell, he accelerated the *Abyss Glider* vertically at the creature's lower jaw.

A strange current gripped Emily, spinning her around into darkness. A quick yelp—and her life was extinguished, her frail form pulverized into mangles of flesh against the roof of the shark's mouth.

A second later, the nose cone of the *Abyss Glider* smashed hard into the Megalodon's quivering throat.

Gaining the monster's attention, Dief hit full reverse thrust, spinning away and descending quickly as the formidable creature swallowed its meal and turned to pursue.

The passengers of the *Lady Washington* scrambled over each other as they ascended the heavy cargo net, climbing desperately into the arms of the *William Beebe*'s crew.

Hugh Wheeler was the last to reach the ship. Watching his daughter climb to safety, he remained in the water, sobbing at the loss of his mother.

Dief zigzagged along the bottom, glancing quickly over his shoulder to make sure he was being followed.

The Megalodon rammed the tail wing, driving the AG-1 sideways into the mud. Dief rolled the sub, then raced for the surface.

Jonas and Mac watched the *Abyss Glider* leap from the sea like a sailfish. Seconds later, the creature's head burst the surface, its open jaws snapping shut on empty air as the sub plunged midwing first into the bay.

Jonas ran to the cockpit and grabbed the radio.

"Celeste, Captain, somebody come in!"

"Jonas, it's Celeste—"

"Celeste, you have to order that gill net removed before Dief gets killed—"

"Maren is ready to harpoon—"

"Listen to me! The bay's too shallow, there's no

room for Dief to maneuver. Retract those nets before he's killed."

"Okay—okay."

Maren looked up from the harpoon gun to see one of the fishing trawlers begin hauling in the southern end of the gill net.

"Celeste—no!"

"Take your shot, Michael. Just do it quickly."

Dief rolled the sub 360 degrees as the Megalodon bit into his portside midwing, shearing off the Kevlar appendage like husk from corn. Knowing he could no longer elude the faster shark, Dief circled back to seek refuge behind the *Lady Washington*.

The radio crackled.

"Dief?"

"Be quick, Celeste—"

"The southern end of the gill net's open."

"Thank God." Dief turned south, veering away from the *Lady Washington*, accelerating toward the open ocean.

A shadow passed overhead. He looked up—and screamed—as the hideous upper jaw clamped shut on the clear nose cone of his sub.

With a tremendous pop, the LEXAN bubble imploded, sending a river of water slamming into Dief's face, driving the breath from his chest. A roar—then a sickening crunch—as the Kevlar and LEXAN sub was pulverized around him, a shard from the crushed nose cone slicing deep into his upper arm.

The Megalodon released its bite and began circling its prey, waiting for it to die.

Dief thrashed in his harness, unable to free himself from the crushing embrace of his upside-down coffin. Reaching to his right, he managed to grab hold of the pony bottle, shoving the regulator into his mouth and opening the valve to the emergency supply of air. After gagging into the mouthpiece, he calmed himself and sucked a life-giving breath.

The glow appeared to his left. Looming through swirls of mud, he saw an ivory head drift closer. The snout pushed against the wreckage, pressing against Dief's chest. With both hands, the submersible pilot futilely attempted to push the sixty-two-thousand-pound behemoth away. A surprisingly strong current caught his left hand, sucking it into a giant nostril.

In surreal motion, the mouth stretched open before him, the nine-foot maw blotting out the sunlight.

Richard Diefendorf said a quick prayer. Then he spat out the regulator and inhaled the sea as the Angel of Death came for him.

Michael Maren swore aloud as the alabaster form streaked past the *William Beebe*, racing for the southern end of the inlet.

After circling twice, the creature finally sensed the obstruction was no longer there. Seconds later, the Megalodon was gone.

Risky Business

Mariana Trench

Terry wiped the sweat from her brow, then continued twisting an iron crossbar. Another fifteen minutes passed before she was able to wrench one end of
the bed frame free. Aided by the additional leverage,
the other end followed quickly.

She stood, slapping the two-foot hollow bar in her
hand, feeling its weight against her open palm. It wasn't
nearly as good as the Russian's hunting knife, but at
least she wouldn't be unarmed.

Terry checked her watch: 2:10 a.m. She eased open
her cabin door and listened. Hearing only the sounds
of the *Benthos*'s generators, she crept barefoot into the
hall, iron bar held tightly within her right fist, her heart
thumping wildly in her chest.

*Access tube or companionway? The Russian prefers
the tube . . .*

She tiptoed to the companionway, listening. She

could hear the voices of the crew talking in the galley, discussing the immense prehistoric fossil the *Prometheus* had unearthed hours earlier. Entering the sealed stairwell, Terry lifted the watertight hatch at the base of the staircase and descended quietly, closing the seal behind her.

Level F. Ship's stores, equipment rooms, and the nuclear reactor. Keep going . . .

Terry opened the next companionway hatch, listening carefully before heading down the last flight of stairs which led to G deck, the only level considered off-limits to all but Benedict's personal staff. She held her breath, again hearing only the hum from the ship's generators. Creeping barefoot across the tile floor, she darted down the empty corridor to the entrance of the submarine docking station.

Terry pressed her ear to the watertight door. Realizing the futility of the gesture, she held her breath and pushed open the door, entering the vault. The empty circular room yawned back at her. Heart fluttering, she ran to the conning tower of the *Prometheus* protruding out from the center of the docking-station floor. Pulling open the sub's outer hatch, she climbed down the ladder and into the vessel.

The sub was dark, save for the fluorescent glow coming from dozens of control consoles. She crept forward, listening, terrified at being alone in a docked sub surrounded by sixteen thousand pounds per square inch of water.

Locating the computer console, she sat down, then booted the system. All day Benedict Singer had infuriated her, playing with her emotions, manipulating her like a puppet.

This time, it was her turn.

The Geo-Tech menu appeared on the screen, just as it had hours earlier. Using the mouse, she highlighted TOKAMAK. She was about to press ENTER when she heard a noise in the docking chamber above.

Footsteps!

Her heart pounding out of control, Terry searched desperately for a place to hide. She hurried to the rear of the sub, smashing her shin painfully against another console before ducking into the bathroom.

She heard the seal open. Whoever was out there was descending into the *Prometheus!*

Terry was convinced it was the Russian. Wiping the sweat from her palms, she gripped the iron bar tightly in both hands and raised it over her head.

She could feel the vibrations of the man's footsteps. She heard him pause at the computer station, then continue moving aft, approaching the bathroom.

Aim for his head, one good shot, then don't stop till he's dead . . .

The door began opening—

Terry swung the iron bar toward the head of the silhouetted figure.

The man sideswiped the bar, then grabbed her arm and twisted it expertly behind her back. Terry started to scream, but her assailant was too quick, clamping his hand over her mouth and nose, cutting off her breath.

"Terry, it's Heath!"

The viselike grip released her. She bent over, gasping for air.

"You okay?" he asked.

She nodded, still out of breath.

Heath inspected the iron rod. "Yeah, this would have hurt." He handed it back to her. "Better save it for Sergei."

"What are you doing here?"

"I saw you leave your room and figured this might be where you were heading. A very dangerous move. Come here. I want to show you something."

He led her by the arm to the computer station. "The GTI file you were about to access requires a security code. Failing to enter the correct code within sixty seconds would have resulted in all sorts of security devices going off."

Terry stared at the monitor, sweat dripping down both sides of her face. "Why did you follow me? Are you trying to protect me from the Russian?"

Heath grinned. "Sergei won't be bothering you tonight. I slipped him a little something in his tea at dinner. Right now, he should be sleeping like a Russian wolfhound. Tell me why you were accessing the Tokamak file."

She sat down next to the computer. "Benedict's been toying with me ever since we arrived on board the *Benthos*, and I'm tired of it. This afternoon was the worst. I don't know if he's intending to let me live or die, but I decided it was my turn to screw with him for a change."

"What do you know about Tokamak?"

"Nothing."

"Terry, I can't help you if you lie to me."

"I'm not lying. Who are you? Do you really know Jonas?"

Heath rubbed the sweat from his brow. "I don't know him personally, but we both worked together on a deep-sea project for the Navy about eleven years ago."

"Eleven years . . ." The realization dawned on her. "The Mariana Trench dives?"

Heath nodded. "It was a top-secret mission. To this day, Jonas still has no idea what it was really about. Shaffer and Prestis—the two men who died when Jonas panicked in the abyss—they were my colleagues."

"So you're with the Navy?"

"Not anymore."

"But you're not a paleobiologist—"

"Tell me what you know about Tokamak."

"CIA?"

"Terry, I can't help you if you won't cooperate."

"You are CIA, aren't you?"

"Terry, enough. Right now, you're endangering both of our lives."

"Look, I told you, I really don't know anything about Tokamak. When I was aboard the *Titan*, I . . ." She smiled, embarrassed. "I guess you could say I did a little covert operating myself. I stumbled across some kind of high-tech lab hidden within the bowels of the *Titan* and—"

"Within the *Titan?* Where?" Heath seemed excited. "How were you able to access it? What was inside?"

She told him about the stairwell hidden within the ship's old missile silo, then described the lab.

"This large machine," Heath asked, "did it look like a giant toroidal—a giant doughnut?"

"Yes. How did you know that?"

"Jesus . . ." Heath rubbed his face again. "How familiar are you with fusion?"

"As in atom bombs?"

"No, no, that's fission. Fusion is the process that powers the sun and stars. It occurs when two atoms of hydrogen, usually an isotope of deuterium and one of tritium, are heated at super-hot temperatures until they fuse together, releasing an incredible amount of energy. When this happens, matter enters a new state—plasma."

Heath turned off the computer. "We're probably still a good twenty-five years away from placing a fusion reactor online, but the potential benefits are enormous. Imagine an energy source that's virtually inexhaustible, environmentally friendly, and produces no combustion products, greenhouse gases, or even by-products that can be made into weapons."

"Sounds too good to be true."

"Some bureaucrats might agree. We're still in the experimental phases and it's very costly, but things are progressing. To make fusion happen, the atoms of deuterium and tritium must be heated to temperatures exceeding one hundred million degrees, then be held together long enough for fusion to occur. The sun accomplishes this using gravity. On Earth, we have to use a magnetic field to confine the gases."

"So what's a tokamak?"

"Tokamak means toroidal chamber in Russian. Coils wrapped around the outside of the toroidal or doughnut create a magnetic field inside the chamber, which, in turn, stabilizes the fusion plasma—"

"Now you're way over my head. Just tell me how Benedict is involved."

"Hear me out. The main challenge of fusion is to be able to contain the hot plasma for a sufficient amount of time. This relates to problems with the fuel itself, specifically tritium, which is radioactive. Several years ago Israeli Intelligence learned of a secret meeting between Benedict Singer and a Saudi millionaire, part of a terrorist organization linked to attacks on the United States, as well as other bombings, including the ones on the Kenya and Nairobi embassies. At this meeting, Benedict demonstrated a prototype fuel that created a fusion reaction said to have been off the scale of any energy reaction previously accomplished. This millionaire and his Arab associates were so impressed that they agreed to finance GTI's work in exchange for partial control of the technology. With their backing and influence, Benedict has been able to recruit some of the brightest minds in Russia and the Middle East to help him construct what may turn out to be the world's first true tokamak fusion reactor."

"What happens if Benedict succeeds?"

"If he succeeds, he'll change the balance of power for decades to come. Up to now, fusion has been a shared technology among the world's nations, a united effort to pool our resources for the common good. Fusion would legitimize their influence on our entire global economy. It would be the equivalent of Hitler developing the atomic bomb before the United States. It's vital that we determine what Benedict's mysterious fusion fuel source is, and whether it's stable. CIA's been following him for years, attempting to infiltrate his organization. We got our first break when Benedict contacted Scripps in search of a paleobiologist."

"Obviously, you're not a paleobiologist. Aren't you afraid Benedict will see through the charade?"

"I have a working knowledge in the field, enough to get by. So far, things have gone okay, although the first real challenge to my cover just came up."

"That fossil?"

"Yes. The object is an incredible specimen of a prehistoric reptile I've never seen before. Benedict's demanding that I come up with answers to its origin, and fast."

"Could it have been related to the species that chased after us today?"

"Too early to say. I'm probably in way too deep. But I need to provide Benedict with information soon, before he suspects something."

"What can I do to help?"

"For one thing, stay the hell away from these computers," Heath advised. "The CIA believes that Benedict's fusion fuel may be aboard the *Benthos*. There's some kind of storehouse located on G deck that's off-limits to everyone except Benedict and his piranhas. If I could just get a look inside, I'd know what he's up to."

"Wish I could help, but right now I'm just struggling to keep from being killed." Terry gave him a nervous smile. "Maybe you could kill Sergei for me, you know, in the line of duty."

"I'll run as much interference for you as I can without jeopardizing my cover, but I can't help you unless you stay in your cabin. Tonight was very foolish. I suggest you speak with Benedict about joining him on board *Prometheus* again. You know, appeal to his ego, speak some Latin to him or something. With any luck, you'll be topside in a few days. So no more chances, okay?"

"Okay."

They exited the sub, Heath escorting her back to her quarters. The CIA agent said good night, then returned to his own cabin, unaware that the microlens hidden in the ceiling had recorded their every move.

Mixed Emotions

The morning sun glared off the aft deck, forcing the passengers and crew of the *William Beebe* to squint.

Jonas felt an ache in his chest and a harsh lump in his throat as Captain Morgan closed the prayer book, concluding the ceremony honoring their fallen shipmate.

Mac grabbed Jonas's arm and pulled him aside, tears of anger welling in his eyes. "GTI made arrangements for me to pick up another chopper, but first I have to file a report with the FAA over yesterday's accident. Figure I'll be gone all day. When I get back, I want you to tell me how we're going to exterminate that damned shark of yours."

Jonas nodded and watched him go.

Jonas could sense Celeste's approach from the aroma of jasmine lotion on her deeply tanned skin. A beige one-piece romper hung from her bared shoulders, the cut of her loose-fitting top revealing the inviting cleavage. She stood barefoot, a pair of sandals dangling from her fingers.

Jonas caught himself staring. She didn't seem to mind.

"Are you going somewhere?" he asked.

"We're meeting in ten minutes in the galley. Since it looks like we're stuck in port for at least the next fifteen hours, I thought you could help me pick up a few supplies in town."

"I don't think I'd be much company."

She looked up at him, her blue eyes glistening. "I'm upset, too. That's why I need to get off this boat for a few hours."

"Let me think about it," he said, following her to the galley.

Jonas nodded to the captain and Harry Moon, then set his breakfast tray on the table, taking an empty seat across from Dr. Maren. Celeste set her tray down next to him.

"I'm having a GTI representative meet with Dief's family," Celeste said. "They'll take care of funeral arrangements and other financial needs."

"Celeste, the Tanaka Institute called," Captain Morgan said. "They said your package should arrive onboard sometime this evening."

"What package?"

"I've arranged for another of the Institute's *Abyss Gliders* to be delivered. I know Dief's death is still on everyone's mind, but we'll need the sub to position the net beneath the Megalodon once she's captured."

"And who do you expect to pilot the sub?" Jonas asked.

"I'll be piloting it," Maren said.

"It's not like piloting the Alvin," Jonas said. "Once the Meg's unconscious, you may have to descend three or four hundred feet just to get the net beneath her."

"I know what has to be done, Taylor. Celeste, can we dispense with the small talk and get this meeting started? Unlike some of you, I've got tons of work to do."

Celeste nodded. "Start by bringing Jonas up to date."

Maren rubbed his eyes. He looked hungover. "Short and sweet, we lost SOSUS."

"What's that mean?" Jonas asked.

"Lost, as in the signal no longer exists. The transmitter must have been torn away from the Meg's hide when she was struggling to break free from the trawl net. No matter, we'll find her."

"Yeah, and how will we do that?" Jonas asked.

"We'll follow the coastline around Vancouver and Alaska until we track her down in the Bering Sea."

"You think the Bering Sea's just a little pond? How do you expect—"

Celeste stopped him. "Jonas, if I have to, I'll arrange a fleet of choppers to track her—"

"Might as well call out the Air Force, while you're at it. Christ, Celeste, this voyage could go on for months."

"No thanks to you," Maren said, a bit too loudly.

"You're blaming me?"

"The plan worked perfectly, we had her trapped in the harbor. The shark was exhausted. Another five minutes and I would have harpooned her. If you hadn't ordered Celeste to remove the gill net—"

"The shark was attacking those rafts," Jonas said. "If it hadn't been for Dief, a lot more people would have died."

"I disagree," Maren said. "The creature had already fed. It wasn't hungry, it only attacked the Tall Ship because it felt threatened. I don't know what you said to Diefendorf, but it was enough to send him into the sea with the sub. For all we know, the *Abyss Glider* may have actually spooked the creature."

"And what's that supposed to mean?"

"It means that you panicked, Taylor. Had you said nothing to Dief, the *William Beebe* would have been able to rescue those passengers without the Megalodon going ballistic, and we still could have harpooned the creature, to say nothing about the fact that Diefendorf would still be alive—"

Celeste watched Jonas's face turn red with anger.

"—but then, you always seem to panic when it comes to these creatures," Maren said. "And, unfortunately, somebody always dies as a result."

Jonas lunged across the table and grabbed the young scientist by his shirt, lifting him clear out of his chair with both hands. Captain Morgan and Harry Moon interrupted Jonas, prying his fingers loose.

Maren turned to Celeste, visibly upset. "Celeste, I've had enough of this guy's attitude. If you want me to do my job, keep this baboon out of my way." He glared at Jonas, straightened his torn shirt collar, and marched out of the galley.

Jonas stormed out to the main deck, his hands trembling in anger.

Celeste watched him go, then headed to Dr. Maren's room. Without bothering to knock, she opened the door.

He was next to the bed, removing his torn shirt.

She reached up and fingered his bruised throat.

He gave her a boyish grin. "At this rate I'm going to need a new wardrobe. So? Did I do good?"

"You'll win the Oscar," she said.

"And what happens when he bashes my skull in?"

"He won't, at least not when there's a crowd around. Stay to the high ground."

"I'm not afraid of Taylor. It's his psycho friend, Mackreides, who bothers me."

"Leave him to me. As for Jonas, I'll let you know when I want you to piss him off again."

Maren slipped his arm around Celeste's waist, pulling her close. "And what about us? You were supposed to come by my cabin last night. What happened?"

She slid her arm around his shoulders, giving him a playful squeeze. "I like to tease my prey before I eat them," she whispered, running the tip of her tongue along his bruised neck. "Guess I wasn't hungry last night."

Celeste removed his hand from her waist, whispering into his ear. "*Varium et mutabile simper femina.*"

"Another one of your mentor's sayings?"

"It means: Woman is ever a fickle and changeable thing. Be patient with me, Michael darling. I'm worth the wait. In the meantime, redirect that libido of yours and help me recapture my fish."

* * *

A cluster of television and newspaper reporters waiting on the wharf suddenly turned and ran in unison toward Jonas as he stepped out onto the main deck. Leaning over the starboard rail, they called out questions as the photographers clicked their cameras.

Jonas ducked back inside the boat.

"Going ashore, Taylor?"

Jonas turned, startled by Harry Moon. "Celeste asked me to help her run a few errands."

"Then you'd better take this." Harry handed him a cellular phone. "You've made a few more enemies over the last twenty-four hours. The ship-to-shore number's already programmed into memory, just hit ONE and SEND. Check in with us every once in a while, so we know you're okay."

Jonas pocketed the phone. "Thanks."

He watched Harry go as Celeste approached from the other end of the corridor. "Come with me into town," she said. "Anything's better than dealing with the press."

Jonas nodded.

Celeste took his arm, leading him to a launch docked along the *William Beebe*'s portside bow. They climbed down into the craft and hid beneath a canvas rain cover as the driver started the boat's engines. Five minutes later, they arrived, unnoticed, along the far side of the Westport Marina.

For the next six hours, they visited wholesale purveyors, ordering supplies and arranging the goods to be delivered aboard the ship. By late afternoon they had finished, stopping to rest at a park bench facing the ocean. The sun bathed the wharf in a golden light, casting a warm glow across Celeste's amber skin. Jonas watched as she fed popcorn to the seagulls.

"I really needed to get off that boat," she said. "Could I ask you one last favor? We passed a restaurant a few blocks back on West Haven Drive—"

"The Islander?"

"Yes. Let's go there for dinner." She smiled. "It's on the company."

"Okay."

"You look tired. It's still early, why don't you close your eyes for a few minutes and relax."

Jonas laid his head back and shut his eyes, the sound of the sea calming him. Within seconds he was asleep.

When he awoke, the sun had turned into a crimson ball, setting quickly along the horizon. Celeste was nuzzled against him. "Have a nice nap?"

Jonas straightened himself and stretched, feeling refreshed. "God, it's so nice to fall asleep without having a nightmare."

"See what happens when I watch over you."

They waited until the sunset faded to violet, then headed to the restaurant. The maître d' led them to a candlelit booth facing the water.

Celeste leaned forward. "Jonas, I need to tell you something. I feel very comfortable around you, like I could talk to you about anything. I've never had that kind of relationship with a man before. You know I'm also very attracted to you."

"I'm married—"

"Yes, but be honest. Are you happy? Is Terry happy?"

"We shouldn't be discussing this right now."

"Why not? I told you personal things about my life."

"Celeste, I love my wife, is that so hard for you to understand?"

"No, but is it so hard for *you* to understand that Terry wants to move on."

Jonas picked up the menu, feeling uncomfortable. "I had a nice time today. Why screw it up now?"

"I'm trying to help you—"

"No, you're trying to manipulate me into believing that Terry wants a divorce."

Celeste smiled. "Okay, I confess. I do have an ulterior motive. The truth is, I think you and I could be very happy together." She glided her fingertips over the candle's flame. "Jonas, forget me for a moment. Just answer this question honestly—how did your first marriage end?"

"My first marriage? Why do you want to know about that?"

"Just answer the question. Did you leave her, or did she leave you?"

"If you must know, she left me. She was having an affair with one of my best friends."

"And why do you think that happened?"

"What are you getting at?"

She reached forward and touched his hand. "What I'm about to say may seem harsh, but I want you to think about it. A woman's love for a man dies when her partner stops paying attention to her. Women like Terry need constant attention. If you don't give it to them, they'll eventually find it from someone else. I don't know what happened to your first marriage, but I think your marriage to Terry failed because you still feel guilty over what happened eleven years ago."

Jonas pulled his hand away. "I feel guilty about a lot of things."

"But eleven years ago was the quintessential moment in your life—the day your obsession with death first began. Two people died under your command. Knowing you, I'd say you probably blamed yourself for their deaths and ruined your first marriage in the process. Then, four years ago, you refocused your guilt into hatred, blaming your misery on these sharks."

Jonas stared out the window. "She died."

"Who died?"

"Maggie, my first wife. She was killed four years ago by the Megalodon."

"I'm sorry."

The waiter interrupted. Celeste ordered for both of them while Jonas continued staring at his dark reflection in the bay window.

"Jonas, are you okay?"

"Can we talk about something else?"

"Okay." She leaned forward. "Maren pissed you off earlier, didn't he?"

"The guy's a jerk."

"Yes, but he's an intelligent jerk. I need him around until we recapture the creature."

"And why do you need me around?"

She smiled. "Maren's a boy. You're a man."

Jonas felt her toes rubbing against his calf. "Celeste—"

"Sorry." She drained her glass. "How is Masao Tanaka doing?"

"Not well."

"Perhaps the stress of the Megalodon's escape was too much for him. Maybe he should retire."

"I think the news of his daughter descending into the Mariana Trench is what triggered his heart attack, not the shark escaping."

"Why should Tanaka be concerned about Terry? Doesn't he think the *Benthos* is a safe ship?"

"It's not the *Benthos*. His son, D.J., was killed in the Trench four years ago."

"*Prastitye*, I had completely forgotten." Celeste picked at her Caesar salad. "Jonas, tell me, how many more of these sharks could really be down there?"

"I don't know. I'm sure there's a few."

"And the *Benthos*—is it vulnerable to attack?"

"I can't say. I know Benedict designed the vessel to take a beating, but who knows what else is in the abyss."

"Now you've got me worried. The Trench is so huge . . ." She paused, staring at her water glass. "Jonas, where was it that you first ran into the Megalodon?"

"You mean four years ago?"

"No, the very first time you saw one of the creatures. Eleven years back, when you were piloting the *Sea Cliff*."

"It was a remote location. We nicknamed the site the 'Devil's Purgatory'."

Her eyes lit up. "Devil's Purgatory. Do you remember the exact coordinates?"

"Yes, but I can't discuss it. The mission was classified, and the Navy's already pissed off enough at me."

"You know I'm only interested because I'm worried

about Benedict and the *Benthos* crew. They're family, all I have left. What if the *Benthos* is exploring the same area of the Trench— this Devil's Purgatory?"

"What if they are?"

"Don't you think the chances of them running across another Megalodon may be greater? Don't you think we should warn them to stay away from that location?"

"There's no reason to think that area could be any more dangerous than another. Besides, I told you, I can't give out the coordinates."

"But if another creature the size of Angel is down there—"

"Nothing as big as Angel's in the Trench. That I can assure you."

"But still, you said there may be other sharks. Jonas, I promise I won't tell a soul. I'm just worried. Earlier I said I trusted you. Don't you trust me?"

"It's not a question of trust, Celeste. Top secret means top secret. Masao's like a father to me, but I couldn't reveal the coordinates to him, either."

"Fine." She slammed down her fork. "Just forget I asked."

"Don't be mad."

"I am mad, and I'm disappointed. I thought we were friends."

"We are."

"If Mackreides asked you for the coordinates, would you tell him?"

"Celeste—"

"I don't understand how some obscure piece of information that's more than eleven years old could possibly hurt the United States Navy."

"That's because you don't know what the mission was about."

"I don't want to know what the mission was about. In fact, I couldn't care less. I told you, I'm just worried about the people on board the *Benthos*."

"Terry, let's change the subject."

Celeste frowned. "You just called me Terry."

"I did?" Jonas rubbed his eyes. "I'm sorry. Freudian slip. I'm just very tired. Can we talk about something else?"

"I have a better idea. Let's not talk at all."

Harry Moon greeted them as they boarded the *William Beebe*.

"What happened to all the reporters?" Jonas asked.

"Dr. Maren spoke with them briefly. Glad you're back, we're about ready to shove off. Maren's been driving the captain crazy since the new *Abyss Glider* was delivered two hours ago. He was ready to send out a search party for the two of you. I think he's afraid the creature's getting too far ahead of us."

"I pay Maren to worry," Celeste said.

Jonas reached into his pocket, removing the cellular phone Harry had given him earlier.

"Just hang on to it for the duration of the trip," Harry said.

"Jonas, I'm exhausted," Celeste said. "Would you mind walking me to my cabin?"

They strolled across the deck, pausing to admire the new *Abyss Glider*, which had been assembled and mounted on its sled in the stern.

Jonas stared at the one-man sub, the blood draining

from his face. "What in the—what the hell is this thing doing onboard?"

"What are you talking about?"

"Don't mess with me, Celeste, you know damn well what I'm talking about. This is an *AG-II*, the deep-water model. What the hell is it doing here? Did you order this?"

"Jonas, calm down. It was the only sub the Institute had available on short notice. It may not be as fast as the *AG-I*, but it'll still do the job. Is there a problem?"

"Hell—yes, there's a problem—there's a big problem! Damn it, Celeste, I told you about my nightmares and now you've brought an *AG-II* aboard? Are you toying with me?"

"Jonas—"

"That sub is my coffin!"

She grabbed him by the arm. "Stop this nonsense. It's not your coffin. You're not even the one who's going to be piloting it."

She followed him inside as the *William Beebe*'s engines growled to life. "Jonas—wait. I'm sorry. Are you all right?"

"No. Do me a favor, just leave me alone. I can't—I can't think straight."

"Come with me, I know just what you need." She led him to her cabin door. "Come in and have a quick drink, it will settle your nerves."

"Not tonight."

"Jonas, the night's still young. Allow me to apologize the right way." She reached her hand around his waist, pressing her groin to his.

Jonas pushed her away. "Don't. Look, I told you, I love Terry."

"Did you also love your first wife after she stopped loving you? Stay with me tonight, Jonas. You don't have to make love to me if you're not ready. Just let me watch over you while you sleep. I'll keep your nightmares away."

He stared at her, her breasts heaving, her lust intoxicating. *So beautiful . . . so dangerous.*

She unbuttoned her shirt. "No one could love you the way I could," she whispered, reaching for his pants.

Jonas grabbed her wrists, feeling his own hands trembling with desire. "Knock it off, Celeste. This isn't going to happen."

"I know you want me, Jonas—"

"Good night, Celeste."

She watched him head down the hall. "Jonas, I bet you'll think of me tonight when you're alone."

Jonas ignored her. He pushed open his cabin door, not noticing Dr. Maren watching from the end of the corridor.

The Spider and the Fly

Mariana Trench

Heath Williams continued to search his computer files, frustrated at the lack of pertinent information available on ancient marine reptiles. At least he knew what monstrous prehistoric species the immense fossilized section of skull belonged to. Unfortunately, he also knew that wouldn't be enough for Benedict. He typed in another command, accessing Jonas Taylor's theories on *Carcharodon megalodon*.

He looked up to see Sergei enter the lab.

"Sergei, back here." Heath directed him into the back room and closed the door behind him.

Hearing the door close, Terry sneaked out of the lab's supply closet and into the outer corridor, heading up to the bridge to find Benedict.

"You wanted to speak?" Sergei said, eyeing Heath suspiciously.

"Yes. I've now dated this fossil and completed my taxonomy work. Based on the measurements of this skull, I'd say we're looking at a creature whose dimensions match those of the life-forms that chased the *Prometheus*. I'm almost certain that the animals swarming after the sub come from the same lineage as this fossil. Benedict needs to know that we're dealing with pack hunters that are probably faster and more cunning than *Carcharodon megalodon*—and perhaps even more dangerous. I strongly recommend that all future submersible missions into the Trench be postponed until we can figure out a way of dealing with these creatures."

Sergei scoffed, already knowing Benedict's reply.

"You wish to board the *Prometheus?*" Benedict's emerald eyes became laser beams, seeking to penetrate her innermost thoughts.

Terry turned away from him to face the LEXAN observation window. The bioluminescent creatures of the abyss twinkled in the pitch-black water like a bizarre night sky. "I know it seems like a strange request, given what happened yesterday, but I just feel like it's something I should do. What was it you said? Yield not to misfortune?"

Benedict thumbed his goatee. "And the presence of these mysterious life-forms no longer bothers you?"

"Of course it bothers me," Terry said. "I have a healthy dose of fear, just like the crew of the *Prometheus*. But I'm not going to allow that to interfere with my responsibilities. I'm willing to face my fears."

"Fortune favors the brave, is that it?"

"If your men can do it, so can I. Of course, I'm not in it for the money."

"And you believe this is the reason my crew risks their lives, for money?"

"I just assumed so," she said. "Most of them don't appear to be scientists, so I'm guessing they're well-paid hired hands."

"Well-paid, yes, but what good is money if one is dead? You and I risk our lives because we believe in the humanity of our mission. These men are different, recruited for their talent, handpicked and trained by me because their lives had long ago become meaningless, lacking all purpose and direction. They were lost souls, something you can't even begin to relate to. They had forfeited everything in life, their miserable existence without meaning or value. I gave them what they desperately needed: a reason to live." His eyes opened wide. "My presence now fills voids manifested through years of narcotics and alcohol and child abuse. I have shown them that an honorable death is better than a disgraceful life. In doing so, I became both their Devil and their God, for they fear me as much as they love me—and that, my dear, is true power."

"So you prey on their fears, is that it?"

Benedict stroked his goatee as if mulling it over. "Do I prey upon their fears? Perhaps. Man, after all, is predatory by nature. After two million years of existence, we continue to slaughter ourselves, be it in the name of conquest, or religion, or some other justification, all of which are rooted in the power of fear."

"Don't these men have families?"

"I am their family. They will remain in my employment and care until the day they die."

"And Celeste?"

Benedict shot her a malicious grin. "Celeste is a different animal entirely."

"What if these men wanted to leave?"

"They could go if they wished. Those that have done so in the past quickly return to drugs or booze or whatever personal problem gave me cause to recruit them in the first place. Try to understand. The tragedy that befell these men robbed them of their self-discipline. I've given each a new lease on life. In exchange, they've turned their free will over to a higher power."

"Which is you?"

"Yes. I am like the spider. Having enticed the condemned fly into my web, I offer sweet salvation in a spiderweb, only fear and death. If you ask me, your organization sounds more like a cult, and you're nothing more than another megalomaniac running it."

"Please, if you wish to parley, then kindly shunt the emotional side of your brain so we may converse like intellectuals. Like all true leaders, I am first and foremost a student of human nature."

Benedict moved toward the immense LEXAN window, staring into the abyss. "Have you ever wondered how certain men throughout history, despite every conceivable hardship, managed to rise above their peers to change the world? Genghis Khan, Napoleon, Lenin, Hitler, Pol Pot, Saddam Hussein—these men all understood fear, a state of mind so powerful that it can move mountains and land a man on the Moon just as easily as it can obliterate a person's resistance with but a single negative thought."

He turned to face her. "What is it that man truly fears? Poverty, criticism, ill health, loss of a loved one, old age . . . of course, let's not forget the ultimate fear: death. Think about it, without fear, we'd have no need for religion or war. Then again, fear is the great motivator, isn't it? Had early man never experienced fear, we would have never developed as a species."

"Are you saying that you have no fear?"

Benedict shook his head. "I have mastered my fear, but it will never be absent. Courage and understanding, that is the key. Fear is nothing more than the dark side of thought, it has substance only in the mind. We create it, and we alone can destroy it. But because most men never master their fear, they spend their lives living in its thrall. My crew follows me into the depths of hell because they fear my wrath more than anything else they can imagine."

What the hell did he do to instill such fear? Terry smiled nervously. "Look, I just came to ask you if it would be all right to spend my last day in the abyss aboard the *Prometheus*. If it's a problem—"

"Fear makes us do things we might never agree to do, doesn't it, my dear?"

"I really don't know what you're talking about."

"Oh, I think you do," he said, drawing closer. "I can smell your fear. It paralyzes your thoughts, your ability to think, to reason."

He stood over her, his penetrating gaze fracturing her will. "You're afraid, aren't you? Afraid of what Sergei may do when he finds you alone."

"Yes," she confessed. "Can't you keep him away from me?"

"Sergei is an animal. I've warned him, but he feeds off your fear—it intoxicates him as much as his alcohol. You must learn to focus your energy on solutions, not the problem itself."

"Solutions? Give me a gun and I'll blow his head off. How's that for a solution?"

"And spend the rest of your life in prison? I think not. Sergei is not your true enemy, Terry, fear is. It will steal your willpower, diminish your strength, immobilize your defenses. To control it, you must first understand it, recognize its subtleties, and find its weakness."

"I don't understand."

Benedict moved closer. He took her hand in his, rubbing the sweat along her open palm with his thumb. "Fear creates stress, which in turn causes a series of psychological changes to occur. Heart rate and breathing increase, raising the oxygen supply and pumping more blood to the muscles. Blood sugar rises, increasing energy. The pupils dilate, improving vision, while the flow of neurotransmitter secretions increases to improve the speed of reactions. Nature designed these physiological changes for primitive man to survive in the jungle, to fight back when challenged. But the evolution of our species only took place when we learned how to engage our minds."

"The challenges facing civilized man are more emotional than physical. When confronted with obstacles, our society of weaklings tends to choose flight over fight. Instead of focusing on solutions, modern man chooses to escape reality, and the battle is lost before it is ever begun. Flight becomes fright. Drugs and alcohol subdue the physiological changes of fear, but in doing so, dull the thought process. Succumbing to our fears, we disarm ourselves of the one tool that can lead us to victory, the very process necessary for solutions and the one that brought our species out of the jungle in the first place."

Benedict released her hand. "The true battle is here, in the mind," he said, pointing to her temple. "Force your mind to create solutions. Face your fear—and defeat it."

He started down the access tube, then stopped. "You and I both know the true reason you wish to join us this morning aboard the *Prometheus*. Choosing the lesser of two evils is not always the best way to live one's life, but under the circumstances, it may be your best solution. Therefore, the invitation is extended. We depart in fifteen minutes."

Ten minutes later, Terry descended to G deck, still uncertain whether she was intending to board the *Prometheus* or not. She followed the long white corridor toward the docking bay, then stopped.

Down the hall to her right, Sergei was swiping his magnetic pass card across the security lock of the vault-like storage room. He saw her just as he was about to enter.

Face your fears . . .

Terry forced herself to continue walking.

Sergei waited, leering at her.

"Wipe that smirk off your face," she said. "Mess with me, and you're messing with Benedict."

Sergei stopped smiling.

Terry continued past him, exuding attitude, then entered the docking area, her heart racing wildly. Taking several deep breaths, she descended into the *Prometheus*.

Benedict looked up from his charts as she climbed down into the cabin. "Captain, our last passenger has arrived. Take us out."

"Aye, sir. Rig ship for dive."

Benedict continued leaning over the light table, his eyes glittering up at her. Perhaps it was the emerald eyes, or perhaps the mouth that hung open in a frozen smile, but for a moment, Benedict's hairless face appeared like the head of a snake, poised to strike.

"Welcome to my web, said the spider to the fly."

"I'm not here because I'm afraid," she lied. "Since I'll be returning topside tomorrow, this will be my last day in the abyss, my last chance to explore the Trench."

"Of course. You're here because you want to be here, even though death may arrive at a moment's notice. Ah, but the madness of one person drives many mad."

"Do you object?"

"Not in the least. As I stated earlier, your presence is welcome." He flashed her a Cheshire-cat smile. "*Morituri te salutamus*—we who are about to die salute thee."

Without asking, she took her place at the computer station. Moments later, the deep-sea submersible pulled away from its docking bay and glided into the Trench.

For the next four hours, the *Prometheus* moved through darkness, dropping to the seafloor every kilometer or so to extract a sample of sediment and rock.

"Each sample will be examined onboard the *Benthos* by our geologists," Benedict had explained. "Results of the tests help us map out the Trench while determining which terrains are best suited to support the next series of UNIS robots."

Fighting drowsiness, Terry stretched, then made her way aft to the bathroom. She closed the door and stared at her reflection in the mirror.

"Hang in there, girl," she said aloud. "By this time tomorrow, you'll be back onboard the *Titan*, then on your way home to Jonas."

She relieved herself, then washed her face.

Without warning, the submersible suddenly turned hard to starboard, tossing her sideways against the aluminum storage locker. Regaining her feet, she hurried from the bathroom as the vessel turned once more.

Standing between the radioman and sonar, Benedict had a tense look on his face. The other members of the crew were watching him.

"What's happening?" she asked one of the men.

"The *Titan* located the creatures. Instead of going after us, they're heading for a location between us and the *Benthos*. Looks like they finally figured out how to isolate us."

Terry took her seat, the news draining her of her strength.

Does Benedict fear death?

She stared at him, the expression on his face exuding annoyance.

"Four objects now on sonar, sir. Two kilometers and closing from the north. *Benthos* still a good five kilometers behind them." The seaman looked up. "They've got us, sir."

"Stay focused, gentlemen," Benedict said.

Minutes passed in silence. The cabin grew warm, the air heavy with the pungent smell of perspiration.

"Life-forms approaching seventy yards to starboard. Stand by. Sir, three of the four just broke from the pack, closing quickly. The fourth is circling behind us."

"Intelligent creatures," Benedict muttered. "Helm, stay on course."

"Aye, sir."

Terry's eyes strained to penetrate the darkness. Unable to see ahead, she focused on the beam of light aimed at the passing seafloor.

Seconds later, she was startled to witness a prodigious girth glide into view beneath the sub.

The flattened mud-brown dorsal surface of the immense head appeared first, the skull as large as the *Prometheus*'s bow. Two forefins, which were attached to a streamlined body, tapered back, ending with two paddling hind limbs and a short but muscular tail.

"It just passed under the sub!" she yelled.

The closest crewman turned. "You saw it? How big—"

"As wide as the sub, nearly as long. It moved through the water like a giant crocodile."

Without warning, the *Prometheus* was slammed broadside.

Terry was thrown sideways against the window, smashing her elbow hard against the titanium plating.

"*Benthos* now three kilometers to the south. ETA seven minutes."

The sub lurched forward, jolted from behind.

"Captain, one of the creatures is attacking the screw. I'm losing helm control—"

An insane screech of metal filled the cabin. The sub began rolling to port, then shuddered, the interior lights flickering off.

Enveloped in suffocating darkness, Terry covered her ears against the deafening shrill of the damaged screw.

The screeching ceased.

Terry felt the sub dropping. Grabbing the armrests of her seat, she nearly wrenched them off. Her breathing became labored, sweat pouring down her face, her skin crawling in the pitch-dark cabin as the *Prometheus* fell to the bottom of the world.

"Screws completely gone, sir," a shaken crewman called out. "We're dead in the water."

"Release ballast plates—"

"Belay that, Captain," Benedict yelled. "We'll be safer on the bottom."

Dropping between two black smokers, the sub plowed bow first into the seabed. The rest of the hull struck bottom seconds later.

Terry began hyperventilating as the vessel came to a complete stop, resting in silence and blackness on the floor of the seven-mile-deep Trench.

A backup generator switched on, bathing the cabin in red light.

Terry felt a prodigious force nudging the outer plates. She glanced out her window, stifling a scream—

An iridescent crimson eye the size of a grapefruit peered in at her.

"Mr. Singer, hull temperature exceeding two hundred eighty degrees and rising fast. These vents will cook us—"

"Here comes the *Benthos!*" sonar called out. "Sir, the creatures are scattering."

Terry wiped tears from her eyes as she breathed a sigh of relief.

"Captain, inform the *Benthos* that we no longer have propulsion," Benedict ordered. "Once they've aligned the docking bay over us, we'll drop ballast and rise straight up into the docking clamps. Make sure the docking arms are stretched to full capacity. We'll need all the leeway we can get for this maneuver, and we only get one shot at it."

"Understood, sir."

A few moments later, Terry felt the *Prometheus* ascend vertically from the seafloor. She whispered a prayer of thanks as the hydraulic docking arms of the *Benthos* guided the sub back into the safety of its bay.

Tigers of the Deep

Mariana Trench

"There's nothing left to repair," Captain Hoppe said, staring into the abyss from the observation deck. "Whatever attacked the *Prometheus* literally tore the screw off the driveshaft."

Benedict stroked his goatee, deep in thought. "Contact the *Titan*. Inform them I want to complete the sub and crew exchanges twelve hours ahead of schedule. I expect the *Epimetheus* to be in the water and descending within the hour. Captain Warren, assemble your crew aboard the *Prometheus*, your shift is over. Lacking propulsion, you'll have to allow your sub to drift free from the docking bay. Wait for the *Benthos* to clear, then drop your ballast and free float topside for repairs."

"Aye, sir," Captain Warren said. "What about the girl? She's expecting to ascend."

"For now, the girl will remain aboard the *Benthos*."

"Benedict, what harm would it do to let her go?" Captain Hoppe asked. "She knows nothing—"

Benedict's eyes seemed to sizzle. "Are you questioning me again, Captain Hoppe?"

"I only—" Benedict's piercing gaze cut off the man's objection. "No, sir."

"Sir, what about these creatures?" Captain Warren asked.

"Where's our paleobiologist?"

"Williams should be in his lab," Hoppe said quietly.

"That's where I'll be. Gentlemen, carry out your orders. Oh, and Captain Hoppe, have Sergei join me in the lab."

CIA Agent Heath Williams slipped the microcassette into a hidden compartment in his duffel bag, then finished packing his belongings.

"Going somewhere, Professor?" Benedict asked, entering the lab.

"Mr. Singer, you startled me. Yes, I heard the *Prometheus* was surfacing early. As I told you when you hired me, I have to be back at Scripps Institute this week for a series I'm hosting on the distribution and diversity of Cretaceous Chelonoidis. But I'll be returning the following week. The section of fossilized skeleton you recovered—it's absolutely incredible."

"Is that so?"

"Yes. I left you a complete report detailing the species—"

"I detest reading reports, Professor. I prefer to hear

verbal details directly from the source. So, if you don't mind."

"Of course not, uh, if I have time. When will the *Prometheus* be leaving?"

"Not until you and I have completed our discussion, so take your time."

Heath led him to the back room where the immense grayish-black object lay beneath surgical lights. Four steel tables had been positioned together to support the relic, which was over ten feet long and eight feet wide, rising upward of five feet at its highest point.

"What we're looking at," Heath said, "is a cross-section of a skull from an extinct order of marine reptiles known as *plesiosaurus*. There were two major subspecies of *plesiosaur*, which differed if the lengths of their necks and in their feeding habits. This particular specimen is a member of the superfamily, *pliosauroidea*, a short-necked, carnivorous breed considered by paleobiologists to have once been the tigers of the Mesozoic seas. As you can see, these monsters possessed extremely large heads with short necks, which streamlined their bodies for swimming. The jaw muscles were quite strong, the teeth were particularly hideous— needle-like cones, slightly curved and razor-sharp, protruding out of the jaw like those of our modern-day crocodile. Here, take a look for yourself."

Heath pointed to the narrow end of the skull.

"It's a little difficult to see because the jaws themselves have been so severely crushed by the predator that killed it, but if you look here, you can still see fragments of four-inch teeth."

"And you call this a pliosaur?" Benedict asked, examining the jaw.

"Actually, I've identified this particular animal as a Kronosaurus, the largest of the known pliosaurs. The species dates back to the early Cretaceous, more than one hundred million years ago. Until *Carcharodon megalodon* came along, these monsters were the true lords of the sea. Kronosaurus dominated the warm shallow seas along the landmass that eventually became Australia. Fossilized evidence indicates the creature's length reached more than forty feet. This animal was four to five times heavier than a *Tyrannosaurus rex* and could probably have eaten one for breakfast."

"And this was the creature's skull?"

"Just a section, beginning about its midjaw, extending back to its forelimb girdle and upper rib cage. See these two holes," Heath stated as he pointed along the dorsal skull. "It's hard to tell because they're crushed, but those were the creature's orbital bones, or eye sockets. Kronosaurus's head was flat-topped, with a set of powerful jaws larger and more destructive than that of T. rex. Each upper and lower jaw contained twenty to twenty-five teeth. The rest of the body was ellipsoidal, very streamlined, with two pairs of elongated limbs, which acted like wing-shaped flippers. The torso tapered back, ending in a short, muscular tail. The rather large limb girdles we've collected from other fossils indicate the creatures were pursuit predators, capable of swimming very fast through the sea."

Benedict stared at the fossil with respect. "How old is this specimen?"

"That's what's so incredible. The animal we're looking at inhabited these waters less than two thousand years ago. What's more, this animal shows clear anatomical adaptations to its environment." Heath pointed to the crushed rib cage along the wider end of the skull. "Again, it's difficult to tell because of the overwhelming damage, but these grooves along either side of the gastral rib cage appear to be gill slits."

"Gill slits? I thought this was a reptile?"

"It is, or rather, it was. What you're looking at is a prehistoric marine reptile that adapted to a deep-water habitat by growing gills. This particular species apparently evolved over tens of millions of years in order to exist within the unique environmental conditions of the Mariana Trench."

"Then you believe the *Prometheus* was attacked by Kronosaurs?"

"As unbelievable as it sounds—yes. Look, we know that most of the dinosaurs disappeared worldwide at the end of the Mesozoic era, about sixty-five million years ago. The ancient marine reptiles disappeared about the same time, but their extinction was more gradual, due to a steady drop in sea temperatures."

"Reptiles, being cold-blooded, rely on the sun as their main source of energy and heat. Scientists always believed that life couldn't exist without the sun. The discovery of hydrothermal vents in 1977 changed all that. Now we know that bacteria and other sea creatures of the abyss are able to utilize sulfur and other chemicals that spew out of hydrothermal vents. Instead of photosynthesis, these creatures rely on chemosynthesis."

"You're not telling me anything new, Professor."

"I realize that sir, but everything I've just said leads up to an incredible theory I have about the Trench."

Heath pulled up a U.S. Geological Survey map of the Western Pacific. A red line circled the arching chain of the Mariana Islands. The dark outline of the Mariana Trench ran parallel, just east of the landmass, as if shadowing it.

"We know the Mariana Trench, Ridge, and the adjacent Mariana Islands were all formed by the continuous subduction of the Pacific Plate thrusting beneath the Philippine Plate. This tectonic process has probably gone on for billions of years. At one time, the Mariana Islands, which are a classic example of an active chain of stratovolcanoes, were all, in fact, underwater. One hundred million years ago, the area from here to the Australian landmass was a warm tropical sea teeming with all sorts of prehistoric species of fish and reptiles. And at the top of the food chain were the Kronosaurs."

"Sixty-five million years ago, an asteroid collision set off a series of mass extinctions. Sea levels dropped and the air cooled, as did the water temperatures. Kronosaurus, being a reptile, suddenly found the sun no longer capable of sustaining its body temperature. Desperate for warmth, many of these creatures would have ventured into the deepest warmer depths of the Mariana Trench, where the superheated waters rising from hydrothermal vents act like a primordial furnace, allowing the marine reptile to maintain its body heat."

"Interesting," Benedict said, stroking his goatee. "So the Mariana Trench became an oasis for certain prehistoric species of marine life."

"Exactly."

"This animal, Professor—what killed it?"

"The only natural enemy the Kronosaurus had was *Carcharodon megalodon*. Even though the sharks didn't evolve until much later in the Cretaceous, Megalodon was bigger, meaner, and better equipped to handle changes in water temperatures. Fossilized records of Megalodon teeth indicate the sharks continued to thrive in oceans all over the world up until the last ice age, about one hundred thousand to two million years ago."

Heath glanced at his watch. "I've read Jonas Taylor's theories on how *Carcharodon megalodon* managed to survive extinction after the last Ice Age by inhabiting the warm bottom layers of the Mariana Trench. The one thing I always questioned was how these enormous sharks could survive, isolated in the abyss, with only a limited food supply. It turns out that the food supply wasn't limited at all. Kronosaurus had been proliferating in the Trench for tens of millions of years, long before the first Megalodon ever sought refuge in the gorge. Of course, once Megalodon moved into the Trench, the hunters became the hunted."

Heath pointed to a series of holes lining the rib cage of the fossil.

"See these holes?" Heath said. "They're bite marks. This Kronosaurus was killed by a Megalodon. The shark clamped its jaws onto the animal's head and upper torso, chomping through bone in one powerful bite that not only crushed its prey's spine, but actually severed the marine reptile in two. I'll bet the reason these Kronosaurus now hunt in packs is to defend themselves against Megalodon attacks."

"So the *mysterium trememdium* is finally resolved. And how do you propose we defend ourselves against this pack of Kronosaurus?"

"In the Mariana Trench, size matters. The Kronosaurs are nearly as large as the *Prometheus*, so they'll continue to attack. But even four of these beasts are no match for the *Benthos*, the largest moving thing in the Trench. My advice is simple: Keep the *Benthos* close at all times, even if it means delaying the completion of your mission."

"I understand."

Heath turned as Sergei entered the lab.

"Sergei, wait for me in the corridor, please," Benedict said, "I'll be right with you." He turned back to Heath, extending his hand. "Better get down to G deck, Professor."

Heath smiled, shaking Benedict's hand.

Instead of releasing his grip, Benedict placed his left hand over the inside of the paleobiologist's wrist, feigning a gesture of warmth.

"One last question before you go," Benedict said, positioning the fingertips of his left hand over the man's pulse. "Have you ever heard of Devil's Purgatory?"

Heath's eyes locked onto Benedict's, the CIA agent's pulse racing.

"Devil's Purgatory? No, never heard of it. Sound like a kid's ride. Why do you ask?"

Benedict smiled, releasing the Professor's hand. "No reason. Again, thank you, and have a safe journey. Your information has helped me to see things much more clearly."

Terry hastily tossed her belongings into her travel bag. Word had spread quickly about the *Prometheus*'s early departure and she was determined to be one of the first onboard.

A knock startled her.

"Who is it?"

"Sergei. I am to escort you to sub."

Terry felt herself break into a cold sweat. "That's okay, I'm fine, thank you."

"I wait for you here," replied the Russian.

Terry sat down on the edge of her bed, her body trembling. She stared at her travel bag, tears of frustration and anger welling in her eyes. She knew that Sergei had no intention of escorting her to the sub.

The message had been delivered, its meaning quite clear: Terry was now a fly in Benedict's web. She would not be permitted to leave the *Benthos* alive.

Seafood

Jonas opened the cabin door. Mac entered, giving him a scowl. "Late night?" he said accusingly.

"Meaning?"

"Meaning, I hope you're more focused on avenging Dief's death than on sleeping with Celeste."

"You're way out of line. Celeste and I went into town to pick up supplies. We had dinner, that's all. Nothing happened, and nothing will."

Mac held up his hands. "Fine. My fault."

"And as far as killing the Meg, you don't have to lecture me on being focused. I'm Captain-freaking-Ahab, remember?"

"Have you come up with a plan?"

"Yes."

"Good." Mac rubbed the back of his neck. "Look, I'm sorry, Jonas. I'm just a bit on edge."

"I know. Dief was a good guy."

"Yeah, he was." Mac pinched his nose, wiping back a tear. "We should have blown this damned fish away years ago."

"Is your new chopper ready?"

"Yeah."

"Then let's go find Angel."

Vancouver Island
10 miles south of Barkley Sound

Andrea Jacobs held up her hand, signaling the rest of the group to stop paddling. She pointed to a spot one hundred yards ahead.

Turning around in the seat of her kayak, she glanced back at the others and smiled.

Her husband, Ronald, gave her a thumbs-up in the kayak directly behind her. Karen McNeil, the group's leader, slid her craft into position to his left. Andrea's staff writer, Shirley Kollin, gave an encouraging wave from the front of her two-seat kayak, her husband, Jon, seated behind her, busy checking his camera.

Andrea maneuvered the bow of her kayak to face south. Then she sat back and waited, her adrenaline pumping.

It had taken more than two years of prodding before Andrea's travel editor had finally agreed to green-light a feature article on Vancouver Island. Lying to the west of the city of Vancouver, parallel to the main coast of British Columbia, the island, the largest in the eastern Pacific, possessed the kind of dramatic geography, variety of wildlife, and contrasting weather conditions that made it an ideal spot for vacationers who enjoy rugged, get-back-to-nature experiences. Arriving in

Port Hardy by ferry, the two couples had spent their first week hiking mountain trails and exploring the granite peaks and alpine glaciers, which ran like a spine along the center of the island. Andrea had photographed majestic snowcapped mountain peaks, hordes of nobly crowned elk, bald eagles soaring in flight, and even several black bears pulling salmon from a stream— but it was whales she was really after—big ones. That meant exploring the cold and hazardous ocean waters off the island's western coastline. Andrea had to convince Karen McNeil that their group was experienced enough to handle the rigors of sea kayaking, the best method for getting close to the pods. They had put in at Pacific Rim National Park that morning, staying relatively close to shore as they traveled north through rough coastal waters.

Now all their effort was about to pay off.

Andrea pulled the hood of her drysuit over her head, then positioned her face mask and snorkel. Her heart fluttered with excitement. Securing the underwater camera around her neck, she grasped the paddle tightly and waited.

With a great *kwoof* of air, the killer whales surfaced, the shiny hooked black dorsal fins of the females dwarfed by the three-foot blade-like fins of the males. Remaining close to the surface as they closed on the kayakers, the pod of Orcas rose and dived in a gentle, rhythmic pattern.

Andrea sucked in a deep breath of air and rolled sideways, plunging herself and the rotating kayak into the icy Canadian waters. Suspended upside down, secure in her seat, she watched in awe as the pod emerged through the misty deep-blue underworld.

Aiming the underwater camera, she quickly snapped off a dozen pictures as low-frequency whistles and high-pitched clicking sounds filled the water all around her. As the pod glided to her right, a thirty-three-foot male appeared out of the mist, moving in to take a closer look. Andrea's heart pounded wildly in her chest as the incredible creature hovered five feet away, the mammal's mouth large enough to engulf her entire upper torso in one bite. She took several more pictures, overwhelmed by the sheer majesty and intelligence of the creature, then watched as it swam away, disappearing into the blue haze with the rest of the pod.

Pushing down hard with the paddle, Andrea flipped herself over, feeling her husband's assistance along the back of the kayak. She spit out the snorkel and gasped for air, her face tingling from the cold.

"That was absolutely incredible!" she announced to the group.

Her husband tossed her a towel. "You take years off my life every time you do that."

"Isn't the water freezing?" Shirley asked.

"It's really not that bad," Andrea said. "The dry suit keeps me warm. My cheeks just freeze up a bit." She turned to Karen. "I thought you said Orcas preferred the eastern coast of the island."

"Our local pods do," the group leader said. "Johnstone Strait, which is on the northeastern side of the island, is the summer home to thirteen resident Orca pods. The group that just passed by are transients."

"How can you tell?" Jon asked.

"Only transients stay to the ocean side of the island.

They prefer to hunt seals and sea lions on their way to the Bering Sea. Our locals prefer fish, and their pods are much larger in number."

"Orcas are great, but you can photograph them at SeaWorld," Andrea said. "What I want to see are the big whales."

"They'll be a little farther out," Karen said. "What I suggest we do is continue to stay within a half-mile of shore. In about an hour we'll cross Barkley Sound on our way to Ucluelet. At that point, we'll be in open ocean and should run into some grays, perhaps even a pod of humpbacks. Are you sure you're up to handling six-to-nine-foot swells?"

"We'll be fine," Andrea said, winking at Shirley. "If the men can't handle it, we'll leave them ashore."

Jonas watched the shadow of their helicopter pass over Cape Flattery lighthouse. Moments later, they were flying over water, heading northwest, approaching Vancouver Island.

"Welcome to Canada, eh," Mac said.

Jonas ignored him, staring at the ocean.

"What's the matter, Jonas? You've hardly said a word all afternoon."

"I've just got a lot on my mind."

"Celeste, or the shark?"

"Both."

Mac lifted his sunglasses and looked Jonas in the eye. "Take my advice and keep your distance from both."

"I told you. I'm not interested in Celeste."

"Come on, pal, you're not the least bit attracted?"

"No comment."

"She came on to you last night, didn't she?"

Jonas grinned. "You might say that."

"And you just turned her away."

"Told her I wasn't interested. We'll never be anything more than friends."

"Friends? Christ, Jonas, wake up. You'd be better off sleeping with her once and getting over it rather than elevating her to a position of trust."

"Actually, we've had some pretty interesting talks."

"Aw, well ain't that sweet. Maybe you guys can take an aerobics class together when you get back to Monterey."

"And what makes you such an expert on women? I don't know anyone who thinks with his pecker more than you do."

"Hey, even my pecker's smart enough to know when someone's playing me for a fool. You think Celeste would be shoving her chest in your face if she wasn't after something? No offense, pal, but you ain't exactly Mel Gibson."

"Maybe she's lonely."

"Wrong. Celeste is cold-blooded. She doesn't give a damn about anyone but herself. If she's making nice with you, it's only because she needs you."

"Needs me for what? Maren's handling everything."

"Don't fool yourself. There's a reason she brought you along, and it's not to play footsies under the breakfast table. Stop being taken in by all that false charm she turns on and off like a faucet. The *William Beebe* ain't the *Love Boat*. Celeste is nothing more than a female version of Benedict."

"That's another thing. She told me Benedict has had his way with her sexually since she was fourteen. I can't tell if she loves him or fears him."

"Probably both." Mac banked to the west, guiding the helicopter across the Strait of Juan De Fuca toward the Canadian border.

Jonas focused his binoculars on Vancouver Island, looming ahead on the horizon. "Okay, Ann Landers, tell me something. If Celeste fears Benedict, why won't she leave him?"

Mac grinned. "I'll answer that one for you in one word: power. He's got it, and she wants it. I'll bet she's still spreading her legs for him."

"Then why is she interested in me?"

"I told you, Jonas, she wants something. You've heard the saying that men use love to get sex, and women use sex to get love. Well, Celeste uses sex to manipulate people into doing what she wants. And that's when she's the most dangerous."

The chopper descended over the southern tip of the island. "Should I head over deeper waters or follow the coastline?"

"Coastline." Jonas focused on a pod of Orcas making their way north. For the next several minutes, they rode in silence; Jonas scanning the surface. Somehow, he hoped to detect some type of disturbance or whale remains that would indicate the presence of the elusive albino predator. He felt frustration building inside. Angel hadn't been sighted in nearly three days.

This is hopeless . . .

"Mac, do you think people can change?"

"Oh, boy, she's really got her claws into you, doesn't she?"

"Actually, I was talking about me."

With a resounding blast from its horn, the ferry, *M.V. Lady Rose*, pulled away from the docks at Bamfield, continuing its ten-hour round-trip journey to Ucluelet.

Fourteen-year-old Kevin Blaine rested his forehead on top of the polished wooden rail, feeling the reverberations of the ship's engines as he kicked the iron support post with his foot.

"Kevin, knock it off," his older sister, Devon, yelled. "You're annoying the other passengers."

"I'm bored. Why can't I skateboard?"

"I told you, it's too crowded on deck."

"How much longer till we're in Ucluelet?"

The nineteen-year-old grabbed her brother by his arm. "Kevin, will you shut the hell up, you're driving me crazy. I swear to God, if Mom and Dad ever make me take you to Port Alberni again, I'll kill you first."

"I'm hungry."

"Here," she said, slapping a ten-dollar bill into his hand. "Now go. I don't want to see you again until we dock."

The predator made its way north against the strong currents of Imperial Eagle Channel, remaining close to the rocky coral bottom as it continued its search. Swinging its elephantine head from side to side, the Megalodon inhaled a troughful of sea, its olfactory senses detecting the faint acrid odor or urine.

A half-mile away, an adult male sea lion pirouetted gracefully just below the waves. At just over six hundred pounds, the mammal feared only the Orca pods. Survival instinct told the agile bull just how far it could stray from shore in order to escape attack. With visibility at over just thirty feet, the large male, always on the lookout, would not venture more than fifty yards from shore.

The hunter moved swiftly along the seafloor, quickly closing the distance between itself and the heartbeat of the sea lion. Ascending slowly beneath its prey, the Megalodon searched the sunlit surface, homing in on its unseen meal.

Sensing danger, the sea lion propelled itself quickly toward shore.

The female detected a dark silhouette of movement along the surface. She launched upward from the bottom, whipping her muscular tail in swift calculated strokes.

The bull registered the disturbance below. Trapped on the surface, it twisted and thrashed, attempting to deflect the impending bite of the unseen predator.

The Megalodon burst through the surface, eyes rolled back, jaws fully hyperextended, engulfing the sea lion in one horrific bite. The pinniped's blubbery girth was instantly crushed beneath the fifty thousand pounds per square inch of pressure, sending streams of blood and excrement gushing out from between rows of razor-sharp teeth.

* * *

It was just after four in the afternoon when the five kayakers moved beyond the last of the Broken Group Islands of Barkley Sound. Heading into open ocean, Ronald Jacobs noticed a bald eagle circling overhead as they passed the final vestige of land for the next several miles. He stopped paddling, following the flight of the majestic bird until it perched in the upper branches of a fir tree three hundred yards away.

"Okay," Karen said, "it's four miles to Ucluelet. Watch for swells, it can really get nasty out here."

"Looks like we've got company," Jon said. He pointed south. A ferry was approaching in the distance.

"That's the *Lady Rose*," Karen said. "She'll be taking us from Ucluelet back up the channel to Port Alberni tomorrow afternoon."

"We're not leaving until I can get some underwater photos," Andrea said. "What happened to those whale pods you promised me?"

"There are forty to fifty grays that spend the spring and summer months feeding between Barkley Sound and Clayoquot Sound, which is another thirty miles to the north. There are always a few minke whales about, as well as humpbacks. Be patient," said Karen, "we'll spot something before too long."

Kevin Blaine leaned over the starboard bow and spit, watching the wind carry it twenty feet back before it hit the water. Most of the other passengers on the *Lady Rose* were either napping on the rows of wooden benches or had gone inside to get out of the weather.

He stared at the blue ocean, hoping to see a whale, when an ivory blur, half as long as the ferry, soared into view well below the surface. Kevin leaned out over the rail as far as he could, gawking at the creature, which was moving parallel to the boat.

Seconds later, it descended, disappearing from sight.

Kevin ran to his sister, who was lying on one of the benches, working on her tan.

"Dev, I just saw something huge. I think it was the Megalodon!"

"Go away."

"You're not listening—"

"Why don't you make yourself useful and get me a diet Coke."

Kevin ignored her and ran back to the bow.

"There," Karen said, pointing ahead to their left. "Looks like we're in luck. They're feeding off phytoplankton blooms."

"What's that?" Ronald asked, paddling harder to keep up with his wife. He paused as a series of seven-foot swells lifted his kayak, soaking him with freezing water.

"It's that white stuff that looks like bathtub foam," Karen said, rolling with the swell. "Every spring the sun causes the phytoplankton to bloom like crazy. Small larvae and fish feed off it, attracting baleen whales."

They approached to within fifty feet of the feeding pod.

"What kind of whales are these?" Shirley asked.

"Grays. I count five, maybe six adults, and a calf. Let's not get any closer."

Andrea pulled the dry suit hood over her head and positioned her face mask. She checked to see that her camera batteries were fully charged. "Wish me luck," she said, rolling sideways into the ocean.

Even wearing the drysuit, the chilly water took her breath away. She looked around, realizing immediately that she was still too far away from the pod to see anything. Then, just as she was about to roll upright, she spotted a ghostly form gliding through the deeper waters directly beneath her, heading toward the whales.

Paddling hard, Andrea pulled herself back into an upright position. "I can't believe it," she said, water pouring off her face. "I just saw a beluga whale!"

"Are you certain?" Karen said. "Belugas usually don't venture this far south."

"I'm telling you I saw it." She picked up her paddle.

"What are you doing?" her husband asked.

"The beluga was heading toward the pod. I need to get closer. I'm too far away to shoot."

"Too late," Shirley said, pointing.

The grays had stopped feeding.

"Something's spooking them," Karen said. "They're closing formation."

Without warning, the pod began moving en masse toward the kayakers.

"Oh, God—stay close and hold on!" Karen yelled.

The thirty-ton leviathans tore up the surface as they accelerated at them, sounding seconds before they would have struck the kayaks. The four boats tossed wildly about, spinning and crashing into one another.

Andrea sucked in a lungful of air and rolled sideways, her camera already positioned in front of her mask.

A series of eight-to-ten-foot swells rolled at them,

lifting and dropping the kayaks precariously. And then the sea calmed, the whales out of sight.

"Everyone all right?" Karen asked.

"I'm freezing," Shirley said. Jon removed a towel from one of the watertight compartments and handed it to his wife.

Ronald turned to Andrea's kayak, which was still inverted. "At least someone's enjoying herself."

"Let's go home, Shirley," Jon said. "I've had enough wilderness to last me a lifetime. The next time your magazine wants to do a wildlife piece, suggest Manhattan."

Ronald reached out to help his wife flip her kayak right-side-up. That's when he saw the cardinal-red cloud pooling around the craft.

"Andrea!" Ronald spun the kayak over—and screamed.

Shirley stared, then turned and retched over the side. Karen and Jon looked on in shock, clutching their mouths.

All that remained of Andrea Jacobs was a gushing scarlet stump of mangled flesh, the lower torso still wedged in the kayak, severed at the stomach.

Ronald stopped screaming as the seven-foot stark-white dorsal fin surged out of the surf. It circled the group twice, then submerged.

"It's the Megalodon," Jon rasped, holding on as the kayaks were lifted by another series of swells. He leaned forward and caught his wife's head as she fainted.

Ronald's eyes bugged out as an unearthly glow appeared beneath him. He gasped in horror as the enormous head rose vertically to his left, engulfing the remains of his wife and her kayak in its powerful jaws. Two vicious chomps—and the shark slid back into the sea, leaving only a paddle and a section of bow bobbing on the surface.

"Move!" Karen yelled. "Split up!" She paddled south, heading for the ferry.

Jon watched her go, then reached forward and slapped his wife hard across her face.

"Shirley, wake up," he yelled, shaking her. Feeling her stir, he released her head and began paddling toward Ucluelet, two and a half miles to the north.

Still in shock, Ronald Jacobs remained motionless in his kayak and wept.

Jonas focused his binoculars on the ferry, then spotted something else. "Looks like a kayak. It's heading straight for the ferry—"

"Jonas, behind the kayak—one o'clock!"

Jonas searched the ocean. "Oh, crap . . ."

"Hold on—" The helicopter soared past the *Lady Rose* as Jonas desperately attempted to hail the ferry on the radio.

Alone in the bow, Kevin watched the woman paddle furiously toward the boat. He ducked instinctively as the helicopter soared overhead, then spotted the dorsal fin and realized what was taking place before his eyes.

Spinning around, he searched the deck, locating the life ring. He tore it from the rail as the *Lady Rose* swung to port to intercept the woman.

Groaning out loud, with her shoulders, arms, and back aching from the anaerobic effort, Karen switched sides, paddling on her right as she headed toward the ferry. Blisters on her hands began bleeding; her tears and the splashing saltwater were blinding.

Fifty yards . . .

She focused on the bow, her mind racing, wondering how she would possibly reach the rail that towered fifteen feet above her head.

Then she spotted the boy tying off the rope.

The predator rose, jaws agape, its eyes focused on the silhouette of the fleeing kayak. In the murky water, the figure resembled another sea lion. The Megalodon closed to within forty feet, then detected the larger creature changing course, approaching its prey.

Kevin felt the ferry cut its engines. He looked up to see three members of the crew running toward him.

Calling to the woman below, he reached out and tossed her the ring.

Physically exhausted, her arms trembling, Karen guided the kayak alongside the moving ferry. She managed to free her lower body from the boat but was unable to muster the strength to pull herself upward.

The three crewmen pushed Kevin aside and grabbed the rope.

Karen felt herself being hauled upward. She held on tight, praying the monster would spare her.

A crowd gathered. Unable to see, Karen climbed up to straddle the rail.

Mac hovered the chopper eighty feet above the deck of the ferry. Jonas watched the scene below, breathing a sigh of relief as the crew reached out and pulled the woman to safety.

"Can you get off a shot with the grenade rifle?" Mac asked.

Jonas peered down the scope of the weapon, searching for the creature. "She's too deep to see, and I'm getting a bad reflection from the sun. I can't tell how close she is to the ferry."

Reaching beneath the seat, he pulled out a large handgun resembling a starter's pistol. Lodged in the barrel was a small transmitter attached to a seven-inch barbed hook. He pulled the safety off the pistol, then activated the transmitter.

"Where'd you get that?" Mac asked.

"Had the Institute deliver it while we were in port. It only transmits over a three-mile radius, but—"

Without warning, the Megalodon rose from the sea, its vertical momentum sending its upper torso high into the air as its jaws clamped down on the empty kayak. Falling forward, the leviathan slammed sideways against the ferry, its weight knocking the *Lady Rose* hard to starboard.

Most of the ship's passengers and crew found themselves sprawling on their backs. Kevin Blaine had squeezed his legs around the rail, holding on precariously as he gawked at the gargantuan beast, its huge pectoral fin so close he could have reached out and touched it. As the creature's upper torso slammed hard against the side of the ferry, the rail jolted out from under him and he tumbled forward, twisting in midair, catching a glimpse of blue sky before plunging into the icy sea.

Afraid he might hit the ferry, Jonas lowered the grenade rifle and grabbed the pistol. In one motion he aimed and fired, the barbed arrow and transmitter exploding from the barrel, puncturing the Megalodon along its exposed underbelly.

Bouncing off the vessel, the monster rolled sideways back into the water.

A strong swimmer, Kevin quickly righted himself underwater and kicked hard to the surface. More cold than scared, he looked up, waiting for someone to appear at the rail with a rope.

Devon picked herself up off the deck and rushed to the rail, shocked at having witnessed her brother fall. She quickly spotted him treading water, waving at her along the surface.

"Kevin, hold on—" She saw the end of the nylon rope tied off on the rail and started pulling in the slack, the life ring appearing from across the deck. Grabbing the flotation device, she tossed it overboard.

The ghost-like demon had reappeared. Gliding gracefully on its side, it opened its mouth, its lower jawline moving silently across the surface. A channel of water streamed into the dark tunnel of the widening orifice.

Devon freaked out. A dozen passengers yelled and

screamed in her ear as she motioned wildly for Kevin to grab the life ring.

Kevin's smile disappeared as he saw the expression of terror on his sister's face. He turned around.

The ivory head, lying on its side, was barely visible. A small wake closed, revealing a black hole in the sea, outlined by pink gums and sickening teeth.

A rush of panic washed over him. Ignoring the life ring, he tried to swim away, but an overpowering current grabbed him, dragging him backward in the water. For a surreal moment, Kevin felt the bizarre feeling of sliding feetfirst down a hole, water rushing along either side of him.

A torrent of ocean washed over him, pushing him downward. Daylight disappeared. For a suffocating moment, the boy clawed in complete darkness along the slimy surface of the monster's tongue.

And then he tumbled backward, crushed into oblivion.

Jonas slammed his face against the cockpit door and howled in rage as the creature disappeared beneath the waves.

Mac shifted the hovering chopper to autopilot, too shaken to even grip the joystick. For the next several minutes, the two men could do nothing but seethe, their eyes closed tight, the horrifying scene refusing to cease replaying in their minds' eyes.

"Chopper, come in, this is the captain of the *Lady Rose*. Chopper, come in—"

"What," Jonas said, not recognizing his own voice.

"Chopper, the woman we rescued says there are two

more kayaks out there. Half a mile northwest. Reply, please, over—"

Jonas looked at Mac; his friend's face was red with rage. Mac gripped the joystick, the airship leaping forward. "We're on it," Jonas yelled, his own adrenaline pumping.

Retracing the woman's direction, they searched the ocean, quickly spotting the kayak. The chopper swooped downward.

Mac hovered the copter just above the surface, watching a series of incoming swells. "Do it fast, Jonas—"

Jonas unbuckled his harness and moved back to the cargo bay. Pulling open the sliding bay door, he reached out for the unconscious man and grabbed hold of one of his arms.

Jonas hauled Ronald Jacobs from his kayak and into the chopper—as the airship leapfrogged over an eight-foot swell.

"Is he alive?" Mac asked.

"He's breathing, but he's in shock."

Jonas covered the man with blankets while Mac circled to the east, looking for the other kayak.

Out of breath, and his muscles trembling from lactic acid buildup, Jon Kollin was forced to stop paddling.

"Shirley, I need your help," he rasped. He rubbed the sweat from his eyes and tried to focus on the sliver of land, still a half-mile away.

Shirley dipped the end of her oar into the water, attempting to paddle. "Jon, I can't, I'm going to be sick again."

Jon was looking behind them, watching the ferry in

the distance. "Something's going on back there." He reached overboard, splashing water onto his face, the cold helping to revive him.

"Shirley, look at me." As his wife turned, he drenched her with an oar-splash of water.

"Damn you—"

"Now pick up your paddle and help me row," he ordered.

The Megalodon continued circling below the ferry, waiting for more prey to appear, when a thrumming sound resonated somewhere in the distance. The baritone vibrations continued, enticing the shark away from the boat to investigate.

As it closed on the source, the beating abruptly ceased. The shark circled, confused, waiting for the voodoo-like beats to reappear. Instead, another sound caught the creature's attention, this one moving along the surface.

The female whipped its caudal fin, homing in on the remaining kayak.

Jon glanced up from paddling to see the reassuring glow of lights coming from a building situated at the entrance to a private pier. "Straight ahead, Shirley," he yelled, stroking harder. "We're almost there."

Shirley turned, then stopped paddling, staring at the expanse of ocean behind them.

"Shirley, don't stop—"

"Jon . . ." Her brown eyes widened with fear.

The dorsal fin was closing on them.

* * *

Jonas continued listening to the beeping of the homing transmitter as he scanned the choppy surface, the fading light from the setting sun making it difficult to see.

"Signal's weakening. Try circling back."

The helicopter banked away from the Broken Group Islands, racing for the southernmost tip of Ucluelet.

"Mac—there." Jonas pointed. "Looks like they're heading for that pier."

"And look who's escorting them in."

The muscles in Jon Kollin's back burned, his forearms ached. His hands were so sore from bleeding blisters that he could barely maintain his grip on the paddle.

A sudden movement caused him to turn to his right. Out of the sea rose a three-foot wake, buffeting the kayak sideways.

The ghost surfaced, gliding effortlessly on its side, its luminescent skin tinged with an orange glow from the fading sunlight. A soulless gray eye looked up at Jon from just below the waterline. The jaw quivered open, exposing the points of its teeth.

Shirley shrieked.

Adrenaline and fear drove Jon's oar through the sea. He continued staring at the shark as he paddled, mesmerized by its impossible size. Tearing himself away, he searched for the end of the pier.

Forty yards ahead.

The fish slapped its tail along the surface and submerged.

"Oh, God—oh, God—this is it," Jon yelled. "It's coming up from under to attack, just like it did before. Shirley, free your legs from the kayak and get ready to jump."

She stopped paddling, twisting her body loose.

"I'm free, now you," she called out, balancing on her knees as she paddled.

Jon fought to pull his lower body from the boat, his legs feeling numb from sitting too long. His arms shook with exhaustion and adrenaline. As one leg pulled free, he saw the water turn white beneath them.

"Shirley, jump—jump!"

The Megalodon's head launched from the sea, its eyes rolling back as its jaws widened to sandwich the kayak. Shirley and Jon felt their boat rising beneath them and jumped. The giant bear trap of a maw snapped shut, crushing the empty kayak as the two boaters flew through the air and tumbled into the sea.

The blast of freezing water sent Jon into action. Righting himself, he quickly kicked to the surface, only to feel the creature's submerging bulk momentarily drag him back down again.

Jon's mind screamed at him to kick harder. He resurfaced, relieved to see his wife already swimming to the pier less than twenty feet away. He raised a dead-tired arm to stroke, terrified to find he could barely move, his muscles heavy as lead.

Shirley reached for the edge of the dilapidated dock and pulled herself up, scraping her arms as she rolled onto the decking. She sat up, chest heaving, and screamed as loud as she could, "Jon, swim faster!"

Below the surface, the Megalodon shook its head to and fro, unable to locate its prey among the remains of the kayak. A second later, it homed in on the telltale vibrations along the surface. The shark turned, whipping its head and tail back and forth in an effort to regain its forward momentum.

Jon had reached the edge of the pier but was beyond exhaustion, unable to even raise his hand out of the water to pull himself to safety. Shirley reached down and grabbed her husband's wrist. Tug as she might, she was unable to budge the two-hundred-pound man.

Then she saw the surface churn thirty feet behind him.

The terror in his wife's bulging eyes was enough. Adrenaline pumping, Jon scrambled onto the pier, then grabbed Shirley by her waist and leaped sideways.

The head of the rampaging beast struck the wharf, obliterating two of the wooden pilings, sending an entire section of the deck crashing into the sea, Jon and Shirley with it.

Like a mad bull lusting after blood, the Megalodon turned its jaws upon the swirling debris, chomping along the surface as it blindly searched for its prey.

Jon pushed his wife up a short wooden ladder as four-foot waves crested over his back. As he climbed onto the damaged pier, he turned to see the shark gliding in from behind.

He grabbed Shirley's hand and ran, hearing the dull thud of their footsteps across the weathered wooden planks, the crashing sea on either side of them.

Sensing the vibrations of its fleeing prey, the Megalodon slipped beneath the pier, homing in on the source of the sounds.

Jon turned as the pier shook. The decking behind them exploded into splinters as the monstrous shark, in its madness to feed, smashed its triangular snout upward through the wooden planks.

"Faster," he yelled, trying his best not to stumble as he pulled Shirley toward the gated entrance to the private pier. "Damn it—"

A fifteen-foot-high chain-link construction fence blocked their escape. The barrier continued to their right, fastened to the side of a seafood restaurant situated on an adjacent pier.

Jon tried the gate while his wife ran to the side of the restaurant, pounding on a metal fire door.

Without warning, the wooden planks beneath his feet fractured, driven upward by the predator's conical snout.

Jon grabbed onto the fence, clutching the aluminum links between his fingers, holding on for dear life as the decking beneath his feet collapsed into the sea. Swirling below the dark waters and splintered planks was a white glow.

"Jon, this way!"

Jon swung himself sideways, stepping gingerly over the gap and onto a wooden walkway bordering the side of the restaurant. Shirley grabbed his hand, pulling him through an open gate and onto the pier supporting the main dining area of the restaurant.

"Shirley, wait, we're going the wrong way—"

"There's a balcony out back. We have to go through the restaurant to get off the pier."

Shirley led him past bay windows encircling the glass-enclosed banquet room. Startled patrons looked up from candlelit dinners, unaware of the creature circling beneath the pier.

Shirley banged on the outer glass balcony door. Jon saw the luminescent fin rise.

A waiter walked toward the door, shaking his head. He pointed to the side, directing them to the front entrance—as a tremendous force shook one of the pilings supporting the pier.

Jon banged on the thick glass. "Open this door, or I'll kick it in!"

The waiter backed away as another man, obviously a manager, approached unlatching the door.

Shirley yanked open the door; Jon practically pushing her into the lavish dining room. They stood there, dripping wet, catching their breath.

"*Madame*, you cannot—"

"Get everyone out of here," Shirley yelled, "the pier's collapsing!"

Shirley led her husband past the stunned diners, searching for the way out.

"*Madame, monsieur*—"

"You heard my wife, Frenchy, get everyone off this—"

With a colossal boom, the entire restaurant shook in an earthquake-like upheaval that shattered the bay windows and sent patrons and their entrees toppling onto the floor.

Above the din of protests and screams, Jon heard a tremendous crack, as one of the damaged pilings collapsed beneath the pier.

The restaurant began to tilt.

Jon grabbed Shirley's hand and ran, pushing and shoving through a maze of tables and dozens of people now scrambling toward the front entrance.

Hovering high above the melee, Jonas and Mac could only watch as the back end of the restaurant cracked off and collapsed, tumbling into the sea.

Solutions

Mariana Trench

Sergei waited in the corridor outside Terry's door until the *Prometheus* pushed away from its docking sleeve.

"Decided to stay, eh?" called out the Russian in broken English, laughing sadistically as he made his way down the corridor.

Terry sat on the floor, fighting to remain calm.

The knock startled her.

"It's Benedict."

She wiped her face and opened the door.

"My dear, why on earth are you still on board?" he asked innocently. "The *Prometheus* departed early this morning."

"Who are you kidding? Your Russian goon's been sitting outside my door for the last few hours—"

"Sergei?" Benedict shook his head. "I didn't know."

"Sure you didn't. Is this how you get yourself off, Benedict, by screwing with other people's emotions?"

Benedict's eyes flashed a warning. "We'll speak again after you've regained control of *your* emotions."

She watched him disappear down the corridor. Terry slammed the cabin door shut. She waited ten minutes, then reopened it and made a dash for the companionway. She ascended two levels and ran through the corridor leading to Heath's lab.

Terry knocked, then pushed open the door. The room was empty. Locking the door behind her, she hurried through to the adjoining room, looking for the government agent.

The fossilized skull stared back at her.

Distraught, she left the lab and headed upstairs to B deck.

She spotted Captain Hoppe in the control room. Remembering how he had stood up to Benedict, she approached, pulling him aside.

"Are you all right?" he asked. "You shouldn't be here—"

"Can I speak with you in private?"

"The *Epimetheus* should be arriving momentarily," the captain said, more for his crew than for her. "Come upstairs. We'll watch her as she descends."

Terry followed him up the access-tube ladder into the observation deck. She waited impatiently while he activated the observation dome, retracting the titanium outer covering from the reinforced LEXAN glass.

"Speak quietly," he said. "The walls have ears."

"Benedict's keeping me on board like some kind of prisoner—"

"I know."

"Can't you help me?"

"I'm—I'm not sure."

"Where's Heath? What happened to him?"

"The paleobiologist? I believe he left earlier this morning aboard the *Prometheus*."

Her heart sank. How could he have left without taking her?

"Captain, please, I have to get off this ship."

Hoppe appeared nervous. "What can I do?"

"Radio the authorities for help."

Hoppe shook his head. "All comm links aboard the *Benthos* and her subs are routed through the *Titan*. There's no way to bypass the system."

Terry felt tears of desperation welling in her eyes. "Can you pilot the *Epimetheus*?"

The question seemed to perturb the captain. "We wouldn't get very far. We certainly can't outrun the *Titan*—"

"How close is the nearest island."

"About a hundred and twenty nautical miles due west of our present position."

"We could make it."

Captain Hoppe turned to face the abyss. He nodded toward a faint light in the distance. "Here comes the *Epimetheus*," he muttered.

"Captain, please—"

For a long moment, Hoppe stared at his dark reflection in the glass. "I've been with Benedict for more than twenty years. He took me in. At the time I was a useless alcoholic who had just killed my wife and little girl driving drunk." Hoppe looked into her eyes, wiping back a tear. "I guess my daughter'd be about your age now."

"You'd be saving my life."

"I want you to return to your cabin and remain

there. Don't speak to anyone. I'll meet you on G deck
at three hundred hours."

For the next fourteen hours, Terry remained locked
in her cabin, anxiously awaiting her chance to escape
her benthic prison.

Benedict had wasted little time. The moment the
Epimetheus had docked, he ordered the sub into the
Trench, this time keeping the *Benthos* hovering close
by. Terry heard the sub redock sometime after midnight. At this point, she had no idea what Geo-Tech
was doing in the abyss, but had decided the deployment of the UNIS robots was nothing more than a
clever ruse to disguise Benedict's own personal quest.

At ten minutes before three in the morning, Terry
opened the door to her cabin, the iron bar clenched
firmly in her right fist. Barefoot, shoes in hand, she
quietly made her way down the two flights of the companionway, stepping out onto G deck.

She waited in the barren corridor and listened.

*Someone's voice . . . coming from the hangar. Cap-
tain Hoppe?*

Hurrying down the deserted corridor, she approached
the watertight door, surprised to find it slightly ajar.
She peeked through the crack and saw Captain Hoppe
squatting on his knees by the far wall, his back to her.

Terry entered the hangar, pushing the thick door
shut behind her.

"Captain, what are you doing in here?"

As she touched the man's shoulder, he tumbled
sideways, blood gushing from his severed throat.

Terry's scream was stifled by Sergei's hand.

"What kept you?" whispered the Russian, taking her from behind. He grabbed a fistful of her long hair, then pressed the blade of his hunting knife to her throat with his free hand.

"We have a little fun before I kill you, *da*? Drop the weapon."

The iron bar clanged onto the floor by her feet.

"Now remove your pants," he whispered, his tongue flicking in her ear.

Terry felt the blade of his knife cut her neck, drawing blood. Reaching to her waist, she unbuckled her jeans slowly, her mind racing.

"Push them down, down to your ankles."

She wriggled the skintight jeans down over her hips, bending to maneuver them over her calves, casually slipping her right foot out of the pant leg.

Panting like an animal, Sergei maintained a grip on her hair while placing the knife between his teeth, freeing one hand to pull his own pants down around his ankles.

Retrieving the knife, he pressed the point to her spine. "Bend over. Spread your legs."

Terry leaned forward, registering the point of the knife at her back. She spread her legs apart, shifting her weight, preparing herself.

Sergei returned the knife to his mouth, then leaned in very close.

Now!

Terry mule-kicked upward with her free leg, slamming her heel into Sergei's exposed genitals.

The Russian howled in pain.

Dropping to one knee, she strained to reach the iron bar as Sergei yanked her backward by her hair. Grabbing it, she spun around and—as hard as she could—slammed it into the Russian's skull.

Sergei dropped in a heap, blood seeping from the top of his head.

She backed up, then hit him again, hearing a satisfying crack.

For a long moment she stood over him, wanting to scream in defiance at the vile creature. Instead, she bent down and pulled her pants back up, then leaned over the Russian and checked for a pulse.

Still alive . . .

The iron bar poised above her head, she searched the man's pockets with her free hand, removing a magnetic pass card from his shirt.

The Russian began to stir. Lunging awkwardly, he grabbed her leg.

She let out a half scream, then bashed his knuckles with the metal bar.

Sergei moaned in agony, releasing his grip.

Terry ran to the watertight door leading to the corridor. Verifying it was sealed, she entered the hangar control room, locking the hydraulic door behind her.

She scanned the control panel, locating the flood valves, and twisted them counterclockwise.

Seawater poured in from ventilation pipes in the hangar's flooring. Sergei rolled over and got to his knees, clutching his head.

Staggering to his feet, the Russian killer sloshed through ankle-deep water, making his way to the watertight door leading to the corridor.

Terry searched the control panel. The red light verified both the corridor and control room doors could not be opened while the hangar was flooding.

Sergei tugged at the corridor door like a drunk, then noticed Terry sitting in the control room. He pressed his face to the reinforced LEXAN porthole, his eyes exuding a predatory malevolence. He swung his fist, pounding the glass.

The water rose to his waist.

Sergei banged again.

She watched as his hatred changed to fear. He pounded harder, becoming desperate. The water level rose above his neck. He pressed his face to the glass and leered at her.

The water level reached the ceiling. The outer doors opened. Terry watched Sergei grab his head a second before his skull imploded like a ripe melon.

She turned away, then slumped in the operator's chair, emotionally exhausted. The remains of the two mutilated bodies drifted slowly toward the open hangar door, heading for the waiting darkness of the Trench.

A movement caught her eye. Terry shrieked as a colossal brown head suddenly appeared from the abyss. Flat crocodile-like jaws opened wide, revealing a frenzied row of hideous pointed teeth.

Terry froze, watching in fascination and terror as the forty-foot prehistoric marine reptile pushed its head into the hangar and snatched Sergei's remains in one gargantuan bite. The beast spun upside down as it swallowed, spewing shards of flesh in all directions.

Luminous scarlet eyes searched the hangar for more food.

The remains of Captain Hoppe moved past the beast into the Trench. The freakish reptile pushed itself away from the hangar door to follow, gliding away like a sinuous eel.

Still shaken, Terry pressed the controls, sealing the hangar doors.

All thoughts of boarding the *Epimetheus* and stealing the sub disappeared. Dying aboard the *Benthos* was far better than facing the terror circling outside.

Terry heard the hydraulic rams activate, forcing water out of the hangar and into holding areas located throughout the *Benthos*. Long minutes passed as the chamber finished draining.

She waited until the panel lights turned green, then exited the control room, inhaling the humidity left behind by the sea. Walking along the damp floor, she inspected the room, verifying the absence of any evidence she had been there.

She held her breath, hearing a strange noise. It was a deep scratching sound, coming from outside the hangar door.

Terry ran from the chamber, sealing the corridor door shut behind her.

Bait

It was dawn by the time Mac's helicopter touched down on the deck of the *William Beebe*. Harry Moon greeted them, escorting them to the control room.

Jonas saw Dr. Maren and Captain Morgan leaning over a chart of the Gulf of Alaska. Celeste was on the other side of the room, arguing with someone on the ship-to-shore.

"You guys look like hell," said the captain.

"Been there," Mac muttered.

Celeste slammed down the receiver. "Dammit. The Canadian authorities are holding us responsible for the deaths of the female kayaker and the kid who fell off the ferry."

"We are responsible," Jonas said.

"That's nonsense," Celeste said.

"If a lion escapes from a zoo and kills someone, the zoo's responsible," Mac said.

Celeste rolled her eyes. "Well, thank you so very much for enlightening me. You'll be happy to know that the Canadian Coast Guard has now decided to handle the situation themselves. They've dispatched a cutter and two helicopters to locate the shark and kill it."

Maren scoffed. "Screw the Canadians. By nightfall, the female will have moved into Alaskan waters and out of their jurisdiction."

"Why are we changing course?" Jonas asked.

Maren pointed to the map. "From Vancouver Island, there are two distinct routes migrating whales take to the Bering Sea. We now know the Megalodon is following the main route, along the Canadian and Alaskan coastlines. I expect the shark to continue heading west until she reaches the Aleutian Islands, at which time she should follow the whale pods north, right into the Bering Sea. The *William Beebe* is now following an alternate route, a shortcut used primarily by gray whales. Our new heading is much quicker, cutting across the Gulf of Alaska, placing us ahead of the shark. This will allow us to cut her off here—at Cape Chiniak, Kodiak Island."

Jonas studied the map. "And once we get ahead of her, how do you plan to locate her, let alone draw her close enough to the ship to hit her with your harpoon."

"Change of plans," Celeste said. "We're going to drug the monster by using bait."

"What kind of bait?"

"Sea lions," Maren said, "the creature's favorite delicacy. When we get to Kodiak Island, three freshly killed sea lion bulls will be loaded onboard. I'm going to surgically implant large dosages of anesthetic into each carcass. We'll hook the bait, attach it to the winch by steel cable, then drag it along the surface until the Megalodon takes it. Within five minutes of consuming the drugs, the shark will be out cold."

Captain Morgan studied the map. "When do you estimate the monster will reach Cape Chiniak?"

"If she continues her present speed, maybe three to four days."

"Then I suggest we go on shifts," Harry said.

Maren nodded in agreement. "I'll put together a schedule."

Valley Memorial Hospital
Monterey, California

When Sadia Kleffner entered her employer's private room, she was surprised to see him sitting up in bed, a nurse tending to him.

"Masao, how do you feel?"

"Sadia, thank God. Kindly inform this nurse that I must leave here immediately."

"Just sit back and relax, Mr. Tanaka. You're not going anywhere until the doctor says."

"But I feel better—"

"I'm sure your doctor will be glad to hear that. Now lie back down before I tie you to the bed."

Masao glared at the nurse, then lay back, giving in to the larger woman.

Sadia sat down on the edge of the bed. "They finished replacing the lagoon doors yesterday. King Kong himself couldn't get through these."

Masao watched the nurse leave. "What is it, Sadia? I know when you're hiding something."

Sadia broke eye contact. "There's been another death. A young boy."

Masao shut his eyes, feeling the strain on his chest.

"The media's on the warpath. Things are getting nasty."

"Have you heard from my daughter?"

"I finally got through to the *Titan*. They claim Terry decided to remain on board the *Benthos* for another week."

"What? She's still in the Trench?"

Sadia could see the older man's hands trembling. "Masao, they assured me everything is fine."

"No, something is wrong. I can feel it. Where is Jonas?"

"Heading into the Gulf of Alaska. They're attempting to intercept the creature at Kodiak Island. Oh, and we delivered the *AG-II* as per Celeste's orders."

"The *AG-II*?" Masao opened his eyes. "Why the abyssal sub?"

"I don't know. Celeste specifically requested the *AG-II*."

Masao shook his head. "Sadia, listen to me carefully. I want you to contact Commander James Adams at the Navy base in Guam. Tell him I wish to meet him immediately. Make arrangements for me to fly out as soon as possible."

"But the doctor hasn't discharged you yet."

Masao sat up, removing an IV tube from his arm. "I'm discharging myself."

"Masao—"

"Sadia, my children's lives are at stake. Now hand me my clothes before Nurse Ratched returns."

Cape Chiniak
Southwest Coast of Kodiak Island

Celeste stood by the starboard rail, watching as the last of the three sea lion carcasses was lifted from the hull of the fishing boat and onto the deck of the *William Beebe*, then packed in ice.

Maren joined her, handing her a telegram. "This message just came from the *Titan*."

Celeste opened it. "It's from Benedict."

"What's it say?"

"*Age quod agis*—to the business at hand."

"What's that supposed to mean?"

"It means he's losing patience with me."

"Don't worry," Maren said, slipping his arm around her waist. "We'll capture the Megalodon very—"

Celeste pushed his arm away. "I told you, not in public."

"Why not? Are you afraid Taylor might see you? Don't deny it, Celeste, I see the way you look at him."

"Jealousy doesn't become you, Michael. As Benedict says, tend to the business at hand." She checked her watch. "What time am I scheduled on lookout?"

"I gave you the noon till six shift. Harry will relieve you until midnight. Then Taylor and Mackreides take over from twelve to six a.m. It worked out nicely. You and I will be able to see each other late at night without Taylor knowing."

"Idiot." Celeste's eyes blazed in anger. "I'll deter-

mine if and when we'll be together, not your hor-
mones. I specifically instructed you to put Jonas and
me together."

Maren cowered back. "I know, but Taylor insisted
he and Mackreides take the midnight shift. What was I
supposed to do?"

Celeste watched the fishing boat move away from
the *William Beebe*. "The two of them are up to something. Where's Jonas now?"

"Last time I saw him, he was with Mackreides in the
chopper."

"Find him. Tell him that I'm very upset, that I'm
worried about the *Benthos*. Tell him I need to speak
with him in my cabin right away."

"What about us? What about tonight?"

"Business before pleasure. Now do as I say."

Maren peered into the cockpit. Finding it empty, he
walked around to the helicopter's cargo-bay door and
slid it open.

Empty.

As he was about to secure the door, Maren noticed
the butt of what appeared to be a large rifle lying beneath a blanket. He climbed inside, then pulled back
the blanket, exposing the rest of the rifle.

"Son of a—"

Making sure no one was watching, he slipped in the
back of the chopper and went to work.

"You're insane," Mac said, closing the cabin door
behind him.

"It's risky, but it'll work," Jonas said. "It's the only way I know I'll have a clear shot at the Megalodon."

"Exactly how close are you planning to be?"

"Fifty, sixty yards."

"And what's to prevent the creature from attacking you?"

"The shark won't even know I'm in the Zodiac. Instead of using the raft's engine, I'm going to allow the *William Beebe* to tow me, just ahead of the bait."

"You are insane. Look, at least let me go with you."

"You can't. I need you watching the sea from above. The transmitter will tell me when she's in the area, but you'll be able to spot her before I do."

"I still think this plan of yours is too risky."

"Maybe, but this madness has to stop. Tonight I end this, one way or the other."

They were interrupted by a knock. Mac opened the door.

Celeste stood in the corridor, her makeup streaked with tears. "Oh, I'm sorry, I didn't mean to interrupt—"

"Celeste, what's wrong?" Jonas asked.

"When you have a chance, I need to talk to you."

"I'm just leaving," Mac said, rolling his eyes.

Celeste stood by the porthole, her eyes glistening with tears. "Jonas, I don't know where our friendship is going, but I need your support. I need you to trust me."

"What's wrong?"

"I've been thinking about the nightmares you've been having. Maybe we shouldn't ignore them. I know this sounds crazy, but for my own peace of mind, I need to warn Benedict about the Devil's Purgatory."

Jonas shook his head. "All of a sudden you believe in my dreams? I thought you said it's just my guilt—"

"Terry's still aboard the *Benthos*."

"What?" Jonas grabbed her arm. "Why didn't you tell me that before? Why the hell is she still in the Trench?"

"According to Benedict, Terry absolutely refuses to leave until the last UNIS is deployed."

Jonas felt weak. He sat on the edge of his bed, rubbing his temples. "I want to speak with her."

"You can't. Only the *Titan* can communicate directly with the *Benthos*." She sat down next to him, massaging his neck. "Jonas, give me the coordinates of the Devil's Purgatory. Let me warn them."

Jonas was silent.

"You still don't trust me, do you?"

"It's not a question of trust."

"Then your word to the Navy is worth more than Terry's life, is that it?"

"Now you're worried about Terry?"

"I'm worried about Benedict and the crew of the *Benthos*, the only family I have. Do I have to remind you that these people are seven miles beneath the ocean, that the slightest breach in their hull would—"

"Celeste, stop. I'm the last person who needs to be lectured about the Mariana Trench. Look, I need to think—let me think about this, okay?"

Celeste turned away in frustration. "Fine. Sit here and do nothing. But if something happens to those people, I'll never forgive you."

Surrounded by impenetrable darkness, Jonas lost all sense of direction. Pressing his face against the cold LEXAN glass, he stared into oblivion, waiting for the Angel of Death to appear.

A faint glow circled in the distance. Jonas couldn't tell if it was below or above him, only that he was moving toward it. The light grew larger, the shape taking form. Jonas began trembling, a knot of fear tightening in his stomach.

The being seemed to sense his presence. It broke from its circling pattern, the triangular head moving silently toward him, its ghostly, luminescent skin frightening against the pitch blackness of the abyss.

Jonas fought to draw a breath. Terrified, yet unable to turn away, he watched his tormentor open its grotesque jaws, exposing the cathedral-like gullet.

An object appeared from within the beast's mouth. In surreal motion it was expelled from the jaws, rising toward him.

An escape pod?

The clear coffin-like tube stopped several feet below him. Jonas could see the silhouette of a figure within. A man, totally naked, his face hidden in shadow.

The glow from the beast diminished, allowing the features of the face to come into view. Jonas screamed, staring at the lifeless figure—of himself.

Jonas lifted his head from the suffocating pillow and shut off the alarm clock. He rolled onto his back, the vision of his own lifeless body lying in the escape pod refused to go away. Still trembling, he sat up, his skin drenched with sweat.

He looked at the clock: 11:35 p.m. Still feeling

claustrophobic, he limped to the porthole, pulled back the drape, and opened the window. A blast of Arctic air filled the cabin. Jonas felt a light drizzle. Sealing the porthole, he began pulling on his wet suit.

He knew he was in for a bad night.

The rain was coming down harder by the time he walked out on deck. He adjusted the hood of his parka, then crossed the slick aft deck.

Mac was speaking with Harry Moon by the big winch. Harry nodded to him. "Miserable enough night, huh?"

"I hope it doesn't get any worse," Jonas said.

Harry looked up. "This rain should ease by two or three. Not much to do, really. Just watch the line and try to stay awake. If that monster of yours decides to take a bite, you'll know it. Just give her as much line as she wants and pray those drugs take effect."

"I know the drill," Jonas said.

"Then I'll say good night. Celeste is set to relieve you at six."

Jonas waited until Harry had disappeared inside. Then he reversed the winch and reeled in the bait, while Mac headed for the chopper to retrieve their equipment.

Jonas watched as six hundred thirty pounds of dripping sea lion carcass was dragged up from the sea. He stopped the winch, then grabbed the two-inch-thick steel line and swung the waterlogged bait over the transom, releasing enough cable to allow the load to flop onto the deck.

The steel cable ran through the sea lion's mouth to a three-foot hook piercing the lining of the stomach. A porous ten-gallon elixir of drugs had been surgically placed within the animal's digestive tract. An additional dozen pouches containing more anesthetics had been hastily sewn along the blubbery hide.

Maren's taking no chances.

Mac returned with the grenade rifle. Jonas unlocked the storage compartment, removing a small suitcase from the crate. Opening the case, he extracted a powerful wireless underwater speaker. Mac stretched the sea lion's mouth wide, allowing Jonas to shove the instrument into the animal's esophagus.

"Let's test it." Jonas reached into the suitcase to power up the sound system. A deep baritone thrumming rose from the carcass. Jonas turned up the volume, the voodoo-like acoustics causing the lifeless mound of blubber to gyrate across the slick deck.

"Damn thing's dancing," Mac said. "How far away will your shark be able to hear this racket?"

"Sound travels much farther underwater. There's no telling how acute the Megalodon's senses are, but I'd guess she'll be able to detect these vibrations quite a distance away." Jonas wiped the rain from his face. "Help me get this bait back into the water."

He restarted the winch. The carcass rose off the deck. Mac pushed it out over the side as Jonas released three hundred feet of cable. The sea lion disappeared into the night, its pounding reverberations echoing in the dark.

"My turn," Jonas said.

"Jonas—"

"Mac, don't, we've already been through this. Just help me with the Zodiac."

Extending out along either side of the ship's mid-deck were small winches designed to launch the motorized rubber rafts known as Zodiacs. Jonas climbed aboard one, attaching a long coil of nylon rope to the bow of the craft.

"There's two hundred feet of rope here," Jonas said. "Allowing for the ship's draft, that should place me a hundred and fifty feet in front of the bait."

Mac shook his head, handing him the grenade rifle. "That translates into two Megalodon body lengths, not much room if you ask me. It'd be safer if I piloted the Zodiac."

"I told you, towing's better. The sound of the Zodiac's engine would attract Angel."

Mac passed him the walkie-talkie. "I'll keep the chopper at one hundred feet, but I'm also going to trail the rescue harness, just in case you need to get off this raft in a hurry."

Jonas forced a smile, then removed a remote headset from the case. He placed it over his ears, pausing to listen.

"Anything?"

"No, she's not in range yet. You realize this could be a long night."

"Just don't fall asleep in the boat, Ahab." Mac released the catch on the A-frame's pulley, allowing the Zodiac to drop straight down to the sea.

Jonas reached up and released the boat from its harness. Taken by the *William Beebe*'s wake, the raft drifted quickly behind the research vessel, which was moving southwest at just under three knots.

Using the length of rope, Mac guided the Zodiac behind the stern. He secured the end to the iron guardrail, allowing the raft to be towed halfway between the *William Beebe* and the trailing bait.

Jonas situated himself within the rubber raft, which glided silently along the surface of the dark Alaskan waters with barely a ripple. A cold rain continued to fall from the overcast sky, the northern air sending shivers down his spine. Sitting low in the boat, he propped a life preserver against the bow and leaned back, facing the engine.

The length of steel cable running from the *William Beebe* to the bait hovered two feet over his left shoulder, disappearing 158 feet behind the raft into the gray-black mist-covered sea. As his eyes became accustomed to the dark, Jonas was able to trace the line of cable to a small patch of froth, created by the sea lion carcass moving through the surface waters. He heard and felt the deep thrum produced by the underwater speaker, pulsating beneath the waves like a heartbeat.

Jonas aimed the rifle, focusing the gun sight on the froth of water.

"Dinner's ready, Angel," he whispered, "come and get it."

Twenty-two miles to the northeast of Cape Chiniak, the 382-foot ferry *M/V Kennicott* continued its journey south along the Alaskan Marine Highway. Unbeknownst to the ship's eight hundred passengers and crew, an ivory glow now shadowed the vessel as it made its way to Kodiak Island.

Entering the Gulf of Alaska, the Megalodon had instinctively increased its speed, a primordial response to the colder ocean temperatures. Evolutionary adaptations that had allowed the giant species to stave off extinction up until the last Ice Age now served to protect the supreme hunter in response to the cold. Chemical secretions within the creature's nervous and circulatory systems boosted the shark's capacity to contract its muscles. These swifter, more powerful muscular contractions generated additional heat energy, which raised the Megalodon's blood temperature six to eight degrees. Enlarged pericardial arteries circulated this increased body heat to the internal organs, while the predator's sheer mass helped insulate its core temperature from its colder environment.

Gliding just above the thermocline, Angel continued crisscrossing the *Kennicott's* wake, searching for food. Although the female's rise in visceral temperature had increased her digestive process, the progression of her estrus cycle, combined with the shark's decreased metabolic rate due to the cold, had left her feeling sluggish. It had been three days since the creature had last fed, and in her weakened state, she could not risk attacking a large pod of whales.

As Angel continued her westerly trek behind the ferry, pressure-wave detectors began sensing familiar vibrations. Aroused, she began beating her caudal fin faster, struggling at first to accelerate her incredible mass. After several dozen powerful thrusts, she managed to increase her forward momentum, reaching a cruising speed her torpedo-shaped body could maintain with little effort. Gliding beneath the ferry, the Megalodon raced ahead, following an acoustical beacon her instincts told her would lead to food.

2:56 a.m.

"Jonas, you still alive?"

Jonas looked up. Though he could hear the rotors beating, the chopper was invisible in the dark cloudy sky. He reached a numb hand for the walkie-talkie, pressing it to his face.

"I'm still here. How you doing up there?"

"Wind's picking up a bit. As long as there's no lightning, I'm fine. What about you? You must be a popsicle by now."

"The wet suit's keeping me warm, but the seas are getting rough."

"Listen, pal, how 'bout we reel you in and call it a night before you catch pneumonia."

"No," Jonas shouted. "No more nightmares, no more people dying. I told you, I'm ending this tonight, once and for all."

"And what if your monster doesn't show, Ahab?"

"She'll show. Out." Jonas shoved the walkie-talkie into his jacket pocket.

Two-to-three-foot waves now rolled the raft from side to side. The increased wind drove the rain harder against his face.

Maybe she won't show . . .

Jonas stared into the pitch, the choppy sea appearing lead-gray against the black sky. For at least the hundredth time he replayed the nightmare in his mind's eye, seeing himself dead in the escape pod.

More images flowed into his mind and he became consumed in a waking dream. He saw himself standing in the rain as the coffins of the two Navy men he had killed eleven years ago were lowered into the ground.

He saw himself on board the *Magnate*, staring into the demon's mouth, powerless as he watched his ex-wife Maggie being dragged beneath the waves. He saw himself in a courtroom, lawyers accusing him of reckless endangerment as throngs of onlookers chanted, "murderer, murderer." And then Terry, teary-eyed, lying in a hospital bed, grieving the loss of their stillborn child.

Terry looked up at him, her intense Asian eyes staring through him with the same mixture of sadness and hatred he'd seen in the grieving spouses and parents, the siblings and children.

Jonas opened his eyes, panting hard to catch his breath. The rain had subsided.

Jonas sat up, kneeling on one of the seats. Unzipping his wet suit, he urinated over the side.

"Okay, Angel, here I am," he whispered. "Come and get me."

Celeste rolled out of the bed and headed for the shower.

Maren admired her figure as she walked to the bathroom. "Can I join you?"

She turned to face him. "Michael, no offense, but I don't think you're up to it. Now go back to your cabin. I need my sleep."

Maren climbed out of the bed, slipped on his clothes, and left.

Beep.

The noise startled Jonas awake. He adjusted the headset and held his breath.

Beep . . . beep . . . beep . . .

Grabbing the grenade rifle in one hand, he reached for the walkie-talkie with the other. "Mac, I just got a signal!"

Mac searched the black expanse of ocean. "I can't see her glow yet. Listen, try to stay calm, don't give your position away."

"I'm fine," Jonas said, nearly hyperventilating as he scanned the sea.

The beeps grew louder.

Angel snorted the sea, her directional nostrils homing in on the microscopic particles of urine. Rising to forty feet, she circled her prey from below, choosing to remain at a safe distance while her senses surveyed the environment.

"There she is," Mac shouted. "She's circling just below the surface, sixty feet off your starboard side. Hold on, Jonas, she's passing beneath you—now!"

Jonas held on, feeling an immense tug from below as the creature's moving girth momentarily drew the raft sideways. Leaning overboard, Jonas saw the swish of a luminescent tail fin as the beast circled away to his right.

"Jonas, you there?"

"Shhh." Jonas turned the volume down. "Where is she?"

"She disappeared below."

Jonas felt his heart pounding, the pulse in his neck throbbing. He gripped the grenade rifle tighter.

"Jonas, she's surfacing behind the bait—"

Jonas pressed his eye tighter against the rifle's scope.

"Thar she blows!" Mac yelled.

The Megalodon's snout rose out of the water behind the sea lion, its jaws biting down on the lifeless tail, severing it from the upper torso.

Targeting the immense head, Jonas held his breath—and fired.

Click.

His heart skipped a beat. He re-aimed and squeezed the trigger again.

Click. Click—click.

"Son of a bitch, the gun's not firing!"

And then Jonas's heart leaped into his throat as the Zodiac suddenly stopped dead in the water. The sea lion carcass, still being towed by the *William Beebe*, raced at him on a collision course,

Mac saw the raft stop, then stole a glance at the *William Beebe*'s stern, spotting a solitary figure disappearing inside.

"Your rope's been cut. Hang on, Jonas, I'm coming—" Mac dropped the airship straight down, aiming the harness for the raft.

Jonas held his breath, waiting for the harness. Instead, he saw the Megalodon's snout bearing down on the approaching sea lion carcass and his drifting Zodiac.

Angel's jaws opened—

Jump!

Jonas leaped from the Zodiac and grabbed the steel cable with both hands. The sea lion carcass struck the drifting Zodiac, tossing it upside down.

Sensing movement, the Megalodon instinctively bit the raft, bursting it in its mouth.

Jonas held on to the cable like a fallen water skier refusing to let go. His lower torso bounded painfully against the frigid surface, the slick line cutting and sliding through his butchered hands. With a thud that took his breath away, the remains of the sea lion rammed into him from behind, sending spasms of pain through his injured leg.

Jonas slipped beneath the half-eaten carcass, wrapping his legs around the bouncing bait as his back slapped painfully against the surf. Blinded by the darkness and freezing water, no longer able to feel his exposed hands, he felt his blood turn to lead while his skin seemed to sizzle beneath the wet suit.

Way to go, idiot. You've killed yourself!

The Megalodon shook the remains of the Zodiac from her jaws and raced after her fleeing prey.

Mac's helicopter soared along the whitecaps, beads of cold sweat streaming into the pilot's eyes as he desperately attempted to line up the dangling harness with the moving bait. Realizing the task was impossible, he grabbed the radio, shouting at the *William Beebe* to respond.

Wedging the sea lion's head between his knees, Jonas gained enough leverage to push his right foot into the shredded remains of the upper torso. The canister of drugs had fallen into the sea, but he could feel the three-foot hook with his instep. Standing on the steel curvature, he raised his head above the dark waves and gasped for air, his muscles shaking uncontrollably.

To his horror, he saw the luminescent snout rise up

behind him. Jaws and upper gums extended outward, reaching for him.

The thought occurred to let go. Instead, he torqued his body sideways, swinging the shredded carcass away from the lunging mouth. Chomping down on empty sea, the predator rose again, this time hyperextending its open jaws to engulf the sea lion and Jonas in one humongous bite.

Jonas shut his eyes. His nightmares had been wrong. He would not die with his wife in the Trench, but here, now, alone, on the open sea.

A thunderous roar overhead—the tip of the helicopter's landing gear clipped the towering dorsal fin. The collision cut a deep gash along one side of the fin, sending the chopper spinning wildly out of control.

The predator submerged.

Mac fought the joystick, unable to control his yaw. The landing gear struck the sea, then bounced upward before its rotor could hit water. Struggling to regain altitude, realizing he was seconds away from stalling, Mac managed to pull the chopper up and over the *William Beebe*'s stern, crash-landing the heaving bucket of bolts against the lower deck.

Jonas held on and waited to be eaten. *I'm sorry, Terry, I was so stupid . . .*

Mac dragged himself from the cockpit and ran to the winch where Harry and Maren were waiting.

"Mackreides, what the hell are—"

Mac shoved Maren aside and reversed the winch.

"Are you crazy—"

"Get the hell out of my way—Jonas is out there!"

* * *

The Megalodon was moving in three hundred feet of water, swimming directly below her prey. Instincts told her the sea lion was either wounded or dead, but it had struck back, forcing the hunter to reevaluate. Hungry, the female rose again, homing in on the thrashing movements of her prey. This time, instead of going for the kill, the predator would bite and release, then circle back and wait for her quarry to die.

In his delirium Jonas imagined himself being drawn upward and out of the sea. Then everything went black.

Mac climbed along the outside of the rail and reached for his friend when the lifeless body toppled backward toward the sea.

The crook of Jonas's right knee caught in the curvature of the hook, suspending his body twenty feet above the water like a piece of meat. Mac reached out precariously and grabbed him around the waist as the luminous glow rose beneath him.

The beast launched itself from the ocean, jaws agape, its upper torso rising alongside the stern of the moving ship. Mac jerked Jonas away from the open maw, practically tossing his friend's body over his shoulder and onto the deck.

Missing its prey, the shark clamped down onto the A-frame. For a surreal moment, the creature held on, its stark-white belly leaning against the transom as its immense bulk fell backward, dragging the winch, A-frame, and twenty feet of splintered decking over the side in a mangled heap, the screech of twisted steel screaming in the night.

Mac pulled Jonas close and ducked as the entire winch and cable assembly seemed to jump overboard.

"Jonas—Jonas, wake up!" Mac checked his airway. "Damn it, he's not breathing! Harry, get the doc, I can't feel a pulse. Harry, dammit, get the doctor!"

The stern of the *William Beebe* looked like it had been struck by a tornado. Standing in the midst of the debris, mesmerized, were Harry and Maren. Ignoring Mac, they continued staring at the white dorsal fin until it disappeared beneath the vessel's churning wake.

Intruders

Mariana Trench

Terry woke up screaming. She sat up in bed, her heart pounding, her T-shirt drenched in sweat.

The loud banging on her door continued.

"Who—who is it?"

"Benedict. Open the door."

Oh, God, he knows . . .

"Just a minute."

Terry slipped on her jeans, then pulled her hair back into a ponytail and opened the door.

As if examining a crime scene, Benedict's piercing eyes were on her immediately. "You screamed, and you look quite pale."

"I just had a bad dream. I haven't had a good night's sleep since we've been in the Trench. When can I expect to leave?"

"Soon enough. Finish dressing and come up to the observation deck, there's something I wish to show you."

She closed the door, listening to make sure Benedict had left. Locking the door, she reached into her pants pocket and removed the magnetic security card she had taken from Sergei the night before.

Where to hide it?

Using her nail file, she made a three-inch incision along one of the seams of her mattress, then carefully pushed the card inside. After making the bed, she finished dressing and headed up the companionway stairs.

Her arrival on the bridge was net by a dozen silent gazes. "'Morning," she mumbled as she climbed the access tube's ladder to the upper deck.

The observation room was dark, the only visible radiance coming from outside the bay window where the red glow of the *Benthos*'s exterior lights revealed the abyss. She saw Benedict's silhouette against the background of the Trench.

"Be sure to seal the access tube behind you," he said in a soft, yet firm voice. "Approach slowly. Their eyesight is surprisingly quite good."

Terry followed his orders. She sealed the watertight hatch, then slowly crossed the darkened room to join him by the enormous observation window.

"No matter what you see, no sudden movements," Benedict warned.

"What are we looking at," she whispered.

"Be patient and observe."

The abyss surrounding the *Benthos* was bathed in a soft red glow, the seafloor appearing in shadows sixty feet below the hovering ship. A petrified forest of black smokers loomed along the edge of darkness. Tall and very thin, each primordial stack billowed brownish mushroom clouds of soot, scalding water, and sulfurous minerals.

Terry saw movement—an enormous shadow circling the seafloor, the life-form itself concealed beneath the *Benthos*. Recalling the creature that had entered the hangar, she grew terribly afraid.

More movement, this time from above their heads, as a seventeen-foot gulper eel slithered down along the LEXAN glass, its outstretched funnel-like mouth trailing after a silver hatchet fish. Rather than chase its quicker prey, the dark brown eel curled the tip of its long whip-like tail in front of its jaws. Instantaneously, an orange-white glow ignited at the end of the tapering tail.

Attracted by the light, the hatchet fish did a quick about-face and darted right into the eel's awaiting mouth.

Terry was about to say something when a shadowy presence glided majestically up along the rising curvature of the *Benthos*'s hull.

Benedict reached out and grabbed her wrist, preventing her from fleeing.

The underside of the flat vile head appeared first, revealing a glimpse of Tyrannosaurus-like teeth. Formidable jaw muscles flexed, stretching open the crocodile-like mouth.

With an almost snakelike quickness, the colossal reptile engulfed the gulper eel in two successive snaps. With a graceful pirouette, the creature swam off, one of its enormous paddle-like appendages slapping the LEXAN glass as it disappeared from view.

"The species is called Kronosaurus," Benedict said, anticipating her question. "They are a short-necked breed of pliosaurs, a prehistoric marine reptile that dominated the Mesozoic seas until *Carcharodon megalodon* evolved seventy million years ago. I've counted six of them, all circling the ship."

"I thought they were afraid of the *Benthos?*"

"Apparently, their appetites have overcome their fears."

"I don't understand." Terry felt droplets of sweat break out along her neck.

Benedict turned, his emerald eyes grilling her. "It seems they've had a taste of flesh, my dear. Apparently they must have enjoyed it."

Terry's mind raced. "The *Proteus*—these creatures must have attacked the sub and eaten the remains of the crew."

Benedict contemplated her response, the answer seeming to satisfy him.

"Are you going to postpone the next mission?"

"*Mais, non, madame. Je maintiendrai*—I will maintain. The *Benthos* continues its trek north through the Trench, the *Epimetheus* and her crew are readied for deployment. I assume you will be joining them?"

"Joining—no, of course not. How could you even think of deploying the *Epimetheus* with these monsters waiting out there?"

Benedict moved slowly toward the control panel along the opposite wall. "So, you now prefer Sergei to these creatures?"

"No, it's just—"

"Then I expect you aboard the sub. We depart in twenty minutes." Benedict reached the controls, activating the titanium outer seal, which slowly began closing over the observation window.

"Benedict, wait—" Terry whirled toward him.

From the darkened perimeter, another Kronosaurus suddenly glided into view. Headfirst, the thirty-four-thousand-pound beast launched its attack upon the diminishing section of glass, its luminous eyes sparkling in the red lights.

She looked back at Benedict, who stared wide-eyed at the approaching carnivore, a sadistic leer stretched across his face.

Terry cowered back as the creature opened its mouth, its flat tapered jaws stretching higher than the window.

A high-pitched whine of hydraulics—and the titanium doors slammed shut over the glass. A thunderous thud echoed through the room as the Kronosaurus struck the dome.

Terry turned to find Benedict standing by the control panel grinning at her, his cleanly shaven head glistening beneath a ceiling light.

"Perhaps surveying the Trench may have to wait after all."

She watched him unseal the hatch and climb down the access tube's ladder as a succession of massive blows pounded the exterior of the *Benthos*.

Second Chance

Iliuliuk Health Clinic
Port of Dutch Harbor
Unalaska, Alaska

"Welcome back."

Jonas opened his eyes on the plump face of an Aleutian nurse.

She gave him a warm smile, then opened the blinds, allowing the morning sun to filter into the room. "There, that's better. I'll bet your throat hurts."

Jonas nodded.

"I'll get you some water, but first let's unstrap those arms."

Jonas looked down at his wrists, which had been secured to the bed rail by Velcro straps. His fingers, wrapped in gauze, felt strange.

"The doctor says you'll be fine, although you did give all of us quite a scare." She held a cup of water to his mouth.

Jonas took a few sips, the liquid soothing his parched throat. "What happened?" he rasped.

"Apparently you decided to take a swim in the Gulf of Alaska. The extreme cold caused hypothermia. Your body shut down."

"My heart stopped?"

"At one point you were dead. Good thing your friend knows CPR. By the time you arrived by chopper, you were breathing but your core temperature and blood pressure had both dropped dangerously low. "Then your heart stopped again in the OR. But we've got good doctors on staff. They got you pumping again, and the extreme cold helped minimize the potential damage to your vital organs."

"Wait, are you saying I was . . . dead?" Jonas closed his eyes, trying to remember what he had assumed was a dream.

"For a minute or two. You've also suffered some severe frostbite. Your fingers and toes are heavily blistered."

Jonas wiggled his fingers, registering a tight soreness.

"The doctor's a bit concerned about the toes on your left foot. He wants to keep an eye on it, just to make sure gangrene doesn't set in. And that left leg of yours, my goodness. Everyone on staff wants to know what caused those nasty wounds."

"Fishing accident," Jonas whispered. "How long have I been in here?"

"Three days. Your friends are back on their boat, somewhere in the Bering Sea. We've been keeping them informed by radio. I'll have our switchboard operator contact them to let them know you're conscious."

The nurse fluffed his pillow, then left.

Jonas closed his eyes, allowing her words to sink in.

I died . . .

An incredible sadness overwhelmed him. He thought back to everything that had happened in his life over the last eleven years since he had first escaped death in the Mariana Trench. Guilt had pushed him into becoming a paleobiologist, his ego needing to prove to the world that his actions aboard the *Sea Cliff* had been justified. His preoccupation with the creatures had destroyed both his marriages. Now his blind hatred had led him to the brink of death.

God's giving me a second chance . . .

The nurse returned several hours later, placing his lunch on a tray table next to his bed. "I hope you're hungry. By the way, your girlfriend, the pretty blonde—"

"She's not my girlfriend."

"Okay. Well, whoever she is, she'd just arrived and is anxious to see you. Should I ask her to wait until you've finished eating?"

"No, send her in."

Celeste entered a moment later, her long platinum hair hanging down over a black turtleneck sweater. She leaned over, kissed him gently on the cheek, then pulled a chair up close to the side of his bed.

"Here, before I forget." She took a cellular phone from her purse, placing it on the bureau. "Harry insisted I bring this to you. He wants you to call him when you're ready to be picked up. So, did you see a white light, or were you headed in the opposite direction?"

"I remember a white glow, but it had teeth. I pulled a really stupid stunt, didn't I?"

"Not only that, but you were trying to kill my shark. All this time I thought I could trust you. The truth is, you never cared about me, you were just using me so you could get close enough to the Megalodon to kill it."

"Celeste—"

"Don't lie, just admit it."

"Fine, yes, I admit that I accepted your offer because I wanted to kill the Meg. As far as caring about you, I've never led you on. I told you up front that I love my wife. You're the one who's been coming on to me."

"I'm attracted to you. Is that a crime?"

"I'm married—"

"What if you weren't?"

"What?" Celeste's tone had sent a shiver down his spine.

"You heard me. What if Terry wasn't in your life? Would you have still turned me down that night?"

Be careful, Jonas . . .

"Celeste, you're a beautiful woman and I'm a stuffy old scientist. It just wouldn't work out. What I appreciate most about you is your friendship. The time we spent together really did mean something to me. And you were right. I've blamed these overgrown sharks for everything bad that's happened in my life over the last eleven years."

"I told you—you're obsessed."

"Terry and Mac have been telling me the same thing for years, but I just ignored them. Guess I actually had to die to realize that my anger and guilt were blinding me. I think Mac summed it up best when he called me Ahab. Celeste, I was so anxious to throw my life away, just to kill an overgrown fish." He laid his head back and closed his eyes. "I want to apologize if I misled you."

She touched his cheek. "It's okay."

"Things are going to be a lot different from now on. God's given me a second chance and I'm taking it."

She eyed him suspiciously. "What does that mean?"

"It means I'm done. Finished. No more Megalodons in Jonas Taylor's life. I've officially retired."

She pulled back. Her nostrils flaring. "Don't get righteous on me, Jonas Taylor. You just can't walk away. Not after everything that's happened. We still haven't recaptured your shark."

"My shark? As I recall, it was your shark—"

"You know what I mean. You have to stick it out—you owe me that."

"Let the creature be."

"Are you delirious? She stood, spilling his orange juice all over the floor. "Jonas, how many people have died since this shark of yours escaped from the lagoon? Don't you think we owe it to the public to track it down before more innocent people are killed?"

"Celeste, it's a shark, for Christ's sake. It's in its own natural habitat. Humans are not the staple of its diet. We just seem to get in the way—"

"You're wrong. It's your fault these creatures escaped the Mariana Trench." She pushed her index finger into his chest. "You and Tanaka are responsible for these monsters surfacing."

"Whoa, I don't believe I'm hearing this. What happened to your advice about not feeling guilty over what happened?"

"You shouldn't feel guilty—as long as you do the right thing. And the right thing is to help me recapture Angel before she kills again."

"Why me? Because I happened to be the unlucky jerk who accidentally crossed paths with these killing machines eleven years ago? Listen, I've already helped capture one Megalodon and kill another. I'd say I've hit my quota as far as prehistoric sharks are concerned."

Celeste paced back and forth like a caged animal. "You have a responsibility to the Institute, Jonas, to all who died."

"How much is enough? You said it yourself. My life has been preoccupied with these creatures for way too long. Sorry, Celeste—no more hatred, no more guilt, all of that died on the table with me three days ago. This is the new Jonas Taylor, I'm reborn. And as far as my responsibilities to you and the Institute, I tried to warn you. I told you to dope the creature up until we could seal the gateway permanently."

Celeste sat on the floor, laying her head on his bed. "Please, Jonas, I need your help."

"That's the thing, Celeste, you don't really need my help. Maren can handle everything. Personally, I think Angel's too big to capture, plus she's in estrus, which makes her even more dangerous. If you want my advice, continue searching the Bering Sea. She'll turn up, sooner or later. It's just a matter of time."

"You're wrong. We haven't seen a trace of her since your accident, and we're not the only ones looking.

The Coast Guard's out in full force, and there must be a thousand fishing vessels out there, as well. No one's spotted the shark, not even a trace of a dead sea lion or whale. Even Maren's baffled."

"The Bering Sea's a big place. Offer a reward to local fishermen. I'm sure someone will sight her real fast."

Celeste laid her head on his hand, emotionally drained. "So that's it? You're just walking away?"

"That's right." He pulled his hand away. "I'm going to heal up, get my strength back. Then I'm going to California to start my life again with Terry."

Celeste looked him hard in the eyes. "Okay, Jonas, I understand how you feel. You've gone through a very traumatic, emotional experience and I don't blame you for just wanting out. But there's something you can still do to prevent innocent people from dying."

"What's that?"

"Your own wife's still on board the *Benthos*, along with people I care very much about. As long as they're in the abyss, they're in danger."

"What are you asking me to do?" Jonas said, struggling to sit up.

"Be the friend that you claim to be. I haven't been able to sleep at night since you told me about Devil's Purgatory. Call me neurotic, but I'm worried sick. I'm getting terrible premonitions about that location."

"Celeste, the gorge is over fifteen hundred miles long and more than forty miles wide."

"I'm a woman, Jonas. Don't try to reason with my emotions."

He lay back, feeling exhausted. "Okay, Celeste, what are you asking me to do?"

"Before you turn your back on your responsibilities, give me the same peace of mind that I've tried to give you. Tell me the location of Devil's Purgatory. Maybe it means nothing to you, but knowing the *Benthos* will avoid that area of the Trench will allow me to sleep at night. I think you, more than anyone, can appreciate that."

Jonas closed his eyes, debating whether to pass on the information. As far as he knew, the Navy was no longer interested in the Mariana Trench. What harm could it possibly do to give her the coordinates and get her out of his hair, once and for all?"

Then he remembered Mac's words of warning.

"I'm sorry Celeste. I just can't give out the location." Jonas watched her face turn scarlet in anger.

"You know what, Jonas? You and the United States Navy can go screw yourselves!"

He cringed as she knocked over his tray table and lunch before storming out of the room.

Michael Maren was staring absentmindedly at the chart of the Bering Sea when Harry Moon entered the control room.

"Those orcas just took the last sea lion carcass," Harry said. "Now what?"

Maren looked up. "How the hell should I know?"

"You're the expert. You said the creature would be here."

"She's out there. She's just not showing herself. Maybe all those helicopters and boats and Coast Guard cutters have her spooked. Mark my words—sooner or later, she'll show herself."

"You look wiped out. Why don't you get some sleep?"

"Yeah, I think I will. When's Celeste due back on board?"

"Three hours."

Maren left the control room, heading out on deck. As he adjusted his parka against the driving wind, he heard someone calling his name.

"Dr. Maren, over here."

Maren looked to the helo-pad. He saw Mackreides attempting to lift a large cardboard box into the cargo bay of his helicopter.

"Hey, Doc, please. It'll just take a moment."

Maren walked over warily. "What do you want?"

"I need a hand with this box, my back's killing me."

Maren reached down and lifted the box, which weighed less than forty pounds. "You needed my help lifting this? What's the matter? I thought you were a tough guy?"

"I told you, my back's out. Would you mind putting it inside?"

Maren turned, tossing the lightweight cardboard box against the far wall. "Now, if that's all, I'll—"

Mac picked him off his feet, tossing him headfirst into the compartment.

Maren rolled over, then sat up, rubbing his head. "What's your problem—"

The tip of Mac's boot connected with Maren's solar plexus, driving the breath out of him. Before he could regain his senses, Mac had bound his wrists together with a nylon cord. Lifting the younger man to his feet, he looped the end of the cord several times around an overhead support in the ceiling of the chopper, forcing Maren to stand.

Maren struggled to free himself. "Why are you doing this?"

Mac climbed into the cockpit and started the engine. "It's simple, Doc. Screw with my boy, you screw with me."

The helicopter rose away from the *William Beebe* and headed north.

"Wait a second! Goddamn it. Where are you taking me?"

"Sight-seeing. I find Alaska quite beautiful, don't you?"

"Enough already. Why are you doing this?"

Mac ignored him. The helicopter flew east over the Bering Sea, then north, soaring over snow-covered peaks and lush valleys.

Celeste looked up from her magazine as the nurse approached Jonas's room.

"Excuse me, is that for my fiancé?" Celeste pointed to the lunch tray.

"Your fiancé?"

"Yes, Dr. Taylor."

"Oh, well, yes, as a matter of fact, it is."

"May I?"

The nurse smiled, handing her the tray.

Celeste returned her smile and waited until the nurse turned her back before she removed the two yellow pills from her pocket.

Jonas was watching the news.

"Hi, I'm back," Celeste said as she breezed into the room.

He shut the television off. "I thought you returned to the ship."

"I felt bad. We're supposed to be friends, and here I was, yelling at you. All I want is for you to be happy."

"Thanks, Celeste. I feel the same about you."

She leaned over and kissed his forehead. "Here," she handed him the two pills and a glass of juice. "The nurse is trusting me to make sure you take these. She says it will help you to regain your strength."

Jonas swallowed the pills. "So what are you going to do?"

She pulled a chair up next to his bed. "The *William Beebe* is on its way to the nearest port for repairs before we go out—"

Jonas felt himself growing tired as Celeste droned on for the next ten minutes.

"—and I've taken your advice and offered a five-thousand-dollar reward for the first person who spots Angel. I'm sure it won't be long till she reappears."

Her words began echoing in his head.

Celeste watched his eyes roll back. "Are you okay?"

Jonas rubbed his temple. "I don't know. I feel really tired . . ." He shut his eyes.

Celeste leaned forward, whispering in his ear. "Jonas are you attracted to me?"

"Yes."

"Do you trust me?"

"No."

"But you'd love to sleep with me, wouldn't you?"

His mind went limp. "Yes—but I can't," he mumbled, the sodium pentothal taking effect. "I love Terry. I won't cheat on her."

"Jonas, Terry's in the Mariana Trench. She'll die unless we warn her about the Devil's Purgatory. Jonas, don't let her die."

Jonas clenched his teeth, trying hard to focus through his delirium. "I don't want her to die."

"Then give me the coordinates—quickly." She patted his cheek. "Jonas, the Devil's Purgatory—"

He felt himself drifting off, his mumbled words belonging to someone else. ". . .the northern gorge . . . twenty-two degrees . . . forty-five minutes . . . North latitude . . ."

"Yes, go on!"

"—one . . . forty-six . . . degrees . . . thirty-three . . . minutes . . . East Longitude."

Celeste kissed him hard on the mouth, then ran from the room.

Two hours passed before Mac slowed the airship, circling above an expanse of grassland spotted with wildflowers. A snow-capped mountain range sculpted the horizon to the northeast, a forest of pine trees blanketed the south.

The chopper touched down.

"Where the hell are we?" Maren yelled.

"Ever hear of a town called Bethel?"

"No."

"Me neither, but according to the map, it's somewhere south of here, maybe thirty, forty miles." Mac pulled open the cargo-bay door, then tossed the cardboard box out.

"What? Now what are you doing?"

"I just thought you'd like your personal belongings with you. I took the liberty of clearing the stuff out of your cabin. Don't bother thanking me, it was my pleasure."

"You're not leaving me here?"

"Why not? It's pretty country, though you may want to keep an eye out for bears."

"I'll die out here."

Mac untied the rope from the support, dragging Maren from the chopper.

Maren dropped knees first onto the half-frozen, muddy ground. "Mackreides, wait. Okay, I confess. I was the one who removed the firing pin from Taylor's weapon. But I swear, I didn't cut that rope."

"Then who did?"

"I don't know—"

Mac walked back to the chopper and shut the cargo-bay door.

"Wait, Mackreides, don't leave! If you don't believe me, ask Celeste. I was with her the night Taylor was attacked."

"Sounds like a motive to me. Celeste's been coming on to Jonas. You became jealous and tried to kill him."

"No, I mean yes, I was jealous, but I didn't cut the rope."

Mac studied Maren's face. He pulled out his Bowie knife.

Maren flinched.

Mac grabbed him by the wrists and cut his bonds. He reached the cockpit and pulled out a knapsack, tossing it at him. "There's a map inside, along with matches and a few other supplies. If our paths ever cross again, I'll kill you."

Mac climbed back into the cockpit.

Maren ran to the cockpit door, finding it locked. "Mackreides, don't do this!"

Mac turned, his smile widening across the square-cut jawline. "Have a nice walk."

Desperate, Maren grabbed onto the landing struts. The chopper lifted, tossing him to the ground.

Maren sat up and watched the helicopter disappear over a cluster of pine trees. A brisk northern wind howled through the trees, the cold air sending shivers down his spine.

He looked around, the seriousness of his predicament finally sinking in.

"Damn you, Mackreides," he screamed, running after the chopper, his voice echoing in the distance. He stumbled over a hollow log, righted himself, then started kicking it, cursing and yelling.

He stopped after several minutes when his foot started throbbing. He opened the knapsack and pulled out the map Mackreides had left him, unfolding it.

"You son of a bitch!"

It was a map of Cleveland.

Maren ripped it in half and started walking, limping noticeably.

Jonas opened his eyes. Celeste was gone, the room dark. For the first time in as long as he could remember, he felt at peace. In his mind, he imagined what he would say to Terry. He would offer to move, sell the house, just pick up and start their lives anew anywhere she desired. He'd get a job with normal hours, be home on weekends, whatever it took, as long as they could be together.

A deep rumbling interrupted his thoughts, shaking the room around him. He sat up as the window rattled in its frame. A cup of water spilled across his tray.

Seconds later, the vibrations ceased.

The nurse re-entered, smiling. "You okay?"

"Was that an earthquake?"

"Just a minor tremor. We get them all the time. Most people just ignore them. You should've seen the last time ol' Makushin erupted, my goodness. Ash all over everything."

"I didn't realize there was a volcano on this island."

"There are active volcanoes all over the Aleutians. After all, we are part of the Pacific Rim."

Jonas stiffened, a terrible thought racing through his mind.

"Are you okay, Mr. Taylor?"

"No, nurse, wait, please, I need your help . . . I need access to a computer."

"My son has a laptop—"

"Could I use it? Please, this is very important. It's a matter of life and death!"

Mousetrap

Mariana Trench

Benedict Singer leaned over the circular light table, his emerald eyes looking more animal than human in the fluorescent glow. To his left was Vladislav Prokovich, newly appointed captain of the *Benthos*; to his right, Dr. Liu Kwan, professor of plasma physics. The three men stood before the huge computerized bathymetric map of the trench and the surrounding Mariana Islands.

The volcanic island chain appeared as a long arcing landmass running north to south. Millions of years ago, the islands had risen from the ocean floor, driven upward as the Pacific tectonic plate subducted beneath the Philippine Plate. Shadowing the islands to the east was the world's deepest trench, the snaking gorge divided by a rising shelf that served to separate the deeper northern and southern halves of the abyss by an expanse of some thirty miles.

A blue dot within the southern region marked the present location of the *Benthos*. Benedict placed an X in red marker over an area in the northern Trench. "According to Celeste, Jonas Taylor indicated this area to be the site of the *Sea Cliff* dives. Vladislav, at full speed, how soon could we arrive?"

Vladislav Prokovich fingered the permanent eye patch covering his left eye socket, a lasting remnant of the Afghan war. "It will take us thirty hours just to reach the canyon wall. The *Benthos* must then ascend thirteen thousand feet to exit the gorge, then travel another twenty-eight miles north along this stretch of seafloor before descending into the northern region of the abyss. From there, another twenty hours to Devil's Purgatory . . . Seventy-two hours, perhaps less depending on the currents."

"It would be helpful to have the *Titan* begin gas chromatography readings of the Devil's Purgatory before we arrive," Kwan suggested.

Prokovich shook his head. "*Nyet*. It's not wise to allow the *Titan* to move ahead while these creatures continue to attack us."

"Why not?" Kwan asked. "The hull of the *Benthos* is impregnable."

"True, but the gasoline tanks and ballast attached to the cowling beneath the ship are quite vulnerable, as is the *Epimetheus*," Prokovich said. "The additional hours do not justify the risk."

"The creatures will abandon us once we begin our ascent," Benedict said. "Instruct the *Titan* to continue to shadow us until that time."

"What about the girl?" Prokovich asked. "With Sergei dead, is it wise to allow her free rein of the ship?"

"What you call free rein is only an illusion," Benedict corrected. "My eyes follow her everywhere."

"Then why did you allow her to kill Sergei?"

"I merely permitted the situation to play itself out. The girl was cunning. Sergei careless. Alcohol ruined him long ago. He deserved to die."

"We could post a guard—"

Benedict patted the sides of the younger man's carrot-red crew cut. "Don't worry yourself, Vladislav. The girl is my subject, a desperate mouse trapped in an inescapable maze. As a student of human nature, I am observing her without her knowing it, studying her responses to stress."

"She knows too much," Kwan said.

"But who can she tell?" Benedict asked. "While she's alive, the option remains to use her as a hostage, should an unexpected situation arise. Upon completing our mission, my little mouse will be dissected and properly disposed of. Until then, allow her to roam within her cage."

3:20 a.m.

Terry paused, her heart racing as she listened to muffled voices from the nuclear-reactor room on F level. Unsealing the watertight door, she climbed down, closing the hatch behind her, finally emerging on G deck.

She entered the deserted corridor. Heart pounding in her throat, she moved quickly down the hall to a set of security doors guarding the entrance of what she had been told was a storage facility. Pulling out Sergei's pass card, she swiped the magnetic strip.

The door clicked open.

Terry entered a dimly lit corridor. She allowed the door to seal shut behind her, then followed a narrow walkway, leading to a door on her right. She listened, then opened it, revealing an empty locker room. Along three of the walls were a dozen semiprivate changing areas. Hanging from hooks within each cubicle were one-piece bodysuits similar to those she had discovered aboard the *Titan*.

Moving through the empty locker room, Terry followed a carpeted passage past a tiled bathroom and shower stalls, finally arriving at a steel door. A warning sign in English, Russian, Korean, and Arabic was posted above the door:

"AIR SHOWER REQUIRED
BEFORE ENTERING FUSION LAB."

Ignoring the warning, she entered, closing her eyes as a gust of air blew hard against her face. It subsided as she moved beyond the threshold, entering the small antechamber. Benches lined either side of the ten-by-fifteen-foot room, a windowed door situated at the far end. Pressing her face against the dark glass, she peered inside.

It was a lab, but like none she had ever seen. At the center of the room was an object that resembled a six-foot black glass cube. Surrounding the apparatus was a myriad of computers and vacuum pumps. Positioned along the ceiling, high above the cube, was a device that looked like a powerful industrial laser.

Seeing no one inside, Terry pushed open the door, experiencing another blast of air as she entered the air-conditioned lab. Moving past the computers, she noticed rows of aluminum examination tables, covered with piles of potato-shaped black rocks. Terry picked one up, examining it.

"Manganese," she whispered, recognizing the nodule.

"Correct."

Terry spun around, startled to find herself face-to-face with Benedict Singer. Caught in the act, she stood defiantly before him, waiting to receive her punishment for misbehaving.

"You seem to be in the habit of these early-morning strolls," Benedict said. "In the future, I'll thank you to observe our rules of hygiene before breaking into our secured facilities, a courtesy you extended when you broke into the Tokamak lab aboard the *Titan*."

Terry felt herself losing her nerve. "What are you doing, Benedict? Are you going to kill me?" *That was stupid . . .*

"Kill you? For breaking and entering? A bit harsh, don't you think—oh, but then you did murder Sergei, didn't you?"

"He was raping me!"

"Attempted rape justifies murder?"

"He would have killed me, just like he killed Captain Hoppe."

"*Sancta simplicitas*, is that it, my dear?" Benedict circled her like a vulture. "It's unimportant. Your heinous act shall remain a secret."

"What do you want with me?" she said, fighting to remain in control of her emotions.

"What do I want?" Benedict repeated, as if contemplating the question. "You know, to be honest, I'm not quite sure. I suppose I'm still gauging your value. Your physical prowess in the hangar certainly impressed me, to say nothing of your daring aboard the *Titan*. What say we test your intelligence? Tell me, what is my true interest in the Mariana Trench?"

She stared into his eyes, refusing to shirk. "The Mariana Trench falls within the boundaries of the Exclusive Economic Zoning Laws. You're using the deployment of the UNIS systems as cover while you illegally mine manganese nodules from the abyss."

Benedict's eyes flashed their approval. "Very good. But why am I going to such an elaborate expense just to mine some poly-metallic nodules?"

"You're obviously not after the manganese, or even nickel or cobalt, for that matter. There must be something contained within these nodules that relates to fusion."

"*Bravo*. Walk with me." Benedict swept her along with his right arm, leading her toward the ovoid chamber. "Tell me, have you ever heard of Helium-3?"

"Only that it's extremely rare."

"Rare would be an understatement. Most scientists believe there is only enough of the isotope on Earth to fill several cups, although much of the element has been discovered on the Moon. Of course, lunar mining would obviously be a vast undertaking."

"Why is Helium-3 important?"

Benedict smiled. "Because it's the key, my dear, the key that unlocks the secret of fusion energy, the greatest technological challenge of our time. Although mankind has come far since Einstein first deduced that mass can produce energy, our major challenge has been to contain the hot plasma required to reach fusion temperatures of one hundred million degrees."

"And you've resolved the problem?"

Benedict leaned back against one of the aluminum tables. "Not I, but two brilliant physicists, Professors Dick Prestis and Michael Shaffer, the former being a onetime colleague of mine."

"Prestis and Shaffer—those names sound familiar."

"They should. They were the two men who died aboard the *Sea Cliff*, a Navy submersible your husband was piloting eleven years ago in this very Trench. Fortunately for me, they took their fusion secret with them to the grave."

"Does Jonas know about any of this?"

"God, no. Not even the Navy was aware of what these physicists were really up to."

"Jonas told me they were measuring abyssal currents in order to bury used plutonium rods."

Benedict grinned. "A clever cover story, but far from the truth. Years earlier, Prestis and Shaffer had made a startling discovery while analyzing manganese nodules, these particular specimens having been dredged from the seafloor more than one hundred years ago by the *H.M.S. Challenger*."

Benedict pressed a button on the control panel next to the cube-shaped machine, causing one entire side to hiss open. Taking a manganese nodule from one of the piles, he placed it on an elevated tray within the machine.

Terry looked up to see the barrel of the laser protrude away from the ceiling.

"Put these on," Benedict instructed, handing Terry a pair of protective eyewear. After sealing the glass box, he returned to the computer console and activated the laser.

A brilliant beam ignited within the chamber, visible through the transparent black glass. The nodule, immersed within the intense beacon, began heating up. A suction pump inside the chamber began to draw out the gas.

"Although we don't fully understand how these nodules complete their enrichment process, we know that primordial gases are vented from certain hydrothermal vents in the Pacific. One of these gases is Helium-3, which has been degassing from the earth ever since our planet was formed. As the manganese, minerals, and superheated waters are pumped out of the hydrothermal vents, nodules are formed, often trapping inert gases within the rock."

Data began flashing across the computer monitor, listing the metals and chemical compounds found in the nodule.

"Prestis and Shaffer used a process similar to the one you're witnessing on the manganese nodules retrieved by the *H.M.S. Challenger* in the 1870s. What they found must have startled them. Trapped within the rock was a unique blend of Helium-3 and deuterium, a fuel mix the physicists soon discovered to be compatible with a long-burning fusion reaction."

Benedict switched off the laser. "All of the nodules we've collected were dredged from a precise location known only to Prestis and Shaffer, a remote area within the Mariana Trench they jokingly referred to as Devil's Purgatory. For their secret dive, the *Sea Cliff* was equipped with a long suction device designed to collect the nodules from the seafloor. I suspect it may have been the vibrations given off by this vacuum pump that attracted the Megalodon to their sub in the first place."

"My God—"

Benedict shut off the computer. "Prestis managed to collect a half-dozen nodules before the creature showed up and attacked. The Navy confiscated the nodules but had no idea as to their value. It was years after the two scientists' deaths before I finally managed to obtain a few of these particular rocks, testing them in my own lab to reveal their secrets."

Benedict picked up another rock. "Searching for the Devil's Purgatory in the vastness of this Trench has been the equivalent of locating a needle in a haystack. Unfortunately, the coordinates were made known only to a handful of Naval officers—and, of course, the pilot of the *Sea Cliff.*"

"Jonas? Jonas would never tell you."

"He already has, or to be precise, he's told my protégée." Benedict flashed a triumphant smile. "Don't be so surprised. Celeste can be quite persuasive."

"I don't believe you."

"Believe it. We're on the way to Devil's Purgatory as we speak."

Terry shook her head. "I don't understand. Why all the secrecy?"

"You answered that question already. The EEZ laws prevent other nations from mining the nodules. Forbidden fruits are the sweetest, *n'est-ce pas?*"

"So who benefits from all this? Who do you really work for?"

"Benedict Singer works for no one. My 'partners' happen to be a small coalition of Arab investors who have generously provided GTI with the human resources and financial means to complete a venture of this scope."

"Investors? You mean terrorists, don't you?" Terry blurted out the words, wishing she could retract them.

Benedict's eyes locked on hers. "I see I've underestimated you again. No matter. In response to your statement, labeling one a terrorist or freedom fighter depends more on one's politics than actions. Were the British colonists of the late 1700s any less violent? My new Arab affiliates allow me to monopolize the world's new power source in ways the Western world never would. I am, by nature, an explorer. I desire access to new frontiers. As such, I have no interest in seeing my resources bound by judicial and legislative branches."

Benedict grabbed her arm, escorting her out of the lab. "Within the next forty-eight hours, the *Benthos* shall arrive in Devil's Purgatory. With the combined mining efforts of the *Prometheus* and the *Epimetheus*, we should be able to clear the seafloor of nodules fairly quickly. Thanks to the Tanaka Institute, the *Benthos* will ascend from the abyss without the United States or Japan having a clue as to what our actual mission was."

Terry felt ill, her hands trembling. "What are you going to do with me?"

"I haven't decided. You've grown on me, becoming a pet project of sorts. The thought had occurred to me to allow you to live out your days aboard the *Benthos*." He smiled. "Tell me, my dear, do you find me the least bit attractive?"

Ring of Fire

Jonas shielded his eyes from the swirling debris as the helicopter touched down on the hospital parking lot. Waving to his nurse, he pulled open the passenger door and climbed into the familiar cockpit.

"You look pretty good for a dead guy," Mac said.

Jonas gave his friend a quick handshake. "Mac, I—"

"Forget it. I'll just add it to your tab, which, by the way, is getting quite full. Seriously, though, I'm glad you finally got your head screwed on straight. For a while there, I was thinking about changing my name to Ishmael."

Jonas buckled his seat belt as the chopper lifted off. "How far are we from the *William Beebe?*"

"A few minutes. We docked last night in Dutch Harbor. By the way, Celeste left the ship early this morning."

"Celeste is gone? Where'd she go?"

"A GTI chopper picked her up. Captain Morgan says she took her belongings with her."

"That makes no sense," Jonas said, spotting the *William Beebe* in the distance. "Why would she just leave after repairing the lagoon and spending so much money on recapturing the shark?"

"I don't know. Maybe it has something to do with her leading you on while she was sleeping with Maren."

"Celeste and Maren? Who told you that?"

"Maren, just before I dropped him off on a nature walk across the Alaskan frontier. He confessed to removing the firing pin on the grenade rifle, but swears he had nothing to do with cutting the line to the Zodiac."

"Did you believe him?"

"Yes, which means there's someone else on board who's not real fond of you. Any clues?"

"No." Jonas rubbed his eyes, trying to absorb everything at once. "I don't get it. Why would Celeste come on so strong if she was sleeping with Maren?"

"Who the hell knows? I say good riddance to both of them."

They joined the captain and Harry Moon in the control room.

"Taylor, good to see you in one piece," the captain said. "Now what's all this about changing our course?"

"I need you to take us to the Mariana Trench as quickly as possible."

"Sorry. My orders are to complete repairs on the ship, then return to the Bering Sea to recapture the creature."

"The Megalodon's not in the Bering Sea," Jonas said. "She's headed for the Trench."

"If Dr. Maren were here, I think he'd disagree," Harry said, eyeing Mac suspiciously.

Jonas searched through the ship's charts, removing a bathymetric map of the Pacific Ocean.

"Harry, I'm sure you're familiar with the Ring of Fire?"

"Uh, actually, no."

"Really? I'd have thought different. Doesn't matter—" Jonas spread out the plastic chart. Using a red dry-erase marker, he drew a line up the South and Central American Pacific coastlines clear up along the Pacific-Northwestern coast of the United States, continuing around Canada, Alaska, and the Aleutian Islands, then across the Pacific and south down along the coast of Japan to Indonesia.

"This is the Ring of Fire, a seismic area situated around the Pacific Rim that is home to more than four hundred active volcanoes. Deep within the Earth, above the core and mantle, are roughly fourteen tectonic plates that float like giant continental rafts across our planet's crust. Dynamic collisions along these plate boundaries produce earthquakes and violent volcanic eruptions, the most powerful occurring along this seismic ring."

"What does all this have to do with the Megalodon?" Harry asked.

"During the last Ice Age, the ocean temperatures dropped, killing off most of the Megalodons. The surviving members were able to inhabit an abyssal, insulated layer of warm water continuously being fed by hydrothermal vents at the bottom of the Mariana Trench.

But the Trench itself is part of the Ring of Fire, a convergent plate boundary created by the subduction of the Pacific Plate pushing beneath the Philippine Plate."

"What's your point?"

"My point, Harry, is that these sharks are equipped with sensory systems that can use the Earth's own magnetic field, along with seismic vibrations in the fault lines to orient themselves over long distances. When Angel's mother escaped from the Trench four years ago, she instinctively headed east, first following the Hawaiian island chain, later moving north along the Central American coastline until she reached the Monterey canyon. All of these locations are part of the Ring of Fire, as is the route Angel's been following since she escaped from the lagoon."

"I thought she was following the migratory course for whales," Harry stated.

"So did I. Now I'm convinced the shark bypassed the Bering Sea. I think she continued southwest, following minute seismic vibrations emanating from the Aleutian Trench. Look here," Jonas pointed to the coast of Alaska, "if Angel continued to follow the Aleutian Trench, she'd cross the Northern Pacific and run directly into the Kamchatka and Kuril Trenches. These gorges continue southwest past the Kuril Islands before becoming the Japanese Trench—again, all part of the Ring of Fire. The Japanese Trench empties into the Mariana Trench, the species' home over the last million years or more."

"It's like the shark's following some sort of underwater highway," Mac said.

"I don't know, Taylor," Captain Morgan said. "This

monster could still be following the cetacean summer migration."

Jonas looked up at the captain. "The Megalodon's not following the whales. The female's entered a powerful state of estrus. Like some kind of giant salmon, she's using the Ring of Fire to navigate her way back to the Mariana Trench in order to breed."

"Taylor—"

"Captain, please. My wife's in the Trench. I need to get her out of there before it's too late."

Western Pacific
21 Miles Southwest of Kamchatka Peninsula

The captain of the twenty-eight-foot research vessel *Cachalot* turned his ship into the wind, allowing his crew to drop sail and drift in the five-foot seas. A cold breeze whistled across the mast. The rising three-quarter Moon peeked out from behind a cloud bank, casting its luminous glow on the ship's decking

Inside, sound engineer Janis Henkel adjusted her headphones and listened, reminding herself not to look at the *Discovery* camera pointing in her direction.

She turned to face her husband. "Bruce, according to my latest calculations, 'Mad Max' is now sleeping in eight hundred feet of water, hovering vertically below our boat. If his pattern holds, he should remain at rest for at least another three hours before continuing north."

"And . . . cut," said Norton Binder, the *Discovery* producer. "Very good, Jan. Is the sperm whale definitely asleep?"

"That's what I just said."

"Great, then let's use this opportunity to retake a few of the scenes we talked about earlier. Bruce, are you ready?"

Jan's husband, biologist Bruce Henkel, clipped the microphone to his shirt, then adjusted his collar. "I'm ready."

"Good," Norton said. "Now this is just voice-over, so don't worry about the camera, just read right from your notes. Josh, are you set?"

"Sound level's fine," the cameraman called out. "Anytime."

Bruce cleared his throat. "Reaching a length of sixty feet and weighing up to forty-five tons, the male sperm whale is undoubtedly the most formidable predator on the planet. It was back in the early nineteenth century that whalers first hunted these leviathans, targeting sperm whales for their enormous yields of oil. Unlike baleen whales, the aggressive sperm bulls often fought back, their actions no doubt inspiring Herman Melville's classic tale, *Moby Dick*."

"Great, much better than the last take," Norton said. "Go to the next passage."

"Larger and more aggressive than their female counterparts, bull sperm whales usually travel alone, their deep descents making the elusive hunters difficult to track in the open ocean. In order to learn more about these predators, the *Cachalot* will remain under sail, making as little noise as possible as we track the creatures with underwater microphones mounted in the ship's keel. Like their dolphin cousins, sperm whales use pulses of sound called echolocation to see their environment, a sensory system unique to toothed whales.

Over the last four days, our expedition has been tracking an enormous bull we've nicknamed Mad Max. By listening in on the whale's underwater vocalization, Jan can pinpoint Max's location anywhere within a five-mile radius."

"Cut. Okay, folks, I'd say that was a solid day's work. Josh and I are going to call it a night. Be sure to wake us if anything interesting happens."

Jan watched the two men head for the guest quarters. She felt Bruce's strong fingers massaging her back. "That feels wonderful. I suppose this means it's my turn to stay up all night and listen to Max snore?"

"It is your shift." Bruce kissed her on the back of the neck, then crawled into bed.

Gliding silently in the southerly flow of the *Anadyr* current, the female continued her southwesterly trek along the Asian coast, passing the Kuril Islands in six hundred feet of water. Far below the creature loomed the depths of the Kuril Trench, its deepest point, the Vityaz Deep, dropping to almost 34,600 feet.

Using the Aleutian Trench as a bearing, the albino predator had crossed the Northern Pacific, following the Kamchatka Trench to the southwest. Moving past Cape Lopatka, the shark suddenly found itself swimming into the path of a thousand whales, all migrating north to their summer feeding grounds in the Sea of Okhotsk.

Like a hungry wolf descending upon a flock of sheep, the Megalodon's sudden presence sent an immediate panic through the frightened pods. The whales quickly established an alternative route, allowing the supreme hunter a wide berth, but not before she had slaughtered and fed upon a fin whale and her calf.

Gliding through waters east of the Japanese island of Hokkaido, the Megalodon now detected new vibrations, the faint, yet powerful heartbeat of a creature the shark immediately recognized as another predator. Seventy million years of primal instincts took over. The challenger's presence within the big female's domain had to be dealt with.

Agitated, the Megalodon increased her speed.

The male sperm whale hovered vertically, motionless in eight hundred feet of pitch-dark ocean. Though silent and at rest, the whale never truly slept, part of its brain was always on constant alert.

Something approaching in the distance aroused the large bull. Opening its eyes, it slapped its enormous fluke several times, leveling itself out.

The sperm whale shook its gargantuan head, rousing itself awake. Using its sonar-like clicks, it quickly located the charging Megalodon. The bull circled, shaking its head as it awaited the arrival of its challenger.

Jan Henkel closed her journal, then took a sip of coffee from her mug. The coffee was cold. As she stood to rewarm the beverage in the microwave, intense clicking sounds began chirping from the hydrophone.

"Bruce, wake up! It sounds like Max is on the move again."

The biologist rolled over in bed, still groggy from lack of sleep. "Tell that whale to go back to sleep."

Jan listened intently to the headphones. "This is bizarre. He's not moving off, he's just circling around and around, two hundred feet below us."

"Think he knows we're here?"

"I don't see how. I think we may be witnessing an undocumented type of sperm whale behavior."

Bruce rolled out of bed. "Okay, I'll wake up the *Discovery* guys."

The sperm whale waited until the Megalodon closed to within several hundred yards before breaking from its defensive pattern. Beating its muscular fluke up and down furiously, the bull charged the albino shark, attempting to ram it with its mammoth head.

Sensing danger, the Megalodon banked sharply and circled away. The bull gave chase but, unable to catch its quicker adversary, returned to its defensive posture.

Though faster than the sperm whale, the Megalodon could not attack the larger bull without risking a crushing butt to the head or a devastating blow from its powerful fluke.

The two behemoths continued circling, measuring each other, the bull occasionally making a run at the luminous shark, which darted away, only to return, looking for an opening.

"What's happening?" Norton shouted, holding onto the mast as the boat began spinning in the whirling seas.

"Something else is down there with Max," Jan yelled.

"Another whale?"

"No, we're only registering one set of clicks. Whatever it is, it sure has Max agitated."

"We need to stay clear in case they breach," Bruce said as he gunned the boat's engine.

The *Cachalot* stopped spinning, its bow moving toward the edge of the turbulence.

Although evenly matched in size with the Megalodon, the sperm whale had one shortcoming not shared by its opponent—being a mammal, it required air. Continuing to circle, the bull worked its way toward the surface to blow.

The Megalodon banked, launching its attack from below.

Darting upward, the shark clamped down on the whale's small rounded pectoral fin, holding on like a pit bull. Mad Max bucked wildly as rows of serrated teeth sank into its appendage.

The crew of the *Cachalot* turned to see the great head of the sperm whale plow upward through the surface. Then another creature appeared, this one snowy-white, thrashing alongside. Before the crew could react, they found themselves in the middle of a battleground between two colossal titans.

The sperm whale flung its head from side to side, sending eight-foot swells crashing against the small sailing boat. As waves began cresting over the side, Bruce grabbed his wife, gripping the wheel with his other hand. Meanwhile, the bull's fluke slapped the sea only feet from the *Cachalot*'s bow.

Rolling sideways, the sperm whale fought furiously to shake its assailant loose, slapping its tail at the Megalodon, which was thrashing about and tearing at the mouthful of flesh and bones clenched in its jaws.

The bull's pectoral fin was no match for the shark's teeth, which quickly punctured the thick muscle of the whale's appendage clear down through the bone. Shaking its head savagely from side to side, the Megalodon tore the sperm whale's severed forelimb from its body, sheering with it a bloody chunk of blubber.

Savagely wounded, the bull whale whipped its enormous head around to face the shark, its long narrow jaw snapping in wild spasms as the enraged cetacean attempted to bite the Megalodon's snout.

Blood and froth rained upon the crew of the *Cachalot*. Jan grabbed hold of her husband as the craft plunged sideways down a ten-foot trough. As the bow lifted precariously, she caught sight of the Megalodon's ghastly upper jaw appear to jut forward from its mouth and slam shut on the sperm whale's lower jaw in a bone-splintering bite, crushing it with a sickening crunch.

The eighty-five-thousand-pound bull heaved its girth in agony along the surface, lashing out with its tail, while the remains of its mangled, dislocated lower jawbone dangled painfully below the underside of its head.

Dark waves rolled over the *Cachalot*'s transom, depositing a slick film of whale oil and blood across her deck. Bruce gunned the engine, distancing the sailboat from the tortured whale, which thrashed across the surface.

The bull whale turned belly-up to die. The alabaster dorsal fin raced past the *Cachalot*'s bow and disappeared. Bruce cut the boat's engines, terrified the sound might attract the creature. Moments later, Mad Max heaved in a final spasm of pain as the Megalodon launched its attack from below, burying its teeth in the whale's back. A sickle of caudal fin lashed back and forth along the surface, sending lather in all directions.

The crew of the sailboat huddled together on deck, horrified by the brutality of the attack and by their own vulnerability. Only Norton looked away, stealing a glance at his cameraman to make certain he was still filming.

For the next twenty minutes, the Megalodon continued its assault on the bleeding mass of blubber that had been Mad Max. Gradually, the torrent along the surface pushed the *Cachalot* farther from the carnage. Bruce and his crew raised one of the sails, distancing themselves further from the nightmarish beast.

As the boat sailed away, Jan spotted a half-dozen lead-gray dorsal fins emerge from the darkness.

Rather than approach the carnage, the great whites circled, waiting patiently for their larger cousin to finish feeding.

Desperate Hours

Mariana Trench

Terry climbed the access-tube ladder, entering the observation deck. Benedict was behind the bar, pouring himself a drink. Captain Prokovich, seated on a barstool, gave her a look that made her want to retreat back down the passageway.

"Ah, there you are," Benedict said. "You're just in time. The *Benthos* is about to begin its ascent along the canyon wall. What can I get you to drink?"

"Nothing."

"Nothing? Nonsense." Benedict poured her a double shot of vodka, then walked around the bar, shoving the glass into her hand.

"*A votre santé*—to your health." Benedict tossed back his drink, then said something in Russian to Captain Prokovich.

Terry left the drink on the bar. She watched the one-eyed man descend to the bridge, sealing the hatch behind him.

Benedict walked over to the control panel. He switched off the interior lights, then activated the retractable dome.

The titanium barrier parted. A red glow from the exterior lights revealed the sheer rock face of the canyon wall, surrounded by the impenetrable darkness of the abyss.

The *Benthos* slowly ascended.

Terry stifled a scream as two enormous Kronosaurs glided past the bay window. Seconds later, a metallic boom jolted the ship.

"They're getting more aggressive," Terry whispered.

"They don't want us to leave. For some reason, they see us as a source of food." Benedict picked up her drink from the bar and handed it to her, escorting her to the window. "Watch. As we continue to rise closer to the current of hydrothermal soot insulating the bottom layer, the creatures will go into a positive frenzy."

Terry focused nervously on the forty-foot Kronosaurus slowly maneuvering between the face of the canyon wall and the observation window.

"Benedict, that one looks like it's going to charge—"

As if in reply, the beast turned, rushing directly at them.

"Here it . . . Benedict, what are you waiting for? Shut the dome!"

Benedict remained impassive.

The monster's head grew immense, its eyes becoming specks of fire in the artificial light. Terry's heart pounded. She turned to run—

Benedict pressed a button on the tiny remote control in his hand. Instantly blazing white lights shot out from the *Benthos*, the blinding beacons igniting the abyss.

The charging Kronosaurus pirouetted sharply, its upper torso quivering as if it had been struck by a ten-thousand-volt charge. Terry watched the creature nearly collide with the canyon wall, then disappear into the inky gorge.

Benedict laughed.

Terry drained her glass, then, feeling light-headed, collapsed into a crushed velvet chair. "You enjoy taunting me, don't you?"

"It's the schoolboy in me," Benedict said, flashing a triumphant smile. "Another drink?"

"No." She watched the turbidity of the water increase as the *Benthos* ascended through the dense layer of sulfur and minerals hovering above the Trench like a blanket of smog. She heard faint crackling sounds, like pebbles colliding against the exterior window.

And then they were through, rising above the hydrothermal layer, continuing to ascend along the face of the primordial canyon.

"The Kronosaurs won't follow?"

"No, they can't leave the hydrothermal layer," Benedict said. "The vents are the life-support system of the abyss. Without them, the entire chemosynthetic food chain dies."

For a long moment, she felt him staring at her. Then he descended to the bridge, leaving her alone with her thoughts.

Benedict's never going to let me off this ship alive. It's up to me to save myself. I need to find a weapon. I need to kill him before he kills me . . .

An hour passed in eerie silence.

At 24,312 feet the *Benthos* rose majestically above the canyon's summit and over the small plateau separating the northern and southern regions of the Mariana Trench. Like a gigantic man o'war, the great ship moved through the darkness, heading north, its exterior lights punching holes in the abyss, revealing a gray barren expanse of seafloor covered in sediment.

Terry stared into a seascape devoid of life, a veritable Death Valley beneath the waves. She imagined her lifeless body drifting along the bottom, her waterlogged flesh picked apart by dozens of white crabs.

Hyperventilating, she clutched her hair as tears poured down her face, a cold sweat breaking out all over her body. Hugging a sofa cushion, she curled into a ball and closed her eyes, rocking back and forth.

It took several minutes for Terry to regain her composure. She opened her eyes, staring at the ceiling.

That's when she noticed the lens of the remote camera, focusing on her from the panel above.

Pacific Ocean
625 Nautical Miles northeast of Devil's Purgatory

Jonas and Mac stood at the stern of the *William Beebe*. Sheets of plywood had been nailed into place over the damaged deck, a temporary wooden barrier serving as a rail. The cool night air whipped against their backs as they stared at the ship's churning wake.

"How soon until the Meg enters the Trench?" Mac asked, turning his face as he soaked a rag in his hand with a clear liquid.

"The report said Angel attacked the sperm whale off

the coast of Japan. At the rate she's moving—a couple of hours, at the most."

"We'll fly out at first light." Mac checked his watch. "You ready?"

Jonas stared at the dark surface of the ocean, remembering his last encounter with the shark. "Yeah, let's get this over with." He followed Mac into the ship, then up a flight of stairs leading to the officers' quarters.

Mac knocked on the cabin door.

After a minute, Harry Moon opened the door, dressed in a T-shirt and boxers.

"Fellas, it's kind of late."

"Sorry, but this is a bit of an emergency," Mac said. "It'll only take a minute."

Harry looked at them suspiciously. "All right, come in." He opened the door, allowing Mac and Jonas to enter.

"So what's the emergency?"

"Somebody tried to kill me last week," Jonas said.

"What?" Harry looked shocked. "When?"

"That night off the Alaskan coast," Mac said.

"When you were attacked in the Zodiac? Are you sure?"

"We're sure," Mac said, circling about the small cabin. "The rope supporting the Zodiac was deliberately cut."

"We know who did it," Jonas said, "but we need your help dealing with the guy."

Harry seemed nervous. "Maybe we ought to inform the captain?"

"No, we'd rather handle this ourselves," Jonas said

as Mac whipped his arm around Harry from behind, pressing the rag of ether to his face in a viselike grip.

Harry opened his eyes and found himself on his back, staring up at the winch that had once held the Zodiac. He tried to speak, but a hand towel had been shoved in his mouth, duct tape covering his lips. Struggling to sit up, he realized his ankles and wrists were also bound in tape.

"Evening," Mac said, slipping the end of the rope around Harry's waist. "Nice night for a swim."

Jonas leaned over Harry. "You should have known about the Ring of Fire, Harry, that's basic knowledge to someone who's supposed to have a background in oceanography. I did some checking with some friends at Woods Hole. Turns out you've never been involved with the SOSUS program or the Institute. Fact is, you only received this assignment hours before the ship left port when the real first officer mysteriously had to leave town to resolve a family matter. I don't know who you are, but you're about to become bait, just like you made me."

Wide-eyed, Harry began mumbling something incomprehensible.

"What'd he say?" Mac asked, reversing the winch, the line pulling Harry to his feet.

"I think he said he forgot his towel," Jonas said, tearing the tape from Harry's lips.

Harry spit out the gag. "It wasn't me, I swear! Don't do this . . ."

"You'll have to do better than that," Mac said, pushing him out over the side.

Jonas released the winch.

Harry uttered a scream as he plunged feetfirst into the sea.

Ice-cold water exploded the breath from his lungs as he was dragged through the blackness of the Pacific. He swallowed a gulp of seawater, the icy liquid scalding his skin as if a thousand daggers were stabbing him. The rope around his waist went taut, jolting him sideways, sliding up beneath his armpits to tighten in a viselike grip as the boat continued pulling him four feet below the surface.

Twisting wildly, Harry grabbed the rope in his bound hands and desperately inched his way toward the surface. His muscles felt like lead weights, his body convulsing in spasms.

Unable to make headway against the force of the churning sea, Harry released the rope, slipping back beneath the waves to drown. Just as he was about to pass out, the rope hauled him painfully from the sea.

Mac reached out and pulled him aboard.

Harry flopped onto the deck, gasping for air, shivering uncontrollably.

"Next time, we cut the rope," Mac said.

"Wa-wait," gasped Harry, fighting to speak. "I'm C-C-CIA."

Jonas and Mac looked at each other. "Bull."

"It's true. Le-let me warm up inside and I'll prove it."

"Prove it here," Mac said, tossing him a wool blanket.

Harry pulled the blanket around his shoulders. "The cell phone I gave Jonas—it has a miniature microphone and transmitter inside. I was monitoring his conversations with Celeste Singer. You told her about Devil's Purgatory—"

"I did?"

"In the hospital. You sounded delirious. She must have drugged you."

"Son of a bitch—"

"What's Devil's Purgatory?" Mac asked.

"The location in the Mariana Trench where I piloted the *Sea Cliff* eleven years ago. What's so important about that spot that she would drug me, and you'd want to kill me?"

"Celeste recruited you for this trip just to get the location from you," said Harry, his teeth chattering. "I knew she was getting close. Cutting the line to the Zodiac seemed an opportune way to keep you from spilling your guts."

"I told you that witch was after something," Mac said. "I say we forget about having him arrested and let this piece of crap swim with the fishes."

"Wait." Jonas knelt down to face Harry. "What's in the Devil's Purgatory that's so important?"

"I can't tell you that—"

Mac restarted the winch.

"Okay, wait—I'll tell you, but only because we could use your help."

"First, you try to kill me, then you want my help? You got a lot of balls, mister."

"They're probably turning blue about now," Mac said.

"Benedict Singer has your wife," Harry said, shivering. "If you want to see her alive again, you'd better untie me."

Devil's Purgatory
Mariana Trench

Like a flying saucer descending through a cloudy night sky, the *Benthos* dropped through the layer of soot, reentering the isolated deep underworld of the Mariana Trench. Red lights revealed a forest of jagged black smokers, each billowing mushroom clouds of minerals and superheated water, the stacks rising more than eighty feet off the prehistoric seafloor.

Benedict Singer stood impatiently over Professor Kwan, awaiting the results of the Gas Chromatography detectors.

"Excellent," Kwan reported. "We've detected plumes of tritiugenic Helium-3 being vented from the seabed throughout this area."

"We found similar plumes at least a dozen times."

"Not like these, Benedict. Not with the same concentration of Helium-3. I'd say we have definitely arrived."

"Sir, *Epimetheus* ready to launch," Captain Prokovich said. "We also have an incoming message from the *Titan*."

Benedict walked to the closest computer terminal and typed in his access code. A scrambled message appeared. He entered another code word to translate the cryptogram:

CELESTE SINGER ETA: NINE HUN-
DRED HOURS. PROMETHEUS RE-
PAIRS COMPLETE, ADDITIONAL
EXTERIOR LIGHTS MOUNTED.
CREW PREPARING FOR

DESCENT. LAUNCH TIME TWELVE HUNDRED HOURS.

"Excuse me, sir," Prokovich interrupted. "The captain of the *Epimetheus* says the girl is in the docking area, requesting permission to board."

Benedict smiled in amusement. "Our mouse is preparing to play her last card. Instruct Captain Warren to welcome Mrs. Taylor aboard."

"Aye, sir."

Terry climbed down into the *Epimetheus*, taking a position adjacent to the pilot's seat.

"Rig ship for dive," said the captain.

"Aye, sir. Seals tight, depressurizing hangar sleeves."

Terry studied every movement, memorizing every switch as it was activated.

"Release docking clamps."

"Aye, sir, clamps release, sub is now free of docking station."

"Engage shaft, take us out."

Terry held on as the engine started, propelling the *Epimetheus* away from the *Benthos* toward its destination in the Devil's Purgatory.

Camouflaged by the abyssal darkness, the family of Kronosaurs glided effortlessly above the warm seafloor, the adult female taking the lead. At forty-nine feet and twenty-five tons, she was nearly a third larger than her mate and twice the size of her surviving female offspring. With her two smaller companions trailing along either side of her pelvic girdle, the behemoth reptile guided her pack in a tight triangular configuration through the gorge.

The streamlined V formation was used by the creatures to conserve energy, the big female's girth creating a channel of water that actually towed the two smaller pliosaurs forward. More important, swimming close together gave the sensory appearance of a much larger creature to the Kronosaurs' voracious enemy, *Carcharodon megalodon.*

Being cold-blooded "fish-lizards," the creatures followed a swimming pattern that kept them moving in and out of the hydrothermal vents. Seventy million years ago, the species' primordial ancestors had required the heat of the sun to warm their bodies. Adapting to life in the abyss, the surviving genus now used the superheated waters of the vents to keep their body temperatures elevated, their gills allowing them to breathe in the sea.

Propelling themselves forward using wide downward strokes from their front flippers, the pliosaurs were fast, efficient hunters, their dark coloring making them nearly invisible in the blackness of the Trench. Only the glow of their luminous nocturnal eyes gave away their presence, crimson specks that lured unsuspecting fish mortally close to their powerful crocodile jaws. The creature's vision, surprisingly good for a deep-sea dweller, was capable of distinguishing the darting movements of bioluminescent fish up to two hundred feet away.

But when it came to stalking prey within the abyss, the Kronosaurs relied on an entirely different sensory faculty. Located within the creature's external brain tissues, situated in close proximity to the nerve endings, was a high concentration of iron oxide magnetite crystals. Like miniature magnets, the crystals allowed the creatures to continuously orient themselves within the Trench by using the Earth's natural magnetic force fields. Over millions of years, this sensory system had evolved to the point where the Kronosaurs could detect minute disturbances within the canyon's magnetic field, disturbances created by schools of fish or giant squid—or by their mortal enemy.

Traveling south on their endless quest for food, the Kronosaurs sensed strong disturbances along the seafloor. With a unified downstroke of their forelimbs, the three creatures moved as one to investigate.

Terry stared out the tiny porthole, her mind racing. Over the last four hours, she had watched the vacuum tube of the *Epimetheus* inhale manganese nodules and sediment from the Cetaceous seafloor. At these depths, the process was extremely difficult. To pull in a cubic foot of rock in sixteen thousand pounds per square inch of water pressure required a one-thousand-horsepower engine running for four minutes. Every so often the suction process would cease, allowing one crew to remove the precious rocks from a pressurized holding chamber beneath the sub while another serviced the equipment.

The bounty had proved so plentiful that the crew had surpassed their hold limits an hour ago. Benedict has refused to allow the sub to return to the *Benthos*. Now dozens of ten-gallon buckets overflowing with nodules littered the narrow passage, forcing the captain to climb over the rocks just to get to his control console.

For the hundredth time, Terry repeated the piloting sequence over and over in her head like a mantra. Closing her eyes, she imagined herself sneaking into the docking station later that night, slipping into the sub and sealing herself in. Within minutes she would free the sub of its docking clamps, making it impossible for Benedict to prevent her escape. First, she'd maneuver the *Epimetheus* away from the underbelly of the *Benthos*, then ascend quickly to clear the hydrothermal layer, removing herself from the creatures' habitat. Then she'd head west, remaining in four thousand feet of water to elude the *Titan* before surfacing to run aground somewhere along the Mariana Island chain. In her mind's eye, she saw herself climbing out of the hatch to behold a tropical island. Ditching the sub in shallow water, she'd wade to shore, the sun bathing her in its warm glow, her nightmare over forever . . .

The radio squawk startled her.

"Captain, the *Titan* has detected a single life-form moving quickly in our direction. Too big to be a Kronosaurus. Range, sixteen kilometers and closing fast."

Terry's heart pumped hard and fast. A single large bioform meant a Megalodon!

"What are Benedict's orders?" the captain asked.

"He wants us to continue mining the nodules while the *Benthos* maneuvers into position directly above us."

"Inform the *Benthos* that we are filled to capacity now," the captain said.

"Benedict's orders are to continue mining," relayed the radioman.

* * *

The three Kronosaurs circled the strange creature from a safe distance, evaluating their prey. Sensing the larger *Benthos* approaching in the distance, the pliosaurs split up. The male and the female offspring closed, intent on driving their prey away from the larger creature and toward the big female, which remained circling in the shadows.

The *Benthos* descended, dwarfing the *Epimetheus* within the confines of its three dangling pillar-like legs, which came to rest on the bottom. One hundred feet above the submersible, the abyssal docking station spread its wing-like clamps to full capacity, waiting to guide the *Epimetheus* safely to the docking clamps, which would then raise the sub, sealing its conning tower within the pressurized chamber above.

Four strobe lights ignited from the *Benthos*'s hull, piercing the blackness like a lighthouse beam.

Terry focused on one of the vertical shafts of light. Fifty feet from her window, she saw a great gust of sediment swirl upward from the bottom.

Before she could react, the two Kronosaurs slammed headfirst into the starboard side of the *Epimetheus*, rolling the vessel hard to port.

Terry screamed, tossed backward in total darkness, landing hard across buckets of manganese nodules. One of the crew fell over her, pinning her legs against the rocks.

"Cease mining!" the captain ordered. "Drop weight plates—"

Red emergency cabin lights switched on as the sub rolled upright.

Terry moaned in pain as she tried to sit up. Pushing the unconscious crewman off her legs, she struggled to her feet.

A droplet of water fell from a titanium plate above her head.

Oh, my God . . .

The *Epimetheus* rose straight up from the bottom and into the bosom of the *Benthos*, its conning tower guided into the docking sleeve by the tightening clamps.

From his vantage behind the eight-inch LEXAN glass within the docking bay's control room, Benedict watched the top of the conning tower rise up into position in the flooded chamber. Brass seals moved into place around the sub's dorsal fin while docking clamps lifted the *Epimetheus* into its locked position.

Powerful pumps forced the water out, draining and depressurizing the vault within minutes.

Terry squeezed her way toward the conning tower. She watched impatiently as Captain Warren ascended the ladder, waiting for the all-clear alarm to sound from above. Bending down, she stole a glance out another window.

An immense shadow was circling close by, gathering speed.

The metallic bell sounded. Captain Warren opened the hatch.

Terry forced her way up the ladder and into the damp vault. She saw Benedict in the control room, speaking into a microphone.

"Captain, instruct your men to unload the nodules into the docking chamber."

"Sir, the *Epimetheus* took a beating. Can we wait?"

"Now, Captain!"

Terry ran to the locked vault door and banged her fist against the unyielding metal. "Let us out!"

Several men had already climbed out of the sub, only to be pushed back down the conning tower by their captain. "Form a line," he ordered. "Get those rocks off the sub!"

White buckets filled with black potato-size rocks were carried out from the conning tower. From below, the adult female Kronosaurus glided beneath its motionless prey. Captain Warren gave Benedict a desperate glance. "Sir, we could really use some help."

Benedict watched the exhausted men struggle to lift the rocks from the sub. "Prokovich, send some of your men into the chamber to assist."

"Aye, sir." The Russian pointed to two men.

Terry heard the titanium bolts click back into place. The door swung open and two burly men pushed past her, hustling into the vault.

With a tremendous surge, the fifty-thousand-pound female Kronosaurus drove its skull upward into the belly of the *Epimetheus*.

Red lights flashed, sirens wailed. Terry dove through the vault doorway, the door slamming shut behind her with such force that it propelled her through the air and into the far wall of the outer corridor. As she raised her head, a deafening roar echoed through the passage. Her body trembled and, for a bizarre moment, she found herself bouncing six inches off the floor as the *Benthos* shuddered beneath her.

She struggled to her feet and ran into the control room.

"Oh, God—oh, my God . . ."

Its titanium hull compromised on impact, the *Epimetheus* had instantaneously imploded under sixteen thousand pounds per square inch of water pressure. As the sub folded in like a crushed aluminum can, the sea rocketed upward, blazing into the sealed docking-station vault, killing everyone. The air inside compressed, superheating to thousands of degrees in a millisecond. It was the ten-foot-thick layer of titanium surrounding the chamber that prevented the *Benthos* from imploding with the force of a small nuclear explosion.

A swirling torrent of debris-infested water whipped around the circular inner walls of the flooded chamber, searching in vain for a way to pierce the titanium plating that safeguarded the rest of the mother ship.

As Terry watched, the whirlpool of brackish water began unraveling, revealing its devastation. Disfigured jellylike corpses slammed against the LEXAN window, their empty eye sockets leaking rivulets of gray matter and blood. Pockets of imploded skin disfigured the bodies, masking the frozen expressions of horror from the victims' unrecognizable faces.

Terry turned in disgust and fled with the others, all

gagging as they escaped into the adjacent corridor for air. Only Benedict remained, staring at the kaleidoscope of human body parts and floating excrement.

"*Naturam expellas furca, tamen usque recurret,*" he whispered, wiping a tear from a lashless emerald eye. "You may drive nature out with a pitchfork, but she will keep coming back." He closed his eyes. "*C'est la guerre.*"

Revelations

Base Commander James Adams adjusted his gold-rim glasses as he walked out from behind his desk to greet Masao Tanaka, motioning his secretary to close the office door behind him.

"Mas, it's good to see you. I want you to meet someone. This is Dave Ross."

A short, slender, intense-looking gentleman in his early forties stood and offered his hand. "Mr. Tanaka."

"Mr. Ross is with the CIA. He has something he wants to discuss with you . . . regarding Terry."

Masao sat. "I'm listening."

Ross pulled his chair around to face the older man. "Mr. Tanaka, what's said in this room stays in this room, are we clear on that?"

"Go on."

"About four years ago Israeli intelligence learned of a secret meeting that took place in the Sudan between a small group of terrorists and your partner, Benedict Singer. Six months later, construction began on the *Benthos*, the *Prometheus*, and the *Epimetheus*, construction paid for by funds discreetly channeled into Geo-Tech from the organization of a Saudi millionaire.

"Eighteen months ago the NSA intercepted a communication that revealed the nature of Singer's meeting. It turns out that Benedict Singer had discovered a fuel source capable of sustaining fusion energy."

"What do you mean by 'sustain'?"

"Scientists have been experimenting with fusion power for some forty years," Ross said. "Their biggest challenge has been in containing a plasma of charged tritium or deuterium while its atoms fuse into helium. Singer's new fuel source stabilized within the shifting magnetic fields of his tokamak reactor, creating a sustained output of fusion energy. In layman's terms, he broke the fusion barrier."

Masao raised his eyebrows, impressed.

"The United States, Russia, Japan, and the European Union have been working for years to complete the ITER, which stands for International Thermonuclear Experimental Reactor," said Ross. "Singer's discovery changes everything. This new fuel source puts him thirty years ahead of ITER and the rest of the world."

"Masao, the Arab coalition bankrolling Benedict Singer represents an organization responsible for bankrolling acts of terrorism," said Commander Adams. "We simply cannot allow these factions to monopolize fusion."

"What does all this have to do with me—or my daughter, for that matter?"

Ross leaned forward. "The Saudi didn't spend over a billion dollars so GTI could explore the oceans or deploy your UNIS robots along the seafloor of the Mariana Trench. The source of Benedict's fusion fuel originates in a remote area somewhere within the gorge. The *Benthos* allows Benedict to steal the fuel from within our own territorial boundaries, EEZ laws be damned. It's the equivalent of the United States slipping into OPEC countries in order to steal their oil."

Masao closed his eyes in thought, absorbing the information. "I don't understand. If the CIA knows what Benedict is up to, why allow him access to the Trench?"

"Two reasons," Ross answered. "First, we only just learned the source and the true nature of this fusion fuel. Second, controlling access into a seven-mile-deep, fifteen-hundred-mile-long gorge is a lot more difficult than it sounds. We just weren't prepared."

Commander Adams walked out from behind his desk. "The *Benthos* is so deep that it's impossible to detect using our satellites. Sonar reconnaissance is difficult at best, the ship's engines barely give off a signature, and even if we could detect her, how would we reach her once she descended into the Trench?"

"What about depth charges?"

"Even if we could pinpoint her, I doubt the explosion would cause much damage. Her hull is one hundred eight inches of titanium."

Ross interrupted the explanation. "Our biggest fear was that Geo-Tech would simply transport the *Benthos* into international waters and enter the Mariana Trench undetected somewhere along the bottom. Fortunately,

MOSSAD's informants revealed that Benedict Singer was searching for a scientific expedition—an excuse to legitimately enter the Trench that would allow him to utilize the *Titan* to shadow the *Benthos* along the surface as a safety precaution."

Commander Adams forced a smile. "These gigantic sharks of yours became the wild card that saved us."

"Wait a moment—" A dark revelation suddenly dawned on Masao. "The new UNIS project, the lucrative JAMSTEC contract?"

Ross shot Adams a look. "We needed to provide Benedict with a legitimate opportunity to access the Mariana Trench. The completion of the UNIS project seemed a perfect fit."

"My God—how far did you people go? The class-action lawsuits, the outrageous monetary awards—the court denying our right to appeal . . . You bastards set my company up, didn't you? You wanted us to go bankrupt!"

Masao stood, kicking back his chair. "You used my Institute to bait Geo-Tech—to entice them to buy us out in order to give them an excuse to legally enter the Trench."

Commander Adams stepped in between Masao and Ross, afraid his friend might actually strike the CIA director. "Masao, calm down, the CIA has assured me that reparations will be made. Try to understand—"

"Reparations? James, do you know how much damage they've inflicted on my family?"

"It couldn't be helped," Adams said. "You must understand what was at stake—"

Masao's face turned red with rage.

"Mr. Tanaka, your daughter's life may be in danger," Ross said. "If you want to help her, I advise you to sit down and let me finish."

"If anything happens to my daughter—"

"Sir, let me finish."

Adams nodded to Masao, replacing the elder man's chair.

Masao sat.

"I'm genuinely sorry for what we put you and your family through," Ross said. "Try to understand that this is not just a CIA operation, that the Japanese, Russians, and Europeans are involved, as well. Benedict would have suspected we were on to him if the United States or Japan had approached him directly. We used the Tanaka Institute as a buffer. Timing was everything. Did we push you into bankruptcy? The lawsuits were real—"

"But the closing of the Institute? The freezing of our assets?"

"No comment. Let's just say we wanted to make sure you were desperate enough to contact Benedict Singer for assistance once JAMSTEC offered you the lucrative UNIS contract. Only Geo-Tech possessed the resources necessary to complete the project, not to mention the money to bail you out of your financial difficulties. You were forced to sell, and we knew Benedict would grab the bait—hook, line, and sinker."

Masao took several deep breaths, attempting to calm himself.

"The biggest problem we faced," Ross continued, "was figuring out what the fusion fuel source was. We got a huge break when MOSSAD managed to get one of their operatives aboard the *Proteus*. Unfortunately, the sub imploded, killing the agent before he was able to transmit the information."

"One thing we did learn," Adams said, "was that Benedict entered the Mariana Trench not knowing the exact location of the fusion fuel. It turns out the *Proteus* had been designed to conduct a thorough search of the canyon floor. Its destruction added months to GTI's timetable."

Ross stood. "Two days before the Megalodon escaped from your facility, NSA intercepted a coded transmission from the *Titan* to Celeste Singer mentioning Jonas Taylor."

"Jonas?" Masao looked up. "What does Jonas have to do with this?"

"Eleven years ago, your son-in-law piloted a series of dives into the Mariana Trench aboard a Navy submersible called the *Sea Cliff*," Commander Adams explained. "It was on the last of these dives that Taylor apparently ran into one of these Megalodon sharks and panicked. The two scientists aboard were both killed. Turns out they were both fusion physicists, Dick Prestis being a former colleague of one Benedict Singer."

"Once we realized the connection, the rest was easy," Ross said. "Analysis of the remaining manganese nodules collected by the two scientists during the *Sea Cliff* dive revealed inert gases trapped within the rocks."

"The fusion fuel," Adams added.

Ross leaned against the commander's desk. "Knowing the exact location of these particular manganese nodules changes everything. We've begun preparing our own remote submersible robots to mine the rocks ourselves, hoping to avoid a direct confrontation with Singer, who still wields a lot of power in the financial and political world."

"But the *Benthos* is already in the Trench," Masao said. "How did you possibly expect to force Benedict out without him becoming suspicious?"

"By instituting JAMSTEC's investigation of the *Proteus* accident," Ross answered. "We were hoping to use that as an excuse to force Benedict out of the Trench before he could locate the nodules. Unfortunately, your daughter sent JAMSTEC a positive report regarding Geo-Tech's activities in the Trench, while Jonas unknowingly spilled his guts about the secret location of the dive site to Celeste Singer. Thanks to your son-in-law, the *Benthos* is now on its way to collect the nodules, and there's nothing we can do to stop him."

"It doesn't matter," Adams said. "MOSSAD has operatives aboard the *Titan*. Once we know Benedict has found the manganese nodules and loaded them on board, the Navy will move in and confiscate the goods under EEZ law."

"What about my daughter? You said she's in danger."

"As far as we know, she's still on board the *Benthos*, along with one of my best agents," said Ross. "We expect them topside aboard the *Titan* within the next few days. It's very important that we get them off the ship before the Navy shows up, or Benedict may resort to using them as hostages."

"Which is the reason you've revealed the truth

about all of this," Masao said. "You want me to intervene, to pick up my daughter and your agent so the Navy can move in without Benedict becoming suspicious."

"Correct," Ross said.

Mariana Trench

Angel remained just below the thermocline, her luminescent-white skin casting an eerie light as she moved through the dark Pacific waters. As she continued south, a strange tingling sensation began buzzing within her nervous system, causing the female to shake her massive head like a horse tossing a fly.

The creature's built-in compass, the Earth's powerful magnetic force field, had suddenly become distorted, the north-south current disrupted by seamounts and other geological formations surrounding the Mariana Trench. These geomagnetic anomalies were instantly recognized by the shark's ampullae of Lorenzini. Locking onto the primordial landmarks, the Megalodon began descending in a wide circular pattern, allowing her thirty-one-ton muscular girth to gradually adjust to the dramatic changes in water pressure.

Icy water bit into the creature's thick hide. Ignoring the pain, the female swam faster, the additional propulsion momentarily warming her. Down and down she descended, her core temperature dropping dangerously low. Finally, the animal plunged through the dense layer of floating minerals and sulfur, entering the warm hydrothermal waters of the abyss.

Gliding just below the cloudlike ceiling of silty debris, Angel cast her moonlike glow upon the ancient gorge, just as her ancestors had over the last one hundred thousand years. The female descended, warming herself in the dissipating heat flowing from the Earth's furnace before continuing south along the canyon floor.

Hours later, the Megalodon's receptor system detected another life-form approaching quickly. The female turned to intercept, heading for the source of the vibrations that were rapidly stimulating her reproductive system.

Looming out of the darkness ahead was a male Megalodon. At fifty-eight feet and forty-six thousand pounds, the shark was distinctly smaller, though quicker than its would-be mate. Avoiding a head-on confrontation, the male circled warily, then came up from behind the big female.

Highly stimulated, Angel permitted the male to slide up along her left flank.

With a thrust of its tail, the male shark lurched forward, biting into the female's left pectoral fin, beginning the act of copulation.

Angel arched her spine and inverted, rolling over the male Megalodon's dorsal surface to swim on her back as she twisted below her smaller mate.

The two prehistoric great whites now swam belly-to-belly, the male on top.

Mounting its mate, the male slid one of its two rigid claspers into the female's cloaca as it reestablished a biting grip upon her inverted pectoral fin. For several minutes the two predators remained locked together in insemination, the male biting deeper in a futile attempt to control the vicious female.

Copulation complete, the exhausted male slid its clasper free, momentarily releasing its grip on the female's pectoral fin.

Still inverted, Angel lunged forward and snapped her open jaws over her mate's dangling caudal fin, severing the entire lower lobe of the half-crescent-moon appendage before the male could react.

Writhing in agony, the male fluttered the remains of its tail in a futile effort to escape.

Angel rolled over, continuing her attack upon her mate's mutilated tail. Propelling herself forward, she hyperextended her nine-foot maw clear over the anal fin, her razor-sharp lower teeth shredding both claspers, ravaging the male's reproductive organs.

The helpless male shook in convulsions, its lower torso writhing in spasms within the female's jaws. Angel bit down harder and hung on, content to wait until its mate died, the male's warm blood streaming into her open gullet.

Finally, with a brutal thrashing of her head, Angel severed her mate's lower torso.

Trailing a river of crimson, the mangled body of the lifeless male fell from the female's mouth, the head and remains of the upper torso caroming off a black smoker before dropping slowly to the seafloor. Within minutes, swarms of albino crustaceans arrived to devour the remains, the sinister circle of life complete.

Having disposed of the threat to her future brood, the queen hunter continued south along the canyon wall, exploring her new kingdom.

Devil's Purgatory

Mariana Trench

Captain Prokovich paused at the double doors, where the heavy bass notes of Carl Orff's *Carmina Burana* resounded into the corridor. He rubbed the sweat from his palms and ran his fingers through the spikes of his red crew cut. Without bothering to knock, he entered Benedict's stateroom.

Benedict was lying back on a black suede couch, eyes closed, enveloped by the brooding music. Sensing another presence, he opened his eyes and, using the remote, turned down the sound.

"Your men have finished?"

"*Da.*"

Benedict noticed the sullen expression on his captain's face. "You're troubled by our losses."

"It was preventable. We took risks—"

"There is risk in all things great."

"Perhaps we should slow down and better prepare ourselves for these creatures."

"Vladislav, slowing down is a luxury we cannot afford. If we hesitate to complete our mission, ITER will complete it for us. Misfortune puts men to the test. Would you prefer the deaths of our comrades to have been in vain?"

"No."

"Then let us finish the task at hand."

Prokovich led him to the docking bay, which had been hastily drained and cleansed. Benedict smelled traces of ammonia.

Professor Kwan was inspecting several dozen buckets filled with manganese nodules.

He turned to Benedict, smiling. "Our test results were positive. You have found the gift of Prometheus himself."

"How much is here?"

"Enough to supply power to every industrial nation for the next several years."

Benedict shook his head. "It's not enough. We need to acquire the rest before the Americans discover our secret and seal off the area."

"How?" Prokovich asked, pulling nervously at his eye patch. "The creatures are still circling. They won't leave the area with so much of our crew's blood in the water."

Benedict gave him a reassuring look. "As we speak, an array of high-powered lights are being mounted along the hull of the *Prometheus*, lights that will keep the pliosaurs at bay. As an additional precautionary measure, the *Benthos* will ascend to a position only fifty meters above the hydrothermal layer where the creatures dare not venture. From now on, we'll escort the *Prometheus* on her way to the seafloor, then back again to the cold layer as she transports the manganese nodules to the *Titan*."

"Aye, sir. And the girl?"

Benedict smiled. "Now that we've located the nodules, she's no longer needed. She'll be dead before the day is out."

Terry sat on the edge of the bed, staring at the cabin door, now bolted from the outside, preventing her escape. Every few minutes a wave of panic would rush over her, forcing her to pace back and forth frantically until the nervous energy dissipated and she'd again collapse onto the mattress, waiting for her jailer to take her to the execution.

Benedict locked me in for a reason. His mind games are over. He's ready to kill me.

Desperate, she grabbed the desk chair and smashed it repeatedly against the locked door until the furniture broke apart in her hands. She tried the door again and saw the knob had loosened. Encouraged, she searched the cabin for something to pry open the lock.

Terry grabbed the wood desk and flung it over, hoping to break off one of its legs. That's when she noticed the ventilation grill.

Captain Prokovich and his crew stared nervously at the row of closed-circuit monitors whose gray-and-white images revealed the undercarriage of the *Benthos*.

Running the length of the monolith's flat undercarriage was a myriad of pressurized tanks resembling rows of giant pontoons. Half of these containers controlled the ship's ballast by drawing in seawater, allowing the positively buoyant *Benthos* to sink. The other half held gasoline, which, being lighter than water, helped maintain neutral buoyancy.

The three Kronosaurs continued to circle the undercarriage of the *Benthos*, apparently excited by the taste of blood. The sound of the ship's powerful hydraulic rams forcing seawater from numerous catches along the lower levels had caught the creatures' attention. The predators' attention was now focused on the giant pontoons. To their nocturnal eyes, the containers resembled the size and shape of the *Epimetheus*, a lifeform that had proven a bountiful source of food. As the *Benthos* rose away from the seafloor, the predators began biting into the titanium containers.

Benedict entered the bridge. "Report, Captain."

"We've got a new problem." Prokovich pointed to the monitors. "The creatures have begun attacking the ballast tanks."

"The containers are too thick, even for these monsters."

"Agreed, sir, however, it is possible for them to cause an indentation along the surface of the cylinder. If this should happen, the extreme pressures could gain a foothold, increasing compressive stresses."

"And the tank would rupture."

"Aye, sir. We've suffered no damages as of yet, but the creatures appear to be getting bolder."

"Twelve hundred feet to hydrothermal ceiling," a crewman called out.

Benedict watched in fascination as an enormous flat

head appeared in one of the monitors. With an incredible burst of speed, the animal slammed into one of the gasoline tanks, attempting to tear it from the flat cowling undercarriage of the ship.

The sound of metal being forcefully bent could be heard by crewmen working on G deck.

Within seconds the enormous pressure of the Trench exposed the cylinder's flaw. The damaged tank ruptured and imploded, setting off a rapid chain reaction that jolted the *Benthos* sideways. Lights flickered off, and the mother ship was immersed in darkness.

Moments later, red emergency lights blazed on as the monolith's backup system powered on.

Prokovich picked himself up from the floor. The *Benthos* had stopped rising and was now listing ten degrees to port. "Damage report—"

"Sir, ballast tanks B-four through B-eight are gone. We're also losing gasoline from tanks G-five, G-eight, and G-nine."

Another explosion and concussion rocked the *Benthos*. For a long moment, the crew stared wide-eyed at Benedict, uncertain of what would happen next.

Then, as if Mother Nature herself had commanded its return, the great ship began falling back to the seafloor.

Western Pacific

The helicopter soared over the deep-blue Pacific, Mac searching the ocean for the decommissioned Soviet warship. "There she is," he said, pointing to a gray shape on the horizon.

Jonas eyed the *Titan* through his binoculars before passing them back to Harry Moon. "You sure Celeste's onboard?"

"We're sure," Harry said. "Once she found out the location of the Devil's Purgatory, she hightailed it off the *William Beebe*. She never had any interest in recapturing your shark, she only wanted your information."

"And how will you know when Benedict's actually located these nodules?" Mac asked.

"We'll know the moment he begins shuttling his two submersibles between the Trench and the *Titan*. Our objective is to get Terry and our agent off the ship without arousing suspicion. Once Benedict's completed the mining job, the Navy will move in."

Jonas felt a knot in his stomach. "What makes you so sure they'll release Terry?"

"She knows nothing about their operation," Harry said, "and Benedict will want to keep it that way. The *William Beebe*'s right behind us. The last thing Benedict wants is a bunch of civilians hanging around the *Titan* while billions of dollars' worth of manganese nodules are being loaded on board. When Celeste realizes that we're not leaving without Terry, she'll have her brought topside before the *William Beebe* arrives."

"And what if my wife has already figured out what's really going on in the Trench?"

Harry shook his head. "Let's just pray that she hasn't."

Mac set the chopper down on the foredeck next to another helicopter. One of the *Titan's* crew waited until the overhead rotors slowed before greeting the unwelcome guests.

"Please come with me," said a crewman in a somber tone.

As they followed him aft, Jonas could see men working on an enormous white, cigar-shaped submersible situated on a hydraulic platform in the stern. Two arrays of underwater lights were being mounted along either side of the sub's hull.

Jonas noticed the ship's name painted in red across the keel. *Prometheus*. He recalled the name from a course on Greek mythology taken long ago as an undergraduate at Penn State. Prometheus was the Titan god who had stolen the sun's power, giving it to humans to survive.

Benedict's ego's showing . . .

Jonas recognized the frail figure standing by the starboard rail.

"Masao—"

He felt his heart tighten as his father-in-law turned to him, teary-eyed.

"I'm sorry—"

"Masao . . . what happened? Tell me!"

"Terry's dead," he rasped, his almond eyes swollen from crying.

Jonas felt his legs weaken as a shock ran through his gut. Mac and Harry grabbed him.

"What happened?" Mac whispered.

"One of the submersibles imploded," Masao said, choking on the words. "Terry was on board. All hands died."

Jonas felt himself losing control. "Masao, who told you this?"

"I saw it, Jonas. I saw it with my own eyes." Masao placed a trembling hand on his son-in-law's arm, leading him into the *Titan*. A reception area had been set up in one of the rec rooms. A television and computer sat on one of the tables.

Jonas watched black-and-white taped footage taken from a camera mounted in the control room of the *Benthos*'s docking chamber. He saw the conning tower of the *Epimetheus* rise through the floor of the flooded chamber. Moments later, the water receded, the sub's crew emerging.

"There's Terry," Masao pointed.

Jonas felt his heart pounding in his ears at the sight of his wife running across the room and off the screen, reappearing in view a moment later. A momentous explosion—the camera shaking violently—as the chamber flooded, killing everyone instantly.

Through tears, Jonas stared at the swirl of bodies dancing on the monitor. "Where's Terry? I don't see her."

"She's there," Celeste said, entering from the corridor. "Jonas—I'm so sorry."

Jonas turned to face her, his muscles trembling in rage. "What caused this? How did it happen?"

"The *Benthos* was attacked by a pack of monsters."

"Megalodons? You're lying. Megs don't hunt in packs."

"Not Megs. Benedict called them Kronosaurs."

"Kronosaurs?" He slumped into a chair, the blood draining from his face. "My God . . ."

"The *Benthos* is stranded on the bottom. We're rigging powerful underwater lights to the hull of the *Prometheus* to keep the creatures away while we rescue the remaining crew."

"I'm going with you," Jonas said.

"Regrettably impossible. There's absolutely no room. We have to pick up Benedict and a dozen of his crew."

"I'm going down," he repeated, pocketing the USB drive with the video. "I need to see her."

Celeste grabbed his wrist, leading him back out on deck to the keel of the *Prometheus*. "See those scratches and indentations in the hull? Those are teeth marks, Jonas, teeth marks made by the Kronosaurs. One of them tore apart the screw and nearly destroyed this vessel. Do you think I'm lying?"

"I need to see her body for myself!"

"You're upset. Come inside and—"

"Don't touch me. Masao, I didn't see her—"

Masao made eye contact with his son-in-law. "Jonas, come with us, please—"

He allowed Mac and Harry to lead him back to the helicopter.

"Jonas, listen to me, darling," Celeste called back. "There are no bodies. The abyss swallowed the remains."

Terry wedged another coin into the groove of the third bolt. Gritting her teeth, she strained to turn the screw, ignoring the pain coming from her swollen fingertips.

After several tries, the bolt loosened.

Not bothering with the last screw, Terry bent open the hanging ventilation cover and peered inside.

The aluminum shaft appeared to run parallel to the corridor, connecting each cabin with the deck's ventilation system. The duct itself was only eighteen inches square. She saw a reflection of light coming from the next cabin down, the grid a good fifteen feet to her left.

Taking a deep breath, she pushed her arms and head through first, then exhaled, forcing her shoulders into the cramped space.

Within seconds she became pinned, her shoulders wedged in too tightly against the shaft's narrow walls. Rolling painfully onto her back, she placed her arms across her chest and rounded her shoulders, freeing up enough space to pull her legs inside.

Arching her lower back, Terry used her feet to push her body through the shaft, waddling through headfirst until she reached the next ventilation cover. She looked in through the grid, finding the cabin empty, but could not gain enough leverage with her arms to free the bolted cover. Squirming farther down the shaft, she rolled onto her side, lined up her feet, and began kicking.

It took several minutes of perspiring labor before the cover gave way. She pushed her feet through the opening, then inched her way in backward, contorting her upper body as she pulled herself into the deserted cabin.

Terry had felt the explosions and the impact of the *Benthos* as it had landed hard on the seafloor. She suspected the ship was stranded. That meant their only chance for rescue was the *Prometheus*.

She remembered the closed-circuit surveillance cameras positioned around the ship. Escaping from her cabin was one thing, making her way to the docking station without being spotted by cameras or crew was something else entirely.

Terry noticed a white lab coat and hard hat hanging

in the closet. A wild idea came to her. She ran into the bathroom and scrubbed the makeup from her face with soap and water. Using the male occupant's shaving razor, she cut off a lock of her hair, then searched the sink for something sticky.

Toothpaste!

With her finger she smeared a light coating of toothpaste on her face, outlining sideburns and a mustache. Slicing the lock of hair into smaller pieces, she fashioned her disguise, praying the toothpaste would hold.

It did.

Terry undressed, changing quickly into the man's shirt, pants, and a pair of rubber work boots. Tying her hair in a tight bun, she positioned the hard hat, then put on the lab coat.

She looked at herself in the bathroom mirror, touching up the facial hair.

Up close, the disguise was useless. But from a surveillance camera . . . it just might work, or at least buy her some time.

Heart pounding, she opened the cabin door and stepped into the empty corridor, trying her best not to walk like a woman.

The *William Beebe* arrived several hours after the *Prometheus* had begun its descent into the Devil's Purgatory. Back onboard the research vessel, Jonas remained alone in his cabin, replaying the video of the implosion over and over, pausing each time where the camera jumped.

Mac entered with a bottle of Jack Daniel's.

"Where's Masao?" Jonas asked.

"The doctor gave him a sedative." Mac shook his head as his friend rewound the tape. "Stop torturing yourself."

Jonas pushed PLAY, then reduced the speed. "Watch carefully."

Humoring his friend, Mac watched the monitor. He saw Terry move out of camera range, then reappear.

Jonas pointed. "There. See how the tape jumps!"

Mac moved closer, kneeling before the screen. "Rewind that again."

They watched the scene once more, the image jumping just before the implosion.

"Unbelievable," Mac said. "They edited the video."

"Terry's alive."

Mac looked into Jonas's eyes. "I'll rig the *AG-II* to dive."

Descending to a position fifty meters above the ceiling of the hydrothermal layer, the captain of the *Prometheus* activated his sub's new array of underwater lights.

Celeste stared out her porthole as the powerful beams illuminated a fast-moving current of muddied water swirling beneath the sub.

"Fantastic," she whispered as the *Prometheus* plowed through the abyssal clouds to enter the Devil's Purgatory.

Benedict stood by the observation window, watching the blazing star approach. So bright were the sub's lights that life-forms living along the bottom seemed to shrivel back into the seafloor as the vessel passed overhead.

Benedict turned as Captain Prokovich climbed up from the bridge.

"You see, Vlad, our plan is working. The three Kronosaurs will not venture toward the light."

"Aye, sir. What are your orders?"

"Have the manganese nodules loaded onboard the *Prometheus* the moment she docks. Then inform Celeste that I wish to see her on the observation deck. Oh, and have the girl brought to the hangar for disposal."

Jonas stood on deck in his wetsuit, inspecting the *Abyss Glider-II* as the crew hooked it up to its winch. Situated on its dry mount, the one-man deep-sea submersible looked more like a jet fighter than a sub. Built for speed, its hydrodynamic design and lightweight construction allowed it to fly through the sea like a manta ray. Although the *Prometheus* would arrive in the Trench first, the *AG-II* would complete its descent in one-fifth the time it took the Geo-Tech sub.

The ten-foot-long craft was composed of two hulls. An outer casing made of Kevlar and reinforced aluminum covered the midwings, twin thrusters, and tail assembly. Within this hull was the LEXAN escape pod, the cockpit of the sub. In the event of an emergency, the pilot could jettison the clear pod from its heavier exterior casing and float topside.

Harry Moon and Mac joined him as he finished his inspection.

"Jonas, what are these two smaller housings beneath your thrusters?" asked Mac, pointing to the tail assembly. "The other sub didn't have them."

"The *AG-I* uses a rocket-like hydrogen booster for quick bursts of speed. To achieve the same effect in thirty-five thousand feet of water, we had to redesign the entire tail assembly. These housings hold two auxiliary propellers, which are powered by a liquid hydrogen and oxygen fuel. This sub's capable of short bursts of speed that would make a torpedo jealous. Came in handy four years ago."

"Maybe this will come in handy too," Harry said, passing Jonas his .44 caliber pistol.

"You think that's necessary?"

"You're not dealing with Boy Scouts down there. Mac told me about the video. If your wife is still alive, Benedict won't keep her that way for long. The weapon's got a full clip. My advice is to shoot to kill and sort out the bodies later. Good luck."

Jonas looked into Mac's eyes. "This is really happening, isn't it?"

"Yeah." Mac averted his gaze.

"Mac—I . . . I just want to thank you, you know, for always being there—"

"Shut up. Just go down and get your wife. I expect to see the two of you back here in time for dinner."

Jonas gave him a bear hug.

Masao was standing by the open rear hatch of the sub. He took Jonas's trembling hands in his own, squeezing them tightly. "Jonas, you know I love you as much as I loved my own son. I know how difficult this is for you."

"She's alive, Masao, but that bastard will kill her unless I stop him."

"Then listen to me carefully. True courage is doing the thing you fear doing most. There can be no courage unless you are scared. But to succeed in battle, you must move beyond fear. Find your warrior's spirit— just as you did four years ago."

"What about my dreams?"

"Use them. Use them to prepare yourself, but don't make them your enemy. Remember, all of the truly significant battles are waged within the self."

Masao gave him a quick embrace, then held open the rear hatch. Jonas crawled into the *AG-II*, sealing himself in the interior LEXAN pod.

Lying prone, he strapped himself into the body harness, then gave a thumbs-up through the clear nose cone of the sub. Seconds later, the *AG-II* lifted away from the deck, swung over the rail, and was lowered into the sea.

The sub rolled wildly in the swells while Jonas waited impatiently for the frogmen to release the vessel from its cable.

This is really happening. With a trembling hand, he wiped the sweat from his forehead. *The Devil's Purgatory . . . the hellhole where I cheated death eleven years ago. It's as if the Trench has summoned me back into its depths to settle the score . . .*

A diver tapped on the nose cone, signaling the "all-clear." Jonas gunned the engines and pushed the joystick forward, the sub descending vertically at a seventy-degree angle.

"All right, you wanted me back—well, here I am!

Just let me hold Terry in my arms one last time, then you can kill me!"

The deep blues of the Pacific melded into the shades of purple then black as Jonas Taylor guided the *Abyss Glider* on its spiraling descent, racing toward his destiny.

"What do you mean, she's escaped?" Benedict asked.

"She managed to pry off the cover to the ventilation duct and crawl through to the next cabin."

Benedict smiled to himself. His resourceful mouse had escaped her maze, a tribute to her ingenuity. Over the years he had placed nearly two dozen subjects in similar desperate, life-threatening situations. In each case, the individual had either succumbed quickly to the prospect of imminent death or had chosen to fight until the bitter end. Benedict had studied his subjects' responses, painstakingly cataloging character traits and personal histories, analyzing strengths and weaknesses until he had developed a set of predictors that he now used to determine which members of his staff would function best in crisis situations. To his surprise, Terry's actions had defied his data, her fight for self-preservation actually making her stronger as her challenges became more difficult.

Such an interesting subject. A pity she has to die.

"Search the ship. Use the closed-circuit cameras in my quarters. I want her found immediately and brought to me. She's earned my personal attention."

* * *

Terry entered G deck's corridor, taking her place in line behind a half-dozen men waiting to enter the docking station, which was now draining and depressurizing with the arrival of the *Prometheus*. Leaning back against the wall, she folded her arms across her chest and kept her head low as Captain Prokovich stormed past her, two staff members in tow.

Beads of sweat dripped down her face. She could taste toothpaste on her lips.

Stay calm . . .

The titanium door of the docking station opened. She followed the crew into the vault.

The conning tower of the *Prometheus* opened. Three men climbed out, shaking hands with the others.

Terry made for the ladder, yielding as another crew member climbed up.

Avoiding his eyes, she slapped the man on the back and descended quickly into the *Prometheus*.

The vessel was empty.

Terry headed for the bathroom. She'd seal herself inside the storage locker and pray no one would look inside during the sub's five-hour ascent.

As she turned the knob, someone inside the bathroom simultaneously pulled the door back to exit.

Terry froze, startled.

Celeste looked up, eye contact unavoidable. "Oops, sorry . . . My God—Terry? Terry, is that you?" Celeste laughed.

Tears of frustration welled in her eyes. "Celeste, please don't say anything. Help me hide inside. Please—"

"Oh, God, if only Jonas could see you now. So, have

you been taking care of Benedict for me while I was gone?"

"Celeste, please—"

"Jonas and I had a great time. You know, I think he was actually relieved when I told him you were dead."

"What?"

"Maybe I should have told him you had a sex change."

Captain Prokovich climbed down into the sub. "Celeste, Benedict is waiting for you on the observation—"

"Vlad, have you lost anything?" Celeste asked, pulling off Terry's hard hat.

In a blind rage, Terry grabbed Celeste by the throat and threw her to the floor, pressing her thumbnails into her trachea.

Prokovich quickly intervened. Grabbing Terry beneath her arms, he tossed her sideways through the open bathroom door.

Terry's head slammed painfully against a pipe beneath the sink.

Celeste sat up, wheezing to regain her breath. A large reddish-purple welt ringed her neck. Prokovich helped her to her feet. "Are you all right?"

Celeste touched her throat, smearing away blood from a small cut. "Lock her in the hangar, but don't harm her, understand?" She tasted her blood. "There's something I need to take care of. I'll join you in the hangar in twenty minutes."

Surrounded by impenetrable darkness, Jonas quickly lost all sense of direction. Through the cold LEXAN nose cone, he stared into oblivion, his mind racing.

Anger had replaced fear, his sense of purpose giving him courage. He knew what was waiting below, but it no longer mattered.

Only Terry mattered . . .

Jonas released the joystick to wipe sweat from his palm.

He checked his depth finder: 10,085 feet.

Not even a third of the way . . .

He pushed down on the joystick.

Celeste took a deep breath, then climbed the access-tube ladder to the observation deck. Benedict was alone, staring into the abyss. She sealed the hatch behind her.

"Why did you do that?" he asked.

"Just thought I'd give us some privacy." She moved behind the bar, pouring them each a drink.

He turned to face her as she finished stirring the contents of his glass. "What happened to your throat?"

"Terry Taylor attacked me aboard the *Prometheus*." She handed him his drink.

Benedict smiled. "Such a resourceful girl. A shame we have to kill her."

"I'll handle it if you don't mind."

"Not at all," he said, finishing his drink.

Celeste moved closer. "You seem kind of melancholy. What's wrong?"

"As Oscar Wilde once said, 'In this world, there are two tragedies. One is not getting what one wants, and the other is getting it.'"

She rubbed her hand along his inner thigh. "Maybe I could put you in a better mood."

Benedict grabbed a fistful of her blond hair, pulling her close. "I missed you."

She smiled, staring into his glimmering eyes. "Then kiss me."

Panting like an animal, Benedict led her to the nearest couch, then stopped, holding the side of his head.

"Benny, what's wrong?"

"I don't know . . . a sudden attack of vertigo."

"Maybe you should lie down."

Benedict staggered forward, the room spinning around him. He looked at Celeste as the realization dawned on him. Staring into her eyes, his emerald gaze seemed more animal than human. "My drink—"

"Just a little something to help you sleep."

He pushed her away, stumbling toward the sealed hatch.

Celeste grabbed the bottle of vodka and smashed it over the bald crown of his head, knocking him out.

Prokovich hastily bound Terry's wrists behind her back with a length of electrical wire, then pushed her into the hangar, sealing the door from the outside.

Staring at the closed hangar door, Terry closed her eyes, remembering Sergei's death.

"Oh, God." She glanced around the sixty-by-thirty-foot cell, empty, save for a half-dozen UNIS robots lined up along the far wall.

Terry found herself breathing hard, her pulse pounding in her head. She struggled to loosen her bonds, seized by the reality of what awaited her.

* * *

Benedict opened his eyes, the pain rousing him from unconsciousness. He was seated in front of the observation window, his wrists and ankles bound tightly around the chair. Blood seeped from the deep gash atop his head.

"Celeste?"

"Right here." She crossed the room and stood before him, sipping a drink.

"Why?"

"Opportunity makes the thief, isn't that what you taught me?"

"Thought this out, have you?" he said weakly, blinking away trickles of blood from his eyes.

Celeste wiped the blood away. "I'm ready. You've prepared me well."

"Perhaps. But our little empire has just gotten a lot larger. You'll need my help."

"I think not. Pardon my bluntness, but I'm tired of being taken advantage of. This organization could stand my touch."

"It doesn't . . . it doesn't have to be like this—"

Celeste stood before him, her eyes blazing hatred. "Looking for a little mercy, Benedict? Funny, I don't remember you giving my mother any mercy."

"Your mother?" Benedict's eyes widened.

"Don't try to deny it. We both know Sergei loves to babble when he's drunk."

"How long have you known?"

"Since I was sixteen. From that moment on, you were mine. Every time I looked into those emerald eyes of yours, I knew I was looking at a dead man."

"Our relationship, our bond, all that I've given you over the years—none of that means anything to you?"

"Why do you think I waited this long?"

"Even after the wound has healed, the scar remains." He shook his head. "How disappointing to learn that, after all I've taught you, you still lack the virtues of honor and loyalty."

"Screw you. All of a sudden, you're the guardian of morals?" She straddled his lap and lifted his chin, pressing the remains of the broken bottle to his throat. "Tell me, was killing that *Muscovite* worth my mother's life?"

"Your mother was a whore. I took her off the street when she was only nineteen. I gave her a life, presented her to your father as a gift."

"A gift?"

"A beautiful gift, one with something special inside. Your father was unable to have children, so I impregnated your mother and gave him a family."

Celeste dropped the bottle and stood, covering her mouth as she backed into the LEXAN glass.

Detecting movement, the adult male Kronosaurus circled along the perimeter.

Benedict gave Celeste a sadistic smile. "That's right. You're my daughter."

A thousand thoughts raced through Celeste's mind at once.

"Your mother was ravishing, the most beautiful woman I had ever met. She was also an invaluable tool, helping me to acquire secrets from your father that eventually led to Geo-Tech's procurement of the Tokamak reactor."

"Is that all she was to you—a tool?"

"No." Benedict blinked away a steady trickle of blood. "I loved her, but she was weak. After your father's death, she again turned to drugs. I found I could no longer trust her with my secrets, let alone care for you. Her last act helped me to remove a potential enemy from the Politburo, a man whose appointment would have blocked our acquisition of the *Titan*."

"So you killed her?"

He stared into his daughter's eyes. "I had restored meaning to her life years before. When she again lost her way, I put her out of her misery. I had something infinitely more valuable. I had you."

"Helluva way to treat your daughter."

Benedict shook his head. "Your beauty captivated me. In my eyes, you were the reincarnation of your mother. My weakness for the flesh—"

She turned to the abyss. "I understand these monsters share that weakness." With the remote control, she turned on the exterior lights.

Benedict saw movement along the periphery. "Celeste, listen to me. We could accomplish great things together. The power of the sun is ours—"

"I'll go it alone."

"Celeste, I'm your blood. I am what you will be, I was what you are."

"I miss my mother."

"*Ultra posse nemo obligatur*—don't bite off more than you can chew."

"Why, Benedict; are you begging?"

"Do you wish me to?"

"No, it's too late. The die is cast, and I have no desire to hold a wolf by the ears." She wiped more blood from his eyes. "If I don't finish you off now, it could be me sitting in that chair one day."

"It appears I taught you too well."

"Must be in the genes."

The male Kronosaur banked sharply, racing toward the observation room window.

Benedict closed his eyes. "*Majori cedo*—I yield to a superior. I suppose the goal of every parent is to see the child spread her wings greater than the nest."

"Then you should be proud."

He opened his eyes and saw movement coming from the abyss. "I think you'd better go."

Celeste turned. Seeing the creature, she kissed Benedict full on the lips, then ran to the access tube and opened the hatch.

"Celeste?"

"Yes . . . Father?"

"I'll see you in hell."

Celeste descended the ladder quickly, resealing the hatch above her. To her right was a keypad that activated an emergency hatch designed to seal off the observation deck from the rest of the ship. She punched in her security code.

Above her head, hydraulics slid a three-ton titanium plate in place over the access tube hatch.

Benedict continued staring into the abyss, focusing on crimson eyes that seemed to grow. From the pitch, a crocodile-like head appeared, its jaws opening wider.

With a thunderous detonation of glass, the creature smashed headfirst through the LEXAN window. The unfathomable pressure instantly imploded Benedict's skull and collapsed the dome of the *Benthos*, crushing the Kronosaurus to death beneath more than twelve thousand tons of titanium. A mushroom cloud of bubbles and blood and debris rose from the flattened upper level as if God himself had crushed the top of the vessel with his heel.

A high-pitched creaking reverberated throughout the ship as the hull of the *Benthos* fought to equalize.

"What the hell happened?" Prokovich yelled.

Celeste waited until the noise died down. "One of the Kronosaurs struck the bay window. Benedict's dead."

An engineer ran over to her. "Hear that creaking sound? The titanium plates are actually shrinking. Stress analysts refer to it as strain. This entire ship could lose integrity and implode at any moment."

Celeste turned to Prokovich. "Vlad, is the *Prometheus* loaded?"

"Yes, but we've got another problem. Sonar has detected an immense life-form heading in our direction. Thirteen kilometers to the north; should arrive at our location within the next eighteen to twenty minutes. Whatever it is, it's huge, at least seventy feet long."

Angel . . .

"How soon can we leave?"

"Ten minutes. But that's not all. The *Titan* is reporting that Jonas Taylor is on his way down in one of the *Abyss Gliders*."

"Jonas? Oh, this is too perfect. Is Terry in the hangar?"

"Yes."

"Captain, contact the *Titan*. Have them patch a call through to Jonas via the *William Beebe*. I'll take the call in the hangar control room, then meet you aboard the *Prometheus* in ten minutes. Alert the crew. We're abandoning ship."

* * *

Enveloped in darkness, Jonas stared into the swirling depths of the abyss, a cold sweat breaking out all over his body. Foreboding gnawed at his gut, the acrid taste of fear dried his mouth.

A glow appeared, circling below. Jonas struggled, fighting to turn the sub.

The head rose upward, jaws hyperextended, teeth bared—

Jonas blinked—staring into empty darkness. With trembling hands, he wiped the sweat from his eyes. "You're hallucinating," he told himself. "Stay focused, you've got to stay focused, stay awake—"

Without warning, a deafening explosion roared in his ears, followed seconds later by a rising shock wave that tossed the tiny sub backward, flipping it nose cone over tail.

Jonas clutched his head, his ears ringing from the blast.

An implosion—had to be the Benthos. God, no—oh, God, please—

Jonas regained control of the sub and raced for the bottom.

Several minutes passed before the ringing stopped and he could hear again.

"Jonas, come in please—"

He switched on the radio. "Masao, that explosion—"

"We heard it too, but Celeste Singer says the *Benthos* is still intact."

Thank God . . .

"She wants to speak to you. She says it's about Terry."

"Patch it through."

After a moment of heavy static, he heard Celeste's voice. "Jonas, can you hear me?"

"Speak."

Staring at Terry through the window of the hangar control room, Celeste switched on the external speaker, allowing her prisoner to hear the conversation.

"Jonas, there's been another accident aboard the *Benthos*," Celeste said. "We're forced to abandon ship. Benedict's dead. Jonas, I've seen Terry's remains. Darling, you don't want to look—"

"I need to see for myself."

Terry heard her husband's voice over the speaker and began screaming his name.

Celeste smiled behind the soundproof glass. "Jonas, I know how important it is for you to be sure. I know you want to get on with your life, and I want to help. Listen, carefully. Running along the lower deck of the *Benthos* is a large hangar. Above the doors is a motion detector. I'm going to set the entry system on automatic. You'll need to do an initial pass-by to activate the system. It takes about five minutes to flood and pressurize the chamber before the doors will open. Once you enter, the hangar will reseal and depressurize automatically. Do you understand?"

"Yes."

"Jonas, this is a difficult time, you losing Terry, me losing Benedict, but I want you to know that I love you and I'll be there for you when you're ready—"

Jonas switched off the radio.

Celeste activated the automatic entry system, then

stepped out of the control room, locking the door from the inside. She walked over to Terry, who was seated on the floor, hands tied behind her back.

"How does it feel to know your husband will be the one who ends up killing you?"

"Shut up."

"Don't worry, Jonas will take care of that after you're gone. We'll probably start a family right away—"

Terry jumped to her feet.

Celeste pushed her back down. "Sorry, one catfight a day is all I'm good for. Oh, in case you were wondering, Benedict really is dead. Don't bother shedding any crocodile tears for him, Benedict earned his way into hell. Anyway, have a nice death."

Terry waited until Celeste had sealed the door behind her. Then she rolled onto her back, squeezing her legs through her bound wrists so that her arms were now out in front of her. More determined than ever, she began tearing into the wire with her teeth, refusing to think about the hangar doors that her husband would activate within the next few minutes.

Celeste climbed down into the *Prometheus*, Prokovich sealing the hatch behind her. The interior of the sub was wall to wall with men, all of whom were standing on top of buckets filled with tons of manganese nodules.

"Rig ship for dive," the sub's captain ordered.

"Aye, sir. Seals tight, depressurizing chamber sleeves."

"Release docking clamps."

"Aye, sir, clamps released—"

The *Prometheus* dropped like a lead weight toward the seafloor.

"Release all weight plates! Engine shaft, full power—"

The sub leveled out, the bow struggling to rise.

"Why the hell are we moving so slow?" Celeste asked.

"We're overloaded," the captain said. "But as long as we're rising, we should be okay."

Jonas switched on his exterior light, staring down into the swirling muck that isolated the hydrothermal layer from the rest of the Trench. He surveyed the darkness, his heart pounding wildly.

Okay, Jonas, no glow means go . . .

Pushing down on the joystick, he guided the *AG-II* through the current of silt.

Jonas held on as the winged sub was tossed about as if caught in a downdraft. Moments later, the *Abyss Glider* punched through the torrent, entering Devil's Purgatory.

Jonas activated his sonar and located the *Benthos*. As he adjusted his course, a torch-like glow began rising up from the seafloor far below and to his left. He headed for the light, knowing it would be the *Prometheus*, a red dot appearing on his screen, marking the sub's position. Two more blips appeared, startling him. Moving much faster, the objects circled up and around to his right, remaining concealed, somewhere in the darkness.

Kronosaurs!

Barely breathing, Jonas stared hard into the abyss, seeing nothing. The blips drew closer, the life-forms seeming to detect his presence.

One of the creatures closed in from behind, the other circled to his right.

Jonas raced for the *Prometheus*.

The circling Kronosaur banked sharply, cutting him off from the submersible.

I don't believe it—they outmaneuvered me! A tightness gripped his throat. The Kronosaurs were not only larger and faster than his vessel, but intelligent hunters, working in tandem.

Pressing down on the joystick, Jonas descended toward the creature blocking his way, all the while focusing on the RANGE TO TARGET indicator on his console.

Three hundred feet . . .

Jonas saw a dark silhouette appear above the light beam of the *Prometheus*.

One hundred feet . . .

He reached for his exterior light switch.

Fifty feet . . .

Now!

Jonas hit the light, then barrel-rolled the *Abyss Glider* around the stunned Kronosaur.

Before he could react, the larger of the two beasts closed in from behind, then suddenly veered away, disappearing with its offspring.

The blips on his radar screen moved off toward the east.

Before he could breathe relief, another blip appeared on the screen. Jonas felt a shiver run down his spine. This object was different—much larger—homing in from the south.

Jonas knew why the Kronosaurs had fled. He stared into the pitch, his pulse racing, waiting for her glow to appear.

The *Prometheus* passed him on his left, the slowly ascending bulk momentarily dragging his sub in its wake. With the blazing array of lights behind him, Jonas could now make out the lights of the *Benthos* glittering eight hundred feet below on the dark sea-floor.

Four hundred feet to his right, Angel's menacing glow appeared, a pinpoint of light quickly growing larger.

Jonas raced for the *Benthos*.

The sixty-two-thousand-pound female entered the battlefield, her senses pinpointing multiple prey. The beast's ampullae of Lorenzini registered the heartbeat of the Kronosaurs, while its lateral line isolated the vibrations generated by the *Abyss Glider*'s twin thrusters.

Ignoring both, Angel homed in on the largest and slowest moving of the three challengers lurking in the female's domain.

Celeste stared out of the porthole, her heart pounding as she waited for the unearthly glow to appear.

"The Meg's closing fast," reported sonar. "One thousand feet—"

Celeste saw the glow. "Captain, do something!"

He slapped her hand away. "Like what? Jettison the crew?"

"Eight hundred feet—"

She turned to Prokovich. "Vlad—"

"It's too late," he whispered. "We're going to die—and for what? A bunch of damn rocks."

The two blips reappeared. The creatures were racing up from the seafloor, cutting Jonas off from the *Benthos.*

He cursed, whipping the *Abyss Glider* in a tight one-hundred-and-eighty-degree turn, ascending back toward the *Prometheus.*

"Oh, hell—"

He saw Angel. She had closed on the Geo-Tech sub and was now circling, a prelude to attack.

"Jonas, can you hear me!"

Jonas hit the radio switch. "I hear and see you, Celeste."

"Jonas, please, there're twenty people on board—can you lure your shark away—at least until we make it above the layer—"

Whomp! The *AG-II* was jolted hard to starboard.

Jonas fought to regain control, glancing at the crimson eye of the devil pressing its face against the nose cone to his left.

Jonas banked hard to starboard.

"Jonas—"

"I'm a little busy right now!"

The adult pliosaur appeared in his headlights out of nowhere.

"Crap—" Jonas whipped the *AG-II* into an inverted three-sixty, as a monstrous set of crocodilian jaws snapped at his tail fin.

Working together, the creatures circled, keeping the *AG-II* between them. Unable to shake himself free, Jonas climbed straight up in a vertical ascent, racing to save himself within the protective lights of the *Prometheus*.

Celeste screamed as Angel rammed her hideous snout against the bow of the sub, tasting her prey.

The sub pitched sideways, its engines straining against the roll.

Angel circled. The creature was inedible, but it was still an enemy.

The sonarman wiped droplets of sweat away from his screen. "Six hundred feet to ceiling—here comes Taylor!"

Jonas raced toward the *Prometheus*, squinting against the blinding lights coming from the sub's hull.

The two Kronosaurs abruptly broke from their attack.

Momentarily relieved, Jonas continued heading for the ceiling, then banked sharply, descending in a wide arc to head back to the *Benthos*.

Jonas craned his neck left and right, his heart racing as he searched the void for the glow, unable to see much of anything because of the bright lights of the *Prometheus*. As he soared past the Geo-Tech sub, Angel's mammoth white head appeared out of the darkness directly in front of him. Her jaws opened wide, revealing a beckoning black void he had seen a hundred times in his dreams.

"Oh, God—" Jonas yanked the joystick backward and to the side. Too late.

The tips of the serrated teeth snapped down on his portside midwing, shredding it cleanly from the hull.

The crippled *AG-II* spun sideways, barrel-rolling over and over, out of control.

Angel turned to follow.

Jonas pushed down on the joystick, plunging nose cone first to escape the faster huntress, hurtling right into the path of the two ascending Kronosaurs.

The startled pliosaurs darted away from the jaws of their immense enemy, dispersing in a wide arc to intercept their escaping prey along the bottom.

Celeste watched the *Abyss Glider* disappear into the darkness below, the Megalodon chasing it toward the seafloor. "How close to the hydrothermal ceiling are we now?"

"We'll be through in two minutes," said a relieved Prokovich. He studied the sonar. "Looks like your friend's not going to make it."

"*C'est la vie.* Wait . . . what about Terry?"

"A deck's implosion has cost the *Benthos* its spherical shape. As we speak, billions of pounds of pressure are pushing against the flattened hull. The bending forces at this depth are fantastic. I guarantee the ship won't last another twenty minutes."

Celeste smiled, picking up the radio receiver. "Jonas, my love, I hope you can hear me. Thanks so much for the help. I promise I'll buy you a lovely tombstone."

Jonas ignored her, too busy fighting to regain control of the out-of-balance sub.

Angel's snout rammed into the tail assembly, her bioluminescent glow lighting the interior of the cockpit as the *Abyss Glider* soared blindly toward the unseen floor of the abyss.

Celeste's voice continued grating on his nerves over the radio.

"Jonas, let's be honest. Don't you wish you would have slept with me that night in my cabin?"

The auxiliary prop . . .

Gritting his teeth, Jonas strained to reach the lever.

Circling upward from the bottom, the big female Kronosaurus raced into the fray, opening its jaws to steal its enemy's meal.

"It would have been the greatest thrill of your life, Jonas, the greatest. You would have fallen in love with me—"

Sensing the Kronosaurus rising toward her prey, Angel opened her mouth, teeth bared as she strained to bite down upon the tail of the *Abyss Glider*.

"—instead, you're going to die. Too bad for Terry, who's still alive aboard the *Benthos*, waiting for you to rescue her."

"What? She's alive—and you left her down there—"

"She's alive at the moment. She'll be dead on arrival—your arrival."

"You bitch—"

"Wish I could have hung around to see the reunion. Give her corpse a big hug for me."

Jonas heard the *Prometheus* crew laughing. His

stomach tightened in knots, a fit of rage rising in his throat as his face flushed in anger. Twisting the lever counterclockwise, he oxidized the tank of liquid hydrogen, igniting the auxiliary propellers.

The *AG-II* shot out of Angel's hyperextended jaws like a torpedo.

The mini-sub streaked past the stunned Kronosaur, then raced upward, soaring by the Megalodon, which turned to give chase.

Jonas grabbed the radio. "Hey, Celeste, don't look now, but I'm about to give *you* the greatest thrill of your life!"

He cut his speed in half, waiting for Angel to catch up.

Celeste stared at the sonar, watching in disbelief as the smaller blip led the larger one out of the depths, on a collision course with her sub.

"Damn you, Jonas!" She grabbed Prokovich's arm. "How close are we to the hydrothermal ceiling?"

She heard the sounds of soot striking the outer hull.

"It's okay," he replied with a smile. "We're in the layer now."

Visibility disappeared. Celeste held her breath, staring out her porthole. Twenty seconds later, they were through, ascending through frigid waters on their way up to the *Titan*.

The crew clapped, tension in the cabin dissipating. Celeste smiled, grabbing the radio. "*Dasvidaniya*, Jonas, my darling . . ."

Jonas accelerated, following the *Prometheus* up through the layer of soot. He looked over his shoulder, seeing Angel's glow rising right behind him. Emerging in the near-freezing waters, he soared up toward Celeste's slow-moving vessel and began circling.

"Hey, Celeste, I found Angel. Where do you want her?"

Celeste turned back to her porthole to see the mammoth creature rise up out of the current of debris. Her father's last words echoed in her mind: *See you in hell . . .*

Jonas waited until the Meg closed within fifty yards of the *Prometheus*. Then he pulled into a tight one-eighty and aimed the nose cone back toward the bottom.

Celeste's eyes widened as the hideous white head opened its immense jaws and wrapped them around the circumference of the spherical observation pod mounted beneath the *Prometheus*.

Titanium plates screeched in protest. The sub's ascension halted, the vessel straining to rise against the added mass of the creature.

With a violent twist of its head, the Megalodon shook its challenger, causing the sub's power grid to overload in a shower of sparks.

Blanketed in total darkness, the helpless crew screamed as they were flung blindly about the pitch-dark cabin, tossed to and fro like rag dolls.

Prokovich fell backward, tumbling into the observation pod. He landed on a pile of squirming arms and legs, his forehead striking the porthole. Opening his eye, he peered through the glass, then screamed, his sanity deserting him.

The sub's emergency lights revealed the pink insides of the prehistoric great white's mouth, which enveloped the spherical pod in a crushing embrace.

Celeste pressed her face against her porthole and looked down at the creature, its hideous gums stretched open around the observation pod, its gray eye rolled back in its head as it futilely attempted to pierce the titanium casing with its teeth.

The tragedy of her life suddenly flashed before her eyes.

Amid the screams of horror, cloaked within the chaos of darkness, Celeste wept, overwhelmed not by fear, but by the emptiness of her own existence.

Unable to bite into its prey, the Megalodon twisted its head back and forth, attempting to tear the observation pod free from the hull.

The edge of a titanium plate loosened—

For a surreal moment, the mass of the *Prometheus* seemed to inhale itself within its own center of gravity.

In an explosion of heavenly light, Celeste's pain was extinguished forever.

Jonas rocketed blindly toward the unforgiving seafloor. Terrified of smashing headfirst into the Trench, he cut off the liquid oxygen, stifling the hydrogen burn, then yanked back hard on the joystick, pulling the sub out of its nosedive.

The *AG-II* leveled out forty feet from the bottom. In his headlight loomed a towering forest of black smokers.

Gritting his teeth, Jonas whipped the sub precariously around the smoking stacks of minerals, which seemed to jump out at him from the darkness. He groaned—as the sub sideswiped a towering mountain of rock, the hydrothermal vent's chimney stack shearing the remaining midwing right off the hull.

With the remaining wing gone, Jonas regained partial control of his craft. He rolled the *Abyss Glider* upright, then soared above the bellowing black smokers.

An imposing shadow loomed ahead behind eerie red lighting, the object too large to be anything but the *Benthos*.

The two blips reappeared, moving to intercept him.

Using her teeth, Terry managed to unravel the coil of electrical wire from her wrists. As she stood, a sickening groan of metal filled her ears.

Along the outer hull of the *Benthos*, titanium plates began buckling like dominoes, creating indentations and minute cavities of space, allowing the unfathomable pressures of the abyss a toehold.

With a deafening crunch, level B imploded, flattening beneath 1,160 atmospheres of pressure.

Terry's scream was drowned out by another explosion as C deck was crushed into oblivion.

A nanosecond later, the *Benthos*'s emergency system activated, its hydraulic compressors slamming twenty tons of titanium plating into place to seal off level D, temporarily preventing the rest of the *Benthos* from collapsing like a house of cards.

Terry squeezed her eyes closed and held her breath as frightening sounds of twisting metal echoed all around her. The memory of the mangled bodies of the *Epimetheus* crew swirling within the flooded docking station overwhelmed her thoughts. Devoid of all hope, she slumped down on the floor and curled up in a ball, waiting to meet her maker.

* * *

Jonas circled the *Benthos*, searching for the hangar entrance. A blue strobe light came into view. He directed the *Abyss Glider* across the beam activating the automatic entry system.

Terry leaped to her feet as seawater began pumping up from a series of baffles beneath the floor. *Oh, God, I'm going to die—I'm going to die . . .*

The madness of the moment became overwhelming. She yanked at the chamber door again, screaming at the hopelessness of the gesture, then sloshed through ankle-deep water toward the far end of the hangar.

She stood there in the rising flood, her entire body trembling in fear, staring at the rows of UNIS robots.

And then an outlandish thought came to her. She refocused her mind, forcing herself to concentrate.

The UNIS devices had barrel-shaped titanium hulls designed to protect the sensitive instruments within from the pressures of the deep. If she could open one up and climb inside . . .

Terry scanned the lid of the first barrel, miserable with the realization that the drill required to loosen the lid's lug nuts was locked inside the control room.

Water rose above her knees.

"Oh, God, please—"

She ran from barrel to barrel, delirious with fright. Then she noticed the last barrel.

* * *

Jonas hovered the *AG-II* outside the hangar in darkness, waiting impatiently for the twelve-foot titanium door to open.

The two blips grew stronger.

Jonas looked to his left and right, nervously scanning the lead-gray dome-like hull of the *Benthos*, just barely visible in the red light. "Come on, faster, damn it!"

A sinewy shadow glided along the bottom, directly beneath the lighted belly of the *Benthos*. Jonas slammed his fist down on the joystick—as the savage head of the adult Kronosaurus shot out from beneath the ship.

Terry cried for joy at the sight of the last UNIS. Whoever had worked on the instrument last had not bothered to secure the lug bolts.

Waist-deep in seawater, she turned the bulky, manhole-size lid counterclockwise, saying a prayer of thanks to the crewman whose carelessness had given her the slightest chance of survival.

A putrid smell rose from the barrel.

She continued twisting, the smell choking her. *A dead rat?* With both hands, she lifted the sixty-pound lid off its seal, releasing a vile stench that staggered her.

Terry turned away, took a deep breath, and reached into the UNIS, feeling what appeared to be a heavy burlap bag.

What in the hell?

Unable to gain enough leverage to lift the bag from

below, Terry slid the titanium lid to one side and climbed on top of the UNIS. Adrenaline pumping, she reached down, using her legs as she forcibly lifted the burlap bag out of the titanium barrel, tossing it into the rising water.

Her ears popped, the pressure inside the hangar rising fast.

Jumping down into chest-high water, she emptied the contents of the bag.

Her bloodcurdling scream was choked off by rising vomit, as the mutilated corpse of Heath Williams tumbled into the water.

Terry pushed the decapitated body away, then rushed back to the barrel, its opening now only six inches from the rising waters. Hoisting herself up, she squeezed inside, crying out in horror.

The inside was too small to fold herself into!

Jonas raced the *AG-II* around the *Benthos*, hugging the titanium dome as the enormous pliosaur closed quickly from behind.

Damn it . . . where's the other one?

Unable to maneuver as close to the hull as its smaller prey, the fifty-thousand-pound marine reptile snapped its jaws, attempting to latch onto the sub's tail fin.

Jonas stole a quick glance to his right, catching sight of the luminous, reptilian eye. A set of streamlined jaws, longer than his sub, opened to reveal rows of deadly sharp, conical teeth.

The Kronosaurus lurched its head sideways, snapping again at its fleeing prey.

Pulling back hard on the joystick, Jonas drove the sub into a vertical climb—seconds before the smaller Kronosaurus came soaring out from around the other side of the *Benthos*.

Climbing up and over the flattened dome, Jonas raced for the hangar door.

Jamming her fingers behind the main circuit board, Terry twisted and pulled from within the hollow barrel, using every last ounce of strength to tear the bulky console out of the interior of the unmanned submersible robot.

Water began pouring into the UNIS.

Bracing her feet against the insides, she jerked backward, smashing her head as she ripped the equipment from its housing.

Terry tossed the circuit board out, then reached up and pulled the titanium cover into position.

In total darkness, kneeling in agony within the cramped refuge, she desperately began twisting the lid along the titanium threads, knowing that the seal had to be perfect in order to prevent the pressures of the abyss from imploding every cell in her body.

For several frightening moments, water continued to seep inside.

Three more revolutions . . . then, mercifully, the flow stopped.

Terry continued turning the lid as tightly as she could, trying hard not to gag at the putrid smell of decayed flesh still lingering within the barrel. Unable to twist the top any farther, she leaned back in absolute darkness, panting in the suffocating confines of what might very well become her coffin.

A muffled sound of hydraulics rumbled in her ears as the giant hangar doors began opening, allowing the abyss to enter the chamber.

Terry began hyperventilating. This was it! She held her head in her hands, trembling in the pitch, waiting for her insides to explode.

The hydraulics stopped.

Sealed in a barrel, seven miles below the surface of the Pacific Ocean, Terry Taylor sobbed, realizing that, but for a final desperate act of survival, her life would have been obliterated.

The one-man sub soared up and over the mangled roof of the *Benthos*, the adult Kronosaur closing from behind. Racing down the opposite side of the hull, Jonas saw a soft glow emanating below to his left.

The hangar door had opened!

Still hugging the titanium surface, Jonas was about to execute a sharp turn into the opening when he spotted the smaller Kronosaur flying at him from beneath the *Benthos*.

Accelerating the *AG-II* away from the hull, Jonas flew directly at the oncoming beast. At the last second, he banked the sub hard into a tight inverted roll and soared into the hangar.

The *Abyss Glider* glanced twice off the far wall before Jonas gauged the interior and yanked back on the joystick, spinning the nose cone in a tight circle before slowing to hover.

Before the hangar doors could close, the smaller

Kronosaur darted inside, crashing sideways into the sub, its girth filling the chamber.

Jonas held on as the *AG-II* rolled upside down, smashing into a row of UNIS robots.

Wedged lengthwise into the tight enclosure, the creature strained to reach its prey as the hangar door sealed shut.

Jonas, suspended upside down within the body harness, could only watch as the beast lashed at him with its tremendous jaws.

He gasped as a headless torso floated by.

With a single bite, the Kronosaur took Heath Williams's body in its mouth, chomping it to pieces.

Jonas shut his eyes to the carnage, as blood and chunks of rotted flesh swirled about the hangar.

The sound of hydraulic pumps caused him to open his eyes.

The Kronosaur pushed the side of its face against the LEXAN nose cone, its crimson eye peering inside.

Jonas struggled to free himself from the body harness, realizing the creature was about to bite into the nose cone.

Then, something bizarre happened. Instead of biting, the Kronosaurus began rolling over and over, its entire torso quivering in colossal spasms.

Jonas saw the water level drop.

The change in pressure!

Heaving wildly, the Kronosaur gave one final lurch, then collapsed under its own weight, blood seeping from every orifice.

Jonas dropped out of the harness and crawled to the rear of the pod. He unsealed the hatch and backed his way out of the sub, struggling to stand.

"Terry!" He continued yelling out his wife's name, slipping several times on the wet floor as he headed for what appeared to be a control room located on the far side of the chamber. Realizing he couldn't reach it unless he climbed over the dead animal's back, he stepped onto the hind flipper, gingerly placed his hands on the scaly slick brown hide.

Trapped within the UNIS, Terry shouted, her muffled screams unheard as she struggled desperately to unscrew the bulky lid in the suffocating darkness. Her chest heaved as she tried sucking in lungfuls of air that no longer existed. A bizarre sensation—as the darkness seemed to whirl around her. And then she slumped forward, unconscious.

Jonas threw his shoulder against the locked control-room door. Giving up, he ran to the watertight door leading into the *Benthos*, only to find that locked, as well.

Above his head, the sound of screeching metal echoed throughout the ship.

A feeling of despair washed over him. His wife was nowhere to be found, his own life about to be crushed into oblivion, Jonas scrambled over the dead Kronosaur's back, hustling to find the gun Harry Moon had given him.

That's when he noticed the console torn out from the UNIS.

Jonas stared at the object, a perturbing thought crossing his mind. Why had Celeste allowed him access into the *Benthos* if Terry was really alive? What had she meant by saying that his wife would be "dead on his arrival"?

Celeste wanted me to enter the hangar. Why? To trigger the mechanism. She must have locked Terry inside!

Jonas searched the chamber, then ran to the rows of UNIS robots. For a long moment, he stared at the lug nuts and torn-out console.

Then it dawned on him.

"Terry, oh, God, please—"

He grabbed hold of the UNIS lid, unscrewing it.

"Terry, can you hear me?"

Jonas lifted the lid, tossing it aside. Reaching into the UNIS, he grabbed his wife's limp arms and pulled her out of the barrel, taken back by the stench of death coming from within.

"Oh, God, Terry, baby, speak to me."

Her face was blue. Tilting her head back, Jonas started mouth to mouth.

The *Benthos* began shaking as if caught in an earthquake.

He checked for a pulse.

Yes—faint.

He continued mouth to mouth, tears streaming from his eyes.

Terry's complexion changed from blue to red. She gagged, slowly opening her eyes.

Jonas trembled with relief, smiling, crying, unable to control his emotions. Terry recognized him, and her eyes filled with tears. Jonas lifted her gently as she hugged him around his neck, refusing to let go. "Jonas—Jonas—I love you so much—"

"I love you, too."

For a long moment, they held each other, oblivious to their surroundings.

A shearing screech of metal screamed somewhere above their heads.

"Terry, the *Benthos* is collapsing. How do we get out of here?"

"Oh, God, we can't," she said with sudden realization. "The control room's locked." She gasped, seeing the dead monster for the first time. "What happened to it?"

"Atmospheric pressure didn't agree with him. Can you operate the hangar doors if we can get inside?"

"I already tried, it's impossible."

Jonas ran to the *AG-II* and crawled inside. Reaching beneath the console, he removed the handgun.

"Come on." Jonas helped her over the dead Kronosaur. "I'm going to blow the lock off, stand back."

Jonas fired twice, rupturing the locking mechanism.

Terry found the iron bar she had used on Sergei. Jonas wedged it in the seal, managing to pry the door open enough to gain a handhold. Together, they pulled back the door enough to allow Terry to slip inside. She scanned the control board, then activated the pressurization sequence.

Seawater began gushing up from the floor. The *Benthos* howled at them in protest.

"We don't have much time," she yelled.

"Help me with the *AG-II*."

Climbing over the beast, they ran in ankle-deep water back to the inverted *Abyss Glider*. Lifting the nose cone, they rolled it right-side up.

"Let's drag it to the hangar door," Jonas shouted, noticing the damaged tail fin and engine mount.

Terry grabbed an edge of the tail assembly and pushed, plodding through the waist-deep water.

"Terry, there's something I have to tell you—"

"Please don't tell me you slept with that woman."

Jonas smiled nervously. "God, no—"

A deep rumbling replaced the sound of shrieking metal.

"Jonas, when the hangar door opens, the *Benthos* will lose what little integrity it has left. It'll crush us like a—"

"Get in and crawl all the way up front," Jonas yelled, opening the hatch for her. Terry scurried into the nose cone, her weight lifting the hatch away from the rising water. Jonas slipped in feet first, sealing the pod behind him.

Lying side by side, they watched the chamber fill above their heads.

Jonas started the engines.

Nothing.

"What's wrong?"

"I think that monster crushed the fuselage. Dammit, the tank of liquid hydrogen ruptured—"

"Jonas!"

The hangar door raised.

Level D buckled, triggering an instantaneous implosion within each deck below.

Jonas grabbed the lever to the emergency pod and pulled hard.

The LEXAN cylinder blasted away from the outer hull assembly and shot out into the darkness—as the *Benthos* imploded behind them, flattening like a pancake. The collapsing titanium shell momentarily sucked them backward before releasing its death grip.

The powerless LEXAN pod began rising in total blackness.

Terry and Jonas hugged each other, breathing heavily into each other's ears.

"Jonas, what were you going to tell me?"

"The Megalodon's here."

"Here? In the Trench? Right now? Oh, God, Jonas—your dreams."

Jonas felt his whole body shaking.

Terry stroked his hair in a motherly way, soothing him. "What happens next?" she whispered.

Jonas opened his eyes wide, still unable to see her face in the pitch. "Angel will detect us just as we approach the hydrothermal ceiling. In my dreams she follows us up, then rises up through the layer to engulf the pod."

"Maybe she won't see us."

"Maybe. Terry, I—I'm so sorry about all of this. I ruined our marriage and—"

She squeezed his hand. "Jonas, you risked your life to rescue me."

"I'd rather die with you than live without you." He leaned over and kissed her.

Angel glided effortlessly just below the hydrothermal ceiling, her bioluminescent glow casting an iridescent reflection against the swirling layer of soot above her body. The massive implosion of the *Benthos* had temporarily driven the predator away. Now she returned, detecting a solitary object rising up from the seafloor. She moved to intercept.

* * *

Jonas leaned out over the navigational console, staring into the blackness of the Trench, waiting for the glow to appear.

Turning to his right, he saw a moonlike radiance moving below dark clouds, approaching fast. *Maybe I'm dreaming again? Wake up!*

Jonas's heartbeat thundered in his chest.

"What is it?" Terry whispered, lying on her back, her eyes closed.

Jonas took her hand and held it tight as the glow materialized into the demonic face of his worst nightmare.

The pod rose up through the hydrothermal layer, spinning wildly in the swirling current. Jonas began hyperventilating.

Clearing the hydrothermal layer, the pod ascended through near-freezing waters. More than six miles of ocean still remained above their heads.

Jonas knew what was coming, and yet he had to look. One last time—one horrible last time—he had to stare death in the face. He squeezed Terry's hand and waited for the luminous triangular head to appear—just as it had eleven years before—just as it had in his dreams a hundred times since.

"Terry, I love you—"

A faint glow pushed through the swirling debris below, growing larger. The shape took form, the unearthly light illuminating Terry's features to a gray silhouette.

Jonas trembled, a knot of fear tightening in his stomach.

Terry held on to him as she turned to stare into the depths.

In deathly silence the face of the Megalodon rose out from the mist, its ghostly white skin frightening against the pitch blackness. The demonic grin cracked open, a cavernous mouth revealing the stretch of dark gums, supporting rows of serrated triangular teeth.

Jonas fought to draw a breath. Terrified, yet unable to turn away, he stared at the cathedral-like gullet, the upper jaw hyperextending away from the widening maw.

A blur flashed to his right. He turned—shocked to see the adult Kronosaurus charging at the pod, its terrible jaws opening.

Jonas and Terry screamed as the carnivore's mouth slammed shut atop the LEXAN cylinder. A grisly grating sound filled their ears as the ovoid pod was ground between the reptile's tongue and the roof of its mouth.

Jonas grabbed Terry and held on as their world went topsy-turvy.

The female pliosaur swam away with her prey but could not swallow it whole. Stretching its savage jaws, the Kronosaurus attempted to reposition the slippery sub between its upper jaw and lower fangs in order to bite it in half.

Jonas and Terry held each other desperately, their eyes squeezed tight, waiting to die, as the pod turned in the pliosaur's gaping maw.

Jonas opened his eyes to see a faint glow, the luminescent light illuminating the razor-sharp pointed Kronosaurus teeth enveloping them on all sides.

Suddenly the escape pod spun out of the reptile's mouth.

Jonas watched in disbelief as Angel lunged forward, snapping her immense jaws over the elongated mouth of the stunned pliosaur.

"Yes! Yes! YES!"

The Kronosaur's lower torso flailed wildly as Angel's immense jaws crushed the crocodile-like head in a smothering embrace.

The pliosaur's dark blood gushed from the shark's clenched jaw. A sickening crunch of bone as the luminous predator splintered the Kronosaur's skull.

Angel paused to eye the escape pod rising away.

Jonas's heart pounded wildly, praying the female would not give chase. For a long moment, he stared into the cataract-gray eye. *Let us go, Angel, let us go . . .*

To his relief, the shark turned, descending back into the Trench, the dead Kronosaur still held firmly within its jaws. With a final flick of its caudal fin, it was gone.

Once more, they were enveloped in darkness.

Jonas choked back tears of joy. He hugged his wife as the escape pod continued to rise.

Jonas lay on his back. Terry nuzzled safely in his arms, her head on his chest. Staring into the ceiling of black sea above, he felt totally at peace. For the first time in eleven years, he was no longer afraid. For the first time, he felt he had a future.

Blackness gradually turned to purple, and then to deep blue.

Terry stirred. He stroked her ebony hair. She drifted back to sleep.

With a powerful whoosh, the pod burst forth from the sea, bobbing on the surface.

Terry sat up, gazing into a scarlet sunset as if waking from a long sleep. She smiled, kissing her husband, nuzzling his neck.

Jonas pushed her aside just long enough to activate the emergency distress beacon.

Ten minutes later, the *William Beebe* appeared on the darkening horizon. An orange Zodiac was quickly lowered into the sea, Masao and Mac climbing on board.

"*De profundis*," Terry whispered, laying her head back on his chest.

"What does that mean?"

"Benedict had it inscribed on his submersibles. It means 'out of the depths.' For so long, my only thought, my only obsession, was to escape from the Trench. I was so scared, always surrounded by death." She leaned over him, smiling. "You saved me, Jonas, you pulled my soul out of the depths. When I saw your face, I felt like my prayers had finally been answered."

"Mine too," Jonas whispered, gazing into her eyes. "Mine too."

Epilogue

The great fish glided through the rising plumes of warm water, her alabaster skin casting an incandescent glow upon rows of billowing chimney stacks. Somewhere ahead lurked the surviving offspring of the adult Kronosaurus the shark had ravaged months earlier. But as the Megalodon neared the edge of the vent field, she was seized by an involuntary spasm that caused her to break from her course.

Thick dorsal muscles contorted, locking Angel's back in a rigid arch that constrained her movements, forcing her to swim in tight circles. Within moments her abdomen began quivering, overcome by a series of monstrous contractions.

Angel stopped swimming, her oviduct widening. Then, with an agonizing push, a completely formed, twelve-foot, one-thousand-pound male pup was expelled from its mother's womb.

With rapid movements of its tail, the young hunter accelerated past its parent and disappeared into the pitch-black gorge. Moments later, a second male was birthed; this one, at nine feet, slightly smaller than its sibling. The pup darted away from its mother's out-stretched jaws, following its brother to the north.

It took the exhausted female more than a dozen strokes of her caudal fin before forward momentum could be re-established. In an instant she was tracking the two male pups through the abyss, intent on killing the very life she had birthed.

Registering the vibrations of their pursuing parent, the pups swam faster, gradually distancing themselves from each other as they darted among black smokers and clusters of tubeworms. For the newborn predators, survival now depended upon their ability to avoid their insatiate mother, as well as the wrathful packs of Kronosaurs.

Unable to catch the faster pups, the female slowed, opening her mouth wide as she struggled to breathe in the oxygen-poor environment. Although she had become used to existence in the shallows, nature had condemned her species to the warm waters of the gorge. The huntress would remain there—provided her hunger could be satisfied.

Angel resumed her southerly course, homing in on the young Kronosaur. One day, perhaps, the predator would kill off the last of these pliosaurs, ending forever the abyssal food chain that had sustained her kind for more than one hundred thousand years. On that day, nature's greatest killing machine would be forced to return to the surface, driven by primal instincts to survive—guided by memories of flesh and blood and bone.